RAGNAROK

RAGNAROK
Twilight Of The Gods III

CHRISTOPHER G NUTTALL

ISBN: 1537636944
ISBN-13: 9781537636948

http://www.chrishanger.net
http://chrishanger.wordpress.com/
http://www.facebook.com/ChristopherGNuttall

Cover by Brad Fraunfelter

www.BFillustration.com

All Comments and Reviews Welcome!

AUTHOR'S NOTE

I'm not particularly fond of books, even alternate history books, that attempt to reproduce foreign accents or make excessive use of foreign terms. Unfortunately, writing a book set in Nazi Germany makes it impossible to avoid the use of *some* German words, including a number specific to Nazi Germany and the SS. I've done my best to keep this to a bare minimum and, just in case the meaning of the word cannot be deduced from context, I've placed a glossary at the rear of the book.

Please don't hesitate to let me know if there's a word I've missed during the editing.

And if you liked this book, please leave a review.

CGN

PROLOGUE

Berlin, Germany, 1950

It was very quiet in the *Reichstag* bunker, deep under Berlin.

Karl Holliston kept his face impassive - and his mouth closed - as the uniformed flunky displayed photograph after photograph on the big screen. Four cities, all in blackened ruins; the charred remains of hundreds of thousands of bodies clearly visible towards the edge of the blast zone. The dead were the lucky ones, Karl told himself; the survivors, if they somehow managed to escape the *Einsatzgruppen* waiting outside the cities, were doomed to die lingering deaths as the radiation worked its dark magic on their bodies. No medical treatment could save their lives, even if the *Reich* cared to try.

And we wouldn't, Karl thought. *They're Untermenschen.*

But no one would have cared about his opinion, if he'd given voice to it. He was just Heinrich Himmler's aide.

"Four cities," Field Marshal Albert Kesselring said.

Himmler showed no emotion as he leaned forward. "Four cities that rose up against us," he said, his voice utterly dispassionate. "I saw no reason to waste the lives of our soldiers in teaching them a lesson."

"The Americans have already announced that they will cancel the trade deals," Speer said, flatly. The civilian licked his lips, nervously. "They're calling it mass murder."

"Tell them to tell it to the Indians," Himmler said. His face twisted into a sneer. "Or to the Japanese."

Kesselring slapped the table, hard. "It was decided that the atomic bomb would not be used…"

"...Unless the *Reich* itself was at risk," Himmler said. "I determined that the *Reich was* at risk."

Speer looked incredulous. "You plan to argue that a bunch of religious fanatics in the desert could somehow threaten the *Reich*?"

Himmler gazed back at him, evenly.

"*Untermenschen* cannot be allowed to revolt," he said. "It would give other *Untermenschen* ideas."

He nodded towards the map. "Or do you believe that we can continue to hold the *Lebensraum* in Russia if the Russians think we can be beaten? That they can drive us out of the lands we won by the sword? Or that we can keep our access to oil if the *Untermenschen* tribes revolt against us? We needed to take strong action and I *took* that action."

"You used nuclear weapons on four defenceless cities," Speer said.

"I destroyed four cities that would have been destroyed anyway, in the fullness of time," Himmler countered. "Were we going to leave the useless *Untermenschen* alive?"

No, Karl thought.

He smiled to himself. The Arabs had been foolish to side with the *Reich*. They might have chafed under British rule - they might have feared and hated the Jews as much as the *Reich* itself - but the *Reich* intended to enslave or exterminate *all Untermenschen*. And the Arabs were definitely *Untermenschen*. They had gleefully assisted the *Reich* in driving out the British and slaughtering the Jews, only to discover that the *Reich* intended to slaughter them next.

"I did what I had to do," Himmler said. "The *Fuehrer's* death made us look weak. If I hadn't taken action, who knows how far the revolt would have spread?"

Karl nodded in agreement. Adolf Hitler might have been declining in his later years - he flinched away from the thought hurriedly, knowing that expressing it meant death - but no one had doubted he ruled the *Reich*. And there had been no designated successor. The three men at the table - Himmler, Kesselring, and Speer - were collectively the most powerful figures in the *Reich*, yet none of them had a strong claim to Hitler's title. Who would take the throne?

Himmler should, Karl thought. *But the other two fear him.*

"Never again," Speer said. "The decision to deploy nuclear weapons will *not* be left in your hands."

"Oh?" Himmler asked. "And you intend to enforce it...how?"

"There will be a new division of the military specifically charged with handling nuclear weapons," Kesselring said. "They will take their orders directly from the *Reich* Council, no one else. There will be no nuclear release without authority from the very highest levels."

That's not an answer, Karl thought.

He weighed up the odds in his head. There were a dozen crack SS units deployed near Berlin, but there were also a number of *Wehrmacht* infantry divisions...all on high alert since Adolf Hitler had died. If the power struggle over who should succeed Hitler turned violent, there was no way to know who would win. Karl had every faith in the *Waffen-SS*, but would Himmler order them to attack the *Wehrmacht*? Or to slaughter the other members of the *Reich* Council and present the *Wehrmacht* with a *fait accompli*?

"The revolution begun by the *Fuhrer* must be completed," Himmler said. "If we have to deploy nuclear weapons to reach our goals, we will deploy them."

Speer looked even paler than usual. "Even at the risk of war with America?"

Himmler snorted, rudely. "Do you really think the Americans would sacrifice New York or Washington for the sake of *Untermenschen*? Or the British? We could turn Britain into a radioactive slagheap and they know it."

He cleared his throat. "The Americans will moan and whine because that is what Americans do," he said. "They won't risk war with us."

"They crushed the Japanese," Speer said.

"Little yellow men," Himmler countered, dismissively. "*We* rule, directly or indirectly, a third of the world. We have millions of men under arms, hundreds of thousands of panzers, aircraft and U-boats; we are far stronger, far more formidable, than Imperial Japan. And we have nuclear weapons. We can destroy them."

"They can destroy us," Speer said.

"They will not risk their existence by waging war against us," Himmler said.

Kesselring tapped the table, sharply. "We have a compromise in mind," he said. "You - the SS - will be given Russia as your private domain. You'll have complete freedom to reshape society any way you choose. In exchange for this, you will accept the position of the *Reich* Council and surrender the SS's claim to nuclear weapons."

Karl looked at Himmler, wondering how his ultimate superior would react. The SS *already* ruled much of Occupied Russia, enslaving or slaughtering the Russians while slowly establishing massive settlements on the soil. Himmler was being offered something he already had. And yet, the SS didn't have an *entirely* free hand. They still had to contend with the *Wehrmacht* and Speer's civilian bureaucracy. To be rid of that, to create a land where the *Volk* could live free and hold up its head with pride...

And we would grow strong, he thought, *as our success attracted more and more Aryans into the Reich.*

It wasn't ideal, he knew. Germany itself would not be transformed so radically. The civilian bureaucrats were already objecting to some of the more important transformations - and their influence would only grow stronger if the SS concentrated on Russia. But the *Reich* Council's control would not last. It would grow weaker and weaker until the true masters took their place at the head of society.

Himmler took a long moment to compose his reply. "You believe this will appease the Americans?"

"This is not about the Americans," Kesselring said. "This is about preventing a civil war."

Karl had to fight to keep his face impassive. He'd known what was at stake - everyone knew what was at stake - but he'd never heard it expressed so bluntly. There were just too many competing factions within the *Reich*, all held in check by Hitler. If the *Reich* Council couldn't put together a compromise to stabilise the *Reich*, the entire edifice would go down into civil war. And *that* would utterly destroy the *Reich*.

"The Americans are not our greatest threat right now," Speer added. "Our greatest threat is ourselves."

Himmler barely moved for a long cold moment. "Very well," he said, finally. "You'll have your control over nuclear weapons."

"You will still have a seat on the council," Speer said.

Karl nodded, inwardly. Speer was the weakest member of the triumvirate. What was control over the economy, over the factories and farms, compared to control over the soldiers, sailors and airmen who fought to expand the *Reich*?

Speer *needed* Himmler to keep Kesselring in line, just as much as he needed Kesselring to keep *Himmler* in line. No doubt Speer expected to slowly extend his influence eastwards, no matter what agreements were made. He'd assume the SS couldn't handle its own economy.

He allowed himself to relax, just barely, as the three men discussed the practicalities of their agreement. It wasn't what he wanted - what he knew *Himmler* wanted - but it was enough to keep the triumvirate happy. And, in the long run, the SS would reshape Russia into a paradise, a good example to the rest of the *Reich*. It might take decades - or more - but eventually the entire *Reich* would follow in their footsteps.

And as long as we never lose sight of our goals, he thought, *we will prevail*.

CHAPTER ONE

East Germany
28 October 1985

The village was a blackened ruin.

Hauptsturmfuehrer Hennecke Schwerk barely noticed as he stumbled through the ruined streets, heading east. He'd lost contact with his unit - all that remained of his unit - two days ago, during the chaotic retreat from Berlin. Now, the handful of men surrounding him were the remnants of a dozen units that had been hammered so badly that they'd shattered, only a handful of troopers surviving long enough to escape the caldron and make their escape to the east. He walked over a body - male or female, it was impossible to say - barely registering its existence. There was no way to know if the dead person had been a loyalist, a traitor, or merely a poor innocent civilian caught up in the maelstrom washing over the *Reich*...

He shook his head, feeling a sudden surge of anger. There was no such thing as an innocent civilian, not now. The world was divided into loyalists, men and women who would give their all to preserve the *Reich*, and traitors, men and women who would tear it down and spit in the face of everything the *Reich* had achieved since Adolf Hitler had taken power in 1933 and reshaped the world. And the traitorous civilians had turned on the *Waffen-SS* and driven them from Berlin, driven them east...

They will pay, he promised himself. *They will pay.*

He shivered as a cold wind blew from the east. They'd been meant to take their winter clothing with them - the *Waffen-SS* had plenty of experience fighting in colder climes - but the offensive had been organised in such a tearing hurry that they'd ended up outrunning their logistics network. East

1

Germany was nowhere near as cold as the Urals - or even the garrison towns near Germanica itself - but it was still cold now. He wrapped his arms around himself as he kept walking, somehow. They'd make it back to friendly lines and then...

The *Waffen-SS* was not supposed to lose. It had *never* lost, not until now. Hennecke had grown up on stories of the black-clad stormtroopers fighting the French, the British, the Russians and a dizzying series of subhuman opponents who couldn't hope to stand up to the *Reich*. The *Waffen-SS* had always taken the lead in fighting, from the coldest realms of Germany East to the darkest depths of Africa. And it had never been bested, not until now.

At least we lost to fellow Germans, Hennecke thought.

The thought wasn't reassuring. He'd been told, time and time again, that none of their opponents could hope to match them, man for man. Even the vaunted British SAS or the American Marines were no match for the SS. But they'd faced their fellow Germans - the softies of the west - in combat...and lost. Berlin had been held so strongly that thousands of blackshirts had died, even before the panzers had come to the traitor's aid. Hennecke knew how close *he* had come to death, more than once. What sadistic god had deemed that he would survive long enough to flee Berlin and join the retreat?

I am strong, he told himself. *I survived because I am strong.*

He shivered, helplessly, as he heard a dull roar in the distance. An engine, he thought; he couldn't tell if it was a panzer or a truck. Watching the panzers come at him had been a nightmare, leaving him with an odd flicker of sympathy for the bandit *Untermenschen* who'd faced the armoured vehicles on the steppes. For once, the panzers hadn't been on *his* side...he didn't want to look behind him, but there was no choice. And yet, there was nothing, save for plumes of smoke rising in the distance.

Perhaps they've given up the pursuit, he thought, numbly. *Perhaps...*

It was wishful thinking, he knew. German soldiers - the *Wehrmacht* as well as the *Waffen-SS* - were taught to take the offensive and *keep* taking the offensive. And if their opponents were in retreat, their formations scattered and their command networks a joke, the soldiers were taught to take advantage of it. How many Frenchmen had gone into the camps, back during the war, because they'd been caught in the open and captured? How many Russians had been mown down by the advancing panzers because their leadership refused to even *consider* the virtues of retreat? He'd thrilled to such tales, back in the past…

…They didn't seem so exciting now.

He glanced up, sharply, as he saw something flicker at the corner of his eye. The overcast skies were clear - thankfully, the enemy wouldn't be able to peer down on them from orbit - but that could change in a hurry. He hadn't seen a friendly plane ever since the *Wehrmacht* had broken the lines around Berlin. The *Luftwaffe* was full of traitors. Almost all of their surviving pilots had sided with the rebels, bombing and strafing the loyalists as they retreated eastwards. Perhaps a handful of soldiers, some wounded, wouldn't be a tempting target, but he knew they couldn't take it for granted. The hatred he'd seen unleashed over the past few months was terrifying.

"Don't get caught by the traitors," his superiors had warned. "They're not taking prisoners."

They kept moving, driven onwards by the grim knowledge that the only way to survive was to reach friendly lines. But where *were* the friendly lines? Hennecke *thought* they were moving east - he'd lost his personal compass somewhere in the retreat - but what if he was wrong? They could be moving north or south…And yet, the devastation surrounding him - the destroyed villages, the shattered roads - suggested that they were on the right track.

But he hadn't seen anyone outside his group for days.

Another farming village loomed up in front of him. Common sense suggested they should walk around it, but he was too tired to care. The village had been wrecked as thoroughly as the previous village, save for the church. It stood alone, surrounded by ruined buildings and piles of blackened debris; outside, a dozen men and women dangled from ropes, their decomposing bodies suggesting they'd been hanged weeks ago. He shuddered, even though he'd seen worse horrors during the advance westwards. Who knew why the villagers had been hanged? And who knew who'd done it?

He didn't bother to issue orders. In truth, he was unsure if any of his companions would *follow* them. Instead, he walked straight into the church and looked around. It felt oddly peaceful, despite the horrors outside; he had to fight the urge to just slump down in one of the pews and collapse. There were few churches in Germany East - he'd certainly never been in one - but, just for a moment, he could understand why the religious took comfort in them. And then he started to search the building, looking for food or drink or something they could use to survive.

"Nothing," he said, twenty minutes later. "Nothing at all."

He shook his head, bitterly, as they made their way back into the cold afternoon. Perhaps it was just his imagination, but the air felt colder, as if winter was coming early. German citizens were meant to keep emergency supplies somewhere within reach at all times - it was something the Nazi Party taught in schools - yet the church had been bare. But then, the coddled folk of Germany Prime felt *safe*. *They* had no reason to believe that they might have to fight for their lives at any moment, that they might be attacked…let alone that the entire *country* might be attacked. The risk of nuclear war had declined, hadn't it?

And so they stopped building shelters and worrying about life after the blast, he thought, bitterly. *And so they turned on the guardians of the Reich.*

He swallowed, hard, as he heard an aircraft high overhead, but when he looked up he saw nothing. A friendly aircraft, perhaps? Hiding within the looming clouds? Or an enemy aircraft hunting for panzers to plink from the sky? He'd heard whispers about entire SS panzer divisions wiped out by enemy aircraft, whispers he'd studiously ignored. But now, all of a sudden, those whispers seemed all too plausible.

Gritting his teeth, he peered into one of the ruined buildings. Someone had already been through it, he realised; they'd torn through a shattered wardrobe, taking clothes and whatever else they could find in a desperate bid for survival. The only remaining clothes were clearly designed for a teenage girl. Normally, he would have been reluctant to wrap them around his body - there was no hope of actually putting them on - but now there was no choice. The laws against cross-dressing - cross-dressers were automatically sent to the camps - were no longer important. All that mattered was staying alive long enough to reach friendly lines.

"Bitch," one of his companions muttered.

He held up a pair of blue jeans, clearly intended for someone a great deal slimmer than the average stormtrooper. Hennecke felt his lips thin in cold disapproval. There was no shortage of clothes from the textile combines in Germany East, but whoever had owned the jeans had preferred to buy American-made clothes off the black market. The single pair in the house - he pretended not to see his companion stuff the jeans into a bag - had probably cost more than everything else in the wardrobe put together. He knew *precisely* what *his* father would have said - and done - if he'd caught Hennecke or any of his siblings with American clothes, but their family lived in Germany East. They knew, all too well, just how cruel and uncaring the world could be.

And besides, buying American clothes helps them to fund wars against the Reich, he thought.

He took one last look at the remaining clothes, then led the way outside. There was no way to know what had happened to the original owner. She might have been evacuated by the rebels, she might have hidden somewhere in the countryside…or she might have been rounded up and shipped to the camps by the loyalists. Or she might have been raped and murdered by prowling stormtroopers. Rape was officially forbidden, but discipline had been breaking down even before the retreat from Berlin. The *Waffen-SS* hadn't known what to do with a rebellion and a civil war, rather than yet another pacification campaign.

Let us hope she made it out safely, he thought.

He was too tired to be angry with her, really. No one had really expected a civil war, not when the *Reich* had held together since 1933. Everyone *knew* the *Reich* would last a thousand years. But now, old certainties were falling everywhere. No one knew their place any longer. Soldiers were turning on their officers, workers were turning on their managers, women were turning on their husbands, collaborator governments were starting to savour the taste of freedom…nothing was the same any longer. And, no matter who won the civil war, it was hard to imagine things going back to the way they were before the rebellion. The old certainties were *gone*.

Darkness was falling when they finally walked into friendly lines. A handful of stormtroopers, looking reassuringly competent rather than refugees; a couple of armoured vehicles, hiding under camouflage netting; an officer, looking as though he was definitely in command. Hennecke was relieved, even though he rather doubted the officer had experienced the maelstrom of Berlin. He had the supercilious air of a man who hadn't had his confidence knocked out of him.

"*Heil Holliston*," Hennecke managed. "*Herr Sturmbannfuehrer.*"

The *Sturmbannfuehrer* looked him up and down for a long moment. Hennecke realised, in a flash of sudden horror, just how awful he must look. He was a *Hauptsturmfuehrer*, yet he couldn't be said to have taken command or done anything, really, apart from lead a handful of men to safety. But he'd lost touch with his unit during the retreat…

"Heil Holliston," the *Sturmbannfuehrer* returned. His gaze moved to the other men. "Go to the tent, report to the officer there. You'll be fed, watered and assigned to new units."

Hennecke felt cold. The *Sturmbannfuehrer* spoke of stormtroopers as if they were animals…

He watched his men go, suddenly wishing he'd never been promoted. It had been a battlefield promotion, the kind of promotion he'd dreamed of before he'd discovered what it entailed. He'd led men into battle; he'd watched them die, even as he'd been spared himself…going back to the ranks would be a demotion, but he would almost welcome it. The war hadn't been what he'd been promised. It had *never* been what he'd been promised.

"You should have taken command," the *Sturmbannfuehrer* said, coldly.

Hennecke said nothing. He knew the *Sturmbannfuehrer* was correct. He'd outranked everyone else in the little group. He could have issued orders, he could have done…done what? There had been nothing he could have done, save for continuing the retreat until they reached friendly lines. But they'd shuffled into the lines like *Untermenschen* slaves doing their best to avoid a full day's work. His men had looked pathetic…

…And so did he.

A pair of stormtroopers seemed to materialise out of nowhere. Hennecke had been so absorbed in himself that he hadn't seen them coming. The two men looked absolutely perfect; their uniforms clean and tidy, their boots and buttons shined until they almost glowed, their faces utterly impassive. It was clear that *they* had never seen combat.

"Take this *swinehund* to the pen and hold him there," the *Sturmbannfuehrer* ordered.

Hennecke had no time to protest before the two stormtroopers frisked him - removing his pistol, his knife and a handful of tools - and then frog-marched him through the concealed camp. It was larger than he realised, he saw; a dozen tents, all carefully hidden under netting and guarded by SS stormtroopers. One tent was clearly set aside for the wounded; he glanced inside, ignoring the grunt of complaint from his escorts, and winced as he saw thirty men lying on the hard ground. A pair of medics were doing what they could, assisted by five young women, but it was clear that they were badly overworked…

He stared in horror until his escorts yanked him forward. He was no stranger to blood and gore, but the sight before him was horrific. Men had lost arms and legs, their bodies hideously mutilated…even if they were somehow rushed to better medical facilities, their chances of ever living a normal life again were slim. It made him realise just how many men might have been killed by their own side - a mercy kill - or left to bleed out and die during the retreat. The medics had strict orders - standing orders - to concentrate on the soldiers who could be saved. There wouldn't be anything, not even morphine, for the ones who had no hope of survival.

And some of the ones left to die could have lived, with proper treatment, he thought.

His escorts kept dragging him forward until they reached the pen, a small region fenced off and guarded by armed stormtroopers. It didn't look very secure - Hennecke was sure *he* could escape, easily - but he knew better than to try. The stormtroopers guarding the fence wouldn't hesitate to shoot him down if they caught him trying to escape - and no one, least of all their superiors, would give a damn. Hennecke was an embarrassment. It was quite possible that he'd be taken out and shot within the next hour. Or perhaps they'd just slit his throat.

There's probably a shortage of bullets, he thought, morbidly.

He glanced at his fellow prisoners as his escorts thrust him into the pen, then marched off to torment someone else. A number of soldiers - he was still the highest-ranking, he noticed - a trio of older men in civilian clothes and a pair of young women. He wondered, as he found a space on the ground, why *they* were being detained. If they were insurgents - or whatever one called treacherous rebels - they would have been shot already. Maybe they were just hostages for someone's good behaviour. Neither of them seemed inclined to talk to him or anyone else.

There was nothing to do inside the pen, so he lay down on the hard ground and closed his eyes. He'd long-since mastered the art of sleeping whenever he had a spare moment, even though the ground was uncomfortable and there was a very real prospect of being shot by his own side. But it still felt as if he hadn't slept at all when he was woken by the guards, who escorted him and the other soldier prisoners out of the pen and down to where a grim-faced *Brigadefuehrer* was standing. He honestly wasn't sure how *long* he'd slept.

"You cowards fled," the *Brigadefuehrer* snapped. His gaze raked over the prisoners, cold and hard and utterly devoid of mercy. "You could have fought. You could have organised yourselves. You could have given the rebels a bloody nose. Instead, you fled."

Hennecke resisted the urge to say something in his own defence. There was nothing he *could* say. The SS was looking for scapegoats. And if they'd chosen him...

"You should be dispatched to the camps," the *Brigadefuehrer* added. "But we have need of you here. You'll be assigned to a penal unit instead. If you survive..."

Hennecke barely heard the rest of the speech. He'd heard horror stories about penal units. A soldier who was assigned to one would be allowed to return to his unit - his record wiped - if he survived a month in the penal unit...

...But the odds of survival were very low.

It might not matter, he told himself. In the distance, he heard thunder - or shellfire. *The odds of any of us surviving are very low.*

CHAPTER TWO

Germanica (Moscow), Germany East
29 October 1985

They had lost.

To lose was unthinkable, but they had lost.

No, Karl Holliston told himself, firmly. *We have not lost. We have merely suffered a setback.*

He sat in his office and studied the map on the wall. It was updated every hour on the hour by his staff, but he didn't need the updates to know it told a tale of disaster. The *Waffen-SS*, the most powerful fighting force on the planet, was retreating from Berlin, pursued by the panzers of the treacherous *Heer*. A handful of units, he'd been told, were fighting a rearguard action, but there was no point in trying to make a stand until the SS was well away from Berlin. Entire formations had been shattered, first by the meatgrinder of Berlin and then by the enemy counterattack. Putting the *Waffen-SS* back together would take *weeks*, perhaps *months*. Karl was all too aware that he didn't *have* months.

Winter is coming, he thought, grimly. *That will buy us some time, at least.*

He glared down at his hands. He'd been a child during the great conquests, back when the panzers had captured Moscow and pushed the borders of the *Reich* all the way to the Urals, but he'd heard stories. His time as Himmler's aide had given him a chance to hear stories his boss had never heard. Men freezing in their uniforms, panzers and their supporting units breaking down because of the cold, even personal weapons failing because it was just too damn cold. The *Waffen-SS* had learned a great many lessons about fighting in the extreme cold over the last forty years. But far too many *Heer* units knew them too.

The office was massive, easily large enough for a hundred men. But he was alone. He knew, all too well, that his position had been badly weakened. No one gave a damn what the ordinary citizen thought - and the average citizen of Germany East was solidly behind the *Waffen-SS* - but his military and political subordinates posed a very different problem. Karl had declared himself the *Führer*, the first true warlord since Adolf Hitler himself; as long as he succeeded, as long as he met no significant setbacks, his position was completely unchallengeable. No one would dare to question him...

But now he *had* suffered a massive setback.

He was honest enough to admit it, at least to himself. The planned reconquest of Berlin had failed, miserably. There was no way, now, to destroy the rebel government. And of thousands of stormtroopers had been killed in the fighting. It was enough to weaken the resolve of a lesser man. Karl knew, all too well, that quite a few of his subordinates *were* lesser men. They'd sell out to the rebels in a heartbeat if they thought they could maintain their power and position. But he could do nothing. Purging every senior officer who *might* pose a threat would not only weaken his command structure, it would almost certainly prompt a coup. There were too many officers, even among the loyalists, who would assume that they too were going to be purged.

His hands touched a thin folder on his desk. Karl picked it up and opened it, reading - again - the nuclear codes for his stockpile of tactical nuclear warheads. His engineers hadn't managed to unlock the launch codes for the missile fields in Siberia, something that bothered him more than he cared to admit, but he had *some* nuclear warheads. And yet, using them might *also* prompt a coup.

He shook his head in frustration. It had been a mistake, he acknowledged now, to allow the stormtroopers so much freedom during the march to Berlin. No one gave a damn about how *Untermenschen* were treated, but the citizens of Germany Prime were *Germans*. The censors had slapped down hard on any whispers of atrocities, yet all they'd managed to accomplish was to give the darker rumours credence. A wave of mass slaughter, of rape and looting... there was no way to deny it, no way to convince the population that he hadn't ordered the SS to punish Germany Prime. Victory would have blown those rumours away. Instead, they'd grown in the telling.

And if you added all the death reports together, he thought sourly, *we would have slaughtered the entire population several times over.*

His phone rang. "*Mein Fuhrer*," Maria said. His ruthlessly efficient secretary was still guarding his door. "The cabinet has arrived. *Oberstgruppenfuehrer* Alfred Ruengeler is being escorted from the airport and will arrive momentarily."

"Understood," Karl said. He forced himself to sit upright, checking his appearance in a small mirror. *Hitler* had never had to worry about how he presented himself to his subordinates. "Have them escorted in when Ruengeler arrives."

Making them wait was petty, he acknowledged, but he didn't dare do anything that suggested he was losing his grip on power. And he wasn't, he told himself firmly. He still controlled a formidable force, he still ruled Germany East...he still had the nuclear devices. There had been setbacks - there was no disguising the fact that there had been setbacks - but he hadn't *lost*.

And I still have my source in the enemy camp, he thought. His private staff had received two more messages from his spy, telling him that the enemy were still trying to consolidate their gains after the Battle of Berlin. *We have not lost.*

He leaned back in his chair as his cabinet started to file into the giant office, Ruengeler bringing up the rear. The man looked torn between defiance and a grim acceptance that he was probably about to die. Karl didn't blame him. He needed a scapegoat for the retreat from Berlin and Ruengeler, the man who had been in command of the operation, was the most likely choice.

Pity I can't put the blame on someone who wasn't there, Karl thought, darkly. *It would be a great excuse to purge some of the unreliable swinehunds.*

His gaze swept their ranks as they took up position in front of him. Territories Minister Philipp Kuhnert and Industries Minister Friedrich Leopoldsberger, two men who had served on the *Reich* Council before the civil war. Both reliable, if only because they knew they wouldn't survive an enemy victory. *Gauleiter* Emil Forster, a stanchly conservative official who could be relied upon to do whatever it took to serve the *Reich*; *Gauleiter* Hugo Jury, a fanatical loyalist; *Gauleiter* Staff Innsbruck, a wavering weakling who should never have been promoted above his level of competence. Karl would have liked to dispose of the man - he was simply unreliable - but Innsbruck had too much support from the lower orders. His position would need to be under-mined thoroughly before he could be purged.

And he wasn't in command when we lost the battle, Karl thought, sourly. It was hard to believe that *anyone* would consider Innsbruck a strong candidate for anything more important than street-sweeper, but *Innsbruck* hadn't lost a major battle. *A pity he can't be used as a scapegoat.*

"Heil Holliston," they said, in unison.

Karl allowed himself a flicker of amusement, although it didn't show on his face. Some of them - Jury in particular - sounded enthusiastic, but others seemed rather more dubious. The *Reich* hadn't had a *real Fuhrer* since Adolf Hitler had died, the *Reich* Council choosing to establish a figurehead ruler rather than fight over who should take the throne. To them, *his* claim to supreme authority was a deadly threat. The power Hitler had wielded had been utterly unconstrained. Karl doubted that any of them were foolish enough to believe that he wouldn't use the power, once he held it. Purging Germany East of those who doubted him would be a good first step.

But it wasn't important, not now.

"Gentlemen," he said. There was no more time for brooding. "Let us begin."

———

Oberstgruppenfuehrer Alfred Ruengeler held himself ramrod straight, even though he rather suspected that he was about to be arrested and marched straight to his own execution. The *Fuhrer* needed a scapegoat for the defeat and there was no better candidate, particularly as Alfred had defied the older man's commands in ordering the retreat from Berlin. There had been no choice - the *Waffen-SS* had been on the verge of breaking - but he knew Holliston wouldn't see it that way. The man had been growing increasingly unstable as disaster followed disaster, a tidal wave of chaos breaking over the *Reich*.

He studied Holliston through impassive eyes. The *Fuhrer* wore a simple infantryman's uniform with a single Iron Cross - Adolf Hitler had worn the same outfit - and he'd cut his hair to resemble the former *Fuhrer* in his prime. And yet, it was easy to see that Holliston was deeply worried. The *Fuhrer* was good at hiding his emotions, but there were enough signs for Alfred to be *sure* he was worried. Holliston would *definitely* need a scapegoat…

...But my subordinates will be safe, Alfred thought. He certainly *hoped* that would be the case. The *Reich* had lost too many good men to go around executing people merely because they'd been too close to the designated scapegoat. *And we are already pulling the formations back together.*

He sighed, inwardly. Tactical defeats were one thing - and the *Waffen-SS* had suffered tactical defeats, no matter what the Ministry of Information said - but the *Reich* had never suffered such a catastrophic setback in its entire history. Even the first Battle of Moscow hadn't been so *shocking*. He'd had to look as far back as 1918 to see a comparable defeat - and *that* had resulted in the end of the Second *Reich*.

"Herr Oberstgruppenfuehrer," Holliston said. His voice was very cold. "Is it true that you ordered the retreat from Berlin."

"Yes, *Mein Fuhrer*," Alfred said. There was no point in trying to lie. He knew the rules. His guilt had to be firmly established to make it clear that he was more than *just* a scapegoat for his superior. And if he played his role, his family would be safe. "I saw no choice."

"Indeed," Holliston said.

There was a long chilling pause. "You did the right thing, *Herr Oberstgruppenfuehrer*," Holliston added. "The *Reich* owes you a great debt."

Alfred felt his expression crack, just for a second. He *wasn't* going to be turned into a scapegoat? Holliston *approved* of his decision? And yet...cold ice ran down his spine as he realised it wasn't anything of the sort. The *Waffen-SS* wasn't led by incompetent fools. It wouldn't be hard for one of Alfred's former subordinates to put two and two together and realise that the *real* blame lay with Holliston. The rivalry between the *Waffen-SS* and the *rest* of the SS would only make it worse. And who knew what would happen then?

"You will continue to hold your position, charged with organising the defence of Germany East in the short term and the reconquest of Germany Prime in the coming year," Holliston continued. "In your opinion, what is the current situation?"

Alfred had to fight the urge to giggle. Reconquer Germany Prime? Right now, he honestly wasn't sure they could defend Germany *East*. Four entire divisions had been shattered in the Battle of Berlin, their panzers destroyed, their supplies expended...Germany East had vast stockpiles of war material, but it didn't produce much for itself. Replacing everything that had been lost in the fighting would take *years*. Hell, merely reorganising the survivors into new units would take far too long.

He took a moment to organise his thoughts. "The last set of updates I saw, *Mein Fuhrer*, had lines being formed west of Warsaw," he said. "Stragglers are being rounded up and funnelled into makeshift units" - thankfully, the *Waffen-SS* had a great deal of experience in throwing together scratch battle-groups at a moment's notice - "while we are massing the remainder of our panzers and aircraft well behind the front lines. Small teams of dedicated commandos have been assigned to impede the enemy, directly and indirectly. As you are aware, experienced teams can cause considerable delay."

As the enemy showed us during the march to Berlin, he thought, grimly. *And blowing up bridges will make it harder for us to take the offensive too.*

"Very good," Holliston said. "And our chances of defending Germany East?"

Alfred knew the right answer. "Very good, *Mein Fuhrer.*"

Gauleiter Staff Innsbruck cleared his throat, loudly. "*Herr Oberstgruppen-fuehrer,*" he said, carefully. "Is it not true that we have lost vast quantities of materiel as well as men?"

"It is," Alfred confirmed. He'd met Innsbruck before; indeed, he was mildly surprised Innsbruck had survived Holliston's assumption of power. The man didn't owe his success to the new *Fuhrer.* "However, there are several factors working in our favour."

Innsbruck lifted his eyebrows. "Indeed?"

"Yes, *Herr Gauleiter,*" Alfred said.

He ticked off points on his fingers as he spoke. "First, the enemy is likely just as disorganised as ourselves," he said. "Their thrusts eastwards are already weakening as they outrun their logistics. They will need time to reorganise before taking the offensive.

"Second, the distance between Berlin and Germanica is quite consider-able," he added. "If they wish to crush us, they will have to thrust eastwards... and do it at a time when winter is coming and the roads swiftly become impassable. Our contingency plans for the defence of Germany East will only make matters worse, for them. By the time they muster the force to launch an invasion of their own, perhaps in spring, we will have our forces solidly in place and ready to stop them."

"But that would require a massive commitment," Innsbruck said. "We would need to conscript more and more young men from the farms."

Alfred nodded, unsure where Innsbruck was going.

Innsbruck turned back to Holliston. "*Mein Fuhrer*, we must discuss peace."

Holliston's face darkened. "Peace? There can be no compromise with traitors!"

"Two-thirds of the young men in my district have already been called up," Innsbruck said, sharply. "Garrison levels have already fallen dangerously low in some places - and winter is coming, winter…when bandit attacks are typically on the rise. My people have already faced a number of raids that came far too close to success. How long can we sustain this commitment without losing Germany East completely?"

Alfred winced. Forty years of occupation hadn't been enough to exterminate the bandits, not the ones stubborn enough to hold on and fight back whenever they saw an opportunity. Most towns and villages in Germany East were practically garrisons, military bases in a sea of *Untermenschen* insurgents and bandits. And he had no doubt that the *Untermenschen* slaves would revolt, if given the opportunity. They were worked to death by their owners. The only thing keeping them under control was the certain knowledge that resistance was futile.

And it might not be futile now, he thought. *We don't have the manpower to keep them in check any longer.*

Holliston made a visible effort to control his anger. "The traitors believe they won the war," he said, sharply. "Do you think they would agree to any terms we might accept?"

And if they did, Alfred asked himself, *how long would it be before they crushed us anyway.*

He sighed, inwardly. Germany Prime had nearly seventy percent of the *Reich's* industrial base, even though it had been decaying for years. Given a couple of years of peace, the traitors could simply out-produce the loyalists and resume the war when it suited them. And ideas from the west would be slipping east all the time…the ideals of the *Reich* would come under threat.

Because they seem easier, he thought. *And very tempting.*

It wasn't a pleasant thought. Germany East was *built* on an ideal, the ideal of transforming a barren country into living space. It had built hard men and women, people who truly *understood* the harsh world around them. But Germany Prime…they'd had it easier for decades. They didn't realise the truth, that one could either bend the world to one's will…or be bent in turn.

"There is *no* prospect for peace," Holliston said. "Do you wish to see your lands returned to the *Untermenschen?*"

He tapped the table sharply. "Does *anyone* wish to surrender?"

No, Alfred thought. He doubted that any of the senior officers would like the thought of giving up their power, even if it *didn't* lead to their execution. *But do they think the war can be won?*

"As long as we have the power to preserve the ethos of Germany East," *Gauleiter* Emil Forster said, "we must not surrender."

Alfred frowned to himself. *Gauleiter* Emil Forster was an older man, one known to be stanchly conservative. He would have expected Forster to consider coming to terms with the rebels, if it was possible. Continuing the war might lead to defeat - or total annihilation. But then, who knew how long Germany East would survive if it still had contact with Germany Prime? Would the Easterners be seduced from their ideals?

"We will *not* surrender," Holliston said. He looked at Alfred. "*You* will take command of the defence. You will ready the troops to resist the coming offensive. *And* you will hold the line."

"*Jawohl, Mein Führer*," Alfred said. He found himself torn between relief and fear. Relief that he hadn't been executed; fear that he'd been given an impossible job. But what else could he say? Defeatism was punishable by death. "Given enough time, we can make Germany East impregnable."

"And you will have something very special to help you," Holliston added. He smiled, unpleasantly. "But for now…I believe we have other business."

And there was something in the way he said it that chilled Alfred to the bone.

CHAPTER THREE

Berlin, Germany Prime
29 October 1985

"That's the latest set of reports, *Herr* Chancellor," Field Marshal Gunter Voss said, as he tapped the updated map. "The SS lines are definitely beginning to solidify."

Volker Schulze, Chancellor of the Greater German *Reich* - or at least the part of it that accepted the authority of the Berlin Government - nodded in irritation. He'd hoped, against experience, that the SS stormtroopers would have broken completely, but they were trained to rebound from defeat faster than any other military unit in the *Reich*. It had been *years* since he'd served alongside them, yet he still recalled how little difference losing the CO - or even the NCOs - had made. The SS, whatever its flaws, had been a meritocracy. A skilled stormtrooper - assuming he had good Aryan blood - had every prospect of rising in the ranks.

"I see," he said, finally. Life had been a great deal less complicated last year, when he'd been nothing more than a factory foreman. "Can you keep thrusting forward?"

"Not until we get our logistics network up and running," Voss said. "*Herr Chancellor*, we simply don't have the logistics to push them further back."

"Work on it," Volker ordered. He knew Voss was right. No one had ever seriously contemplated having to fight a civil war, of all things. The *Reich* had countless contingency plans - everything from an invasion of Britain to a defence of Occupied France - but none of them had ever been put into practice. "I assume we are continuing to harass them?"

"Of course," Voss said. "But we're reaching the point of diminishing returns. Even our air supremacy is under threat."

Volker scowled as he contemplated the map. The *Luftwaffe* had largely joined the provisional government, once the *Reich* Council had lost its grip on power, but the air force had paid a high price for its decision. A number of bases and aircraft had been destroyed, either by sleeper agents or cruise missiles, while the remaining pilots were exhausted and running out of supplies. They had planned for an intensive operational tempo, he'd been assured, but - once again - the *Reich's* planning had not matched reality. He had a nasty feeling that he would have to order the air force to reduce its operations soon, before exhaustion and poor maintenance took an even greater toll on its pilots.

A shame we can't send the navy, he thought. The *Kriegsmarine* had been solidly behind the rebels from the start, save for a handful of warships that had fled harbour and escaped to the east. *They've done very little so far.*

He shook his head in annoyance. It was a foolish thought, unworthy of him. The navy *couldn't* come to grips with the SS, not when the SS was largely landlocked. Maintaining a blockade of the handful of ports in Germany East was largely pointless. The Americans weren't going to sell supplies to the SS. And if the Chinese decided to pour fuel on the fire by shipping weapons to Germany East, there was nothing the *Kriegsmarine* - or anyone else - could do about it.

"Order the *Luftwaffe* to do whatever it sees fit," he said, finally. "If they feel they have to reduce their operational tempo, they can reduce their operational tempo."

Voss didn't argue. That worried Volker more than he cared to admit. He'd been a stormtrooper, but he'd never reached high command. Voss, on the other hand, was a Field Marshal. He'd never hesitated to point out the limits of Volker's experience before...

...And if he wasn't arguing, it meant the situation was truly dire.

Volker looked down at the map, silently translating the pencil-drawn symbols into something understandable. Berlin was safe now, ringed by panzer divisions and infantrymen who'd force-marched from the coastal defences of France to the heart of the *Reich*. But the SS had utterly *devastated* the land between Berlin and Warsaw. The reports pulled no punches, none at all. Every last bridge had been destroyed, every last village and town had been devastated…improvised mines had been scattered everywhere, covered by a handful of commando teams who'd fired a couple of shots at the advancing soldiers, then scattered into the undergrowth and vanished.

And the enemy defence lines are forming, Volker thought, coldly. *They'll be ready for us soon.*

He sighed, then looked up at Voss. "If we leave them alone for six months," he said, "they'll be ready for us."

"Yes, *Herr Chancellor*," Voss said.

Volker rubbed his eyes. He'd often considered emigrating to Germany East; he'd *planned* to emigrate, once he reached retirement age and his children were married off. And he'd *visited*, during his career. He knew just how tough the easterners were. Given time to raise and deploy a new army, they could make the cost of winning the war intolerable. If it had been possible, he would have accepted sundering the *Reich* in two. But he knew, all too well, that Karl Holliston wouldn't accept anything less than the reconquest of the entire *Reich*.

There can be no peace, he thought, morbidly.

"Field Marshal," he said. "Could we win before the first snowfall?"

Voss looked unsurprised by the question. Volker rather suspected he'd been considering the issue himself.

"Perhaps," he said, finally. "We don't know when the snow is going to fall."

"But we could still chew them to ribbons," Volker mused. "They'd either have to abandon vast tracts of land or fight us."

He scowled at the thought. The SS - and the *Heer* - was *good* at slotting newcomers into units and relying on the old hands to teach them the ropes. There was no such thing as a unit *completely* composed of soldiers - or stormtroopers - fresh out of basic training. But if the SS's combat veterans were killed, the SS would have fewer experienced soldiers to teach the newcomers how to fight. It wasn't a pleasant thought, but it was one that had to be faced. A campaign - even a limited thrust eastwards - would make it harder for the enemy to regenerate their forces.

"Yes, *Herr Chancellor*," Voss said. "But if we waited six months, we would also be far stronger."

Volker had his doubts. Germany Prime *might* possess most of the *Reich's* industry, but Hans Krueger had made it clear that their industrial base was on its last legs. The demands of the war hadn't helped, either. They needed to give the machinery a rest; instead, they'd upped the demands to support the military. Pushing the industry any harder might result in a general collapse. And even if they *didn't* have a wave of large-scale failures, they'd still pay a terrifying price for occupying Germany East.

And they might get their atomic bombs up and running, he thought. It was anyone's guess just how long it would be before the SS unlocked their own bombs. A trained engineer, he'd been warned, might *just* be able to remove the PAL system and improvise a replacement detonator of his own. *What will they do if they have working atomic bombs?*

He cursed under his breath. The Siberian missile fields probably couldn't be turned on Germany Prime, but they *could* be pointed at America. And Karl Holliston was insane. Who knew *what* he'd do if he thought he was losing the war? Taking the United States down too might make perfect sense to him. Or perhaps he'd reason that the Americans would retaliate against Germany Prime, giving Germany East a chance to rebuild. Stopping him from using the damned things was worth almost *any* price.

"We have to move now," he said, softly. "If we give them too much time, they will use it against us."

"Yes, *Herr Chancellor*," Voss said. "But I should caution you that we need more manpower."

Volker sighed. Almost every male German in the *Reich* had *some* military skills - thanks to the Hitler Youth - but not all of them had gone into the military. They'd started training volunteers even before the siege of Berlin had begun, yet it would take months before the new recruits were ready for the demands of modern war. There was an entire army in South Africa, but getting it back to the mainland in time for the big offensive was impossible. Even disengaging from the South African War was proving tricky.

"See what you can drag up," he said, finally.

"My staff did have an idea," Voss said. "We could approach the French or the Italians for manpower."

Volker looked up at him, sharply. "Are they mad?"

"Italy and France both have good reason to want to keep Holliston *out* of power," Voss pointed out, dryly. "Fighting beside us would be better than fighting Holliston on his own, later."

"Hah," Volker said.

In truth, he wasn't sure *how* to react. The French could fight well, he'd been told, but they'd lost so badly in 1940 that they'd never recovered. Their infantry had a great deal of experience fighting in North Africa, yet could they stand up to combat in Germany East without panzers and jet fighters of their own? And the Italians were laughable. They'd been jokes back in 1940 and they were *still* jokes. Their empire would have fallen apart *long* ago if they hadn't been backed up by the *Reich*.

And they weren't interested in crushing the life out of their territories, he acknowledged, ruefully. *They might have lost their empires if their subjects hadn't realised that they were better masters than us.*

"If you can convince them to send troops, do so," he said, finally. "But see what they want in exchange."

He shook his head in frustration. The *Reich* simply didn't have many diplomats. A year ago, the subject nations had known to obey - or else - while the North Atlantic Alliance had known better than to lower its guard, no matter what honeyed words came out of Berlin and the *Reich*. Now...he didn't know *quite* how to talk to the French. Barking orders was no longer possible, but he didn't want to let the French walk all over him either...

"They'll want political freedom," Voss predicted. "And the return of Alsace-Lorraine."

Volker nodded. The French had made that demand before, back when Gudrun had tried to come to terms with them. And it was politically impossible. There wasn't a single ethnic Frenchman living in Alsace-Lorraine, not now. They'd all been driven out in 1950, when the *Reich* had been reshaping Western Europe after the war. The French hadn't even had the worst of it. Countries such as Belgium and the Netherlands had completely disappeared from the map. The lucky ones - the ones who couldn't pass for German - had been shipped into French North Africa.

And the unlucky ones were exterminated, he thought, grimly.

He'd been in the SS. He *knew* how *Untermenschen* were treated. And yet it had been a shock to realise just how *many* *Untermenschen* had been slaughtered. The dispassionate remarks in school textbooks utterly failed to convey the sheer horror of what the *Reich* had done. Volker wouldn't shed any tears for *Untermenschen* who had opposed the *Reich*, but how many of the *Reich's* victims had been enemies? How many of the dead had been Germans who had been wounded in combat or born with defects?

"See what they say," he said. "But we can't give them Alsace-Lorraine."

It was going to be a nightmare, he predicted. The *Reich* knew how to handle subject states - they supported the *Reich* and did as they were told, in exchange for what scraps the *Reich* offered them - but independent states? What would happen when the French started to build up their armoured divisions? Or produce their own jet fighters? Or even develop their own nuclear weapons? Would they want revenge for forty years of oppression?

"They may be satisfied merely to know that the SS beast has been slain," Voss offered. He didn't sound confident. "We will see."

Volker sighed. "Begin drawing up the plans to take the offensive as soon as possible," he said. "Even if we don't have the French and Italians in support, we need to move anyway."

Which will weaken us if they decide to take matters into their own hands, he thought. The French had a long way to go before they could stand up to the *Reich*, let alone match it, but what would happen if the German population was thoroughly sick of war? *And they will know it.*

He sighed as Voss saluted and left the room. If he'd known what Gudrun would unleash, when she'd started asking pointed questions, he would have gone to her father and...and done what? Konrad would still have been left in the hospital, trapped between life and death; his parents, his sister, his girlfriend utterly unaware of his condition. It wasn't fair to blame Gudrun, he told himself sharply, for everything that had happened. The underlying weakness of the *Reich*, the steady collapse of the entire structure, had been underway long before she'd been born, let alone reached adulthood.

Her father might have told her not to meddle in politics, he thought. *She might have been pulled out of the university and married to someone he chose, but would it have made a difference? Or would we have fallen harder because no one was prepared to stand up and point out that the Kaiser had no clothes?*

He looked down at the map for a long moment. He'd approved of Gudrun as a possible wife for his son, back when the world had made sense. And then his feelings had grown mixed when she'd made it impossible for him to hide from the truth any longer. Part of him had been angry at her, even though he'd *known* it wasn't her fault. And now she was a prisoner, taken by the SS. Volker knew, all too well, just what the SS would do with her, after everything she'd done to them. He'd hoped Gudrun - or her body - would turn up somewhere in Berlin, but there had been no sign of her.

She's been taken to Germanica, he thought. *And all we can do is hope they give her a quick death.*

There was a tap on his door. He looked up to see his aide, looking grim.

"*Herr Chancellor*," he said. "Minister Krueger is here to see you."

"Show him in," Volker ordered. "And then bring us both coffee."

He schooled his face into impassivity as Hans Krueger was shown into his office. Krueger was a smart man, but he wasn't a *likeable* man. He'd been on the former *Reich* Council and had switched sides, a little too quickly, after the uprising. Volker had no reason to distrust him - Holliston wouldn't give Krueger a quick death if Krueger were captured - but there was something about Krueger that annoyed him. The man was more concerned with his figures than the real world.

And those figures can change the real world, Volker thought. There had been something oddly effeminate about the accountants in the factory, the men who could decide - seemingly on a whim - who was worth keeping and who could be fired. And Krueger had something of the same air about him. He was not a manly man. *He cannot be trusted completely.*

"*Herr Chancellor*," Krueger said. He was carrying a leather folder under one arm. "Do you have a moment?"

"Too many of them," Volker admitted. He wanted to be out there, *doing something*. "Is this important?"

"I've been running the latest set of figures," Krueger said, quietly. He took a seat and opened the folder. "We're looking at a total economic crash within three months."

Volker sucked in his breath. "Are you sure?"

"That's the best-case," Krueger said. "Frankly, we've been pushing everything too hard over the last decade. We simply didn't give our industrial base any chance to breathe."

"I didn't make those decisions," Volker snarled.

"I know," Krueger said. "But we still have to deal with the consequences."

He looked grim. "It gets worse," he added. "Food supplies are starting to run out."

"Then grow more," Volker said.

"We can't, not immediately," Krueger said. "Quite a few farmers were drafted into the army, *Herr Chancellor*. That had an impact on productivity. But we also drew most of our food from Germany East. Germany Prime - alone - cannot feed itself forever. We have already started expanding our farming capabilities, but it will be several years before they make an impact."

He sighed. "And if we have an industrial collapse at the same time," he added, "we will be staring at outright chaos."

"Take food from the French," Volker said, after a moment. "Or buy it from the Americans."

"The French don't produce enough food to meet our demands - even if they were *willing* to meet our demands," Krueger warned. "They never pushed production - they knew we'd steal it. And the Americans will expect us to pay."

"And we don't have any cash," Volker said. The *Reich's* stockpiles of foreign cash had always been very limited. "There's nothing we can use to pay the Americans."

"If indeed they have the food on hand," Krueger added. "They might not be able to meet our demands either."

Volker cursed under his breath. The Americans *had* been helpful, but he couldn't help thinking that the United States would welcome a German collapse. Whoever won the war would need to spend years rebuilding, years the Americans could use to make themselves invincible, utterly untouchable. They were already too far ahead of the *Reich*...

...And they weren't even his *real* problem.

He gritted his teeth. "And if the entire population starts to starve..."

"We lose," Krueger said, bluntly. "We need to take action, quickly."

"And that means we need this war to end, *quickly*," Volker agreed. "And if we don't win soon, we'll lose."

CHAPTER FOUR

Germanica (Moscow), Germany East
29 October 1985

They were scared of her.

Gudrun clung to the thought, even though she felt utterly naked and utterly helpless. The SS was *scared* of her. They had stripped her down to her underwear, searched her so thoroughly that she doubted there was even a millimetre of her body that hadn't been inspected, then chained her up so carefully that she could barely move. And if that hadn't been enough, they'd repeated the search at regular intervals. Did they think she'd somehow managed to conceal a weapon even as they carried her into the very heart of their territory?

She knew it was insane - she knew they *weren't* scared of her - but it was all that gave her hope. They'd driven her east, then transferred her to a plane. She wouldn't even have known they were flying her to Germanica if one of her guards hadn't said it out loud, clearly unaware she was listening. Or perhaps it had been deliberate. They'd *wanted* her to fear...

"They will try to break down your resistance," Horst had told her. It felt like *years* since they'd been students together, plotting how best to bring down the *Reich*. "They will want to make you feel helpless, as if you have lost all control over yourself. And if you let them convince you that you *are* hopeless, you're doomed."

But it was hard, so hard, to keep from feeling helpless. Gudrun had been arrested before, but the SS hadn't known who or what she was. They'd seen her as just another troublemaker, a student in the wrong place at the wrong time...and the experience had nearly proved too much for her. Now...they knew who she was; they knew what she'd done. She had no reason to expert mercy.

And the only reason they went to so much trouble to take me alive, she thought, *was because they want me for something.*

She shivered, helplessly. The temperature had been dropping for hours now, ever since she'd been taken from the airport and dumped into a prison cell, but none of the guards had offered her anything more substantial to wear. Her bra and panties, already torn by the repeated strip searches, provided no protection at all. She couldn't help wondering if she would catch her death of cold before the SS started torturing her, then decided the cold was probably part of the torture. Horst had warned her that they would do everything in their power to break her will, but his words hadn't been anything like enough to convoy the sheer sense of helplessness and futility pervading her body and soul. Her life was definitely no longer her own.

The cell itself was completely empty, save for a bed and a bucket she was too chained up to use. She suspected it was yet another humiliation, although they hadn't fed her anything like enough for it to be a real problem. And they hadn't made any attempt to hide the cameras either, hanging four of them from the ceiling and wrapping them in steel mesh. Absurdly, the sight almost made her giggle. She was chained - and even if she hadn't been, she was too short to reach them, even if she stood on the bed.

But they might have taller prisoners, she thought, Horst was a head taller than her - and she knew the SS prized height. For all she knew, Horst was a dwarf compared to some of his former comrades. Besides, the Slavs she'd seen had all been short and ugly, but was that true of *all* Slavs? *And they clearly don't want to take any risks.*

She forced herself to relax, even though it was futile. Her wrists and ankles ached; the metal belt they'd wrapped around her hips dug into her flesh and she was hungry, terrifyingly hungry. She'd never really gone hungry in her life, even though some of the food she'd had to choke down at school was barely a step or two above the slop fed to prisoners and *Gastarbeiters.* Now, she couldn't help feeling as though she didn't have the energy for anything. It wouldn't be long, she suspected, before she died…

…And the hell of it was that a quick death would probably be a relief.

The cell door opened. Two burly male guards stepped through, glaring suspiciously at her as if they expected her to have vanished somewhere in the last hour. Gudrun resisted the urge to rattle her chains at them; instead, she just waited - reluctantly - as they glanced around the cell, then yanked her to her feet and shoved her through the door. They didn't speak to her, they never did. Only one of her captors had spoken to her since she'd been taken prisoner and Gudrun hadn't seen *her* for days.

She forced herself to stand still as they ran their hands over her body, telling herself - desperately - that it was *Horst* who was touching her. But it was hard to believe it - truly believe it - when their rough fingers were pinching at her flesh and tugging down her panties to check that she hadn't managed to conceal something between her legs. And this time, they were worse. Their hands were rubbing at her clit as if they expected her to enjoy it, their breathing growing deeper and deeper with anticipation as they pushed her over to the table and bent her over. She realised, feeling a surge of fear, that she was about to be raped...

"That will do," a cool voice said.

The guards started, then let go of her. Gudrun twisted her head and saw *Hauptsturmfuehrer* Katharine Milch standing there, looking grim. The older woman - the first woman she'd seen wearing a uniform - looked hellishly intimidating. If she had a *right* to wear that uniform, Gudrun thought, she wouldn't just be as good as a man, she'd be better. And she'd saved Gudrun from a fate worse than death...

...Or had she?

Did they really plan to rape me, Gudrun asked herself, *or was she always meant to save me from them?*

It was impossible to tell. She knew just what horrors awaited prisoners, but she found it hard to believe that the SS guards in Germanica were so undisciplined that they would rape a prisoner without permission. And yet... she couldn't help feeling relief, clinging to Katharine like a drowning man would cling to a lifejacket. But had the whole incident been set up to *make* her cling to Katharine? She had no way to know.

She cursed under her breath as Katharine pulled her panties back into position, then helped Gudrun to walk slowly towards the door. It was hard, so hard, to walk with a chain wrapped around her ankles. If Katharine hadn't been holding her, she would have fallen over several times. And yet…what *was* Katharine doing? Where were they going?

It was a relief to be out of the cell, but the interior of the building wasn't particularly reassuring. She couldn't help remembering the interior of the first prison she'd visited - and her old school, which had probably been designed by the same person. Grey walls, solid metal doors…no signs on the walls, let alone paintings or anything else that would give the building personality. It was completely soulless…she shivered, again, as they reached an elevator and stepped inside. The air was, if anything, growing colder. It was all she could do to keep her teeth from chattering.

She hadn't wanted to talk to Katharine, but she couldn't help herself. "Where are we going?"

The older woman gave her a cold look. "Someone wants to see you."

Gudrun winced as the elevator came to a halt. She had a nasty feeling she knew *precisely* who they were going to see. The doors hissed open, revealing a carpeted hallway leading down to a pair of heavy wooden doors. She stepped gingerly out of the elevator, silently relieved to walk on something other than cold stone; Katharine helped her down the corridor, snarling at her whenever she looked left or right. And yet, Gudrun couldn't help herself. The walls were decorated in portraits of the honoured dead, all looking too handsome and muscular to be real. She caught sight of a man who looked like Horst, drawn against a burning panzer and wondered, suddenly if he was a relative. Horst had never said much about his father, merely that he'd died in the wars…

Two SS stormtroopers stood guard outside the doors, their eyes barely flickering over Gudrun as she approached. They didn't even seem to be aware that she was practically naked! She felt a sudden flicker of anger as Katharine spoke to the guards, realising that she'd been right all along. The guards who had dragged her out of her cell had been acting, giving Katharine an opportunity to play the hero…she pushed the thought aside, sharply, as the doors opened to reveal the largest office she'd ever seen. A single wooden desk was positioned at the far end, a man she recognised from his photographs sitting behind it. And seventeen men were standing against the wall, staring at her.

Gudrun had to fight to keep from cringing. She'd been brought here - chained up, almost nude - to humiliate her in front of the men. Karl Holliston, sitting behind the desk, had planned the whole thing. He didn't think of women as fit for anything, save for being mothers, daughters and housewives. Exposing her was merely the first step towards undermining everything she'd done. It would be hard for any of the men to respect her after they'd seen her in such a fallen state…

She shivered. Two years ago, a girl she'd known - vaguely - had been expelled after allowing her boyfriend to take nude photographs of her. Gudrun and her girlfriends had been horrified. How could she have allowed her boyfriend to take photographs that might - easily - fall into the wrong hands? No one had ever looked at her the same way again. In the end, she'd emigrated to Germany South, where all that mattered was the right bloodline and the ability to bear children. Gudrun had no idea what had happened to the poor girl after that.

Katharine pushed her forward, gently. Gudrun braced herself, stood as firmly as the chains would allow and began to walk towards the desk. The watching men made no sound, no catcalls nor expressions of pity; they just watched as she stepped forward. Holliston's face twisted oddly as he studied her, his expression dark and cold. Gudrun shivered, despite herself. Holliston wasn't interested in anything, but power. He'd do *anything* to keep it.

She came to a halt and stared at him, forcing herself to meet his eyes. She'd met enough powerful men - her father had always seemed all-powerful to her - to know that open defiance was rarely welcomed. Neither her father nor her male teachers had been pleased when she'd talked back to them, although - in all honesty - her mother and her female teachers had been pretty much the same. Hell, it had been harder to predict what would set her mother off…

"Gudrun," Holliston said. His voice was very cold. "Battle-maiden."

Gudrun felt a hot flash of anger. Only Konrad had ever called her that, back when they'd been getting to know one another. He'd said it to tease her…

"You could have borne the *Reich* many strong sons," Holliston continued. "Instead, you chose to bring it down."

It was hard to keep the smirk off her face, despite the danger. Holliston and his ilk had *never* considered that a mere *woman* could be dangerous. Hell, Gudrun had been *eighteen* when Konrad had been wounded. Old enough to marry, old enough to bear children, but not old enough to be considered a responsible adult. She'd practically been a minor child, as far as the law was concerned; she'd certainly enjoyed no greater rights at eighteen than at eight. But then, Holliston probably needed a woman to be a grandmother before he started taking her seriously...

She threw caution to the winds. "The man I was going to marry was wounded in one of your wars," she said. There was no point in trying to hide it. She'd told the story often enough that it had probably reached Germanica by now. "And you didn't even have the decency to tell us what had happened to him."

Holliston showed no visible reaction to her words. "Your boyfriend gave his life in defence of civilisation," he said. "You betrayed him."

Gudrun felt another surge of anger. That comment *stung*. Konrad would *not* have approved of her standing up to the *Reich*. He'd been a loyal SS stormtrooper. *And* she'd married Horst...

"He didn't die," she said. "You kept him alive, unable to heal him and unable to just let him go. You betrayed him."

She forced her voice to harden. "You betrayed *everyone*."

"And you betrayed the *Reich*," Holliston countered. "Or have you forgotten the oath you swore every day at school? And when you joined the BDM?"

"I forgot nothing," Gudrun said. He had a point, she had to admit. She'd been swearing loyalty long before she'd actually known what the words *meant*. "But the *Reich* betrayed its citizens first."

She leaned forward, almost overbalancing and falling over. "Konrad was your *ideal*," she said. "Brave and bold, blonde and strong; I could have been *happy* as his wife, bearing his children and bringing them up while he fought to defend the *Reich*. But instead he was killed in an unwinnable war and you didn't even have the decency to admit what *happened* to him."

"And if that is what you will do to Konrad," she added, "what will you do to everyone who does *not* come up to scratch? Your stormtroopers killed young men in Germany Prime, they raped and abused young women. How can you claim to be fighting for the *Volk* when you abuse it?"

She looked at the other men in the room. "What will happen to your sons? Or to your daughters?"

"Be silent," Holliston said.

Gudrun ignored him. She'd been silent for too long. Eighteen years of her life had been spent accepting that her place in the world would always be subordinate to a man, even though she'd managed to win a place at university.

She'd loved Konrad - she admitted it to herself - but she knew now she would never have been *happy* as a housewife, doing nothing more than cooking his food and bearing his children. And perhaps she would have been left alone if Konrad had gone back to the war and died there.

"You and yours ruled the *Reich* for forty years," she said, turning back to him. If these were going to be her last words, they were going to be good ones. "And yet you're scared to let the people *breathe*. You ran the entire country into the ground! Do you really think I could have gotten *anywhere* if the people hadn't had a cause? You made your own enemies."

She allowed her voice to harden. "You did this to us," she added. "Your entire claim to power is based on a lie."

"I do not expect you to understand," Holliston said. His voice dripped contempt. "You're only a *girl*."

Gudrun bit down on her reaction, *hard*. He *wanted* her to scream at him; he *wanted* her to explode in feminine rage, to prove to his allies that Gudrun was just an emotional girl - a child - whose opinion was too emotional to be valid. But she'd sat on the cabinet, back in Berlin. She'd learned more, she suspected, than he'd ever realised. And keeping her temper under control was only part of it.

"I don't think that anyone has any doubt that I am a young woman," she said, shrugging as through her near-nakedness didn't bother her. "But does that make me wrong?"

She looked up, her eyes moving from face to face. "Does that make me wrong?"

Holliston made no attempt to answer the question. Part of her considered that to be a good thing, a tacit confession that he had *no* answer. But the rest of her knew it wasn't ideal. She could be right - or wrong - and yet it didn't matter. She was still a prisoner, trapped hundreds of miles from her friends and comrades. And even if they knew where she was, getting to her would be almost impossible. She was doomed.

"You will be interrogated until we have drained every last scrap of information from you," Holliston informed her, instead. "And then you will be put on trial for crimes against the *Reich*."

Gudrun almost smiled. A trial? The *Reich* rarely bothered with trials. A criminal was guilty - if he wasn't guilty, he wouldn't be in jail. But she knew *exactly* what he had in mind. He could order her shot at any moment, but that would just make her a martyr. She'd be more dangerous to him in death than she'd ever been in life. He needed to break her - to discredit her - before he killed her. By then, death would probably be a relief.

"Take her back to her cell," he ordered. "And make sure she's held securely."

"*Jawohl, Mein Fuhrer,*" Katharine said.

Gudrun gritted her teeth as Katharine swung her around, then forced herself to walk towards the door. She was damned if she was showing weakness now, despite the humiliation. If she was a prisoner, she'd be a *tough* prisoner...

And maybe I can work on Katherine too, she thought, as she made her way out of the door and back down the corridor. *She might have ideas of her own now.*

It wasn't much, she acknowledged. But it was all she had.

CHAPTER FIVE

Berlin, Germany Prime
29 October 1985

"Are you sure this is going to work?"

Horst Albrecht shook his head, crossly. Kurt Wieland seemed to veer constantly between a determination to leave as quickly as possible and an understandable fear that they wouldn't be able to get past the first set of checkpoints. Horst didn't really blame him for being conflicted - he was an officer in the *Heer*, not someone who *should* be assigned to a stealth mission - but it was annoying. It was quite hard to see how Gudrun and Kurt were actually related.

"There is no way to *guarantee* this will work," Horst said. He glanced down at the forged papers, checking them again and again for any mistakes. It wasn't the first time he'd been an infiltrator, but the consequences for getting caught this time would be far worse. "If you want to go back to the infantry, go now."

He ignored Kurt's flash of anger as he checked the final pair of ID cards. They weren't *precisely* forgeries - they'd been produced at the SS office in Berlin - but they wouldn't match the records in Germanica. The SS had a mania for good records keeping - just about every German had a file, buried somewhere in the government bureaucracy - and a particularly alert officer might wonder why there wasn't a copy within reach. Horst would have been surprised if the SS-run government hadn't started changing everything it could, just to prevent the provisional government from sending spies and commandos into its territory.

But changing all of the ID cards in Germany East would be a long and time-consuming process, he told himself. The ID cards had been changed once, years ago; it had taken *months* before every last set of *old* papers had been collected and replacements issued by the bureaucracy. And *that* had been in peacetime. *There will be so much disruption in Germany East that changing the ID cards will be the least of their problems.*

"They should suffice," he said, finally. "Are you coming?"

"Of course," Kurt snapped.

Horst sighed, inwardly. Kurt had admitted, reluctantly, that he blamed himself for the whole mess. If he hadn't helped Gudrun break into the hospital, Gudrun would never have kick-started the whole chain of events that had led down to civil war. But Horst suspected Kurt was wrong. Gudrun, his wife and lover, was simply too determined to be deterred for long, even by her family's disapproval. She would have found another way into the hospital.

"Very good," Horst said. He would have preferred to go alone, even though he *knew* that having a second pair of hands along might be helpful. He'd been steeped in SS culture and tradition almost as soon as he could walk; Kurt, for all of his undoubted bravery, lacked the background he needed to pass unremarked. "Read the papers and *memorise* them."

Kurt gave him a sharp look as he picked up the first folder. "Do you expect this to be necessary?"

"It depends," Horst said. He smirked, suddenly. "Are you circumcised?"

Kurt glared. "No!"

"Good," Horst said. "It's very rare for *anyone* to be circumcised in Germany East. If you had been, we would have had to alter the file to reflect that."

He picked up his own folder and read it through again, reminding himself of the details. It was a careful balance between truth and lies, classing him as a resident of Germany East on one hand and an SS *Hauptsturmfuehrer* with special orders to report to Germanica on the other. He knew enough about the various special operations divisions to pass for a commando, as long as he didn't run into an *actual* commando. It was all too possible that the person they encountered would know everyone in his unit by name or reputation.

And I won't know all the private jokes and traditions, he thought. *I could be tripped up quite easily.*

"There's a surprising amount of truth here," Kurt said, finally. "Is it *wise* for me to be a native of Berlin?"

"Your accent marks you out as a Berliner," Horst said. Kurt would have lost the accent, if he'd been trained in Germany East. "There's no point in trying to pass you off as an Easterner."

He scowled. Kurt's accent was a problem, even though they'd done their best to compensate for it. There were plenty of SS officers who had been born and trained in Germany Prime, but in these days…they'd just have to hope they didn't run into someone who would be automatically suspicious of a Westerner. It shouldn't be that much of a danger. Karl Holliston had been born in Berlin, after all.

"Never mind that," he added. "Do you know the songs?"

"Most of them," Kurt said. He didn't sound pleased. "We learned them in the Hitler Youth."

"There'll be some verses you weren't taught," Horst said. He couldn't imagine parents being very pleased if their children had been taught the more bloodcurdling verses. "We'll go over that later, just in case we are invited to sing with the men."

Kurt gave him a sidelong look. "Is that likely?"

"The SS prides itself on being one big happy family," Horst said. "There's a great deal of rivalry, of course, but it's never *brutal*."

"Really," Kurt said, sarcastically.

Horst nodded. It was rare - almost unknown - for officers in the *Heer* to socialise with their men, but SS officers were *expected* to spend a great deal of time with their men. And local units would often fraternise with other units. It was supposed to help, when the units were mashed together into improvised battlegroups. The men already knew and respected their new comrades.

"The SS is not the *Heer*," he said, finally. "Don't make the mistake of assuming they're the same, just because they use the same weapons. There's a *lot* of little differences between them."

"And I might slip up because of them," Kurt said. "Perhaps I'll just let you do the talking."

"That would be a good idea," Horst said, dryly.

He put the folder down and opened up the latest set of reports from the front. The SS lines were firming up, unsurprisingly. Horst *knew* the *Waffen-SS*. They would have taken a beating, the defeat would have given them a terrible shock, but they were trained to recover from *anything*. He could imagine the officers moving from unit to unit, collecting stragglers and slotting them into the front lines; filling holes in some units, disbanding others until after the war. And probably doing whatever they could to slow down the advancing panzers as much as possible.

They'll need time to boost morale, Horst told himself. *Stopping a panzer or two won't be enough.*

Kurt looked up. "Do you have a plan?"

"Slip through the lines," Horst said. He tapped the papers. "We shouldn't have any trouble getting our hands on a jeep, once we show them our ID. And then we just head east to Germanica."

"That could take a while," Kurt observed.

Horst nodded. There were just over a thousand miles between Berlin and Germanica. Even if they took the *autobahns,* even if nothing got in their way, it would take at least five or six days to reach Germanica. And he knew there *would* be problems. There were plenty of checkpoints on the *autobahns.*

And even if there weren't, he thought, *they'll be using them to rush supplies and men to the front.*

"So we reach Germanica," Kurt added. "What *then?*"

"We play it by ear," Horst said. In truth, there was no way to come up with a proper plan until they knew the situation on the ground. "I have some... contacts...I might be able to convince to help us. If they refuse - or if we can't meet them - we will have to think of something else."

He scowled. He'd seen the *Reichstag* in Germanica before, back when he'd gone to the city for a Victory Day parade. It was a towering nightmare of stone and steel, protected by some of the finest stormtroopers in the *Reich.* And now, it was playing host to the self-promoted *Fuhrer* of the Greater German *Reich.* He would be surprised if the building wasn't ringed with defences, from antiaircraft guns to antitank weapons. It wouldn't be strange for Germany East.

Kurt cocked his head. "You think we can do it?"

"I think we have to try," Horst said.

He cursed under his breath. Gudrun had trusted him to protect her...and he'd failed. He'd been so wrapped up in his scheming - *their* scheming - that he'd missed the spy right under his nose. And now Gudrun was a captive.

She'd be on her way to Germany East, if she wasn't there already. There was no way he could just let her go. She was his wife, his lover, his friend. He *couldn't* abandon her.

But he knew what would happen if he was caught. The SS might have some difficulty comprehending that Gudrun was more than just a puppet, but they would have no such difficulty with him. Horst was a traitor in their eyes, a young man who had betrayed everything he'd been taught to respect; he could expect no mercy if his former masters got their hands on him. He'd be lucky if he was *merely* tortured to death.

He looked back at Kurt. There *was* a resemblance between him and his sister, Horst admitted, although it was more physical than mental. Kurt's face was a masculine version of *Gudrun's* face, his blond hair cropped short to fit a helmet. And he'd fought well in the war, no one doubted his courage. But it took a different kind of courage to stand up against the entire *Reich*…

"This is your last chance to stay here," he said, slowly. "Do you want to remain?"

"No," Kurt said. "I'm coming with you."

Horst nodded as he picked up the papers. "Where were you born?"

Kurt blinked, then realised what he meant. "Berlin, Braun Hospital," he said. "My parents were Herman and…"

"Don't volunteer information," Horst said. It was something he'd been taught during basic training. *Nervous* people, people with something to hide, volunteered information. "They'll think they're being manipulated."

He bounced question after question off Kurt, silently relieved that Kurt managed to keep his story relatively straight. It helped that much of the background information was actually *true*, but there were still risks. Whoever they encountered *might* know enough to poke holes in the narrative, then rip it apart. There was no way to be sure.

Kurt held up his hand. "Will they ask *all* of these questions?"

"I don't know," Horst said. "There's a war on. They might not have time for a full interrogation. It depends…"

He shook his head. "If they wanted to give you a security clearance, they'd send officers to your home, your school, your training camp…they'd go through your life in minute detail before deciding if they could trust you or not. Some very good people have been denied clearances for reasons beyond their control. But here...if they have reason to be suspicious, they might just toss questions at you to see if you slip up."

Kurt snorted. "What are the odds of us encountering someone who went to the same school as me?"

"Poor," Horst said. "But don't dismiss them entirely."

He picked up the next set of papers. "We're leaving this evening," he added. "Getting through the lines is not going to be fun."

"No," Kurt agreed. "Getting shot by our own side would be embarrassing."

Horst nodded. The *Waffen-SS's* lines had been shattered, but they were already being pulled back together. It was plausible - quite plausible - that a couple of officers would get lost *now*, yet that wouldn't last. The longer they waited, the greater the chance of being asked awkward questions that would lead to certain death. Horst would have liked to go earlier, but without the papers getting through the lines would be impossible. He could only hope the SS hadn't shot Gudrun out of hand.

They won't, he told himself, firmly. It was something to cling to. *They'll want to break her first.*

He gritted his teeth at the thought. Gudrun wasn't a common soldier. She certainly wasn't a common *politician*. She was an *inspiration* to hundreds of thousands of people who had been denied the chance to breathe free, denied the chance to speak their minds to their lords and masters. The SS wouldn't want to kill her; they'd want to turn her against her supporters...

And she might wind up wishing she was dead, he thought. He knew what they'd do to her, just to wear down her resistance before the *real* pain began. *She might even try to kill herself.*

He looked at Kurt. Kurt was an infantryman in the Berlin Guard. He hadn't even seen *fighting* until the civil war, let alone the true horrors of an insurgency. Kurt had no *conception* of just what his sister might be going through, no real understanding of what the SS did to those it considered irredeemable enemies...

And if Gudrun is dead when we arrive, Horst promised himself, *Karl Holliston will join her shortly afterwards.*

"Father," Kurt said, as the door opened. "Have you come to see us off?"

Horst winced. Herman Wieland looked to have aged twenty years in the last few days, although it was clear that he was holding himself under tight control. He had to be worried, Horst knew; he'd been a policeman, a man of power, yet he hadn't been able to protect his daughter. His world had shifted on its axis even before Gudrun had been taken prisoner; now, he was clearly unstable, unsure of his place in the world. Horst didn't really blame him for his doubts. Old certainties were fading everywhere.

"I'm going to the front," Herman said, quietly. "I just came to say goodbye."

Kurt stared. "Father!"

"I'm not as old as Grandpa Frank," Herman said. "I can pull my weight."

Horst frowned. "Berlin still needs policemen…"

"Berlin needs *better* policemen," Herman said, softly. "And I need to do *something*."

"You *are* a good policeman," Kurt said. "Father, I…"

Horst looked at Herman and felt a sudden wave of sympathy. Herman *had* been a good policeman, in the eyes of his family, but much of the city would probably disagree. The *Ordnungspolizei* had been the face of the regime, the iron fist in the iron glove…in many ways, they were more detested than the SS. Herman might not have taken advantage of his position, but far too many other policemen had milked it for all they could get. And now that the regime had fallen, the police were coming under attack.

And there's a war on, he thought, sourly. The enemy wasn't *that* far from the gates. Berlin was practically under martial law. *We don't have time to worry about the police.*

"Good luck," he said. Kurt shot him a betrayed look. "We'll bring her back."

Herman gave him a ghost of a smile. "Have many children," he said. "And name one after me."

"*Father*," Kurt protested.

"And you find a wife too," Herman added. "Someone…someone more suited to the modern world."

Horst kept his expression under control. Generations of German men - and women - had been raised to believe that a woman's place was in the home, that the husband and father was the head of the household and his word was law. But Herman's daughter had triggered a revolution and his wife had started to organise political meetings of her own. He couldn't blame Herman for being confused, for wanting something else. The world had moved on, leaving him behind.

He still loves his family, Horst thought. *But he doesn't know how to relate to them any longer.*

"Yes, father," Kurt said. "If I make it home, I will find a wife."

Herman nodded. He looked at Horst for a long moment, then turned and strode out of the chamber. Horst understood, all too well. Herman blamed him. Gudrun wouldn't have been kidnapped if she hadn't been with him...

There's enough blame to go around, he told himself. *And none of it is very helpful.*

"Get some rest," he ordered. He glanced at his watch, meaningfully. "It starts getting dark around 1800. We have to get through the lines before then."

"I understand," Kurt said. He sounded distracted. "Is he out of his mind?"

Horst bit down a whole string of unhelpful answers. "He was a soldier - an *experienced* soldier," he said, finally. It was true. "And we need as many of them as we can get."

He kept the rest of his thoughts to himself. Herman was fit for his age, but he was no match for an SS stormtrooper. There was no way he'd be able to keep up with the young men for long, although his experience might give him an advantage. But the provisional government was *very* short of experienced manpower. Herman might be needed, if only to teach lessons to the younger soldiers. They were going to war against one of the most formidable military forces in existence.

And he doesn't want to come home, Horst thought. *The modern world has no place for him.*

He shook his head. It smacked of defeatism to him. Giving up was, perhaps, the only true sin. He'd certainly been taught never to give up during basic training. And yet, he understood the impulse all too well. Did *he* fit into the brave new world any better than his father-in-law?

"Go get some rest," he repeated. There would be time to worry about the future *after* Gudrun was rescued and the war was over. "I want to be on our way at 1700."

"*Jawohl,*" Kurt said.

CHAPTER SIX

Berlin, Germany Prime
29 October 1985

"Drink your coffee," Ambassador Samuel Turtledove said. "There are people down there" - he jabbed a finger towards the window - "who would kill for that cup."

Andrew Barton nodded in agreement. Berlin was no longer on the verge of starvation, thanks to vast quantities of food being trucked in from the west, but supplies of everything from coffee to baby clothes were running short. The American embassy was about the only place in Berlin, save for a handful of government offices and military bases, where *real* coffee was freely available. It wasn't very *good* coffee, he had to admit, but it was better than the powdered grit Berliners were being served these days.

"I've had worse," he said. "The...*slop*...I had to drink on the front lines... no wonder the German soldier is so feared."

Turtledove smiled, then leaned forward. "Washington has been breathing down my neck for a full report," he said. "What do *you* make of the war?"

Andrew took a moment to gather his thoughts, sipping his coffee slowly. "I think in some ways we were overestimating the fighting power of the German military," he said. "And in others, we were underestimating it."

General William Knox lifted his eyebrows. "You think we were wrong?"

"The Germans haven't fought a peer power since the final push against Russia, forty years ago," Andrew said. "We had to use a lot of guesswork when we calculated how the average German division would stack up against its American or British counterpart. And a lot of those guesses might have been wrong."

He placed the cup on the desk and leaned back in his chair. "Their panzer divisions didn't strike me as anything like as fearsome as their reputation suggests," he said. "They move fast over open terrain, but even relatively small opposition slows them down remarkably. Their designers insist on having a radio in each panzer, a development they pioneered, but I had the impression that their technology is primitive and easy to disrupt. And their armour has not advanced at the same speed as their antitank weapons."

Knox frowned. "You think their panzers are inferior to our tanks?"

"I think so," Andrew said. "I'm no expert, sir, but I believe our armour is better - our antitank weapons are better too.

"The same seems to be true for their aircraft," he continued, after a moment. "Their air force *was* badly shaken by the uprising, then by the war, but it doesn't seem to have the same flexibility as ours. Their ground-based air defence units are *grossly* inferior to ours; their flak guns are of very little value unless the aircraft fly low, their rockets have a nasty tendency to lose their locks and fly off in random directions. The best system they have, as far as I can tell, is an oversized warhead designed to explode close to an aircraft."

He took a breath. "Technology-wise, we are at least ten years ahead of them," he concluded. "And I think their military would have taken a pasting if we had ever wound up fighting a shooting war."

Knox frowned. "That's not what we were told to expect."

"No," Andrew agreed. "And there is a reason for that, sir.

"They are tough, very tough. Their junior officers have less flexibility than I was told, but they are still good at spotting opportunities and thrusting through chinks in the enemy's defences. Their NCOs are very good at training up young men under fire, sir; I think they're actually tougher than ours, even if their tech *is* inferior. And they *understand* the tech at their disposal. The average panzer can be repaired, more or less on the go, by its crew."

"That's true of our tanks too," Knox objected.

"Not for everything," Andrew countered. "There are things that have to be sent back to the shop - or merely discarded."

He shook his head. "Overall, sir, their toughness may be enough to make up for their technological inferiority."

"There's another point, Mr. Ambassador," Knox said. "The Germans may never have *envisaged* a civil war. *We* certainly haven't planned, let alone exercised, a full-scale invasion of Texas or Montana. The Germans might have proved far more lethal if they'd launched an invasion of Britain or defended the Atlantic Wall against us."

Andrew nodded in agreement. He had no doubt that the Germans had thousands of contingency plans - everything from civil unrest to nuclear war - but those plans would have been shot to hell by the civil war. Units they'd thought they could rely on had turned on their leaders; others had been shattered by internal fighting, priceless weapons and equipment destroyed in the crossfire. The steady collapse of federal authority across the United States, just prior to the civil war, was one thing. *This* was far worse.

They had to put the invasion - and defence - of Germany Prime together from scratch, he thought. *And they did a damn good job.*

"Very true," Turtledove said.

He rested his hands on his desk as he spoke. "Washington has also been asking for recommendations," he added. "Do we continue the program of covert support? Do we go more *overt*? Or do we pull back, now that Berlin is safe?"

"There is no way that the SS does *not* know that we are assisting the Berlin Government," Andrew said, flatly. "They would have lost all doubt, Mr. Ambassador, the moment a Stinger blew one of their aircraft out of the sky. And we should brace ourselves for some kind of drastic reaction."

The Ambassador frowned. "They'd have to be insane to pick a fight with us."

"They would see it as *us* picking a fight with *them*," Andrew said.

"Kicking them while they were down," Knox agreed.

The Ambassador sighed. "So…what do you recommend?"

Andrew frowned. "My contacts tell me that the Provisional Government intends to take the offensive as soon as possible," he said. "They may intend to invade Germany East before winter, before it becomes impossible to continue the offensive. This is probably their best hope of winning the war quickly - and frankly, sir, we should help them as much as possible."

"But continuing the war will weaken them," Knox pointed out. "The longer they fight each other, the easier it will be for their *allies* to desert them."

"There's also the prospect of nuclear weapons being used," Andrew warned. "The longer the war, the greater the chance that *someone* will pop a nuke."

"Or fire on us," the Ambassador said.

"We would have to give the ABM system its first real test," Andrew agreed.

He scowled. No one, not even the President, knew how well the ABM system would handle a *real* missile attack. It had been tested, of course, but only on one or two ballistic missiles at a time. Who knew *what* would happen when - if - the Nazis launched over a hundred ballistic missiles at America? Even if two-thirds of them were intercepted, the remainder would be enough to destroy the United States.

And the President will burn the Reich in response, he thought. *And millions of innocent people will die.*

"My very strong recommendation is that we assist the Provisional Government as much as possible," he said, flatly. "The war needs to be ended as quickly as possible."

"If it can be ended," Turtledove mused. "General...if they launch an offensive, what are the odds of success?"

"Incalculable," Knox admitted. "We simply lack enough information to make a proper judgement. We have no idea how many panzers remain in Germany East, we have no idea how many aircraft are at their disposal, we have no idea how long the SS edifice will remain intact under the pressures of war. And, as Andrew says, we have a great many question marks over the nuclear bombs. It is impossible to say just what will happen when the *Heer* goes east.

"Practically speaking, I'd give them a reasonably good chance of establishing a solid foothold in Germany East before winter intervenes," he added. "I find it hard to imagine that the SS held back *many* panzers and aircraft from their great offensive. But I don't know if they can make it all the way to Germanica before winter. There's plenty of space to trade for time, plenty of strongpoints and fortresses that would need to be reduced...their logistics are going to be a major pain."

"1941 all over again," Andrew commented.

He'd studied Operation Barbarossa during his training and he *still* didn't understand how someone with even *minimal* military knowledge could have signed off on it without a few qualms. The Germans had faced France on roughly equal terms - the French had even had a few advantages of their own - but they'd won through bringing vastly superior force to bear at the decisive point. The Russians...Russia was immense, with plenty of space to trade for time, while the Red Army was staggeringly powerful. And the Germans had come far too close to losing.

And if they hadn't declared war on Japan, he thought, *we might have helped the Russians kick them out of Russia.*

"It's possible," Knox agreed. "We simply do not know."

Turtledove nodded. "And *your* recommendation, General?"

Knox considered it for a long moment. "It should be noted," he said, "that the longer the war rages on, the weaker the Germans will become. And while that *does* raise the spectre of a nuclear release, it also offers the prospect of the *Reich* collapsing and the end of a global threat. Whoever won the war would need to spend years rebuilding, if they *could* rebuild."

He paused, thoughtfully. "But we can probably do business with the Provisional Government," he added. "That is *not* true of the SS."

Andrew nodded. "In this case, the devil we *don't* know is better than the one we do," he said, flatly. "The SS is a devil we know too well."

He sighed. "You've already heard stories of atrocities," he added. "What sort of nightmare will be unleashed if the SS wins the war?"

"That isn't our concern," Knox said. "Our sole concern is protecting America."

"And a friendly regime in control of the *Reich* will be better for America than a regime that hates us," Andrew pointed out. "We can dicker with the Provisional Government."

"Perhaps," Turtledove said. He smiled, rather sourly. "Washington may overrule our recommendations anyway."

"Of course," Knox grunted. "The people in Washington aren't the people on the spot."

Andrew winced. He hadn't been back to the United States since before the crisis had begun, but he *had* been hearing things through the grapevine. *Everyone* wanted to have their say, from Poles and Frenchmen who wanted their countries to be independent to groups that wanted to isolate America from the world or even support the Nazis. And everyone was likely to be disappointed. Poland no longer existed - the Poles who had escaped were the only true Poles left in existence - and France was a shadow of its former self. Andrew suspected it would take generations for the French to recover, even if the Germans pulled out tomorrow...

And while the Provisional Government is better than the SS, he added silently, *they'll still put German interests first.*

Knox was right, he knew. Distance - and wishful thinking - had played a large role in several foreign policy disasters; now, with a nuclear power wracked by civil war, the disaster could be a great deal worse. But the President would have to balance a number of competing factions if he wanted to steer America through the growing crisis…and that might be impossible. There were mid-term elections coming up.

"I shall discuss the matter with Washington," Turtledove said. "Andrew, do you wish to return to the front lines?"

"As long as they will have me," Andrew said. "The chance to watch the war is not one to be dismissed."

"As long as it doesn't kill you," Knox said, dryly.

Andrew shrugged. He was an OSS operative, not an ambassador. The prospect of being scooped up by the SS had always loomed over him, even though - technically - he had diplomatic immunity. It wouldn't be the first time someone had 'vanished' in Berlin, or suffered what looked like a random mugging; he'd known the risks, he'd accepted the risks, when he'd taken the job. The prospect of being killed in battle, even as an observer, seemed cleaner, somehow.

"I know the risks," he said.

Turtledove nodded. "Get a good night's sleep first," he said. "And make sure you eat a good meal before you go back to the front."

Yes, mother, Andrew thought.

He couldn't blame Turtledove for worrying. The Germans would feed him as long as he remained within their ranks, but their rations weren't very good, certainly not by American standards. And he'd been hearing dire rumours about the food situation, rumours that hadn't been quashed by the sudden influx of supplies. It made him wonder, deep inside, if the *Reich* was on the verge of starvation as well as everything else. But there was no way to be sure.

At least until it happens, he thought, coldly.

"Thank you, Mr. Ambassador," he said, rising. "I'll make sure of it."

———

There were times, Volker had to admit, when he thought he understood Karl Holliston's desire for power perfectly.

He was Chancellor, but he wasn't omnipotent; he could make some decisions, but others had to be decided by consensus. And *this* decision, perhaps the most important of all, was one that *had* to be unanimous. There was no way he could push it forward on his own authority.

"We are currently bringing up additional panzer divisions, along with supporting elements and aircraft," Voss said. His finger traced lines on the map as he spoke. "If everything goes according to plan, we will be ready to launch a major offensive in two weeks."

He paused. "We will be thrusting towards Warsaw, but our *principle* objective will be to envelop and destroy the remaining SS forces in the region," he continued. "Once those forces have been crushed, we will reform our divisions and continue eastwards. Our goal will be to capture Germanica before the first snowfall."

There was a long pause. "I acknowledge that there are risks involved," he concluded. "But I believe this offers the best chance for a speedy victory."

Volker kept his expression under tight control, his face betraying none of his concerns. The plan was daring, he had to admit. Perhaps it was *too* daring. Defeat would cripple them as surely as victory would cripple the enemy. And yet...and yet...Voss was right. It offered the best chance for a speedy victory.

"Chancy," Admiral Wilhelm Riess said, finally. The Head of the *Abwehr* didn't sound impressed. "If this plan fails, we will have nothing left."

"We are already raising new units and bringing back others from South Africa," Voss said, tartly. "Defeat will weaken us badly, Admiral, but it will also weaken our enemies."

"And we have to win the war quickly," Foreign Minister Engelhard Rubarth said. "We are already growing weak, Admiral. It will not be long before our puppet states start thinking they can make decisions for themselves."

If they're not already contemplating the possibilities, Volker thought. *Even a relatively minor challenge to our power could prove disastrous.*

"The South Africans are already turning unfriendly," he said. "And if *they* are turning unfriendly, how long will it be before others follow suit?"

"They have friends and allies in Germany East," Riess pointed out. "Of *course* they hate us."

CHRISTOPHER G NUTTALL

Volker nodded. The SS had been the loudest supporter of the South African War, demanding - time and time again - that vast numbers of German soldiers were sent to prop up an increasingly unpopular government. And then they'd *lied* about the war...he fought down the sudden surge of hatred, forcing himself to think clearly. If South Africa turned hostile, they could cause real trouble...

"All the more reason to win quickly," he said. If they won the war in the next three months, they *might* be able to hold the *Reich* together. "Can anyone think of a better option?"

There was no answer. Volker wasn't surprised. There was no compromise - no *reasonable* compromise - that Karl Holliston would accept. Even a negotiated surrender would probably be rejected, unless it was complete, total and utterly unconditional. Holliston didn't just want power, he wanted revenge. And there wasn't a single person, sitting at the table, who would be safe if Holliston won the war. They'd all be *lucky* if they were merely executed.

"So we proceed," he said. "Any dissent?"

"We can shift our goals, if the offensive fails," Riess said. "Can't we?"

"We have contingency plans," Voss assured him. "Merely chewing up the remains of their divisions will make it easier for us to launch another offensive in the spring."

"We will have to be stern with the Easterners," Luther Stresemann said. The Head of the Economic Intelligence Service looked grim. "Far too many of them are behind the SS."

Volker winced. The SS's propaganda offensive was crude, but it was effective. The Easterners *knew* they lived on the edge of civilisation. They wouldn't forsake the SS unless they believed their interests would be protected.

"We treat them firmly, but with compassion," he said, bluntly. "Unless they turn on us."

"They will," Voss said. He sounded very sure of himself. "We have to be ready to take strong action."

"But no atrocities," Volker said. There were fire-eaters who wanted to retaliate for everything the SS had done, but he knew it couldn't be permitted. "I don't want a single incident they can use against us."

But he knew, even as he said it, that it was nothing more than wishful thinking.

CHAPTER SEVEN

Germanica (Moscow), Germany East
29 October 1985

Karl Holliston rarely liked to admit his mistakes. It was, he'd learned as a child, a form of weakness. And yet, he conceded, dragging Gudrun into his office - in chains - had been a mistake. He'd expected a cringing girl, but he'd underestimated her. The questions she'd asked - the questions he'd dismissed - had struck a nerve. Far too many of his subordinates would have asked those questions themselves, if it had been safe to do so.

He scowled as he walked into the Map Room. It would be easy to have Gudrun shot - or tortured - but that would serve no purpose. He needed to *break* her. And he needed to use her to break her friends and allies in the treacherous Provisional Government. But that would take time, time he suspected he didn't have.

"I have received word from one of my agents in Berlin," he said, once the door was firmly closed. It wasn't something he would have said out loud, not normally, but he needed to remind his officers that he had access to sources they didn't have. The *Waffen-SS* had good reason to be annoyed with him. "The enemy is planning an early offensive."

Oberstgruppenfuehrer Alfred Ruengeler frowned. "How early?"

"As in the next two weeks," Karl said, flatly. "They're planning to pocket our forces and destroy them."

Ruengeler turned his attention to the map. "They'll find it hard to get enough forces into position to pocket ours," he said. "We blew all the bridges and mined most of the roads…"

His voice trailed off. "They'd have to erect pontoon bridges as they went along," he mused, slowly. "But if they were determined…and they had enough air cover."

Karl nodded, impatiently. The *Waffen-SS* had concentrated on close support aircraft for the troops, not jet fighters. Normally, the *Luftwaffe* would have provided top cover, but now the remainder of the *Luftwaffe* was on the wrong side. And losses during the Battle of Berlin had been staggering. His few remaining aircraft had been pulled back from the front lines to airbases where they would be held in reserve, implicitly conceding the skies to the rebels…

And if they bring in help from the Americans, he thought, *we will never regain air superiority.*

"We will have to pull back our forces," Ruengeler said. "If we lose the remaining divisions, *Mein Fuhrer*, we will lose the war along with them."

"No," Karl said. "We cannot let the enemy gain a foothold in Germany East."

Ruengeler looked unconvinced. "*Mein Fuhrer*," he said, "if they destroy those divisions, they will gain that foothold anyway."

"It isn't that simple," Karl said.

He scowled at the map. Ruengeler was a military man. He didn't understand the *political* issue - or the looming disaster threatening the entire *Reich*. If the rebels gained control of a substantial section of Germany East, they could use it to undermine his support and encourage his subordinates to overthrow him. The collective loyalty of the senior *Gauleiters* couldn't have filled a thimble. If they saw their power under threat, they would try to find ways to come to terms with the rebels.

And while they will probably fail, he thought savagely, *they will probably bring me down with them.*

The thought made him clench his fists in rage. If he'd assumed supreme power earlier…but he hadn't. There were too many high-ranking officers and party leaders who owed nothing to him, who feared that he would promote his favourites above their heads. Karl couldn't risk alienating them, not yet. But by keeping them around, he was giving them a chance to stick a knife in his back…

The entire edifice is unstable, he reminded himself. *We haven't had a proper Fuhrer for far too long.*

Ruengeler coughed. "*Mein Fuhrer?*"

Karl almost jumped. Ruengeler had been speaking and he hadn't been listening. But he didn't dare ask what the younger man had said. He couldn't show weakness, not now.

"We cannot abandon Warsaw," he said, instead. "The rebels would be able to use it to funnel their troops further east."

"Yes, *Mein Fuhrer,*" Ruengeler said. "But we cannot *defend* Warsaw either."

Karl looked up at him. "We have deployable nuclear bombs," he said. "Perhaps it's time we used them."

Ruengeler hesitated. "*Mein Fuhrer,*" he said slowly, "they have warheads too."

"Yes, they do," Karl agreed. "But will they be willing to use them on their fellow Germans?"

He pointed a finger at the map. "If they push forward and fight a conventional battle," he said, "they will have a good chance of crushing us. Correct?"

"Correct, *Mein Fuhrer,*" Ruengeler said.

"And if we retreat eastwards, we concede too much territory to them," Karl added. "We need a third option."

He studied the map for a long moment. "We let them thrust their spearheads forward, then hit them with the nuclear weapons," he said. "*That* will send them stumbling back in disarray."

"I would need to study the issue," Ruengeler said, slowly. "We have never deployed nuclear weapons on the battlefield."

"Then do so, quickly," Ruengeler ordered. "We have to make it clear that we will not be crushed and broken!"

"Yes, *Mein Fuhrer,*" Ruengeler said.

Karl nodded, then turned and headed for the door. He'd be back later, but right now there was too much else to do. His subordinates needed to be watched, carefully, as they carried out his orders. He needed to nip any problems in the bud before they brought him down…

…Or before someone decided to take advantage of the planned enemy offensive for themselves.

It was an open secret that many of the direct links between Germany Prime and Germany East were still usable. The telephone network had been designed to survive an American attack. He'd closed off some of the exchanges, of course, but many of his powerful subordinates would have little trouble using the network to make contact with friends and allies on the other side of the line. Karl had no trouble imagining a particularly ambitious official planning an assassination, even as the *Heer* marched eastwards. Someone who took the rebels Karl's head would be assured of a warm welcome.

But he won't be able to take it easily, he thought, darkly. *And that's all that matters.*

How the hell, *Oberstgruppenfuehrer* Alfred Ruengeler asked himself in the privacy of his own mind, *did it come to this?*

He knew better than to say it out loud. The *Reichstag* was not a friendly place. There were eyes and ears everywhere, just watching and waiting for someone to slip up so that they could be reported. The merest *hint* of treachery would be enough to land someone in the camps, if they opened their mouth at the wrong time. There was no one Alfred could talk to, even if he'd trusted anyone with his concerns. His closest friends might betray him if they thought their lives - and those of their families - were at risk.

Alfred had been in the *Waffen-SS* for decades. His father had marched him down to the recruiting officer the day he'd turned sixteen, using his contacts to make sure his son didn't have to wait an extra year before being shipped off to the nearest training centre. He'd never considered himself anything other than a soldier; he'd certainly never embraced the attitudes of those charged with monitoring the *Volk*. And yet...

He'd never seen the test sites in Siberia, where the first German atomic bombs had been detonated, but he'd seen photographs from the Middle East. Four cities had been destroyed, their survivors poisoned...they'd been lucky, in a way, that they'd been shot down almost as soon as they'd been discovered. At least they'd been spared a lingering death. And yet, the thought of unleashing such horrors on German soil chilled him to the bone.

But what choice *was* there?

Alfred had fought for the *Reich* in a dozen different countries, climbing up the ranks as he gained more and more experience. And it had shaped his worldview more than he cared to admit. The *Reich* was not perfect - it had many flaws - but it was still stronger than America or Britain. Their enemies embraced a chaotic lifestyle that would eventually bring them down, he was sure.

And if that is true, a little voice whispered at the back of his head, *how come their technology is so much better?*

He shook his head, dismissing the thought. If the rebels and traitors won, the *Reich* would come apart at the seams. He had no illusions about what the *Untermenschen* would do, if they got a taste of freedom. The French would demand their freedom, then the return of territory taken during the last war... it would be utter madness. What was Germany without discipline, without everyone knowing their place?

And the whole crisis was started, he told himself, *by a girl who did not know her place.*

And yet...and yet...

He hadn't looked into her story. He hadn't considered her very important when he'd been on the front lines and now, when he *knew* she was important, he didn't dare try to access the files. But there had been something in *Holliston's* reaction that convinced him that she'd been telling the truth. And that meant...what?

If our soldiers are being betrayed, he asked himself, *what does that say about us?*

He shook his head as he walked into the smaller office and peered down at the maps his subordinates had placed on the table. Warsaw was more than just a city; Warsaw was the communications and transport hub for the entire region. Of *course* the rebels would want it - and *of course* Holliston couldn't just give it up. But to use nuclear weapons? There was very little protective gear in the district. None of the stormtroopers had *any* protective gear...

...But what could he do about it?

Get them what I can, he told himself. *And hope that it would be enough.*

He could try to talk the *Fuhrer* out of it, he supposed, but what could he say that would be convincing? Nothing came to mind, because there *wasn't* anything. The planned thrust eastwards - if the *Fuhrer's* source was accurate

- would either destroy the remaining SS divisions, thus shortening the war, or take a large chunk of Germany East that could be used as a springboard for a spring offensive. Nuclear weapons might be the only way to slow the offensive long enough to rebuild the military...

And there was nothing he could do.

He'd heard rumours, of course, as he'd handed his command over to his second and headed back to Germanica. He'd expected to be turned into a scapegoat for the failure and executed, just to save Karl Holliston from the consequences of his own mistakes. But instead...he was trapped in hell. There was nothing he could do to keep the *Fuhrer* from using the weapons, nothing he could do to save himself and his family if he crossed Holliston. He was trapped...

...And there was *still* nothing he could do.

———

"I'm going to unlock your chains," Katherine said, as she pushed Gudrun into the cell. "If you do anything stupid, you will regret it."

Gudrun nodded, feeling a twinge of relief mixed with fear. Horst had tried to teach her some moves, but Katherine was stronger and *far* faster than Gudrun could ever hope to be. Any resistance would be futile - no, worse than futile. Katherine would use it as an excuse to punish her, to rub her hopelessness in her face. All she could do was wait patiently, take the abuse as best as she could and pray for a chance to escape.

She glanced down at her hands as Katherine undid the cuffs. Nasty purple bruises had formed around her wrists, mocking her. She rubbed at them, cursing the dull ache under her breath. Katherine undid the chains around her feet, then carefully removed the cuffs before Gudrun could think of any way to use them as a weapon. She would have sold her soul for a pistol and a skeleton key.

But getting out of here would still be impossible, she thought, morbidly. *Perhaps I should find a way to kill myself.*

She looked up at Katherine. "Thank you," she said. She didn't want to ask for anything else, but her stomach was rumbling unpleasantly. "Can I have something to eat?"

"Yes," Katherine said. She sounded displeased about something. "Wait."

Gudrun sat down on the bed as Katherine backed out of the cell. If she'd had the energy, she would have laughed. She was too tired and hungry - and aching - to risk attacking Katherine, even if she'd thought she could win the fight. But Katherine was treating her as if she was an incredibly dangerous prisoner...

I can use that, she told herself. *But how?*

It felt like hours before a man stepped through the outer door, carrying a tray of food. He studied Gudrun coldly, his eyes flickering over her as if she wasn't really worthy of his attention, but she felt nothing. Karl Holliston had paraded her in front of his men, trying to humiliate her by displaying her nearly-naked body...she was too far gone to care. The tray was pushed through the hatch in the wire, allowing her to pick it up and examine it. There was nothing apart from a bowl of slop and a plastic glass of water. The slop - she had no idea what was in it - smelt foul and tasted worse, but she ate it anyway. There was nothing else to eat. The water tasted...odd, odd in a manner she couldn't describe. It dawned on her, too late, that the water might easily have been drugged...

...But there was nothing she could do about it.

Her head started to swim a moment later. She forced herself - somehow - to sit back on the bed and lie down before darkness started to overcome her. There was a crashing sound as the remains of the tray hit the floor, but she was too tired and dizzy to care...

...And then she fell straight into the darkness.

―――

Karl Holliston cared very little for sex. Power, in his experience, was so much more rewarding; if nothing else, power could bring willing women to his bed. But he had to admit, as the doctors adjusted Gudrun's position before beginning their examination, that she was a beautiful girl, practically the ideal of German womanhood. Blonde hair, flawless complexion, blue eyes, willowy figure...she would have made a good wife, if she'd stayed in her place. A woman shouldn't be involved in politics. It was no place for her.

He scowled at the pale-faced doctor as he walked into the sideroom. The man was slime, even by the admittedly low standards of the SS. A sadist, a monster, a man with a complete lack of scruples...the SS found him useful, even as much of them found him surprisingly disgusting. Practicing his talents on *Untermenschen* was one thing, practicing them on good Germans was quite another. But there was no denying he knew his job.

"Well?"

"She isn't a virgin, *Mein Fuhrer*," the doctor said. He licked his lips, salaciously. "The rumours that she was married may be true."

"Or she simply gave up her virginity to the first man who came along," Karl snarled. It had been years since he'd worn the black uniform to impress the girls, but he still remembered how easy it had been to get them into bed. "Is she *pregnant?*"

"Not as far as we know, *Mein Fuhrer*," the doctor said. "But if she was married only recently, a pregnancy might not show."

Karl considered it for a moment, then dismissed the thought. It wasn't as if he would have treated her any differently. Pregnant or not, Gudrun was too dangerous to be allowed to live unmolested. Normally, the female relatives of traitors would be shipped east and married off to men struggling to tame the frontier, but Gudrun was a traitor herself. Her mere *existence* was an offense against the natural order.

"Never mind," he said. "How about her health?"

"Generally speaking, *Mein Fuhrer*, she's in rude health," the doctor said. "If there was any starvation in Berlin, *she* wasn't starving. The last few days, of course, won't have been easy for her, but she's not suffered any permanent damage."

"Very good," Karl said. Perhaps the titbit about Gudrun not starving - when the reports indicated that Berlin had been on the brink of starvation - could be used against her. "Can you break her?"

The doctor frowned. "It would depend on just what you wanted, *Mein Fuhrer*," he said, carefully. "*Anyone* can be broken, but..."

"I want her alive, able to answer questions, and ready to condemn her former allies," Karl said, shortly. "She is *not* to be a quivering mass of jelly when we put her in front of the cameras."

"Yes, *Mein Fuhrer*," the doctor said.

Karl fixed him with an icy look. The doctor had a proven track record for breaking his subjects, but not all of them had been useful afterwards. And Karl *needed* Gudrun to be useful.

"If she is useless to me afterwards," he warned, "you too will be useless to me."

The doctor swallowed. "Yes, *Mein Fuhrer*," he said. He'd only survived so long, even in the SS, because of Karl's patronage. If Karl dumped him, for whatever reason, he'd be lucky to live long enough to flee the city. "But breaking her so completely will take time."

"We have time," Karl assured him. "But I want her ready as soon as possible."

CHAPTER EIGHT

Berlin, Germany Prime
29/30 October 1985

The night was bitterly cold.

Horst kept quiet, very quiet, as he led the way eastwards. They'd been shown through the lines surrounding Berlin an hour ago, then warned to keep their heads down as they walked towards the enemy lines. The possibilities of being shot by a roving patrol were higher than Horst cared to admit, particularly if the patrol captured them first. After the first atrocity reports, the defenders had lost all interest in taking prisoners.

Fools, he thought, grimly. *The war will take longer if the enemy soldiers think they can't surrender.*

Kurt was doing better than he'd expected, he had to admit, although that could be just his prejudice talking. Gudrun's brother *had* been an infantryman, after all. He would have been trained to move silently from place to place. His actual *experience* was somewhat lacking, Horst knew, but there was no way to change that in a hurry. All they could do was keep moving and hope they didn't run into trouble until they crossed the lines.

The darkness seemed to press in around them like a living thing as they followed the road eastwards, keeping a wary eye out for vehicles or aircraft. A handful of shapes loomed up in the distance, slowly revealing themselves to be burned-out panzers or trucks; a number of buildings, destroyed in the fighting, bore mute testament to the savagery the SS had unleashed on Germany Prime. Horst knew - at a very primal level - just how ruthless the SS could be, but this was madness. He liked to think he would have switched sides, even without Gudrun, if he'd been forced to witness such a nightmare. But he knew it wouldn't have been easy.

He frowned as he saw a pair of bodies lying on the ground, stripped naked. They were both male, he noted; their SS tattoos clearly visible on their arms. In the darkness, it was hard to tell what had actually killed them - he certainly didn't want to touch the corpses - but the provisional government had been getting reports of other enemy bodies being stripped as the SS retreated. Their comrades would have a better chance at survival if they took everything they could from the honoured dead.

And they wouldn't turn on their own, he thought.

He brooded as they headed onwards, leaving the bodies behind. The SS stormtroopers were taught to be loyal to their units, first and foremost. It was unlikely that *any* of them would switch sides, unless they did it in a body. They'd be abandoning men who *depended* on them. Horst knew *he* wouldn't be comfortable just walking away, if he'd been assigned to the *Waffen-SS*. It was lucky - for Gudrun, for Germany, for *everyone* - that he'd largely been on his own in the university. Even his fellow infiltrators hadn't been his true *comrades*.

The bridges were in ruins, they discovered, as they approached a river. Horst had half-expected to have to swim - which would have delayed them badly - but thankfully there were enough chunks of debris sticking out of the water to allow them to scramble across. He couldn't help thinking that the bridge would need several months of repair work - it would be quicker, perhaps, to start putting pontoon bridges together to rush the panzers eastwards. He tensed as they reached the far side, expecting to run into an enemy patrol, but there was nothing. The entire bridge had simply been abandoned.

They must be concentrating on setting up lines further to the east, Horst thought. *And they may have lost more trained manpower than we thought.*

He scowled at the thought. It had been a long time since the *Waffen-SS* had fought a conventional war, but they must have learned *something* from their advance to the west. The bridge would make an ideal place to give the advancing panzers a bloody nose. He'd certainly seen the tactic practiced often enough during basic training. But instead…they'd just fallen back, abandoning the bridge. It suggested that morale was *very* low.

"We keep moving," he hissed to Kurt. "We need to make contact with their lines before the sun rises."

The night seemed to grow louder as they kept walking, engine noises and the occasional gunshot echoing out in the distance. Horst cursed under his breath - of *course* the stormtroopers would be jumpy - but kept walking anyway. The provisional government had command of the air. Logically, moving panzers and other armoured vehicles around would be done at night. Or so he told himself.

He looked up at the stars, silently checking their position. They were still moving east, if he was correct. It wouldn't be long, surely, before they walked into an enemy position. They *had* to have patrols covering the road. There was no way they would just *allow* the panzers to charge up towards Warsaw, not when they needed to buy time to rebuild their armoured formations. The SS was good at regenerating its units, but even with the best will in the world it would take longer than they had to rebuild...

"Halt," a voice barked. "Hands in the air!"

"Do as they say," Horst muttered, raising his hands. He scanned the terrain ahead of them, but there was nothing to see in the darkness. The enemy had to have dug into the side of the road. He raised his voice a moment later. "Don't shoot! We're friendly!"

A pair of black-clad stormtroopers materialised out of nowhere, one wearing a heavy pair of night-vision goggles on his forehead. Horst felt a flicker of sympathy - the bugs had never been worked out of the system - and then tensed as the stormtroopers glared at them. There was a very real possibility of being taken for deserters - or even men who had lost contact with their units in the chaos - despite the papers they carried. And if they *were* taken for deserters, they might be shot out of hand.

"Identify yourself," the leader snarled.

"Johann Peltzer and Fritz Hanstein," Horst said. "Our papers are in our jackets."

He braced himself as the stormtroopers took the papers and inspected them carefully, using a flashlight to make out the words. Logically, the stormtroopers should send them onwards to Germanica as soon as possible, but nothing was the same any longer. They might wind up being ordered to serve in the SS divisions or...

The stormtrooper saluted, smartly. "You have orders to return to Germanica, *Herr Inspector?*"

"Yes," Horst said. Posing as members of the SS *Inspectorate* was a risk, but very few stormtroopers would want to attract their attention. "We need transport back to the *Reichstag*."

"I'll have you escorted to the camp, *Herr Inspector*," the stormtrooper said. "The *Standartenfuehrer* will arrange transport for you."

"Thank you," Horst said.

He kept his expression under tight control as they were escorted up the road and into an enemy camp. Dozens of tents, all concealed under camouflage netting; hundreds of stormtroopers, most desperately catching up on their sleep before they had to return to their duties. There weren't many vehicles in evidence, he noted, but that proved nothing. The *Waffen-SS* would probably have spread out their panzers, gambling that they would have time to concentrate their forces before the *Heer* began its advance. He glanced into a large tent as they passed and swore, under his breath, as he saw the wounded. The odds were good that none of them would survive the coming offensive.

They picked the wrong side, he told himself.

But it wasn't convincing. No one had expected a civil war, not even Gudrun. Very few soldiers had voted with their feet, even when military bases had turned into battlegrounds; they'd stayed with their comrades rather than following their own inclination. And most of the *Waffen-SS* would be fanatically loyal. They *knew* what sort of chaos would be unleashed by the revolution. The *Untermenschen* would rise up in revolt all over the *Reich*.

He sucked in his breath as he saw a tall man, wearing a *Standartenfuehrer* uniform, standing in front of one of the tents. A *Standartenfuehrer* would not be so easily bullied, Horst knew; he'd want to make it clear that he was in charge, despite the wide-ranging authority granted to the Inspectorate.

"*Heil Holliston*," the *Standartenfuehrer* said.

"*Heil Holliston*," Horst returned. He held out his papers. "We require immediate transport back to Germanica."

The *Standartenfuehrer* looked back at him evenly, then carefully went through Horst's papers, one by one. They should pass muster, Horst knew, but if the *Standartenfuehrer* insisted on checking with Germanica...they'd be caught, before the mission had even fairly begun. And then...they'd be lucky if they were *only* marched out of the camp and shot. It was quite possible that Holliston had marked Horst - and any member of Gudrun's family - down for special attention.

"Very well, *Herr Inspector*," the *Standartenfuehrer* said. "We are sending a convoy of the wounded up to Warsaw in the morning. You may accompany them."

"We need a vehicle that can take us all the way to Germanica," Horst said, firmly. It would be perfectly in character for an Inspector to demand the very best, regardless of the practicalities. "*Herr Standartenfuehrer...*"

"We don't have anything that can be spared," the *Standartenfuehrer* said. He sounded too tired to care that he had just interrupted an Inspector. "You'll have to go with the convoy."

"Very well," Horst said, trying to sound irritated. "We'll inspect the camp while we're waiting."

The *Standartenfuehrer* gave him a ghastly smile. "Make sure you tell Germanica that we need more supplies out here, *Herr Inspector*," he said. "This camp is not going to hold against a determined offensive."

"Of course," Horst said.

He saluted the *Standartenfuehrer*, then led Kurt out of the tent. Dawn was just beginning to glimmer in the distance, a wavering line of light heralding the approach of the day. He resisted the urge to yawn as he nodded to the sentries, then strode over to the medical tent and glanced inside. There were hundreds of wounded, including dozens who were too badly injured to be saved. The others...he shuddered as he recalled some of the horrors they'd uncovered in the files. He had never known - never even *considered* - that the Nazi Regime would kill its own wounded soldiers...

But they did, he thought.

He looked away, unwilling to meet the eyes of men he knew would probably be killed if they didn't die soon. The files had made it clear, written in glowing tones by people who didn't even have the decency to be *ashamed* of what they'd done. Hundreds of thousands of Germans - good Germans, men with the proper bloodlines - had simply been exterminated, murdered by their own government. And that had been the least of it. Children born with birth defects - even *minor* birth defects - had been murdered too...

And we never knew, he told himself. *None of us ever realised what had happened.*

It made him wonder - again - what had happened to his father. Uncle Emil had told Horst that his father had been killed in one of the wars - and Uncle Emil should have known - but he hadn't gone into detail. Did he know what had happened? Or had something been covered up? There was no way to independently verify *anything* they'd been told. For all Horst knew, his father had been so badly wounded that he'd been murdered by his own government.

And I might never know, he thought.

He wandered through the camp, doing his best to memorise the details. He'd probably be called upon to give a report when they reached Warsaw, even if they were given a vehicle and told to make their own way to Germanica. And there might be a chance to slip a report back to Berlin, even though he knew it was unlikely...

Two hours later, they were called over to join a small collection of trucks heading east. The wounded didn't look very comfortable - the trucks had clearly been designed to transport goods, rather than people - but none of them were in any fit state to complain. Horst bit down the urge to make sarcastic remarks - he couldn't help noticing that none of the badly-wounded men were being shipped to Warsaw - as he clambered into the front seat. Kurt followed him as the lorry roared to life. Thankfully, the enlisted man in the driver's seat didn't seem inclined to make conversation.

"Get some sleep," he urged Kurt. "It's a long drive to Warsaw."

He kept a wary eye on the sky as the convoy lurched down the road to the autobahn. It was unlikely that the *Luftwaffe* would deliberately target wounded men, but any prowling pilot wouldn't *know* what the trucks were carrying until it was far too late. Besides, wrecking the SS's logistics network would suit the Provisional Government perfectly. But there seemed to be no aircraft in the sky.

They're digging in, he thought, as they passed a line of stormtroopers working on a trench network. *And getting ready to make us bleed.*

He scowled, inwardly, as they passed more and more signs of enemy activity. Trenches, weapons positions, a handful of panzers dug into the undergrowth so they'd be almost completely invisible, except at very short range.

A number of trenches were being dug by men and women in civilian clothes, people he assumed had been conscripted by the SS during the march towards Berlin. He couldn't help noticing that most of the civilians were middle-aged, with no children, teenagers or elderly. It struck him as an ominous sign.

They could have shipped the children east, if they weren't already evacuated, he told himself, slowly. He *wanted* to believe it. Hell, if there had been teenage boys in the towns and villages, they would probably have been conscripted into the army. *If the children were still there...*

He shook his head, sourly. There were just too many secrets buried in the *Reich's* past. A few hundred children, torn from their parents and raised as Germans in Germany East, would hardly be the worst of them. He glanced at Kurt, then closed his eyes himself. They'd need to be alert when they reached Warsaw.

It felt like he hadn't slept at all when the truck finally lurched to a stop. Horst elbowed Kurt - he'd managed to sleep through the entire drive - then clambered out of the vehicle, just in time to see a small army of medics carting the wounded into the city. A number had died in transit; their bodies were dumped to the side, waiting to be placed in a mass grave. It wasn't common for bodies to be returned to their families, not in Germany East. Horst...had simply never wondered just how sinister the procedure was until now.

Makes it easier to hide something, he thought.

"Herr Inspector," an *Obersturmbannfuehrer* said. "We have readied a car for you to drive east."

Horst allowed himself a moment of relief. He'd feared they would have to take the railway, which would have gotten them there quicker...but forced them to pass through a whole series of checkpoints. Transit within Germany East was heavily restricted. He thanked the officer coldly - as if it was the very least he could do - and then allowed himself to be led outside. The car - a Volkswagen painted black - was already waiting for them. A small flag fluttered from the radio aerial on the roof, identifying the vehicle as an official car; a packet of maps lay on the front seat, just to make it easy for them to find their way to Germanica.

"Try not to drive at night, *Herr Inspector*," the *Obersturmbannfuehrer* warned. "I suggest you stop at settlements along the way."

Kurt frowned. "Might I ask why, *Herr Obersturmbannfuehrer?*"

"There have been a number of reported attacks along the roadside," the *Obersturmbannfuehrer* told him. "It's safer to sleep in a settlement."

Horst nodded, slowly. He'd thought the bandits had been cleared out of the western sections of Germany East, but it was clear they were having a resurgence. And why not? Most of the defenders had been marched west to fight the civil war. Germany East was *huge*. Forty years of occupation hadn't been enough to exterminate every last trace of Slavic resistance.

"We will find a place to sleep in the settlements," he said, frankly. It would be another risk - the settlements might also check their credentials - but it had to be done. "I thank you."

"Just make sure they know we need reinforcements, *Herr Inspector*," the *Obersturmbannfuehrer* said. "We stripped the city bare to support the offensive…"

He stopped talking, suddenly. His words were far too close to defeatist. And defeatism was punishable by death.

Horst winced at the thought. What *wasn't?*

"I'll make sure they know," Horst assured him. "We have orders to give our report to the *Fuhrer* in person."

He climbed into the car and checked it, carefully. It wasn't *that* different from the cars he'd learned to drive when he was younger; indeed, the only *real* difference was a military radio installed beside the steering wheel. Civilians weren't allowed radio transmitters without a special licence. Who knew *what* they might put on the airwaves?

But we will need to summon help if we run into trouble, Horst thought. If an *Obersturmbannfuehrer* was prepared to admit the existence of bandits to a pair of inspectors, the situation had to be worse than it seemed. *And if we do, we might attract far too much attention.*

He turned the key. The engine roared to life,

"Let's go," he said. They'd stop, once they were well outside the city, to inspect the car for hidden surprises. "We'll get as far as we can before it gets dark."

CHAPTER NINE

Berlin, Germany Prime
30 October 1985

"I wish you weren't going," Adelinde Wieland said. "Herman, you have absolutely nothing to prove."

"I'm an experienced soldier as well as a policeman," Herman said. "They *need* me."

"The war will not be won or lost because a slightly-overweight policeman picked up a rifle or not," Adelinde said, curtly. "I may be a *mere* woman, but even *I* know that!"

Herman winced, inwardly. Nothing was the same any more. His daughter had turned the *Reich* upside down, his wife had turned into a politician... he honestly didn't know where to stand. A year ago, he could have forbidden Adelinde - or Gudrun - from leaving the house, secure in the knowledge the law would back him up. Now...Adelinde would laugh at him if he tried. And he had never raised a hand to her before...

He took a sip of his coffee instead, wincing at the taste. They might be living in the *Reichstag* now, but they still couldn't get good coffee. And breakfast had been nothing more than bacon, cheese and bread.

"I have to go," he said, finally. "There's no place for me here."

"Foolish man," Adelinde said. He would have snapped at her, perhaps broken his private rule about never striking her, if he hadn't seen the tears in her eyes. "I don't want to lose you just because you think you have something to prove."

Herman sighed, heavily. "Where else can I go?"

He met her eyes. "I won't be a policeman much longer, even with our... *connections*," he said. He'd never taken advantage of his daughter's position before and he was damned if he was starting now. "The provisional govern-ment will disband most of us after the fighting is over - if we survive long enough to be disbanded. And what can I do then? Stay in bed like Frank?"

"My father died to save our lives," Adelinde pointed out, stiffly.

"He died to save *Gudrun's* life," Herman said. It was irritating. He'd cor-dially disliked his father-in-law almost from the very moment Frank had moved in with them, but Frank had died a hero. "And I don't *want* to be useless."

Adelinde shook her head. "Please," she said. "Don't go."

"I've already given them my word," Herman said. "And you'll find it easier to…to work if I'm not around."

He sighed heavily, feeling an odd surge of bitter hopelessness. *Nothing* was the same any longer. And he was really too old to learn new tricks. He'd thought everything was predictable, a year ago; his sons would serve in the military, marry good women and sire children, while his daughter would become a housewife, bearing and raising the children of a good man. But now his daughter was a revolutionary, the country was gripped by civil war, and his wife wanted a career outside the home. And his entire family had been marked for death.

If I'd stopped Gudrun from going to university, he thought, *would she be free now?*

It was a bitter thought. He'd *known* how much the university meant to her, even though she couldn't really *do* anything with a degree. What sort of man would be comfortable taking orders from a woman? Or hiring one, when there were plenty of male candidates for any given job? He'd honestly thought she was wasting her time. Hell, she could have gotten married at seventeen and had two or three children by now. No one would have thought any worse of her if she'd dropped out of school to marry and have kids. But instead…

"I can't stay here and worry," he admitted. "I have to keep myself occupied."

Adelinde lowered her eyes. "Then take care of yourself," she said. She looked up at him, her eyes wet with tears. "And come back to me."

Herman gave her a tight hug. He loved his wife. He'd loved her ever since he'd married her; he'd loved her, even when money had gotten tight and they'd had arguments that could probably be heard down the street. They'd lived together for twenty-five years; they'd raised their children together. And even now, even when he didn't feel as though he understood the world any longer, he still loved her.

"I'll come back," he promised.

He kissed her once, tenderly, then picked up his jacket and walked out the door, heading down to the gates. The soldiers on duty saluted him as he passed; he saluted them back, then kept walking. He'd never really felt *comfortable* being feted, particularly as he hadn't earned it in his own right. It was why he'd stayed a policeman after Gudrun had become a politician, even though he could have traded on her connections to rise in the ranks. He wouldn't have felt *comfortable* boosting his own position.

And I don't know what's happened to her, he thought, numbly. *Where is she?*

He pushed the thought aside, somehow, as he made his way through the streets. Berlin felt different these days, now the siege was at an end. The massive street parties had faded, replaced by deserted houses as the older members of the city's population were evacuated west and the younger members were pushed into the army. Even the young *women* had been given jobs, helping to clear the streets of rubble and keeping the city running. Herman couldn't help wondering just *what* would happen in the future, now that Gudrun had shown that it was possible for a woman - a woman who was practically still a *girl* - to overthrow the government. Women wouldn't remain subservient any longer.

The camp had been erected on the far side of the city, one of many providing refresher training to young men who had either left the military or had never served past the Hitler Youth. Herman joined the line of younger and middle-aged men and waited patiently until the guard checked his papers, then followed the pointing finger into the nearest set of barracks. A doctor gave him a quick check-up - he couldn't help noticing that he was assisted by a pair of BDM maidens, something that would have been unthinkable in his day - before ordering him into the next room. Herman stepped through the door and joined another line of prospective soldiers, almost all of whom seemed to be middle-aged. He recognised a couple from the police and walked over to join them. The others seemed to be workers from all over the city.

They'll have gotten their release from their employers, he thought, as a trio of NCOs ordered the men through another set of doors and onto the training field. *They wouldn't have been allowed to sign up without it.*

He pushed the thought aside as the NCOs started to bark orders, putting the men through their paces. It was...*kinder* than he recalled, back when he'd been a paratrooper; he wondered, absently, if it was a subtle blessing or an unsubtle insult. He wasn't the young man he'd been in those days, he knew; he was more mature, more controlled, but also less *fit*. He dreaded to think what the Hitler Youth would have done, if he'd turned up in such a state. Public humiliation would have been the least of it.

The memory made him shiver. There had been a boy in his class, a smart boy who'd been unfortunate enough to be a little pudgy. The Hitler Youth had put him through hell, mocking his weight, forcing him to humiliate himself time and time again...in the end, the boy had committed suicide and the instructors had just laughed, pointing to him as a prime example of a weak failure of a man. His parents had done nothing...Herman had no idea if they'd tried and failed, or if they'd hoped the Hitler Youth would make a man of their son. And now...

He could have kicked his past self for laughing. They'd laughed and joked about taking everything that was dumped on them, from endless exercises and forced marches to savage - often sadistic - corporal punishment. His own father had told him that pain was weakness leaving the body. But Herman had never been singled out, never been mocked in front of the entire class. Who knew what would have become of him if he had?

The Hitler Youth will not survive the coming years, he told himself, as the exercise routine finally came to an end. *And the BDM has already been disbanded. Gudrun saw to it personally.*

"Those of you who survived are being assigned to a rifle company," the lead NCO bellowed, his voice shaking the parade ground. Herman looked around and discovered, to his shock, that a third of the volunteers had dropped out. He hoped, grimly, that it meant they'd merely discovered they couldn't continue. "You'll be issued weapons, then marched to the shooting range."

And hope to hell we have enough bullets to sight our rifles properly, Herman thought, as they were marched to the next set of barracks. *If we are short of ammunition, we may be in some trouble.*

He gritted his teeth, feeling his body ache as he marched. Once, he'd marched over forty miles in a single day; now, he felt old and drained from a handful of exercises. Being a policeman in Berlin had seemed hard, but he should have known it was far - far - easier than being a soldier. Old age had crept up on him without him ever realising it. He winced as they walked past a group of younger men, the youngest barely old enough to shave. They looked *far* more energetic than the older men.

But we have to do what we can, Herman told himself, firmly. *There's nothing else we can do.*

──────

"You don't *look* American," a voice said, as Andrew stepped into the office. "That's probably a good thing."

"Thank you, *Herr Oberleutnant*," Andrew said. "Can I pass for a *Heer* officer?"

Oberleutnant Sebastian Riemer looked Andrew up and down thought-fully. "Probably not," he said, after a moment. "Your German is perfect, but your pose is subtly wrong - you'd probably alarm anyone if you tried to take command."

Andrew nodded, shortly. Riemer was unusual for a German soldier, in that he had close family connections in America. It was probably why he'd been detailed to escort Andrew, even though he was a potential security risk. He'd actually been *in* America, unlike almost every other officer Andrew had met. And, compared to the humourless SS officers who'd escorted him around before the civil war, he was a decent man.

Which doesn't mean he won't be loyal to the Reich, Andrew reminded himself firmly. The younger man was blond enough to have stepped off a recruit-ing poster, his eyes so blue as to be almost unreal. *You cannot take the risk of trying to recruit him as a source.*

"We've prepared papers for you," Riemer added, picking up a wallet from the table and holding it out. "Make sure you stick to the cover story if you get caught."

"Understood," Andrew said. Posing as a German officer was risky, but being identified as American after being taken prisoner by the SS would be worse. Karl Holliston was unlikely to give much of a damn about American opinion after the United States had already intervened in the conflict. "I take it I don't have any actual *authority*?"

Riemer shot him a wry smile. "What do you *think?*"

Andrew smiled back as Riemer escorted him through the door and down to the underground car park. A small vehicle - it looked so much like a jeep that Andrew was *sure* someone had stolen the plans from America - was waiting for them, a young soldier in the front seat. He climbed into the back and forced himself to relax as the jeep headed up the ramp and out onto the streets. Berlin seemed almost deserted.

Shortages of fuel, Andrew thought, grimly. *Everything they have has been earmarked for the military.*

He considered it for a long moment. The *Reich* had access to the vast oil fields of the Middle East, but the SS was in a good position to block all shipments to Germany Prime. That left the oil fields in Ploesti, yet they were supposed to be on the verge of running dry. It made him wonder just how bad the shortages were, in Germany Prime. The *Reich* was supposed to have put together a strategic oil reserve that made America's look small, but he had no idea what had happened to it. By now, the demands of war might be making it run dry.

"You'll be attached to a forward command post," Riemer informed him, as they drove past the barricades surrounding Berlin and out into the countryside. "If you want to go further into the field, you may do so - but we cannot guarantee your safety."

Andrew nodded. He'd seen too much of the fighting before the *Waffen-SS* had been driven away from the city, but he'd never realised just how much of the outskirts had been reduced to bloody rubble. Men and women - a surprising number of women - were poking their way through the debris, dragging out bodies and dumping them in the nearest mass grave; military engineers were working over the burned-out panzers, looking for pieces that could be salvaged and put back into service. It looked as though hundreds of panzers had been destroyed in the fighting, although Andrew had no way to know for sure.

A dull explosion echoed in the distance. Andrew glanced east and saw a plume of smoke rising into the air. A pair of aircraft headed eastward at terrifying speed, but evidently saw nothing worth attacking. Riemer didn't even bother to look.

"They've been scattering mines and improvised bombs around as they make their way eastward," he commented. "We've got teams out there scouring for booby traps, but they're very good at hiding them."

"They probably learned from the insurgents," Andrew commented. American troops had had problems with IEDs too, in Mexico. "Don't you have any locals who can help find them?"

Riemer gave him a sharp look. "Most of the locals were evacuated," he said, crossly. "I wouldn't give two rusty *Reichmarks* for the fate of the remainder."

Andrew frowned. The Provisional Government had been filling the airwaves with tales of SS atrocities, although he had a feeling that most of their claims were being taken with a pinch of salt. German civilians were so used to being lied to - so used to being told lies that made it clear that their lords and masters didn't have any respect for their intelligence - that they rarely believed anything they heard on the radio. But Andrew had heard enough - from his contacts and sources - to know that there *had* been atrocities. The Easterners had forgotten that the Westerners were also German.

He kept his thoughts to himself as they passed a line of men, wearing military uniforms and marching east. Andrew couldn't help thinking that they looked surprisingly old for soldiers, although he knew there *were* some *very* long-serving soldiers in the National Guard back home. But then, the *Reich* was short on experienced manpower. They'd probably started press-ganging men who were too old to be front-line soldiers, but could teach the younger men what they needed to know before they went back to the war.

"They've been exchanging bursts of shellfire every so often," Riemer said, as the sound of falling shells echoed in the air. "They just seem to be firing at random."

Andrew scowled. German shooting wasn't as accurate as he'd been led to believe - or so his observations suggested - but he had to admit that the SS could disrupt the Provisional Government's preparations for war simply by firing shells at random. They might not hit anything *important* - it was unlikely they *would* hit anything important - yet they would cause confusion and damage morale. And they might consider anything that slowed down the coming offensive to be worth doing.

If winter comes before the Provisional Government can make it to Moscow, Andrew thought, *the front line will literally freeze for five months.*

He gritted his teeth as the jeep pulled into a military camp. Ambassador Turtledove had gone over the problem, again and again, with Washington. There was something to be said for prolonging the war - the *Reich* would be badly weakened - but it *still* heightened the risk of a nuclear release. Or something else that would upset the balance of power. There were plenty of rumours about other secret weapons...

But most of those rumours are nonsense, he thought. *And they certainly haven't shown any workable hardware.*

He smiled at the thought as he clambered out of the car and submitted to a pat-down from the guards. There were plenty of stories about flying wings - and flying saucers - but the *Reich* had never managed to put them into practice. They'd certainly never managed to duplicate the B2 stealth bomber, even though they'd *known* it was designed to sneak through the vast air defences of the Atlantic Wall...

The irony chilled Andrew more than he cared to admit. It had taken decades - literally - for the panic over German super-science to die down. And why not? Germany had been first to launch a missile, first to put a man in orbit, first to put a man on the moon...

...But they'd never been able to match the United States. Countless billions of dollars had been spent, first in catching up with the Germans and then getting ahead of them...

And now the Germans are tearing themselves apart, Andrew told himself, as he walked into the tent. *And we may have won the cold war without firing a shot.*

CHAPTER TEN

𝔑ear 𝔚arsaw, 𝔊ermany 𝔈ast
30 𝔒ctober 1985

"Get out of bed, *swinehund*," a voice barked. "Now!"

Hennecke Schwerk - who was no longer a *Hauptsturmfuehrer*, even in the privacy of his own head - jerked awake and stood up hastily. The 'bed' was nothing more than the cold hard ground, but he knew better than to try to sneak a few extra minutes of sleep. The *Scharfuehrers* who ran the penal battalions were no better than the men they supervised, handing out kicks and beatings to anyone who dared disagree with them. They snapped and snarled as the soldiers formed a ragged line, waving clubs around as if they were swords. It didn't take much to get hit.

Trusties, Hennecke thought. It was pretty evident to him that the penal battalions were where bad NCOs were sent to die. *And if they get killed out here, no one is going to give a damn.*

"We have some *special* work for you today, ladies," *Scharfuehrer* Kuhn bellowed. Hennecke had only known Kuhn for a couple of days, but he'd already begun to detest Kuhn intensely. "We're going to be digging trenches!"

He waved a hand at a pile of shovels. "Grab a shovel and follow me!"

Hennecke obeyed, hastily. There was no point in trying to resist, not when no one would bat an eyelid if a soldier from a penal unit was beaten to death. And there was no point in trying to desert, either. Making it across the front lines would be difficult - and if he made it, he'd just be shot by the rebels instead. All he could really do was follow orders, keep his head down and hope that he survived a month in the unit. And then he could go back to the regular *Waffen-SS*...

But I won't keep my rank, he thought. Kuhn had made it clear that Hennecke's former rank counted for nothing, not now. *God alone knows where I'll go.*

They stumbled out of the camp and headed up the road, the stragglers yelping and cursing as the *Scharfuehrers* helped them along the way with kicks and swipes from their clubs. A handful of passing stormtroopers stopped to jeer, hissing and cursing at the penal battalion as they marched past. The *Scharfuehrers* ignored them, of course. They probably thought the reminder of just how the rest of the *Waffen-SS* thought about the men in orange uniforms would help discourage desertion. Hennecke would have bet good money that Kuhn and his cronies would have landed in *some* trouble if half the battalion deserted. If nothing else, a group of deserters with nothing to lose would pose a security risk.

"We want a trench here," Kuhn bellowed, as they reached the edge of the front lines. A handful of soldiers were clearly visible, scanning the horizon with binoculars, but there was nothing else in sight. "Follow the lines drawn on the ground and start digging."

Useless makework, Hennecke thought, as he shoved his spade into the ground and started to dig. He'd been taught how to dig foxholes and trenches in basic training, but both of them were useless without armed men to hold the line. *And besides, without antitank weapons, the poor bastards in the trench will just get crushed.*

There was no point in arguing, he knew. Kuhn was marching up and down the line, barking orders and swiping anyone who didn't meet his high standards. Hennecke didn't dare glare at him as he strode past Hennecke's position; he merely kept working, silently promising himself that he'd have a chance to deal with the bastard later. Perhaps, if he returned to the *Waffen-SS*, he could accidentally put a bullet in Kuhn's back. Or maybe there'd be an opportunity to behead him with a shovel…

"Keep working," Kuhn snapped, as he walked past Hennecke again. "These trenches have to be completed soon!"

Hennecke barely heard him. It was cold, but sweat was still dripping down his back as he dug into the ground. He couldn't help thinking of the false spring, the warm weather that was so common in Russia before the snowstorms finally materialised out of nowhere to bury the settlements in snow and ice. He'd had enough experience in the winter to know it was going to be hellish...

He yelped as the club connected with his back. "Keep working," Kuhn ordered. "Think on your own time!"

Bastard, Hennecke thought. He wasn't doing any better or worse than anyone else. Kuhn just wanted an excuse to hit someone, like the tutors in the Hitler Youth. Kuhn - a violent bigoted mindless fool - was overqualified for the job. No wonder he was stuck baby-sitting the penal units, rather than doing something useful with his time. *He probably won't get out of here in a month, whatever he does.*

The sun was high in the sky when Kuhn finally pronounced himself satisfied. Hennecke had hoped for food and drink - or at least some rations - but Kuhn had other ideas. He marched them past the front line and down a road until they reached the shattered remains of a military convoy. A passing aircraft had caught them in the open and strafed them viciously, tearing the vehicles apart as if they had been made of paper. And dozens of bodies, some clearly wounded even before the convoy had been destroyed, lay everywhere.

"Half of you dig a grave," Kuhn bellowed. "The rest of you clear the bodies out of the convoy, then mark down anything that might be salvageable."

Hennecke hurried to join the latter group. He'd done enough digging for one day, as far as he was concerned. The first set of bodies were already spilling out of the vehicle; they were easy to carry out, their tags and ID papers removed before they were put by the side of the road with as much respect as the penal battalion could muster. Inside, other bodies had been badly damaged by the enemy aircraft. Hennecke hesitated over a pistol one of them had carried before deciding that taking the weapon would be pointless. Kuhn would see him concealing it and demand answers - or worse.

"You're not allowed to *touch* a weapon without permission," he'd said, when Hennecke had been dumped into the penal unit. "If you do, you will be shot!"

He finished removing the bodies, then glanced around for anything else that could be salvaged. The vehicle itself was probably beyond repair, but there were some components that could probably be reused, if they could be recovered in time. He wasn't surprised when Kuhn ordered his men to remove anything that might be useful, then carry them back to the camp once the funeral had been completed.

And if I die out here, Hennecke thought as they carefully lowered the bodies into the mass grave, *I'll be lucky if I get any sort of burial.*

The movies he'd watched about the glorious wars of conquest had made it clear that the dead were buried with all honours. But Kuhn didn't bother to say a word over the corpses, merely spit on them before he ordered his men to start covering the bodies with earth. The men were too tired to be shocked, too tired to argue as they buried their former comrades. Hennecke couldn't help wondering if it was worth it. The men had been wounded even before they'd been killed.

"Back to the camp," Kuhn ordered. "Pick up your supplies and go."

Hennecke groaned, but he knew better than to argue. Instead, he looked at the man next to him. He didn't recognise him, although his youth suggested he'd only been in the *Waffen-SS* for a year, if that. His head was completely shaved, his body scarred...

God alone knows why he's here, Hennecke thought, sourly. It was a taboo subject, when the penal soldiers had a few minutes to themselves. No one ever asked why their comrades had been dumped into the unit. *Rape, murder, defying orders, kicking the CO's cat...who knows?*

"Grab a cup of water," Kuhn ordered, as they marched back into camp. "And then you'll have a short break before you go back to work."

Hennecke was far too tired to care. The trenches were already manned; a handful of men, their rifles at the ready, watching for the rebels to advance east from Berlin. He knew - deep inside - that none of those men would survive, when the rebels finally came at them. The trenches might provide protection against infantry, but they wouldn't stop panzers...

Kuhn was as good as his word, somewhat to Hennecke's surprise. There *was* water waiting for them, along with some food rations. But even a man as foolish as Kuhn had to realise that *not* watering his men would kill them, eventually. And besides, they'd be working hard in the afternoon, unless the camp came under attack. Hennecke had no idea what they were meant to do if the enemy attacked. They had no weapons, nor did they know how to escape east...

No one gives a damn about us, he thought, morbidly. *We're just here to work until we die.*

He drank his water rapidly, wishing he had the time to savour every last drop. But he'd seen, on his first day, just how easy it was for some of the men to steal water and food from their weaker comrades. Kuhn and his *Scharfuehrers* didn't seem to care, even though it meant losing manpower to thirst and dehydration. Bastards. Even *he* had been more careful of his men during the advance on Berlin...

The thought chilled him. He knew what he'd done, back when they'd crashed into the village; he'd heard rumours, whispered down the line, about far worse atrocities committed by other units. Perhaps he was being punished for what he'd done, even though his victims had been rebels who could - who should - have sided with the legitimate government. He tried to tell himself that he hadn't done wrong, but somehow it felt hard to believe...

We're not meant to survive long enough to go back to our units, he thought, as he watched two men get into a fistfight. He had no idea what they were fighting over, but he didn't particularly care. *We're just meant to work until we die.*

He shook his head, slowly. He'd been promised a month...

...But even if they'd been telling the truth, how was he meant to survive so long?

———

SS-Obergruppenfuehrer Felix Kortig jumped out of the helicopter as soon as it came to a halt, bare inches above the ground, and ran towards the camouflaged building as through his life depended on it. Behind him, he heard the helicopter rev up its engines and claw its way back into the sky, flying eastwards as low as the pilot dared. He knew, all too well, that the *Luftwaffe* was on the prowl. A lone helicopter would seem an easy target.

"*Herr Obergruppenfuehrer,*" *Sturmbannfuehrer* Friedemann Weineck said. "Welcome back."

Felix nodded, curtly. Weineck had been *Oberstgruppenfuehrer* Alfred Ruengeler's aide before he'd been recalled to Germanica, a weak-chinned young man who might easily have been charged with keeping a covert eye on his boss. And yet, Ruengeler had apparently not only survived the retreat from Berlin, he'd been promoted and put in overall command of the defence of Germany East, leaving Felix himself in command of the front lines. Felix honestly had no idea what to make of it.

"Thank you," he said, as they walked into the map room. The building had once been a farmhouse, but now it was his HQ. He had no idea - he didn't want to know - what had happened to the original owners. "Has there been any update from the pickets?"

"The enemy has been sniping and shelling at us along the front lines, but there has been no major offensive, nor are there any signs that one is imminent," Weineck reported. "A number of our patrols have reported taking fire as they rounded up stragglers and dispatched them eastwards."

Felix nodded in irritation. It had been nearly six days since the SS had fallen back from Berlin, but the divisions had been shattered so badly that stragglers and survivors were *still* making their way back to the lines. Entire *units* had been obliterated, their handful of survivors hastily reassigned to other units…it would take weeks, perhaps months, to sort the problem out, under normal circumstances. But the times were very far from normal. He'd been warned, in no uncertain terms, that the rebels intended to mount a major offensive as soon as possible.

"At least they're still making it back to our lines," he said. "Do we have an updated casualty count yet?"

"Nothing precise, *Herr Obergruppenfuehrer*," Weineck confessed. "We're looking at around seven thousand men unaccounted for, as of now, but…"

"Anything could have happened to them," Felix said. He undid his jacket and dumped it on a chair, then strode over to the map table. "They could have been killed, or captured, or they could have deserted…"

"Yes, *Herr Obergruppenfuehrer*," Weineck said.

Felix looked down at the map for a long moment. It *looked* like an endless series of trenches, running north to south along the border between Germany Prime and Germany East, but he knew it was an illusion. The trench warfare of the first Great War - a war his father and grandfather had both recalled with horror - was an impossibility in the age of modern war, certainly when the territory that had to be covered was truly immense. Mobile warfare had come of age, during Operation Barbarossa; now, he couldn't help feeling as though he was about to learn how the Russians had felt, back when the Germans had crossed the border and thrust deep into their territory.

They'll probe our lines until they find a weak place, then ram their panzers through it, he thought, grimly. *And they will find a weak place.*

He looked up. "Have the panzer divisions reorganised themselves?"

"Yes, *Herr Obergruppenfuehrer*," Weineck said. "We have two divisions positioned here and here" - he tapped two locations on the map - "and a third still working up, but held in reserve here."

"Good," Felix said. "They'll know we're there, of course."

"We have them camouflaged," Weineck protested, shocked.

Felix snorted. He'd seen the sort of orbital imagery the *Reich's* space program had produced - and it was probably fair to say the Americans could do better. No matter how hard the panzer divisions had tried to remain unseen, he had no doubt they'd already been localised by the Americans. And the Americans would have quietly tipped off the rebels...

"But they still have to take Warsaw before pushing further into Germany East," he mused, ignoring the protest. "They don't have a choice. Warsaw is the linchpin of the Polish *Gau.*"

"Yes, *Herr Obergruppenfuehrer*," Weineck said.

"Which means they need to drive at the city, which will force us to defend it," Felix mused. "And yet, if we pull back, they will have to storm the city themselves..."

He shook his head. Storming Berlin - *trying* to storm Berlin - hadn't accomplished anything, beyond breaking a number of irreplaceable divisions. He'd *met* Field Marshal Voss - he *knew* how the older man thought. There was no way he would risk his divisions storming Warsaw. He'd seen *precisely* what had happened to the SS.

"Check with the Warsaw CO," he ordered. "Has the city been readied for a siege?"

"The last report said it was ready," Weineck reported. "But that was before...before Berlin."

Felix nodded, sourly. Warsaw had never been fortified as extensively as Germanica. No one had envisaged the city coming under attack, not when the Americans would have to fight their way through Germany Prime and the Chinese through Germany East if they wanted to reach Warsaw. But even so, taking a city was no easy task. A determined defence could tie up a hostile force for weeks, perhaps months. Stalingrad had been a nightmare; Leningrad had literally starved to death before surrendering.

"They'll want to chew up our forces instead of taking the city," he said. "Or, at least, they'll want to take the city *after* they crush our forces."

He nodded to himself. Ruengeler had said as much, during their last conversation; Felix saw nothing wrong with his superior's logic. The target wasn't Warsaw - Warsaw itself was worthless, even if it *didn't* bleed the rebels white trying to take it. No, they'd want to crush the SS divisions before they could get reinforcements…

"Inform the unit commanders that we will be going with Option Seven," he said, after a long moment. It had been Ruengeler who had drawn up the operational plan, but Felix saw no reason to change it. "We do *not* want to give them a chance to pocket our units."

"*Jawohl, Herr Obergruppenfuehrer,*" Weineck said.

"Very good," Felix said. "Now, about logistics…?"

"We've emptied a number of supply dumps in the *Gau,*" Weineck informed him. "However, we have started shipping supplies west from Germany East. Our logistical situation is poor, but should improve rapidly."

Which is what we get, Felix thought bitterly, *for drawing up a plan counting on victory in a single decisive battle.*

It had been a mistake. It had been a terrible mistake. Hitler wouldn't have made such a mistake, Felix was sure; Himmler, colder and more calculating, would have avoided it altogether. But Holliston had gambled the entire *Reich* on one throw of the dice and lost badly. Deep inside, Felix knew they were going to pay a terrible price for his mistake.

But he knew his duty. The *Reich* had to be preserved, whatever the cost.

Or everything they'd built over the last forty years would be swept away in fire.

CHAPTER ELEVEN

Germanica (Moscow), Germany East
1 November 1985

Gudrun felt sick.

She struggled out of a morass of tiredness, dimly aware - on one level - that something was badly wrong. Her entire body felt wretched, as if she'd drunk herself senseless and then just kept drinking until she plunged into darkness. She coughed and retched, her stomach twisting painfully as she tried to throw up. Her eyes opened, only to snap closed again as brilliant white light sent daggers lancing into her mind. And her body felt filthy...

Her gorge rose. She twisted, remembering - somehow - that she was on a bed, only to lose her balance and fall down to the floor. The sudden shock of pain sent her head spinning, again; she retched again and again, dry-heaving violently until her throat and mouth hurt as much as her stomach. But there was nothing in her stomach to expel. She swallowed, hard, despite the bad taste in her mouth. Her entire body felt weak and frail, as if she had a head cold mixed with savage drunkenness.

I've been drinking, she thought, numbly.

She hadn't felt so...so unpleasant since the night she'd drunk a stein of beer at a friend's house two years ago. Her father had laughed at her, she recalled. He'd pointed out, rather sarcastically, that it was better she learn the lessons of drunkenness now, rather when she was older and raising children of her own. It was one of the few times she recalled her father being less angry than her mother about anything. Young women weren't supposed to drink, her mother had said. It was a masculine art. Gudrun would have argued the point if her head hadn't felt like a fragile eggshell...

Clarity returned with a shock. She was in a prison cell, in Germanica. And she'd been drugged.

She forced her eyes to open, despite the bright light. The cell was just as she remembered: small, cramped and very secure. No one seemed to be standing on the other side of the bars, watching her, but she knew it was just an illusion. There were, no doubt, hundreds of people watching her through the cameras. She would have been horrified at the thought of so many people watching her while she was naked, if she hadn't felt so rotten. It was hard to care about anything when part of her just wanted to curl up and die.

Her body felt weak, but she forced herself to sit up anyway, despite the throbbing pain in her forehead. Perhaps she'd banged it when she fell…she honestly wasn't sure. What had they given her? Horst had talked about drugs, but he hadn't gone into any real detail. He'd seemed to believe that being captured was the end of the world - it would have been, if she'd been identified last time she'd been taken prisoner. Now…her head swam and she grabbed hold of the bed, using the hard metal framework to steady herself. She was damned if she was going to let them break her, not like this…

They can keep feeding you drugs, a little voice whispered at the back of her mind. *You can't eat without taking drugs.*

She shuddered, swallowing hard to fight down the urge to be sick again. They could have jabbed her with a needle at any point, but instead they'd drugged her food. Why? To make it clear that she was helpless? It wasn't as if they couldn't hold her down and inject her with whatever they pleased. Or did they want to avoid damaging her? Or…

It was hard, so hard, to think clearly. The world blurred around her for a long moment, everything going so dim that she wasn't sure if she'd fallen back into the darkness or merely hovered - for a long chilling moment - on the edge of oblivion. She tried to stand, she tried to clamber back onto the bed, but her body refused to cooperate. It crossed her mind, as she struggled, that she must be giving the unseen watchers one hell of a view. But she was too tired to care.

Damn them, she thought.

She heard the outer door opening behind her, but her head refused to turn as the inner door jangled open. Gudrun tensed as…*someone*…stepped into the cell, then cringed as strong hands pushed her against the bed. It was a man, she was sure. She could *hear* deep masculine breathing. And she was helpless, in an utterly undignified position…she had to fight to twist her head enough to see him. A man, wearing a white coat and a mask that obscured his face, was pressing a needle against her upper arm. She tried to fight, but it was pointless. The man took a blood sample, then casually turned and walked out of the cell, closing the inner door behind him. Gudrun slumped against the side of the bed, fighting back tears. It was all she could do not to fall back to the floor.

They can do that to me any time they like, she thought. A sense of helplessness and despair threatened to overwhelm her, mocking her. She'd started the movement that had overthrown an entire government, but now she was utterly helpless. Her jailers could do *anything* to her and there was nothing she could do to stop them. *And to think I thought the worst thing that could happen to me was being exiled to Germany East.*

She almost giggled at the thought. Karl Holliston and his cronies had to be having fits, after losing everything to a slip of a girl! They'd never seen her as a real threat - they'd never seen *any* woman as being fit for anything other than bearing children and raising them. Now…they had to come to terms with what she'd done to them. They might kill her - if they could bring themselves to sentence her to death - but it wouldn't change the facts on the ground…

Her throat cracked. She tried to swallow again, but her mouth was too dry. Her entire body felt dehydrated. How long had she been asleep? She could generally get by on four or five hours of sleep per day, but now? How long had it been since she'd been captured? It felt as if she hadn't had anything to eat or drink for days, yet there was no way to know for sure any longer. Konrad had been fed through a tube. She saw no reason why they couldn't feed her while she was drugged out of her mind.

A thought struck her, sending shivers down her spine. What had she told them while she'd been drugged? Horst had told her that the SS could get anything out of anyone, once they started using the right drugs. Could she have been interrogated? She didn't recall anything past the moment she'd eaten the drugged food, but what did that mean? Could she have been interrogated without any memory of it? And if so, what could she have told them?

But I don't know anything, she thought, numbly.

It was true, she thought. She knew who was on the Provisional Government, but *that* was no secret. The SS had *still* had agents within the

Reichstag, even after the uprising; they'd know who had taken a seat at the table, who had resigned, who had headed east to join the remainder of the former government. She knew who'd been part of the original protest movement, but the SS would know that too. And she *didn't* know anything about the Provisional Government's future plans.

We were concentrating on staying alive, she reminded herself. *We didn't have any real plans for what we'd do after we broke the siege.*

The door opened, again. This time, she managed to turn her head in time to see two more masked men enter the cell, one carrying a tray of food. His companion took her by the arms and hauled her up to the bed, pushing her bare back against the cold stone wall. She shivered, helplessly, unable to avoid a flicker of bitter gratitude as they held a cup of water to her lips and forced her to drink. It tasted normal, as far as she could tell, but that proved nothing. She was sure there were plenty of drugs that had no taste at all.

She couldn't help feeling like an invalid - or a baby - as they fed her, placing the soft food on a spoon and pressing it into her mouth. She'd always feared that she would have to feed Grandpa Frank like that, one day; now, she couldn't help feeling an odd sense of guilt for how badly she'd disliked him, before the uprising. But then, Grandpa Frank had had his own reasons for feeling guilty too. The memory made her look up at the two masked men. What did *they* have to feel guilty about? What had they done to countless helpless victims?

The men finished feeding her and withdrew, as silently as they'd come. Gudrun watched them go, feeling stronger as the food worked its way through her body. It didn't *feel* as if she'd been drugged again, although she had no way to be *sure.* All she could do was hope and pray that she *hadn't* been drugged. Gritting her teeth, she forced herself to stand up and stride from one end of the cell to the other, then back again. Her legs still felt wobbly, as if they were made of spaghetti, but she pushed them forward anyway. Horst had warned her that she would need to do something - anything - to keep her mind together. And yet, the thought of him almost brought her to her knees. Would she ever see him again?

She closed her eyes, leaning against the metal bars as the full weight of what she'd lost struck home. Horst had loved her - no, he *did* love her. He'd turned on his masters, on his comrades, for her. And he'd risked everything just to keep her safe. And now…she tried to imagine what he would do, if he'd survived the ambush. He'd come for her, wouldn't he?

He was born in Germany East, she thought. *He could get to Germanica without problems…*

She shook her head, bitterly. Horst might not have survived the ambush, back when she'd been captured. And even if he *had* survived…Germanica would be heavily defended, with countless stormtroopers dedicated to keeping Karl Holliston alive. If a team of SS commandos hadn't been able to purge the *Reichstag* in Berlin of the makeshift Provisional Government, how could one lone man get into the *Reichstag* in Germanica and get her out?

And if they catch him, she told herself, *they'll make sure his death is slow and painful.*

She heard the outer door opening again and looked up. Two *more* masked men - she thought they weren't the *same* men - were looking at her, their eyes travelling up and down her naked body. She was just too wretched to care, even though she knew they might intend to rape her. The SS wanted to break her - and how better to make it clear that she no longer had any control over herself than by raping her? She braced herself as they came closer, intending to fight even though she knew it would be futile. Perhaps she'd land a blow that would force them to kill her…

"We have to talk," the lead man said. He glanced up at the cameras. "My people are watching us at the moment."

Gudrun stared at her. "What…what is this?"

The man ignored her question. "Is there any way to end the war?"

"You could try talking," Gudrun said. What *was* this? *Who* was he? A friend and ally, or just someone playing a mind game? She had no doubt the SS would use every dirty trick it could think of to break her. "This war could go on for a very long time."

"Your comrades are planning an offensive," the man said. "But whatever happens, the *Reich* itself will be gravely weakened."

Gudrun forced herself to meet his eyes. She was dead anyway, no matter what she said. It was rare for girls of good German blood to be executed - the SS normally exiled them to Germany East, marrying them off to settlers who would keep them in line - but she doubted she'd be that lucky. Karl Holliston would want to make a terrible example of her - or, if that proved futile, shoot her in the head and dump her body in an unmarked grave. There was no hope of survival.

"Does the *Reich* deserve to survive?"

The man shrugged. "*Can* we survive?"

Gudrun fought down the urge to laugh. "Who are you?"

"Some people who want to find a different way," the man said. "We need to know if there *is* a different way."

"Overthrow Holliston," Gudrun said, sarcastically. She doubted the man would do anything of the sort. "And then we will talk."

The man looked back at her, evenly. "And what terms will we receive?"

Gudrun lost it. She started to giggle, helplessly.

"I'm locked in a prison cell, stark naked," she said, when she managed to regain control of herself. Someone had removed the last of her clothing while she'd been asleep. "What sort of terms do you think I could offer you?"

"Your government," the man said. There was a hint of…*something*…in his voice that nagged at her mind. "What sort of terms would *they* offer us?"

Gudrun forced herself to think about it. The Provisional Government would have *liked* to control the entire Greater German *Reich*, but practicality told against it. The economy was in tatters. There was no way the Provisional Government could keep control of the subject nations, let alone keep fighting the war in South Africa. And Germany East? Perhaps, as Volker had suggested, it would be better if Germany East went its own way.

"They would probably agree to your independence from the rest of the *Reich*," she said, finally. She doubted there was any form of compromise that would keep the *Reich* unified, not one that would suit both sides. "As long as you didn't pose a threat to us, we wouldn't pose a threat to you."

The second man leaned forward. "You'd just let us *go*?"

"Yes," Gudrun said. "I don't think we could afford to keep you."

She sighed. "But Holliston is the real problem," she added. "As long as he's alive, there can be no peace."

The first man seemed to shrug. "Are you sure?"

"I'm not sure of anything," Gudrun said. She wondered if she dared ask how long she'd been in the cell, then decided she probably couldn't trust their answers. "But Germany Prime and Germany East have been separating for years. Culturally, you're very different from us. I don't think you'll tamely accept all the changes we've written into the laws..."

"Of course not," the first man said. "Imagine giving *everyone* the vote."

Gudrun snorted. The *Reichstag* had been nothing more than a rubber stamp for the *Reich* Council for *decades*. No one had taken it seriously - a seat on the *Reichstag* was nothing more than a convenient place for the council to dispose of their political enemies. But now, the *Reichstag* would regain its prominence in the *Reich*...if they ever managed to end the war and hold free elections. She could understand why the Easterners might sneer at it...

We gave everyone the vote, she thought. It had been hard, very hard, to convince the Provisional Government that *women* should have the vote. She'd had to fight a long battle to ensure that women, like men, could vote from the age of twenty. *And Germany Prime, the most densely-populated part of the Reich, would have a major advantage.*

She shook her head. There were hundreds of differences between the two regions, ranging from how children were raised to the private ownership of weapons and ammunition. She honestly didn't see how they could come to terms. Holliston might not be popular - she had no idea how popular he was - but the SS was *very* popular. Invading and occupying Germany East might spark an insurrection against the Provisional Government.

"Get rid of Holliston," she said. "And then you can talk to the Provisional Government."

"We shall see," the first man said.

He turned and led the way out of the cell, his companion giving Gudrun one last look before following him. Gudrun watched them go, feeling utterly unsure of herself. Were they genuinely planning to take steps against Karl Holliston? Or were they merely trying to trick her into implicating herself? But it wasn't as if the SS *needed* an excuse to execute her. They already had her at their mercy.

She sighed as she turned and walked back to the bed. There was nothing to *do* in the cell, nothing but wait for something to happen to her. She sat down on the bed, resting her hands behind her head. There was no point in trying to conceal anything from the watching cameras...

Maybe they will overthrow Holliston, she thought. She found it hard to believe that Holliston was universally beloved, particularly after he'd assumed the title of *Fuhrer*. A *Fuhrer* with *real* power would be a nightmare. *And if they don't...*

She shook her head. She wanted - she *needed* - to believe she had allies, people whose interests matched her own. And if she could convince them to turn against Holliston, she might just be able to get out of the cell before it was too late.

And if they are plants, she thought grimly, *it isn't as if I can implicate myself any further.*

CHAPTER TWELVE

Germanica (Moscow), Germany East
1 November 1985

Gudrun, Katherine noted dispassionately as she stepped back into the security room, was bearing up well under the interrogation.

It wasn't something she'd expected to admire in her captive. Gudrun had always seemed like a weakling to her, a foolish female who'd seduced many men from their duty. She certainly was *not* the kind of woman who would openly defy her male relatives, let alone force the men to accept her on her own terms. And yet, there was a hard core of strength in her that Katherine was forced to admire.

Soft, yet unyielding, Katherine thought. *She will bend, but she will not break.*

She kept her expression blank as she stood in the room, watching Gudrun through the security cameras. She'd known far too many women - even women born in Germany East - who would have been humiliated by being forced to remain naked, but Gudrun was neither breaking down nor demanding clothing. And she was keeping herself busy by walking around her tiny cell, even though she *had* to know it was futile. Escape was impossible without outside help, Katherine knew; the *Reichstag* was so heavily defended that nothing short of an armoured assault would be enough to break through the defences and gain access to the inner chambers.

Katherine hadn't had an easy life, even before she'd joined the SS. Her mother had died when she was very young; she'd grown up with her brothers and a number of male cousins, all of whom had treated her as one of the boys. She'd had endless clashes with her teachers over the proper place for a young woman, enduring punishment after punishment for refusing to stay in the space they'd put aside for her. Her brothers had admired her defiance, even after they'd grown old enough to understand the difference between boys and girls. But Gudrun? She'd had an easy life.

In many ways, Gudrun was precisely the sort of girl Katherine despised. She would have married a handsome young man in a black uniform, abandoning her studies and all hope of a genuine career to bear and raise a legion of screaming brats. Her schooling suggested promise - she wouldn't have got into the university without genuine talent - but it would all have been wasted when she got married. And yet, when her boyfriend had been crippled, Gudrun had literally overthrown the regime.

Or, at least, she started the avalanche rolling, Katherine thought, dryly. No one could hope to overthrow an entire government without help, save perhaps for the legendary Otto Skorzeny. *And she didn't even stop after taking her revenge.*

It was odd. Gudrun was a mixture of admirable and detestable traits. A grim determination that Katherine admired, mixed with a willingness to bend and seek compromises that Katherine detested. *Gudrun* would not have stood up to her father, Katherine was sure; she'd have found a way to work around him instead. And she would probably do the same with her husband, if she managed to return to his arms. Horst - oathbreaker, traitor - might not understand the woman he'd married. Gudrun would not be content to be a simple housewife any longer.

I always stood up to the men, Katherine thought. She *had* stood up to her relatives; her strict father, her bully of an older brother, her teachers who had tried to force her to wear dresses and act like a meek little child. *But Gudrun did nothing of the sort.*

It galled her, in some ways, to realise just how much Gudrun had accomplished. And yet, how much of that had been through her *personally?* Katherine had shot and killed the enemies of the *Reich*; Gudrun had manipulated countless Berliners to rise up against the *Reich*, eventually overthrowing the *Reich* Council itself. Katherine had strangled an insurgent with her bare hands; Gudrun had won the loyalty of some very dangerous men - and done it on her own terms. Katherine couldn't help wondering if the Provisional Government understood Gudrun any better than her husband. If she'd been born a man, she would have been running the *Reich* by now.

But if she'd been born a man, there would have been no need for the uprising, Katherine thought.

Just for a moment, she felt an odd flicker of kinship with the girl in the cell. They were both intelligent and capable women, yet they'd both had to fight to gain even a fragment of respect from the men. Katherine wasn't just a good shot, she was a *great* shot; she'd beaten the Hitler Youth's reigning champion, only to have her record dismissed because she hadn't been in the Hitler Youth herself. She needed to be *better* than the men to win respect…and Gudrun, she suspected, had had the same problem.

She turned as she heard the door open, just in time to see Doctor Muller walk into the compartment. Katherine felt her lips thinning with disapproval. Doctor Muller - and she had grave doubts about his doctorate - was a monster. Worse, he was a pervert. He made her feel naked and unclean every time he looked at her, although he was smart enough not to do anything stupid. No one would have complained if she'd drawn her knife and sliced off his balls.

"Katherine," he said. He *never* addressed her by rank. "Our prisoner is doing well."

Katherine scowled at him, leaning forward and meeting his eyes. She had no doubt that Muller enjoyed the perks of his job. Fondling helpless girls - girls he'd drugged into comas - was definitely one of them, as far as he was concerned. And she'd heard whispered rumours about the experiments Muller liked to perform on *Untermensch* women. Katherine held no love for the *Untermenschen*, but there were limits. Cruelty for the sake of cruelty was simply absurd.

"How well?"

"The first dose of the drug should be working its way out of her system now," Muller informed her. "She will already have lost track of the days. The next dose will weaken her resistance to some of our…*other* techniques and then…"

"Just remember that the *Fuhrer* wants her alive and intact," Katherine reminded him. She was due a reward for her service in Berlin. Perhaps she could convince Holliston to let her be the one to finally execute Muller. "Play your games with someone else."

Muller flinched. "I don't know what you mean."

"I know," Katherine said. She took a step forward, deliberately forcing her way into his personal space. "And the *Fuhrer* knows what I mean."

She watched, feeling nothing but disgust, as Muller stepped backwards. The man had no fire in him, no bravery…he loathed women, he saw women as his helpless prey, yet he couldn't even stand up to her. The boys at school had been braver when they'd told her she couldn't play with them because she was a girl.

"I'll go start the next set of treatments," Muller stammered, finally. "I…"

"Go," Katherine said.

She forced herself to watch as he scurried out of the room, then turned her gaze back to the security cameras. Muller wouldn't try to restrain Gudrun himself, of course; he was far too much of a coward to take the risk. He'd have his orderlies do the job before he dared go anywhere near his prisoner. Gudrun would castrate him if he did anything else.

And her mere existence would emasculate him, Katherine thought with a flicker of dark humour, *if he'd been masculine in the first place.*

She cursed under her breath as she watched the orderlies enter the prison cell. Most of the records from Germany Prime had been sealed, after the uprising, but she *did* have a few contacts in low places. Gudrun *had* been engaged to a young stormtrooper - she was listed as his prospective bride in his file, a standard procedure for a young man going to war - and that stormtrooper had been badly wounded in South Africa. The medical report had made it clear that he wasn't going to recover, even before he was shipped back to Berlin. His parents had never been informed of their son's injury.

And if that is true, Katherine asked herself, *how many of Gudrun's other charges are true too?*

It wasn't something she'd ever expected to have to consider. She had nothing but contempt for the weaklings of Germany Prime. Life was safe there, life was soft…she had no doubt that their weakness had bred weakness. They certainly didn't face the risk of constant attack from *Untermensch* bandits…

And yet, was Gudrun right?

She gritted her teeth as Muller walked into the cell, his face twisted into a leer that made Katherine want to hit him. He would enjoy himself playing with a helpless girl, steadily wearing down her resistance…except Katherine had the very strong feeling that Gudrun *couldn't* be broken. It wasn't in

Katherine's nature to submit - she would have sooner died than let a man play with her - but Gudrun might just surprise the doctor. And then...what?

And if she's right about her boyfriend, Katherine asked herself again, *what else is she right about?*

––––––

They were all plotting against him.

Karl Holliston was no fool. He'd *known* that declaring himself the *Fuhrer* would invite challenges, particularly from those who didn't owe their positions to him. Victory in Berlin would have buried all doubts, leaving him secure long enough to make his position impregnable. But now...

It was a delicate balancing act, he had to admit. The more men he conscripted into the army and sent west, the weaker the defences in the east. He had no doubt that they could recover any lost territory, in time, but many of the *Gauleiters* disagreed. *Their* wealth and power depended on them remaining *firmly* in power, which would be put at risk if he weakened the eastern defences. It gave them ample reason to drag their feet, to refuse to send men west, to plot against him. And there were limits to how many of his subjects he could purge.

He cursed under his breath as he studied the map. Germany East was a competing network of fiefdoms, each one operating with considerable autonomy. Himmler himself had set the system up, back when the SS had been granted unrestricted control over the vast swathes of Occupied Russia; he'd parcelled great estates and plantations out to his supporters and the men willing to turn the desolate steppes into genuine farmland. It hadn't seemed a mistake at the time, but now the chickens had come home to roost. Karl couldn't help wondering if his former master had made a deadly mistake.

But we wanted to expand the farms, he thought, sourly. *There was no choice.*

He rubbed his forehead, feeling his head start to pound. Hitler had never faced a civil war, not since the Night of the Long Knives; *Himmler* had narrowly escaped a civil war by coming to terms with his opponents. But *he* had to face a civil war, as well as an internal threat from the *Gauleiters* who didn't support him. And he couldn't even move against them without triggering a major crisis. All he could do was wait and pray that the coming offensive was defeated.

Pushing the thought aside, he rose and strode over to the giant window. Night was falling over Germanica, but the city was still brightly lit. The towering buildings, each one designed in the gothic style that had been so popular after the Third *Reich* had taken control of Europe, were a stunning testament to the city's power. Even the centre of Berlin, designed by Albert Speer and Hitler himself, couldn't match the sheer grandeur of Germanica.

But it will, he told himself. *When we take the city, we will reshape it until all traces of the uprising are gone.*

He smiled at the thought. Victory would bring more than mere power; victory would bring the opportunity to truly make a mark on the *Reich*. Berlin would be purged, everyone who had served in the rebel government marched out of the city and shot, along with everyone related to them. The *Heer*, the *Luftwaffe* and the *Kriegsmarine* would be folded into the *Waffen-SS*, with loyalty to the New Order being placed ahead of everything else. And France, Italy and the other subject nations would be squeezed to the bone to rebuild the *Reich*. They'd been allowed too much independence over the past decade, even before the rebels started trying to dicker with them. They would learn that what little freedom they had was granted by the *Reich*.

And they will lose it if they defy us, he thought.

It wouldn't stop there, he promised himself. The damned university would be shut down, the student traitors marched east and put to work in forced labour camps. Women would be pushed out of the workforce altogether and forced to bear children, with marriages arranged by the state if the parents were unwilling to do it for their daughters. The population of the *Reich* would start to rise again, allowing the remainder of Germany East to finally be brought into the *Reich*. And the war in South Africa would be rejuvenated, with more and more troops sent to Africa until the blacks were finally - ruthlessly - crushed.

The phone rang. He turned, feeling a hot flicker of anger. Who dared interrupt him so late at night?

"Holliston," he said, picking up the phone.

"*Mein Fuhrer*," Maria said. "Minister Kuhnert requests an urgent meeting."

"Oh," Karl said. Territories Minister Philipp Kuhnert was an ally, of sorts. He certainly had nowhere else to go, after the uprising. Holliston trusted him *marginally* more than he trusted any of the *Gauleiters*. "Send him in, along with some coffee."

He kept his face blank as Kuhnert was escorted into the room. A serving girl, carrying a tray of hot coffee, appeared a moment later, placing the coffee on the table before bowing and retreating in haste. She was the daughter of one of the grandees, Holliston recalled; she'd been placed in the *Reichstag*, he suspected, in the hopes she'd catch a senior official's eye and marry him. There were no *Untermensch* servants in the *Reichstag* itself.

I should organise a match for her, he thought, as Kuhnert saluted. *Hitler used to do it all the time.*

"Minister," he said, stiffly. "I trust this is *urgent?*"

"There was a report from the Urals, *Mein Fuhrer*," Kuhnert said, bluntly. "A couple of outlying farms have been overrun and burned to the ground. The men on the spot say that all of the registered weapons have been stolen. They don't know what else might have been taken."

Karl sucked in his breath. "And the farmers?"

"Dead, *Mein Fuhrer*," Kuhnert said. "It was not pleasant."

"It wouldn't have been," Karl said. Slavs were savages. Given a chance, they'd loot, rape and murder from one end of the *Reich* to the other. "Were all the bodies recovered?"

"We think so," Kuhnert said. "Unless there was someone there who wasn't on the registry…"

Karl dismissed the thought with a wave of his hand. The Westerners might complain about having permanent files from birth to death, but Easterners were sensible enough to understand their value. Anyone staying at the farm would have had his presence noted and logged. No, there was no one unaccounted for.

"I've heard a great deal of anger," Kuhnert added. "The mobile reinforcements that should have responded to their cry for help were sent west two weeks ago."

"And so we lost a farm," Karl mused. Losing one farm was annoying, but hardly fatal; losing more, particularly in the east, was a serious problem.

Giving the bandits a victory - even an easy victory - would encourage them. "Can you calm the locals down?"

"I doubt it, *Mein Fuhrer*," Kuhnert said. "They are insistent that forces should be pulled back from the front to confront a more serious threat."

Karl slapped the table. "The rebels *are* a serious threat!"

He glared down at his hands. Germany East was just too damned *big*. If he detached anything less than a full-sized infantry division...he scowled. It would need something *bigger* than an infantry division to make a *real* impact on the bandits. And he couldn't even spare a single division. There was just too much to do in the west.

"If this continues," Kuhnert said, "I don't know what they'll do."

"Something stupid, perhaps," Karl said. He had to do *something*, but what? "Tell them we'll send reinforcements eastwards as soon as we can."

"I don't think they will accept that, *Mein Fuehrer*," Kuhnert warned. "They have good reason to be sceptical of our promises."

"Then make sure they accept it," Karl snarled. His head was *definitely* starting to pound. He was trying to save the *Reich* from those who would destroy it, from those who would give the land back to the Slavs...and he was being badgered by petty details. "We *will* send them reinforcements as soon as we can."

He drank his coffee, knowing it wouldn't be enough to keep him awake. He needed sleep, not...not late nights. And yet, there was just too much to do.

"Tell them that we will do what we can, when we can," he added, firmly. Himmler had been lucky. He'd never had to cope with a civil war. "And make it clear that we don't need the distraction."

"*Jawohl, Mein Fuhrer*," Kuhnert said.

Karl watched him go, cursing under his breath. There was *far* too much he had to do, far too many issues that required his personal attention. And yet, he simply didn't have the time to handle it all. He had no idea how Hitler or Himmler had coped...

I imagine it was easy, he thought, bitterly. *They could trust their subordinates.*

CHAPTER THIRTEEN

Farm #342, Germany East
1 November 1985

"This looks like a small fortress," Kurt noted, as they drove towards the gates. "I've been in military bases that had fewer defences."

Horst shrugged. "It's fairly normal for Germany East," he said. "You never know when you might come under attack."

He felt a flicker of homesickness as they stopped in front of the gates. The farm itself wasn't *that* big, but it was surrounded by a heavy metal fence and a handful of concrete firing positions. It didn't *look* as though they were manned - and the barren fields looked deserted, the crops taken in for winter - yet he knew, from his early life, that they could be manned at terrifying speed if there was an attack. Every Easterner knew he might have to fight for his life at any moment.

"Stay polite," he muttered. "Inspectors or not, we don't want to anger them."

He climbed out of the car, breathing in the familiar smell of farmland. A young girl - a year or two younger than Gudrun, if he was any judge - was walking down the drive towards the gates. She wore a checked dress that showed off both her chest and her muscles, her blonde hair plaited and hanging down to brush against the top of her breasts. And she carried a rifle, slung over her shoulder. Horst knew better than to assume she couldn't use it. Chances were she'd be a very good shot.

And she might be covered by someone else too, he reminded himself. The sky was darkening rapidly. *They might suspect our motives.*

"Greetings, *Fräulein*," he said, once the girl was in earshot. "My comrade and I seek shelter for the night."

The girl looked him up and down, her eyes wary. Horst held out his papers and allowed her to read them, wondering if she'd be able to tell the difference between *real* papers and cunning fakes. It would be ironic indeed if they were caught because a young girl insisted on checking with Germanica before allowing them through the gate. But she nodded, glanced behind the car and then opened the gate. Horst ordered Kurt to drive the car up to the farmhouse, then followed him at a more sedate pace. The girl locked and bolted the gate before walking up beside him.

"It's not been safe out there," she said, gently. "Did you run into trouble?"

"None," Horst assured her. They'd passed a dozen plantations, but they hadn't seen any signs of real trouble. "What have you been hearing?"

The girl didn't answer as they reached the farmhouse. It looked very much like a blockhouse, despite the desperate attempts to make it a little more homey. A middle-aged man was standing by the door, arms folded across his chest. Horst had no difficulty in recognising him as a military veteran as well as an experienced farmer and stern father, not someone who was likely to put up with any nonsense. He couldn't help feeling a flicker of sympathy for the girl.

"Heidi, tell the girl to put more food in the stew pot," the man said gruffly. He looked directly at Horst. "And who are you?"

"Travellers, father," Heidi said. She held out Horst's papers. "They've come from the front."

"Go do as you're told," the man ordered. He scanned Horst's papers for a long moment, then motioned for the two visitors to enter the farmhouse. Heidi scurried ahead of them and vanished in the distance. "I'm afraid we only have a hard floor and some blankets for guests."

"That will be quite sufficient," Horst said, as he followed the farmer into his house. The interior reminded him of his family's house, further to the east. "All we really need is something to eat, something to drink and a place to stay."

"I can do that," the man said. He led the way into a dining room, of sorts. The walls were solid concrete, but all the furniture was wood. "Are you going all the way back to Germanica?"

"That's what our orders say," Horst said.

"Tell them we need more manpower out here," the old man said. He poured three glasses of schnapps and handed them round. "The serfs are getting restless."

"And my brothers have gone to the war," Heidi said, coming back into the room. "Have you seen them?"

"Probably not," Horst said. He didn't miss the look Heidi shot at Kurt. "But the war front was very disorganised when we were called back to Germanica."

He chatted to the farmer, watching - with some private amusement - as Heidi flirted inexpertly with Kurt. She'd probably pegged him as a Westerner from the start, someone who would either take her away from the farm or come to live and work with her, rather than someone who would take her down the road to another farm. He hoped Kurt had enough sense not to do anything stupid, no matter how charming Heidi was. The last thing they needed was a father insisting on an immediate marriage - or worse. There was no way their papers would stand up to inspection at a registry office.

"The girl is late," Heidi said, twenty minutes later. "I'll go fetch her."

She rose and walked out of the room. The farmer motioned for them to rise and take their seats around the wooden table, refilling their glasses as they sat down. A faint slapping sound echoed out of the kitchen; a moment later, Heidi entered, followed by a dark-skinned woman with a nasty bruise on her right cheek. The woman was carrying a large pot, which she placed on the table before bowing and withdrawing from the room. She was so thin, Horst noted, that she looked almost like a walking skeleton.

"I apologise," Heidi said. "You can't get good help these days."

Kurt looked shocked, Horst saw, although thankfully he had the sense to keep his opinion to himself. His family had probably never had a *Gastarbeiter* maid, even though his father could probably have obtained one if he'd wanted. Horst, who had seen too many servants on his father and uncle's farms, took it in stride. It was just part of life in the *Reich*.

"Really, the war is sucking away too many people," the farmer said. "There's a whole plantation just down the road with minimal supervision."

Horst nodded. "It's the war," he said. "As soon as the traitors are defeated, things will return to normal."

He eyed the farmer carefully, wondering just what side the man was on. Talking so freely to a pair of inspectors…did he think himself beyond reproach? Beyond punishment for defeatism? Or was he just too old to care?

A man who had served the *Reich* loyally for decades might be quietly ignored, if he asked too many questions towards the end of his life.

Besides, Horst thought, *who's going to hear him out here?*

Kurt leaned forward. "Can the two of you handle the farm on your own?"

"For the moment," Heidi said. She gave Kurt a charming smile. "But what will happen when spring rolls around and we have to plant more crops?"

"We won't be leaving," her father said, gruffly.

Horst felt a spark of pity. They weren't *that* far from the front. Heidi and her father would probably have to watch their farmhouse converted into a strongpoint, if they weren't overwhelmed by western armies or killed by bandits. The slave might be beaten down…or she might be in touch with outsiders, telling them to wait for a chance to storm the farm. It wasn't as if two people could hold the wire indefinitely.

"I hope your sons make it back," he said, finally.

"So do I," the old man said. "So do I."

————

Kurt had known, from what he'd learned before he'd met Horst for the first time, that Germany East was different from Germany Prime. But he hadn't really *believed* it, despite Horst's words. The farmhouse and the farmers were… *strange*, by his standards; the old man seemed to trust his daughter, allowing her to carry a weapon and even talk to strange men without interference. And Heidi had casually slapped her servant…

It bothered him, more than he cared to admit. His father had never allowed a servant - *Gastarbeiter* or not - to enter their family house, even though his wife had had enough children to qualify for one. The poor girl might be a servant, but still…she didn't deserve to be treated like a slave. And yet…there was nothing he could do.

"I shall withdraw for the night," the farmer said. "Heidi, bring the gentlemen blankets and pillows."

"Of course, father," Heidi said.

She shot Kurt a look - she'd been shooting him looks all evening - and then turned and hurried out of the door. Kurt honestly wasn't sure what to make of her. No girl, at least in his experience, had ever been so forward, certainly not with him. Gudrun would have been grounded for the rest of her life if she'd acted like that - Kurt dreaded to think what their parents would have said, after they found out. But Heidi seemed to live by different rules.

The farmer rose and made his way slowly out of the room. Horst watched him go, then glanced sharply at Kurt. "Be careful," he muttered. "You don't want to get her pregnant."

Kurt looked back at him, feeling his cheeks flush. "We're not going to do anything," he protested. "I don't understand…"

"Be careful," Horst repeated. "I'll explain later."

Heidi returned, carrying a pair of large blankets and pillows. They looked rough, compared to proper bedding, but Kurt had plenty of experience sleeping in foxholes. Pillows and blankets would be practically paradisiacal, compared to cold ground and open air. She spoke quietly to Horst, telling him where to find the bathroom, then started to organise the blankets on the floor.

"You were born in Berlin," she said. "What's it like?"

"It's just like any city," Kurt said. He wasn't a virgin, but the way Heidi was moving was incredibly distracting. There was just something about her that drew him to her, even though she wasn't *quite* the ideal of German womanhood. He'd never seen a girl so muscled in his entire life. "Far too many people to be comfortable."

"Nothing like a farm," Heidi said. "What's it like?"

Kurt considered his answer for a long moment. "Very different from a farm," he said, finally. "I had to go to school…did you go to school?"

"I had a day or two every week at the village," Heidi said. She looked down at the wooden floorboards for a long moment. "That was enough for me, according to father. My brothers didn't get much more until they joined the Hitler Youth."

Kurt smiled. "There are giant shops where you can buy anything you like," he said. "And cinemas and countless places to go…"

"With a girl," Heidi said, deadpan. "Have you taken many girls to the cinema?"

"No," Kurt said, feeling embarrassed. He'd dated a few times, but never seriously. He hadn't even lost his virginity until he'd gone to the brothel, after his promotion. "Life in the city isn't *that* free."

"A pity," Heidi said. "I saw a movie reel once about a city. It looked like paradise."

"Here might look like paradise too," Kurt said. He frowned. "How *are* things out here?"

Heidi sighed. "I don't know how we're going to get through the next year," she admitted, reluctantly. "Father keeps telling me to keep my chin up, but…"

She shook her head. "We need my brothers back if we are going to plant anything," she added, bitterly. "Or we have to hire workers from the east…"

"Or bring in more slaves," Kurt said.

"I don't know if we can trust them," Heidi said. "There are only two of us here. And if we can't meet our quotas…"

Kurt frowned. "What happens if you can't meet your quotas?"

"I'm not sure," Heidi confessed. "We might lose the farm. Or someone might be allocated to work here. Or…"

"I see, I think," Kurt said.

He felt a sudden stab of sympathy for the younger girl. She *wanted* to stay on the farm. He couldn't imagine her having any problems finding a husband in Germany East; she was pretty, smart and knew everything about working on a farm. And it probably wouldn't have been hard for her to *leave* the farm, even without her father's permission. No, she *wanted* to stay on her father's farm…

Would she inherit? Kurt didn't know. In Germany Prime, the father's possessions would go to his sons - there were limits to how much could be passed to the daughters. But in Germany East, who knew? He had a feeling the land might go to whomever could work it.

Horst returned to the room, wearing a faded brown bathrobe that looked two sizes too small for him. Heidi glanced at him, then motioned for Kurt to follow her. There was no sign of the farmer - or the serving girl - as they walked down the short corridor and into a small bathroom. A steaming bucket of warm water sat next to the bathtub.

"We don't have running water out here," Heidi said. She smiled, oddly nervously. "The visitors we get from the cities always comment on it."

"There's hot and cold running water in Berlin," Kurt said. He'd never really appreciated what a luxury it was until he'd gone into barracks, where spending more than a minute under the water was *bound* to attract the wrath of the *Scharfuehrers*. "I always loved standing under the shower."

Heidi nodded as he turned to face her, then moved forward and kissed him, hard. Kurt suddenly found himself torn between his body, which was reacting in all sorts of ways to the beautiful girl in his arms, and his mind, which insisted that kissing her back was a very bad idea. But it seemed a small concern, a very small concern, when she was alive and warm and…

He kissed her back, feeling her shuddering against him. His hands roamed over her dress, feeling her muscles moving as she stroked his back. Her tongue flicked in and out of his mouth as his fingers fiddled with her dress, eventually allowing it to fall to her waist; her breasts bobbled free, jutting out firmly and pressing against his chest. She didn't need a bra, part of his mind noted as his fingers started to stroke her breasts; her fingers were fiddling with his belt, trying to undo it…

Somehow, he pulled back. "Your father," he said. He grunted in shock as she pulled him back, her hands reaching into his underwear to take hold of his cock. "What…what will he say if he catches us?"

Heidi's face flickered with…irritation. "Nothing."

Kurt stared at her. He knew *precisely* what his father would have said - and done - if he'd caught Gudrun making love to a stranger. Gudrun wouldn't have been able to sit comfortably for a week, while the stranger would have been pitched out of the house…if he hadn't been arrested and hauled off to jail. He couldn't believe that any father, *anywhere*, would turn a blind eye. Hell, he doubted his father wanted to *think* about what his *married* daughter did with her husband.

"I'll be leaving tomorrow," he said. It wasn't easy to turn her down, not when he could see her bare breasts and her hand was holding him, but somehow he mustered the will. "I can't leave you here."

Heidi let go of him, her face cycling through a bewildering series of emotions. Tears formed at the corner of her eyes, *genuine* tears. Kurt felt an odd stab of guilt, realising that he'd humiliated her by turning her down. And yet…he couldn't just sleep with her, then leave her behind.

"I'm sorry," Heidi said. She stepped backwards and turned away from him, buttoning up her dress. Kurt forced himself to look away, even though parts of his body were screaming at him for being an idiot. "I thought…never mind."

Kurt reached out and put a hand on her shoulder. "You thought what?"

"We need someone else here," Heidi said, sadly. She refused to turn and look at him. "And if you had stayed with me, you could have helped save the farm."

"I don't know how to run a farm," Kurt said. He felt a sudden surge of pity. Heidi didn't just need a man, Heidi needed a man who would stay on her farm. "And your brothers will come back..."

Heidi laughed, bitterly. "And do you really think they'll be back before it's too late?"

She turned to face him. "Stay with me," she said. "We *need* you."

"I have my duty," Kurt said, bluntly. Did she expect him to give up his job? Or had she simply not thought that far ahead? "But when it's done, I'll see what I can do."

Heidi snorted, then strode out of the bathroom, closing the door firmly behind her. Kurt stared after her, unsure if he should be relieved or angry at himself. Heidi had *definitely* been something different, but he understood her problem. He understood it all too well.

And there's no way I can come back, he told himself, firmly. There was a bit of him that liked her, that admired her willingness to take an awful risk for her father's farm. He wished, suddenly, that he'd met her without deception. *And if I do, after the war, who knows what she will make of me?*

Shaking his head, he washed quickly and headed back to the dining room. They'd have to leave early, in the morning...

...And, unless he was very lucky, he knew he would never see the farmhouse again.

CHAPTER FOURTEEN

Berlin/Front Lines, Germany Prime
3 November 1985

Berlin looked...*different*.

Volker Schulze stood on the roof of the *Reichstag*, peering east. The city was dark and silent, the curfew holding now the series of street parties had come to an end. Armed soldiers were patrolling, he knew, watching for trouble, but none of them were visible as he looked down at the streets. Berlin was holding its breath, waiting to see what would happen next.

They know the offensive is going to begin, he thought, as a cool breeze washed across the rooftop. *And any spies still in the city know too.*

It wasn't a reassuring thought. Berlin had been riddled with spies, even before the uprising; entire *divisions* of informers, ranging from unhappy wives and bratty children to paid provocateurs, had been uncovered in the RSHA's files. The *Reich* had told its citizens, time and time again, that it was good and right to inform on one's friends and family, if they showed signs of disloyalty. And he had no doubt there were rings of spies and informers who had never been listed in the files, not when the different factions in the *Reich* were struggling for supremacy. He would be surprised if Karl Holliston didn't know - already - that the Provisional Government was gearing up for an offensive against Germany East.

But he might not believe the reports, he told himself, although he knew it was nothing more than wishful thinking. *Launching an offensive now is risky as hell.*

He scowled as it grew colder. It would be colder still further eastwards as winter descended, a winter that had shattered entire armies in days gone by.

Volker had fought in the east as a young man. He *knew* how dangerous the Russian winter could be. And yet he'd given orders that ran the risk - the very real risk - of leaving his forces caught outside winter quarters when the snow finally descended. There had been no choice, he told himself, but it still worried him. General Winter had come far too close to beating the Third *Reich* on its own.

There's no choice, he told himself. He'd gone over the facts and figures time and time again, hoping for a better way. But there was none. The SS could not be allowed time: time to rebuild its forces, time to unlock the nuclear warheads, time to subvert the Provisional Government and trigger another civil war. *We have to end the war now.*

He closed his eyes for a long moment, feeling a sudden flicker of bitter envy for Herman Wieland. There was nothing *to* envy. Herman - a man in his late fifties - was going back to the front. And yet, he'd be placing his life at risk, while Volker knew he didn't dare take a rifle himself and join the fight. It felt *wrong*, somehow, to send so many men to their deaths while he stayed behind, in safety. But what choice did he have? *He* was the glue holding the Provisional Government together.

And besides, the nasty part of his mind pointed out, *you won't survive long if the war is lost.*

Volker nodded reluctantly, conceding the point. Konrad was dead already, his corpse laid to rest in a graveyard on the other side of Berlin, but his wife and daughter were still alive - and dangerously vulnerable. He'd had them both sent out of Berlin, their names changed to protect them from the remaining loyalists, yet he knew Holliston would stop at nothing to find and kill them if he won the war. Volker had never spoken to Holliston, but he knew the man's reputation. He would do whatever it took to regain control and stamp his will on the *Reich*.

He felt a faint sensation of guilt as he peered over the darkened city. Thousands of Berliners had been evacuated westwards, now the siege had been lifted, but they still weren't *safe*. And yet he'd made plans to have his wife and daughter shipped to Britain if the war was lost, if the SS recovered Berlin…none of the others in Berlin, save for the remainder of the government, had the ability to protect their families. It felt wrong, somehow, to put his family first, yet what choice did he have? He knew *exactly* what would happen to his family if the war was lost. The remainder of the population would probably be safe if they kept their heads down...

But that might not be true, he told himself, sourly. *All the reports we received from the front lines...*

Volker had no illusions about the SS. He'd *been* a stormtrooper. He knew just how brutal the SS could be. And yet, there had been a savagery unleashed in the last few months that was quite beyond anything he'd ever experienced. Villages smashed flat, towns devastated, men shot, women raped, children marched eastwards to an uncertain destination...it was as if a devil had come to Germany Prime. It was possible that some of the stories were exaggerated - he certainly *hoped* that some of the stories were exaggerated - but there was just too much evidence to support them. He'd even seen photographs of some of the mutilated bodies left behind by the SS.

He shook his head, tiredly. He'd thought he was joining the defenders of civilisation, when he'd joined the SS. And maybe many of the ordinary stormtroopers still believed that they *were* defending civilisation. But their leadership was as corrupt as any other department within the *Reich*, more interested in its own power than in protecting the *Reich* from its enemies. And they had betrayed their loyal servants...

Behind him, a door opened.

"Your aide told me I'd find you up here," Voss's voice said.

Volker didn't turn. "I like looking at the city," he said. "It reminds me of what we're fighting for."

Voss stepped up beside him. "I never liked Berlin," he said. "There were too many people here."

"Perhaps," Volker said. It was true, he supposed. Anyone who wanted to make a name for himself would come to Berlin, given time. There had been no shortage of talk over the last two decades about restricting the growth of the city's population. "But it's also the capital of the *Reich*."

He sighed as he peered towards a particularly dark section of the city. The power distribution network had failed there, after an SS suicide squad had attacked the transformers and destroyed them. Normally, it would have been a simple repair, but there was nothing *normal* about a city under siege. The engineers swore blind they were working on the problem, yet there was a lack of spare parts. And there were several other parts of the city where the electrical supply was hanging by a thread...

And if we can't keep Berlin lit, he thought grimly, *what good are we?*

The thought sent a cold shiver running down his spine. There was no way to avoid the simple fact that the *Reich* Council - in its various incarnations - had ruled the *Reich* for over thirty-five years, ever since Adolf Hitler had died. It had enjoyed a certain legitimacy through sheer longevity. But *his* government had barely been in existence for a couple of months. It certainly didn't control the state as completely as the *Reich* Council had done.

And, in overthrowing the Reich Council, he reminded himself, *we proved that a government could be overthrown.*

He shook his head, bitterly. He'd looked into the hidden history of protest movements within the *Reich* - communists, democrats, feminists - and they'd all ended badly, so badly they'd been scrubbed from history and almost forgotten. Indeed, he'd never heard of women demanding rights after the war. The SS had crushed the movement - the women themselves had been dispatched to Germany East - and everyone had pretended that it had never happened. But the women had been lucky, compared to the communists. *They'd* wound up hanging from meathooks in cellars below Berlin.

Voss cleared his throat. "*Herr* Chancellor?"

Volker cursed under his breath. "I'm sorry," he said. Confessing weakness had always bothered him, but he trusted Voss. The Field Marshal had had ample opportunity to take power for himself after the *Reich* Council had fallen. "I was woolgathering."

"The lead units are in position," Voss told him. "We can launch the offensive at daybreak."

Volker glanced at him. "I would have thought that was a little predictable."

"We don't have the finely-tuned army we'd need to launch a night-time offensive," Voss reminded him. "If we had more time..."

"We don't," Volker said, sharply.

He turned to look at the other man. Voss knew - he was one of the few who did - just how little time the *Reich* actually had. They needed to win - quickly - or they would lose, no matter who came out ahead. Holliston would inherit a broken country if he ever retook Berlin. And yet, Volker didn't dare risk so many men without some guarantee of victory...

Don't be stupid, he told himself, sharply. *There is never any guarantee of victory.*

It was tempting, chillingly tempting, to call off the offensive. He could do it, too. But there would be someone who wouldn't get the message, who would launch an attack without support and get slaughtered for it. And that too would be bad.

"Launch the offensive as planned," he ordered. "Pocket and destroy the bastards."

"*Jawohl, Herr* Chancellor," Voss said.

Volker nodded as he led the way towards the door. He would have liked to convince the stormtroopers to surrender, but he knew that was unlikely. Even without the atrocities to fuel anger - he'd been quietly warned that his soldiers could not be expected to take prisoners - the stormtroopers would be unlikely to surrender without being hammered into the ground first. They were *tough*.

And they will die to defend a man who fled Berlin rather than fight, Volker told himself, bitterly. He'd *been* a stormtrooper. If things had been different, he might have been one of the black-clad men on the other side of the front lines. *And their deaths will be for nothing.*

———

Herman couldn't sleep.

The makeshift accommodation was staggeringly uncomfortable, leaving him with aches and pains even as he tried to catch a few hours of sleep. He couldn't remember having any troubles sleeping on the hard ground - or a handful of blankets - when he'd been a paratrooper, but he'd been nearly thirty years younger at the time. Now...he felt old and frail, even as he tried to sleep. Part of him honestly worried that he wouldn't be able to get up and walk in the morning.

He glanced at his watch, then at his comrades. They seemed to have managed to fall asleep, although some of them might be lingering on the very edge of awareness. He still recalled days from his youth when his comrades had sworn blind he'd been asleep, although he'd been awake and aware - or thought he'd been awake and aware - the whole time. Back then, he'd thought nothing of a forty mile forced march through the mud. Now...

I'm too old for this shit, Herman thought. It was 0530, according to his watch; the offensive was scheduled for dawn, still two hours away. *I could be back home and in bed...*

He scowled as he forced himself to stand up, despite his aching body. There was no point in trying to sleep, not now. He wasn't a young man any longer, able to survive on a few hours of sleep. Carefully, he picked his way to the door and peered outside. The guard was sitting on the ground, snoring quietly. Herman felt a hot flash of anger as he stared down at him, knowing it was sheer luck that an inspector hadn't passed. The entire unit would be in deep shit if their guard had been caught sleeping.

And if we'd been caught by the enemy, he thought, *we'd all be dead.*

He removed the guard's weapon, then hissed at him to wake up. The guard jumped, one hand reaching for the rifle that was no longer there; Herman held it up, fighting down the urge to slam the butt into the guard's face. He was no longer in the police force.

"You fell asleep," he growled. The guard looked younger than him, although not young enough to pass for a fresh-faced young man right out of the training centre. "You could have gotten us all killed."

He scowled as the guard began to splutter excuses. Yes, they *were* in the middle of an armed camp; no, that *didn't* excuse the guard falling asleep. Herman's old instructors would not have hesitated to hand out harsh punishment to the entire unit, even during training; now, in the middle of a war, a soldier could be shot for falling asleep on guard. There was no excuse for doing something so stupid that an enemy could simply walk up to the makeshift barracks and lob a couple of grenades inside.

"Idiot," he said, finally. "Give me a cigarette and it won't go any further."

The guard looked relieved as he removed a pack of cigarettes from his pocket and held them out. Herman took one, his policeman's eye noting the lack of any actual *markings* on the cigarette packet. Probably imported from France and sold on the black market, he decided, rather than purchased legitimately from an authorised dealer. Evading tax would have been a serious crime, two years ago - the authorities would have taken a very dim view of it - but it wasn't a problem now. Besides, Berlin's vast stockpile of cigarettes had been drained by the war. No new shipments were coming into the city.

He borrowed a match to light the cigarette, then inhaled the smoke. It tasted odd, compared to the ones he'd smoked on duty, but he found it hard to care. Doctors might insist that smoking posed a health risk - it was funny how they'd started saying that as the cost of smoking had begun to rise - yet he was a *policeman*. There had always been the risk of a violent death, even before the war. A suspect, knowing he'd be lucky to escape execution, might just choose to fight...

"Two hours," the guard said.

Herman nodded in grim agreement. They'd been told they'd be going to the front after the lead units had punched a hole in the enemy lines, but very little else. The older soldiers had been offended at being told so little, even though they *knew* it posed a security risk. There was just too great a chance of *someone* sneaking out of the camp, finding a telephone and calling his SS masters. Or merely going back to Berlin for some fun. There had been a surprising number of soldiers on punishment duty when the makeshift unit had arrived at the camp.

We're too close to Berlin, Herman thought, dryly.

It was a common problem. Soldiers - bored or aware of their own mortality - had a tendency to sneak out of camp in search of wine, women and song. Herman had often rounded up soldiers who'd made it to the pubs, marching them back to the camps and handing them over to their superiors. It was even a danger in a combat zone, even though the soldiers really should have known better. He'd heard horror stories about young men sneaking out of camp in South Africa, only to be caught, killed and mutilated by the local insurgents.

But the stories could easily have been spread by the higher-ups, he reminded himself. *How better to discourage soldiers from fraternising with the enemy?*

He leaned against the doorway and watched, grimly, as the camp slowly came to life. There would be no formal assembly, not today; units would form up, then march to the front lines and go to war. He wished, suddenly, for a hot bath or even a shower, but he knew they were both impossible. It was a military camp, not a holiday home. There were few luxuries even for the commanders.

"Thank you," the guard said. "I could have wound up in real trouble."

Herman scowled. He honestly wasn't sure he'd done the right thing. Falling asleep in the middle of a camp was bad enough, but falling asleep in a war zone could prove lethal. The guard deserved whatever punishment was meted out to him. And yet, Herman wasn't sure *he* could have coped with *his* punishment. He was no longer able to drop and give a hundred push-ups on command.

"Never mind," he said. "But if you fall asleep on duty again, I'll kick you in the nuts and then slit your throat."

And I mean it, he added, silently. It wouldn't be the first time a dangerously-incompetent soldier had been pushed out or murdered by his comrades. *You put us all in danger.*

He turned and peered back into the hut. There were few buildings still standing between Berlin and the front lines; the hut, he'd been told, had been patched up by the engineers before the company had been told to sleep there. He didn't know if they'd been given the hut because the higher-ups thought they'd need somewhere relatively warm and dry to sleep or if it was an unsubtle insult aimed at the old men. But he had a feeling he'd be wishing, soon enough, that they were back in the hut…

Time to get ready, he thought. Dawn was starting to waver on the horizon. In the distance, he could hear the sound of shellfire and explosions. It wouldn't be long before the first units started to advance on the enemy positions. *We're going back to the war.*

CHAPTER FIFTEEN

Germanica (Moscow), Germany East
3 November 1985

Gudrun started awake...and froze.

She was in a different cell. The cage bars that allowed her guards to watch her were gone, the hard bed was gone...instead, she was lying on a plastic bed, inside a room that reminded her of a swimming pool. She took a long breath as she sat upright and shuddered, unable to hide her revulsion. The room *smelt* like a swimming pool too, bringing back memories of learning to swim at school. She'd dreaded those lessons, but there had been no avoiding them. Or the wet towels snapped across her back and buttocks by the matrons when they thought she was deliberately lagging...

They moved me while I was asleep, she thought, numbly. She looked down and scowled as she realised she was *still* naked. It didn't bother her any longer, not when she knew there was far worse to come. *But why?*

She swung her feet over the side of the bed and stood. Her legs felt oddly steady, even though she knew she must have been drugged again. Perhaps she was growing used to whatever they were feeding her. Or perhaps she'd fallen asleep naturally and they'd just gambled that she wouldn't wake up, while they carried her to her new cell. She glanced around, studying the walls. They were solid plastic, smooth to the touch. She couldn't see any cameras.

They'll still be watching, she told herself, as she examined the door. It was sealed, unsurprisingly, so carefully worked into the walls that she honestly wasn't *sure* she was looking at the door until she traced out the frame. There were no handles, nothing to indicate how the door could be opened from the inside. *They'll be watching me to see what I do.*

She swept her gaze around the room, but saw nothing. The bed was really nothing more than plastic, hard to the touch. And yet it was warm...the entire room was surprisingly warm. It felt almost like a sauna. Did they *want* to warm her up? Or were they just playing games with her mind? She honestly didn't know.

Be grateful it isn't worse, she told herself. She'd had to undergo a medical exam, shortly after arriving - she had no idea how long she'd been in Germanica - and it had been humiliating, far worse than anything she'd experienced in the BDM. *Being in a cell is better than on the examination table.*

She sat back down, shaking her head slowly. Perhaps they were trying to drive her mad with boredom. It wasn't going to work, if that was the case. She'd always been at the top of her class, in school; she hadn't been truly challenged until she'd gone to university and discovered that she wasn't the smartest person in the world after all. Boredom had been part of her life, ever since she'd found out that complaining about the lessons was a good way to be noticed by an angry teacher. And telling him that he'd got something wrong - and he had - hadn't helped either.

Pushing the thought aside, she concentrated on a more important problem. How long had she been in Germanica? She didn't know - it felt as if the entire world had shrunk to her prison cell - but she was a woman. Her period had been a week off, more or less, before she'd been captured. And there was no way they could hide her blood from her.

Or have they drugged me to ensure I don't bleed, she asked herself. *Or did Horst manage to get me pregnant?*

She closed her eyes in pain as the full implications dawned on her. They *hadn't* used protection - how could they, when contraception was almost unavailable save for older couples with more than three children? Horst could easily have gotten her pregnant, before or after the marriage. And if she *was* pregnant...she swallowed, hard. The SS might not harm the baby - the parents were both of good bloodlines - but they would certainly take the child away.

And I've been half-starved, she thought. *My period might be delayed anyway.*

She worked her way through the logic, slowly. If she *wasn't* pregnant, she'd only been in Germanica for a week, more or less. But if she *was* pregnant...

A dull *thump* echoed through the room. She looked up, alarmed. There was a hissing sound, right above her; moments later, a tiny hatch appeared in the ceiling. Seconds later, a stream of water poured from overhead and splashed down to the floor. The puddle spread rapidly until the bitterly cold water was splashing against her bare feet. Gudrun shivered, pulling her feet up until she was sitting on the bed; the water kept rising as more and more poured down into the room. She cursed under her breath, remembering how the matrons had used to push girls into the swimming pool, then forced her legs into the cold water. There was no way to avoid taking a swim.

She started to shiver as the water rose higher. It was cold, so cold...to her horror, the water just kept rising, threatening to drown her. She found herself kicking to stay afloat, her body rising until it was pushed against the ceiling, the water bubbling at her mouth...did they mean to *kill* her? Panic fluttered at the back of her mind as she gasped for air, struggling to pull one last breath into her body. She was going to die in the cell...

...And then the water level dropped so rapidly that she banged her leg against the bed, then landed badly on the wet floor. A grate had opened nearby, draining the water out of her cell; Gudrun was too tired to try to open it, even though she doubted it was a way out for her. Her throat hurt badly; she hacked and coughed, spitting up droplets of water she'd swallowed onto the floor. And it was suddenly very - *very* - cold.

She forced herself to sit upright, wrapping her arms around her legs as cold air blew into the room. Her entire body shivered helplessly, mocking her. The gusts of air - it was hard not to think of them as *wind* - blasted over her body, coming from portals high overhead that opened and closed randomly. She couldn't help a flicker of guilt, remembering how she - and most of the other girls - had teased and tormented those who'd been poor swimmers. Perhaps she deserved to suffer...

Because it was safer to tease them than stand up for them, she thought, bitterly. The matrons hadn't done anything about the bullying. Hell, they'd been bullies themselves. *And none of us wanted the matrons looking elsewhere. We were grateful when the matrons picked on the weaker girls.*

She ran her hand through her wet hair, knowing there was nothing she could do to straighten it out. The entire *Reich* was based on bullying, on the strong tormenting the weak...why should the BDM have been any different? And she'd had more than her fair share of torments too...except that wasn't entirely true. Gudrun's father could have made *real* trouble for the matrons, if they'd stepped too far out of line. Perhaps she should have asked him to defend the other girls.

A low rumble ran through the room. The floor hatches opened, spewing water back up and into the room. Gudrun yelped in shock as the water - scalding hot this time - splashed against her bare skin, then jumped back to get out of the way as the water kept rising. But this time it was too hot, burning her as it rose higher…she scrambled back onto the bed, knowing it wouldn't give her more than minimal protection. And then it started to wash against her feet.

She gritted her teeth, trying not to scream. It wasn't hot enough to do *real* damage - she hoped - but it was hot enough to be extremely uncomfortable. And it was still rising, brushing against her knees. She stood on tiptoe, trying to keep as much of herself as she could out of the water, even though she knew it was futile. The water brushed against her thighs, then her breasts, then finally started lapping at her throat. She kicked desperately as her head bumped against the ceiling, hoping - praying - that the water would be released, again, before she drowned. Or was cooked…

…Instead, water started pouring from the ceiling.

She closed her eyes, expecting to drown at any second. But the water level seemed stable…she realised, numbly, that the hot water was being drained as cold water poured from high overhead. The temperature dropped rapidly, so rapidly that she started to shiver within seconds. She tried to remember what she'd been told about hypothermia, but she couldn't remember anything, beyond the word having been used as a threat in swimming class. It had been enough to make her obey.

And then the water level dropped, again. She found herself sitting on the floor, her entire body shaking helplessly.

They can kill me at any moment, Gudrun thought, as the last remnants of the water drained away into the floor. That had always been true, but now she *knew* it. *They can kill me any time they like.*

She shuddered, forcing her body to stand and lean against the wall. Her skin had gone red, as if she'd spent too long in the sun. She knew the colour would fade, that her skin would return to normal, but she didn't miss the underlying message. It wouldn't be long before they started inflicting more permanent harm on her, if she refused to talk. Or to help them…

Another low gurgle echoed through the room. Gudrun cursed as the water - warm water, this time - began to bubble up from the floor. It was rising slowly, but surely; she knew, deep inside, that she didn't have the energy to keep fighting. Part of her just wanted to give in, to let them drown her. It would be a victory, of sorts. The SS wouldn't have her to parade in front of her former allies. But it would also be a defeat. She would never see Horst again...

She cursed, savagely, then rolled over and drifted on her back. It had been nearly two years since she'd done it - she hadn't gone swimming since she'd left school - but the old skill was still there. She promised herself, if she survived long enough, that she'd hunt down her old matrons and make sure they suffered for their crimes. Shutting down the BDM wasn't enough.

And the water level kept rising...

———

"She hasn't broken yet," Karl Holliston observed.

"No, *Mein Fuhrer*," Muller said. "But she's definitely weakening."

Karl shrugged. Watching a young girl being pushed to the brink of drowning, time and time again, wasn't particularly amusing. If Gudrun had been anyone else - a girl unfortunate enough to have the wrong relatives - he would have ordered her exile to Germany East without a second thought. Muller would have bitched about losing his test subject, but Karl would have taken no notice. The camps had plenty of room for SS doctors who forgot who gave the orders.

But Gudrun *wasn't* someone else.

He shook his head, feeling a blaze of helpless anger. Displaying Gudrun in front of his supporters - the upper leadership of Germany East - had been a mistake. No one had said anything overtly - not yet - but he knew that some of the *Gauleiters* had qualms. Gudrun was a young girl, barely old enough to bear children. They'd been raised to *protect* young women, to treat them as the queens and princesses they were...to issue gentle correction, rather than outright torture. Forcing Gudrun to appear before them, naked and chained, had brought out their protective instincts.

But none of them truly comprehended that Gudrun was a menace. In all honesty, Karl himself hadn't appreciated it until the *Reich* Council came apart at the seams. Gudrun was not a *physical* threat - she certainly wasn't a trained combatant - but that didn't make her any less dangerous. It was the ideals she represented, the truths she told, that threatened the integrity of the *Reich*. And her ability to talk otherwise sensible men into rebellion was truly dangerous. Karl dreaded to think what would happen if the *Gauleiters* managed to talk to her.

"She's going to be pushed right to the edge with the next one, *Mein Fuhrer*," Muller said, breaking into Karl's thoughts. "And then we'll pull her out and start asking questions."

Karl gave him a sharp look. Muller enjoyed his job too much. Karl wouldn't have been too concerned if Muller wanted to play games with *Untermensch* prisoners, but *Gudrun* had to be left alive and reasonably unmarked. She needed to be mentally broken, not physically broken…

"Make sure she is physically unharmed," he growled. "Or else you will be the next one in the drowning room."

Muller flinched. Karl wasn't too surprised. Like most interrogators, Muller was a coward at heart, fearful of the day he'd be put inside his own cells. And he knew *precisely* how Muller liked to entertain himself. How strange it was that a man would be so scared of his own entertainments…if he was on the wrong side. But it was what made Muller so useful to the SS.

And people like him have advanced our knowledge considerably, Karl thought, as Muller headed off to start the next step in his plan. *Where would we be without the knowledge that has come out of the camps?*

He smiled at the thought. Adolf Hitler had wanted to exterminate the *Untermenschen* from the Third *Reich*, but it had been Himmler who had seen the value in doing more than simply *killing* them. Countless *Untermenschen* had been tested to destruction, their lives contributing to a growing archive of knowledge about the human body. Some of it had been futile - the search for a homosexual gene had turned up nothing - but much of the research had actually proven useful. There had even been talk of impregnating *Untermenschen* women with Aryan babies, using them as host mothers to bring the babies to term. Only fears about what might get into the babies had dissuaded the *Reich* from trying the experiment.

Can't have them weakened by their hosts, he thought, darkly. *They might be useless to us.*

His lips thinned as he watched Gudrun being dragged out of the drowning room by her long blonde hair. Too many of the *Gauleiters* would *definitely* disapprove of such treatment, even for a treacherous bitch. Gudrun seemed too tired to fight back, even though she wasn't chained or otherwise bound. And yet, she was holding herself together remarkably well, even after being pushed right to the brink of her endurance. Karl had seen hardened insurgents break after spending a few hours in the drowning room, breaking down and begging for mercy, but Gudrun hadn't broken. She was badly shaken, clearly weakened, yet still holding herself together.

Too weak to strike a blow, Karl told himself, as he watched them drag Gudrun into the next room and shove her into a hard metal chair. *Or is she merely biding her time?*

He shrugged, dismissing the thought. No one short of Otto Skorzeny himself could possibly hope to escape from the cells, let alone break out onto the streets. The *Reichstag* was the single most heavily-defended building in Germanica; hell, the prison complex had only two exits, both sealed from the outside. Gudrun might be able to escape from Muller - Karl rather doubted Muller could handle someone who actually wanted to fight back - but where could she go?

Nowhere, he thought.

He glanced up as a nervous-looking guardsman entered the room. "*Mein Fuhrer*," he said, snapping out a perfect salute. "*Oberstgruppenfuehrer* Ruengeler requests your presence in the War Room."

"Understood," Karl said. "Dismissed."

The guardsman didn't quite flee, but it looked very much as though he *wanted* to. Karl knew, even as he started the long walk back to the War Room, that it was bad news. No one wanted to be remembered as the person who brought bad news...Himmler, for all of his many virtues, had a terrible habit of shooting the messenger. Karl still winced at the thought of a promising young officer who'd been exiled to Germany Arabia for bringing the *Reichsführer* some very bad news. *He* wasn't like that...

...Was he?

"*Mein Fuhrer*," Ruengeler said, as Karl walked into the War Room. "The enemy have begun their offensive."

He sounded surprised. Karl allowed himself a tight smile, despite the situation. Ruengeler, a professional military man if ever there was one, had doubted that the rebels would attack so soon. But Karl, who was more used to politics than war, knew the rebels had little choice but to attack. Chewing up the remaining SS divisions before they could reform was their only hope of a quick victory.

And so they fall right into my trap, he thought.

"Very good," he said, calmly. There was no hope of directing the battle from Germanica - no doubt Ruengeler was worried about him trying to do precisely that - but he *could* keep abreast of the situation. "Do we have an axis of advance yet?"

"No, *Mein Fuhrer*," Ruengeler said. "But it won't be long now."

"Of course not," Karl agreed. He put Gudrun out of his mind. If the battle were lost, breaking her would no longer matter. She could be killed - or exiled, if too many people made a fuss - and then forgotten. "Let's wait and see what they do."

CHAPTER SIXTEEN

Front Lines, Germany Prime
3 November 1985

"Incoming!"

Hennecke Schwerk dived into the foxhole, praying silently that he would be one of the lucky ones as shells crashed down on the position. The rebels seemed to have an unlimited amount of ammunition and, judging where some of the shells were landing, an excellent idea of where the *Waffen-SS* had taken up position. Loud explosions shook the ground, sending pieces of dirt falling into the foxhole; he told himself, firmly, that unless a shell actually landed on top of him there was little chance of being killed. But as the bombardment grew louder, he couldn't help feeling that the earth would cave in on him at any moment.

He risked a glance out of the foxhole as the bombardment lessened, the shells flying over their heads and striking targets further to the east. The town - he'd never learned the place's name - was in ruins, every building that had survived the SS's advance westwards smashed flat by the rebel bombardment as they prepared to move east. He had no idea what had happened to the population, but as their homes burned or collapsed into rubble he found himself hoping that they'd made it out of the danger zone in time.

They'll be coming soon, he thought, grimly. The enemy would be advancing already, relying on the bombardment to force the defenders to keep their heads down. *And we're out here to greet them.*

He scooped up the antitank rocket launcher and scowled as he took up position in the foxhole, peering west. The irony was going to kill him, perhaps literally. He'd battled his way through countless enemy positions where the enemy soldiers had fired a shot or two at him and then fled, only to be landed in the same position himself. But there was a difference; the rebels had had friends and comrades to cover their retreat, while the penal battalion had none. Chances were they'd be shot in the back if they didn't make it back to friendly lines under their own steam.

"Hold position," Kuhn bellowed. "Watch for the advance!"

At least he's not a coward, Hennecke conceded, ruefully. Two of the company's newest members had been shot for attempted desertion, after they'd been caught trying to sneak out of the camp. *But that means he'll just keep us here until it's too late.*

He shook his head in frustration. They'd been issued with antitank weapons, but no pistols or rifles. Kuhn was the only man in the squad with a personal weapon. Hennecke could see the logic - it wasn't as if the squad was particularly motivated to fight if they had a choice - but it was frustrating. Standard doctrine called for infantry to move up beside the panzers, covering them from enemy infantry who were doing…well, precisely what Hennecke and his unwilling comrades were doing. And if they *did* see enemy infantry, they'd have no choice, but to retreat at once.

Which wouldn't be bad, Hennecke thought, *if it didn't run the risk of us being branded cowards.*

He'd been lucky, he knew. The deserters hadn't been the only men to be shot as the officers reasserted control. Being sent to the penal battalion was bad, but a number of other men had been shot - or hanged - just to make it clear that the officers were still in command. They'd pulled the different divisions back together at a very high cost. Hennecke wouldn't have been too surprised if they'd killed one in ten men just to make the point.

They would, if they weren't so short of manpower, he thought. The shells were falling further and further eastwards, hammering the lines drawn up near Warsaw. *They're stuck with us for the moment.*

He flinched as a trio of aircraft roared overhead, heading east. It was hard to be sure, but they looked like jet fighters rather than ground-attack aircraft, probably trying to smash the remaining aircraft defending Warsaw. No bombs fell as they vanished into the distance; he saw a pair of missiles rise up from a position further east, only to fall back to the ground as they lost their targets. They simply weren't good enough to catch modern aircraft.

"Here they come," Kuhn snapped. "Choose your targets, but I'll have the head of any man who fires without my permission."

Hennecke sucked in his breath. Panzers - five of them - were advancing up the road towards the town, their weapons sweeping from side to side as they looked for targets. A handful of mounted infantry followed them, riding in armoured vehicles that would have been safe enough, off a modern battlefield. But he knew from bitter experience that an antitank missile would make short work of them. He wondered, absently, if he should be shooting at the transports rather than the panzers, but Kuhn would strangle him - personally - if he disobeyed orders. The panzers were priority targets.

Doesn't take an idiot to know we're short on panzers, Hennecke thought, as he took careful aim. *They probably want to waste as many enemy panzers as they can before they crash into our panzers.*

He gritted his teeth as he waited for the order to fire. Kuhn might think they had a good chance of landing a blow and getting out, but Hennecke wasn't so sure. They hadn't had time to set up escape trenches, let alone pre-position vehicles to allow them to make a rapid escape. Hell, their sole objective - as far as Hennecke could tell - was to bleed the enemy a little before they got brutally crushed. And there was no *way* they could kill *everyone* coming at them without more weapons...

"Fire," Kuhn bellowed.

Hennecke pulled the trigger. The missile leapt from its launcher - Hennecke rapidly discarded the remainder of the device - and slammed into the nearest panzer, which staggered to a halt. Two more went up in fireballs, a third taking the missile on its armour plating and continuing, apparently undamaged. Hennecke scrambled up out of the foxhole and crawled for his life as the enemy opened fire, bullets snapping through the air bare millimetres above his head. Kuhn was barking orders as they ran, but Hennecke couldn't make out any of the words. All he could do was crawl until he reached cover, no matter how puny it was, then run as hard as he could.

He glanced behind him as the sound of shooting grew louder. The enemy panzers were smashing through the foxholes, crunching their way into the town. He couldn't tell if any of the squad had been killed or captured, although he wouldn't bet against it. They had just been far too exposed for comfort.

Kuhn slapped his back as he ran past. "Run!"

Hennecke nodded. Someone was dropping shells on the town…it struck him, suddenly, that there *had* been a plan after all. The higher-ups had plotted out the town as a target, preparing their mortars to ensure they gave the enemy a hot reception. And his squad had been put in place to delay the enemy long enough to let the mortar crews open fire.

And it worked, he thought, sourly. *But how many of us did it kill?*

———

"We're meeting resistance," the dispatcher said.

"Understood," Field Marshal Gunter Voss growled. He hadn't expected an unopposed march to Warsaw, even *if* the *Waffen-SS* was smart enough to realise that they needed to play for time. "Heavy resistance?"

"Just small ambushes," the dispatched reported. "But they're causing considerable delays."

"Of course," Gunter said.

He studied the map, wishing - just for a moment - that he had a tactical interface like his American counterparts. He'd mocked the concept when he'd first heard of it - both to his comrades and in print - yet he had to admit it might have its uses. American commanders might have less latitude than their *Heer* counterparts - and their superiors would be watching over their shoulders - but their superiors would have a far better idea of what was actually going on

The enemy tactics made sense - indeed, he'd predicted *precisely* what the enemy would do while he'd been drawing up the plans. Standing and fighting would be ideal, from his point of view, but he knew better than to *rely* on the enemy doing what he *wanted* them to do. No commander worthy of the name would allow his forces to be pocketed in a caldron and crushed if he could avoid it. And slowing up his advance would be enough to give the enemy time to pull back and *escape* the pockets.

"Order the advance units to keep pushing forward," he ordered. "And move the secondary units up ahead of schedule. Warn them to keep sweeping the landscape for surprises."

"*Jawohl, Herr* Field Marshal."

Gunter nodded, leaving the dispatchers to issue the orders to the units in the field. The time-delay was a major headache; no matter how quickly he responded to any reports of trouble, events might well have moved on before his orders reached his subordinates. But he had faith in the junior officers leading the advance. They could cope with most matters without needing him to hold their hand.

But they don't see the overall battle either, he reminded himself.

The map was updated, again. Blue arrows were lancing towards Warsaw, punching through the observed enemy defensive lines. It wouldn't be long before the enemy CO had to make a choice between pulling into Warsaw - and being trapped - or retreating further east. Either way, Gunter thought, his counterpart would lose. Unless he had something clever up his sleeve...

"More contacts," a dispatcher called. "Enemy forces are holding the line at..."

"Dispatch aircraft to deal with them," another dispatcher snapped.

Gunter nodded to himself. The *Waffen-SS* was good, but he had enough mobile firepower to flatten them. If they chose to stand and fight, so much the better.

And if they don't, he thought, *we still have enough firepower to give them one hell of a mauling.*

———

Hauptmann Felix Malguth kept a wary eye on his radar screen as the HE-477 flew over the battlefield. There were no SS aircraft in the air, according to the intelligence staff, but it would only take one jet fighter to ruin his day. And besides, the level of antiaircraft firepower the SS had drawn up to protect their lines was truly staggering. He'd seen two of his comrades blown out of the sky, one crashing before he'd had a chance to eject, simply for flying too close to one of their concentrations.

But that didn't stop him playing a major role in the battle.

He smiled, coldly, as he altered course, following the orders crackling through the radio. The SS was making a stand, holding back the panzers as they fought to punch through enemy lines and advance towards Warsaw. Felix allowed his smile to grow wider as he caught sight of the enemy positions, then tipped his aircraft down towards the ground as he released his bombs. A chain of explosions billowed up underneath him as he levelled out, spinning his aircraft through a whole series of evasive manoeuvres. The SS's antiaircraft rockets were pitiful, compared to the American Stingers, but they might still score a lucky hit.

Go get them, boys, he thought, as he saw the infantry run forward. Any survivors, he hoped, would be too badly battered to put up much of a fight. *Don't let them get away.*

A lone farmhouse sat in the midst of a field, looking suspiciously innocent. Felix had learned a great deal over the last month about 'innocent' buildings - it looked, very much, as though the SS had turned it into a fortress. He pointed the nose of his aircraft towards the farmhouse and strafed it, watching with satisfaction as a pair of black-clad men fled the burning ruin and ran for cover. There was no point in trying to pick them off individually, he knew; he turned and headed north, looking for further targets of opportunity as he returned to his base. Once he had a new load of bombs, he'd be heading back out to find more targets...

...And hurting the SS, once again, for what they'd done to the *Luftwaffe*.

———

Andrew had been warned, very firmly, to stay at the rear as *Generalmajor* Gunter Gath led his staff through what had been the outer edge of the enemy's defence line. He did as he was told, keeping his head down as the sound of shooting grew louder and louder. The roads were lined with destroyed vehicles, pushed aside by follow-up units as they headed into the combat zone. He couldn't help wondering just how many of the destroyed panzers could be salvaged.

Panzer armour definitely appears to be somewhat overrated, he thought, silently composing the report he intended to write. He wouldn't actually *write* it until he got back to the embassy, but it helped to plan it out in advance. *German antitank rockets appear to be capable of stopping even their latest panzers, even when striking frontal armour rather than the sides or turret...*

He smiled at the thought. The Germans had never succeeded, if MI6 was to be believed, in duplicating Chobham armour. And it looked, very much, as though the Brits were right. The panzers, once the most feared tanks in human history, had taken hideous losses to weapons their American and

British counterparts would shrug off. But then, it wasn't *that* much of a surprise. Britain and America had lavished billions of dollars on finding new ways to penetrate panzer armour, unaware - until it was too late - that they'd not only beaten the Germans, they'd moved so far ahead that the Germans didn't have a hope of catching up.

A set of orderlies hurried past them, carrying stretchers as they headed west. The wounded, no matter their condition, were being moved all the way back to Berlin, where doctors and nurses were waiting to treat their wounds. Andrew had a nasty feeling that it wouldn't be long before the medical staff were completely overwhelmed, if they didn't start running out of supplies. The *Reich* hadn't asked the United States for medical supplies...

They probably don't want to admit just how badly they're suffering, Andrew thought. He couldn't blame the Germans for trying. If they looked weak, their American counterparts would try to take advantage of them. *But it doesn't take a genius to know that they* are *taking a beating.*

He sucked in his breath as they walked into a village...or something he *assumed* had been a village. There were piles of debris everywhere, but no intact buildings. Even the *church* had been destroyed. It didn't *look* as though the damage had happened recently - there were no fires - yet there was no way to know for sure. Even if the war ended tomorrow, even if Holliston shot himself in a bunker, the Third *Reich* would take years to recover. The United States would have plenty of time to solidify its position.

Hitler wouldn't have gone down so easily, Andrew thought. It was easy to imagine the first *Fuhrer* leading a final defence of Berlin, reverting to the infantryman he once was as British, French and American troops broke into the city. Hollywood had definitely thought so - there were plenty of movies where the *Reich* was defeated, either during the war or shortly afterwards. *But instead he went mad and died.*

He wrinkled his nose as he scented the burial pit. Dozens of bodies had been unceremoniously dumped in the hole, after they had been stripped naked. Their hands were tied behind their backs...he swore, quietly, as he saw the blue tattoos on their arms. SS men, not *Heer* or civilians. They'd been killed by their own side.

"Deserters," *Oberleutnant* Sebastian Riemer said.

Andrew glanced at him. He looked sick.

"How do you know?"

"They've been stripping bodies ever since the offensive failed," Riemer told him. "We've stumbled across plenty of naked bodies. But this…they've all been shot in the back of the head."

Andrew nodded, slowly. He had no inclination to get any closer - the smell was thoroughly unpleasant, even though it was cold enough to keep the bodies from decomposing rapidly - but Riemer was right. The dead men - the *murdered* men - hadn't been killed in battle, they'd been executed. And the only reason the SS would execute its own men was for desertion.

"Crap," he said, finally.

He wondered, as Riemer hurried after his commander, just what it meant. The SS had a reputation for toughness - was that, like so much else, breaking down under the pressures of civil war? It couldn't be *easy* to lay waste to Germany, not when it was *Germans* who would suffer. And then, being defeated had to be a shock too. The SS had lost small-unit engagements in the past, but it had never been defeated in open battle. Its reputation for invincibility had seemed deserved.

But the Reich never had a civil war before, he reminded himself. *How badly did we suffer during the War Between the States?*

"Keep funnelling men towards Warsaw," Gath was saying, as they caught up with him. He was barking orders to his staff, one by one. "Keep the pressure on. I don't want to give them a chance to regroup."

He smiled, rather thinly, at Andrew. "Finding it a little cold, *American?*"

"You've never experienced winter in Alaska," Andrew said, choosing to ignore the fact that he'd never set foot in Alaska either. He'd never gone any further north than Boston. "I'm warm enough, for the moment."

"Good," Gath said. He turned back to peer eastwards. "Let's see how hot we can make it for them, shall we?"

CHAPTER SEVENTEEN

front Lines, Germany prime
3 November 1985

"They're turning our flank, *Herr Obergruppenfuehrer*," *Sturmbannfuehrer* Friedemann Weineck reported. "Their lead elements are already pressing against our defensive lines."

"Order the rearguard to commence falling back, as planned," *Obergruppenfuehrer* Felix Kortig said. "And remind them that they are to refrain from heroics."

"*Jawohl, Herr Obergruppenfuehrer*," Weineck said.

Felix nodded impatiently as Weineck scurried off to do his will, then studied the map carefully. The enemy were showing more determination than he'd expected from a bunch of rebels, but they had to know that time was short. It was already growing colder. It wouldn't be long before the front lines literally froze. The rebels had to make their move now or wait for spring.

And the trap has been set, he thought. *They have no idea what's coming their way.*

He smiled, coldly. The rebels were clearly aiming to isolate Warsaw rather than storm the city - hopefully trapping thousands of stormtroopers within the city defences - their forces trying hard to cut the links between the front lines and Germany East. He'd expected as much, which was why most of his combat-ready formations were withdrawing through the back door before it was slammed shut. And they would push forward, harder, when they realised their enemy was escaping. The retreating units would lead them straight into the trap.

And if they do try to storm Warsaw, he added silently, *they'll be chewed up and spat out by the defences.*

———

Herman felt old as he advanced forward, sweat trickling down his back even though the weather was bitterly cold. The town in front of him was surprisingly undamaged - the *Waffen-SS* hadn't bothered to destroy it when they'd retreated - but that didn't mean it wasn't dangerous. His unit had been detailed to sweep it as the panzers roared past, seeking out the enemy armour before it escaped; he couldn't help feeling, as his gaze swept the streets looking for trouble, that it was a honour he would gladly have foregone.

You wanted to go back to the military, he told himself, sternly. *And here you are, old man.*

He glanced back at his squad, using hand signals to issue orders. If the SS had left a stay-behind unit in the town, they'd reveal themselves as soon as the soldiers began searching the buildings. They wouldn't be able to hide so they could emerge afterwards and snipe at convoys moving east, not when the town was being searched thoroughly. The *Heer* had plenty of experience in making sure a town was harmless before they cleared the roads for military convoys.

Bracing himself, he ran towards the nearest house. There was no sign of an enemy presence; no gunshots, no explosions…nothing to suggest the town was inhabited. A cold chill ran down his spine as two of his men joined him, one kicking down the door while the other threw a HE grenade into the house. The walls shook as the grenade detonated, but held; Herman ran forward, weapon raised, and into the house. It had been devastated - a table and a number of chairs had been reduced to splinters - but it appeared to be deserted. There was no sign of any bodies.

They swept the house quickly, weapons at the ready. There was nothing, save for a few hints that the inhabitants had had time to pack before they left. Herman hoped that they were safe - the *Waffen-SS* had probably shipped them to a settlement further east, rather than a detention camp - but there was no way to know for sure. If they came back, they would have to buy more clothes, he noted. It was easy to see that the house had been stripped of everything usable.

They're probably running short of winter clothes, Herman thought. It was odd - the SS had plenty of experience in cold weather - but it was quite possible that the SS logistics network had broken down. They might not have been able to get winter clothes to the men before it started to bite. *They've taken everything they need to stay alive.*

Pushing the thought aside, he hurried back downstairs and ordered the next section into the town. They'd leapfrog their way through the streets, searching each and every building before finally declaring the town cleared. He had no doubt that *someone* would be ordered to garrison the town, just to make sure the enemy couldn't turn it into a base; he hoped, as the aches and pains grew worse, that his squad would get the job. They weren't young men any longer...

An explosion blasted out, close enough to shake the house. Herman hit the ground automatically, expecting to hear bullets cracking through the air at any second. But there was nothing, save for the sound of distant shellfire. He cursed under his breath as he crawled forward, grimly aware that the enemy might be waiting for him to show himself before they opened fire. Chances were the SS needed to conserve ammunition as much as the *Heer*...they wouldn't want to waste their bullets on walls. But he had no choice.

He peered out of the door and swore under his breath. Someone had packed an IED into the next house, rigging it so the device would be triggered when someone kicked open the wooden door. Two of his men were dead; a third lay on the ground, his body so badly wounded that Herman *knew* there was no point in calling for a medic. It was a dark miracle he'd even survived long enough for Herman to *see* him. He gritted his teeth, then crawled towards the dying man. But he expired before Herman reached him.

I'm sorry, Herman thought. He hadn't known the three men very well, but they had been under his command. And now they were dead, old men fighting a young man's war. *I wish...*

He dismissed the thought, angrily, as he called the next squad forward. The town might be deserted, but it was still dangerous. He had no doubt that the destroyed house wouldn't be the only one to be rigged, which meant the buildings would either have to be destroyed or cleared one by one. And none of his men were trained in removing IEDs.

"Call it in," he grunted, as the squad reassembled. "Tell them we're waiting for..."

He hit the ground, again, as a splatter of bullets passed over his head. Rolling over, he saw a pair of enemy soldiers briefly visible within the church tower before they ducked back out of sight. There *had* been an enemy presence in the village after all! He swore under his breath as he directed his men forward, considering their options. Normally, he would have called in artillery support - or an airstrike - but he had a feeling that the gunners were occupied elsewhere. And using the other buildings for cover was probably out of the question. There was no way to know how many of them had been rigged to blow.

Crap, he thought, grimly. *We need to move.*

He barked out a string of orders, then led the first squad forward while the second opened fire on the tower. Herman doubted they would hit anything worth the effort - none of his men were particularly good shots, even the ex-policemen - but they would force the enemy to keep their heads down. He braced himself as he slipped up to a house, half-expecting it to explode, then moved forward. Two enemy soldiers, clearly visible by the church entrance, lifted their rifles as they approached. Herman opened fire, spraying them both with bullets, then ducked back as another bullet cracked against the wall, missing him by bare millimetres.

We're not going to get into the church, he told himself, as he unhooked a pair of grenades from his belt. *They'll have everything sealed.*

He tossed the first grenade through the nearest window, then threw the second as soon as the first exploded. A third explosion shook the ground a second later, detonating with such force that the entire building began to collapse. Herman had a brief vision of a man falling to the ground before he vanished into the rubble. He stayed back as the church fell to pieces, then peered forward carefully. The threat seemed to have vanished.

"Got a message from HQ," the radioman said, as Herman watched the debris settle. "They want us to leave the rest of the town alone, but hold position."

Herman allowed himself a moment of relief. HQ would probably send *someone* to check the town for unpleasant surprises, eventually. The owners, whoever they were, might just be able to get back to their homes, even though they *had* been looted. But then, who cared about the looting as long as the buildings themselves were intact?

They're not all intact, he reminded himself, darkly. *And the fighting may sweep back over them at any moment.*

He motioned for his men to follow him on a brief patrol of the village, then peered into the distance. Smoke was rising from the direction of Warsaw, reminding him that there was a major offensive underway. He could hear everything from explosions to gunshots, echoing in the air; brief flashes of light flickered and flared before vanishing into nothingness. He'd seen war before, during his service, but this was different. Whoever won the battle, whoever won the war...the *Reich* itself would lose.

This is Ragnarok, he thought numbly, as a formation of aircraft roared overhead. *The twilight of the gods.*

———

"The advance elements are encountering more and more booby traps," the aide reported, grimly. "They're slowing down."

Field Marshal Gunter Voss gritted his teeth in frustration, although he wasn't too surprised at the news. Reports from prowling aircraft had made it clear that the *Waffen-SS* was retreating, trying to get as much of its mobile forces out of the caldron as it could before it was too late. Gunter couldn't blame them, either. It was what *he* would have done, in their place. Allowing entire *divisions* of panzers to be pocketed and destroyed would shorten the war.

They learned from us, he thought, cursing the irony. The Provisional Government had used delaying tactics to slow the SS juggernaut during its advance on Berlin - and now the SS was using the same tactics to slow *his* armoured thrusts. *And they may get away with it too.*

He chewed his cigar as the next set of updates flowed into the HQ. Warsaw itself was important, but he wanted - he *needed* - to crush the SS's mobile forces. He had no doubt he could starve Warsaw out, if nothing else, but Warsaw was irrelevant as long as the enemy panzer divisions remained largely intact. And time was not on his side. Putting the offensive together at such speed had been hard enough, but he knew he couldn't sustain the advance indefinitely.

And if we don't destroy their mobile forces, we will have to go into winter quarters and prepare for a spring offensive, he reminded himself. *And even if we win, we will lose.*

"Order the panzers to avoid towns and other likely ambush sites," he said, after a long moment. "And move up additional infantry to sweep the region."

"*Jawohl.*"

Gunter gritted his teeth. "And tell the panzer commanders to keep pushing forward," he added. "They are to stop for nothing."

"*Jawohl,*" his aide said.

It was a race now, Gunter saw. His forces had to race to encircle and pocket the SS, while the SS needed to break out of the trap before it was too late. And he had a nasty feeling he might just lose. He'd expected the SS to stand and fight, not start retreating. They'd practically started falling back as soon as the offensive began, sacrificing their best chance to savage *his* forces.

But they are not fools, Gunter reminded himself, sternly. Karl Holliston had no formal military experience, but whoever was in tactical command on the other side would be a very experienced SS officer. *They might have decided to give up Warsaw while withdrawing deeper into Germany East.*

He shook his head. "Order the third-line units to begin their advance," he added. "Tell them to thrust forward as hard as they can."

"*Jawohl.*"

Gunter felt his scowl deepen. The SS were already struggling to delay his armoured pincers; now, they'd have a *third* armoured force advancing against their fortified positions. It would put immense pressure on their lines, but the SS were renowned for their discipline. They might break - or they might not. Either way...

The battle isn't over, he told himself, firmly. *And they haven't escaped yet.*

———

"Get up," Kuhn snapped. "They're coming!"

Hennecke scrambled out of the trench and joined the other soldiers as they started to move eastwards, once again. A handful of stormtroopers took up position in the trench, ready to bleed the enemy - again - before joining the retreat. Hennecke was surprised *he* and the other penal soldiers hadn't been issued more weapons, but there were apparently shortages everywhere. The pressure of the offensive was steadily breaking through the lines.

He forgot dignity - and training - as he heard shooting breaking out behind him, lowering his head and running for his life. Other soldiers fled too, trying desperately to get away from the armoured spearheads before it was too late. Hennecke had heard stories - gruesome stories - of panzers crushing unarmed men beneath their treads, something the *Einsatzgruppen* had done in Germany East to force insurgents to talk. Why *wouldn't* the rebels do the same? Everyone *knew* they hated the SS.

The ground shook, violently, as three aircraft roared overhead, splitting up as a couple of missiles lanced up towards them. Hennecke would have shaken his fist after them, if he hadn't been trying to run; it would have been just about as effective as the antiaircraft missiles, perhaps more so. Ground to air missiles were one thing, he supposed, but what the *Reich* needed was ground-to-*aircraft* missiles.

"They're coming," another voice shouted. "Run, damn you!"

Hennecke ran as the sound of shooting grew louder, forgetting everything but the desperate need to survive. If they made it to the next set of defence lines...

...What then?

He almost stopped running. He knew what would happen when they reached the next set of lines, *if* they reached the next set of lines. The remaining penal soldiers would be put to work digging more trenches and foxholes, only to start running again when the enemy caught up with them. And it would happen, over and over again, until he died or the war came to an end. Part of him just wanted to give up, to sit down and wait for death...

...And yet, part of him still wanted to live.

Two more aircraft flashed overhead, flying west. He allowed himself a moment to hope they were friendly, although he knew it was unlikely. There hadn't been a single friendly aircraft in the sky since the enemy counterattack at Berlin. But they were heading west...

Shaking his head, he forced himself to keep running. There was no other choice. If he sat down, he would be killed; if he deserted, he would be killed. The only hope for survival was to keep running...

…And, after everything he'd gone through, all he wanted to do was survive.

———

"The enemy spearheads are reaching Point Thor," Weineck reported. "Their secondary units are advancing against our front lines…"

"Good," Felix grunted.

He sucked in his breath, feeling a flicker of unwilling admiration for the *Heer*. They'd put together a full-scale offensive in a terrifyingly short space of time, then aimed it directly at the weakest point in his lines. Under other circumstances, it would have been a complete disaster, even if he *did* manage to extract most of his forces. Now…

"Send the signal to the special units," he ordered. "Code Thor-Loki-Odin. I say again, Code Thor-Loki-Odin."

Weineck nodded. "*Jawohl.*"

He didn't understand, Felix knew; he didn't know what was coming. But *Felix* did.

And so we change the world, he thought, grimly. It wasn't something he'd ever expected to do. *Who knows what will happen next?*

———

Strumscharfuehrer Ruediger Fondermann had never expected to be called upon to do his duty, even though he'd endured nearly a decade of intensive training and conditioning to make sure he *could* do his duty when - if - the time came. Everyone had thought that the special units would never be used, not after the *last* time the genie had been allowed to escape the bottle. But he had his orders and he would carry them out.

He took a long breath as he stood and walked over to the device. Countless books and movies had described them as monstrous bombs, no different from the gravity weapons deployed by the *Luftwaffe*, but it was really nothing more than a metal box. He flipped open the hatch and gazed down on the small keypad, his fingers carefully tapping in a code he'd been given an hour before he'd departed Germanica. A single mistake, he'd been warned, would trigger the bomb's security features, rendering it useless. But there was no mistake...

"You'll have half an hour, after you engage the arming sequence, to find shelter," he'd been told. There was a secondary code for immediate detonation, but he'd been warned not to use it unless there was a very strong chance of falling into enemy hands. The rebels wouldn't show him any mercy, if they realised what he'd been ordered to do. "Put the code in, then get moving."

He braced himself, silently plotting out his path to relative safety, then tapped in the final code...

...And the world went white.

CHAPTER EIGHTEEN

front Lines, Germany Prime
3 November 1985

The enemy were in full retreat, *Hauptmann* Felix Malguth thought as he spotted a bunch of black-clad soldiers fleeing west. There was no point in strafing them, but he had no compunction about flying low over their heads and giving them a scare. Maybe they would be so terrified that they would be easy meat for the groundpounders, when they finally arrived. They seemed to be slowing down as the day wore on…

…And then there was a brilliant flash of white light.

Felix barely had a second to realise what had happened before the world went completely black. A nuke. He'd been looking directly towards a nuclear weapon as it detonated. And now he was blind…panic yammered at the back of his mind as he tried, desperately, to recall how he'd been flying before he'd been blinded. He might be heading straight towards the ground, or…he fumbled, desperately, for the ejector handle. It wasn't safe, but it was the only way to survive…he'd just have to hope he landed on the right side of the line. Friendly troops might just get him to a medic in time to do something. The SS would probably watch and laugh as he struggled to find his way home.

The shockwave struck the aircraft a second later. Felix lost control completely, the aircraft flipping over as it started to disintegrate. There was a tearing sense of pain, a flicker of light even in the complete darkness…

…And then there was nothing.

Herman had been looking northwards when there was an unbelievably huge detonation, a flash of brilliant white light that - just for a second - sent everything into sharp relief. He threw himself to the ground automatically, not sure what had happened but completely sure it was bad. The ground shook violently a second later, so violently that a number of houses in the town collapsed into rubble, a couple exploding as emplaced booby traps were detonated by the near-earthquake.

He clung to the earth, praying desperately as the shaking went on and on. What had happened? Had the SS deployed nuclear weapons? He hated to imagine it, but he couldn't think of anything else that could create such an effect. Stockpiling a vast number of conventional explosives might have been enough - he'd seen some immense stockpiles explode during his military service - but the SS was short on everything. Surely they wouldn't have stockpiled so many explosives when there were so many other demands on their resources?

The shaking slowly came to an end, the thunderous noise fading into nothingness. It was suddenly very quiet…Herman rubbed his ears as he rolled over, half-convinced that he'd been completely deafened. But he could hear someone screaming in pain and shock…he forced himself to sit up and peer eastwards. A giant mushroom cloud, glowing an eerie red, was hanging in the air, mocking him. Just for a second, he fancied he saw a laughing face within the blaze before it vanished into the cloud. Another mushroom cloud could be seen further in the distance…

A nuke, he thought, numbly. *They detonated a nuke - two nukes.*

He pulled himself up and half-walked, half-stumbled towards the screaming man. He was rubbing his eyes desperately, as if he thought he could somehow massage them back to life. Herman realised, to his horror, that the man had been looking towards the blast when the warhead went off, that he'd been blinded…there was no way to give a blind man back his sight, he thought. The medics couldn't do anything for the poor man, but try to make him comfortable…

"Stay still," he said. The victim was shaking like a child who'd been hurt for the first time, tears dripping down his face as he kept rubbing his eyes. "Please, stay still."

"I can't see," the man said. "I can't *see*."

"I know," Herman said. He gritted his teeth, feeling suddenly out of his depth. He was a policeman, not a doctor. Normally, if someone was injured, he would call for help from the nearest hospital. But the nearest medics were too far away to do any good. "Keep your hands off your eyes unless you want to make it worse."

He briefly considered securing the victim - for his own good - as the remainder of the squad assembled itself. Only one man had been blinded, thankfully, but several had been injured by flying debris. And there were other dangers. Herman had heard stories about men who'd been involved in cleaning up the Middle East, after four cities had been destroyed by nuclear blasts. They'd all had health problems in later life…

"There's nothing on the radio, but static," the radioman reported. "I can't get in touch with anyone."

Herman nodded. He knew very little about *how* an atomic bomb worked, but he *had* been given a fairly comprehensive briefing about their effects, back during his training. It would be days, perhaps weeks, before radio communication became reliable again. Until then, they would be out of touch with higher command. And there were other problems too…

"We hold position," he ordered, finally. "And I need a volunteer to take a message to HQ."

———

"Jesus Christ!"

Andrew stared in horror as the mushroom clouds took shape, unable to escape the feeling that he was looking at the end of the world. The nuclear genie had been allowed out of the bottle - once - and millions of people had died. Now, two *more* nuclear weapons had been detonated and…and he had no idea how many people might have been killed. Or sentenced to a long and lingering death. It was impossible to be *sure*, but it looked as though both weapons had detonated on the ground…

And that means fallout, he thought. *Everyone in the vicinity is in deep shit.*

Cold ice ran down his spine. He'd been briefed extensively on nuclear weapons when he'd taken up his post and he knew enough about them to worry. A groundburst would have sucked up plenty of debris, irradiated it as it passed through the blast, and then scattered the resulting dust in all directions. The soldiers on both sides would be in deep trouble. Even taking a breath could mean swallowing radioactive poison. And the population of Warsaw was - perhaps - in worse trouble. They might have to evacuate the entire city.

And I'm not safe here either, he told himself. His skin crawled, although he was fairly sure it was his imagination rather than floating radioactivity. *I might be breathing in poison too.*

He looked towards *Generalmajor* Gunter Gath. The German was barking orders into a radio, but the screech of static was enough to tell Andrew that the *Heer* had lost all control over the battle. Chances were the *Waffen-SS* would launch a counterattack in the chaos - they'd presumably expected the nuclear blasts, although neither MI6 nor the CIA had picked up on the preparations - and the *Heer* would have to fight, even in the midst of stunned disorientation.

Or they might have already broken the offensive, Andrew thought. It was hard to be *sure*, but it looked as though the devices had been positioned alarmingly close to the lead spearheads. God alone knew how many frontline combat soldiers - and panzers - had been caught in the blasts and vaporised. *The Provisional Government's grand offensive might have just failed.*

He shuddered. It had been nearly thirty-five years since nuclear weapons had been used, since humanity had realised just how dangerously powerful their weapons had become. America had recoiled in horror from the thought of using nuclear weapons, even as it had built up the largest and most dangerous arsenal on the face of the planet. But the *Reich* had had a different view of nuclear weapons. They were just another tool to use when necessary...

...And they might just have been enough to save Germany East from a quick defeat.

He shuddered, again. Countless theorists had claimed that a nuclear deterrent rendered a country invulnerable. It was why Britain and India had worked so hard to build up their own nuclear arsenals. But nuclear weapons hadn't been enough to stop the Falklands War, nor had they prevented the German people from rising up against their government. They clearly had their limits.

"Send runners to the advance elements," Gath ordered, finally. He sounded bitterly frustrated. "Tell them to fall back to the western lines - the offensive is to be discontinued."

Andrew wasn't surprised. The *Heer* had been shattered by the blasts, even if the physical damage wasn't as bad as Gath clearly feared. There was no point in pressing the offensive after the blasts, not until the soldiers had had a chance to regroup. And by then winter might have swept over the *Reich*.

And who knows what will happen, Andrew asked himself, *if the offensive has to be delayed until spring.*

He swallowed, hard. The entire world had just changed. If Holliston was mad enough to use nuclear weapons on his fellow Germans, there was no reason why he wouldn't be able to use them on the United States. And he *did* have a number of ballistic missiles under his control, even if he didn't have the launch codes. Given time, Andrew had been warned, a competent engineer would be able to bypass the security protocols…it was clear, now, that someone had already succeeded in unlocking and arming the tactical warheads. What would happen if Holliston decided to fire on America?

The President will have to ask that question, Andrew thought. *And I'm glad I won't have to come up with an answer.*

———

Why the hell, Field Marshal Gunter Voss asked himself, *didn't I see that coming?*

He stared down at the table, barely hearing the endless stream of reports flowing into his headquarters. Two entire divisions broken beyond repair; four more badly crippled…countless men killed, wounded or exposed to radioactive dust…it was disaster on an unthinkable scale. The *Reich* hadn't suffered so badly since the Hundred Days, when British, American and French soldiers had crushed the might of Imperial Germany and brought the Second *Reich* to an inglorious end. Now…

I should have seen it coming, Gunter told himself. *I knew how ruthless Holliston could be…*

He didn't need to look eastward to know that the mushroom clouds were still drifting in the sky. Holliston had been *staggeringly* ruthless. Countless stormtroopers would already have been exposed to radioactive dust, even if they kept retreating rather than rallying and trying to launch a counterattack. And the citizens of Warsaw, loyal to the SS even if they weren't loyal to Holliston personally, would have been *drenched* in radioactivity. He dreaded to think just how many people might have been condemned to die in screaming agony over the months and years to come…

Maybe it won't be that bad, he thought. *They improved the tactical nuclear warhead design after the first blasts…*

He bit down on the thought, angrily. The nuclear weapons dropped on four Arab cities had been *designed* to spread radioactive fallout, but he doubted the original designs could be improved *that* much. To believe otherwise was just wishful thinking. No, Holliston had sentenced thousands of loyalists - military and civilian - to death, just to protect Germany East from invasion. And he might just have succeeded. Voss's grand plan to pocket the enemy troops lay in ruins.

We thought it was unthinkable, he told himself. *And we were wrong.*

He looked up at the map, then down at his hands. He'd known, of course, that the *Reich* had to take a ruthless line with *Untermenschen*, but he hadn't cared to know the details. Of course not. The *Heer* had honour, something the SS notably lacked. And yet, the SS's willingness to do truly horrific deeds should have warned him that they might be prepared to unleash nuclear weapons, just to ensure they came out ahead.

They were happy to arrest countless Germans for crimes against the Reich, he thought, numbly. *I should have taken that as a warning.*

He pushed the thought out of his head, angrily. There would be time for a post-mortem afterwards, if they survived so long. Right now, he needed to deal with the disaster washing over his troops before it was too late.

"Contact the remaining units," he ordered. "They are to fall back and take up defensive positions."

He scowled. Gath should have thought to do it already, if Gath was still alive. The communications network was in such a mess that he honestly didn't know who was still breathing, who was wounded and who was dead. But if he hadn't, Gunter had to issue the order. The offensive had come to a screeching halt. All he could do now was salvage as much as possible and hope for the best.

"Order the reserve medics to be prepared for heavy casualties," he added. He cursed under his breath as the full implications struck home. The *Reich* had a number of medical units trained to deal with weapons of mass destruction, but nowhere near enough to cope with the sheer scale of the catastrophe.

"But they are to apply nuclear protocols before taking the wounded into Berlin or any field hospital."

The protocols might kill them, a voice whispered at the back of his head. *Just washing them down to remove contamination might drive them over the edge.*

He told the voice to go away, sharply. There was nothing else he could do. People caught in a cloud of radioactive dust would wind up with dust settling on their clothes. Washing them down might not save *their* lives, but it would save others. And yet, if they had been badly burned by the blast…

"And send an emergency message to the Chancellor," he added. "I need to talk to him as soon as possible."

"*Jawohl.*"

"Message from *Generalfeldmarschall* Brandenburg," another aide called. "The *Luftwaffe* has lost every plane that was over the blast zone."

Gunter nodded, unsurprised. Few aircraft could hope to fly near a nuclear blast and escape unscathed. The Americans claimed their latest bombers could fly to the *Reich*, drop an atomic payload on their targets and return in time for dinner, but hardly anyone believed them. There *were* a handful of intercontinental bombers in the *Luftwaffe's* ranks, yet Gunter had always been sceptical of their value. They'd have to fly all the way to America, sneak through the most formidable network of air defence bases in the world, drop their bombs and somehow make it back home. ICBMs sounded a great deal more practical, when it came to launching nuclear weapons at the United States.

And dropping smaller bombs wouldn't be worth the effort, he thought, sourly.

"Order the *Generalfeldmarschall* to get a couple of recon birds up as soon as possible," he said, pushing the thought aside. He needed to know what the *Waffen-SS* was doing, despite the risk to the pilots. "I want recon reports!"

"*Jawohl.*"

———

Hennecke hadn't known what to expect when he'd been ordered to take up position in a trench, but the colossal explosion - and the giant mushroom cloud - had left no doubt as to what had happened. Someone had detonated a nuke, perhaps two nukes; the enemy offensive had weakened, then stopped altogether. They'd been caught in the blast…

"Well," someone said, from the rear. Hennecke couldn't tear his eyes off the cloud as it loomed over them. "What do we do now?"

"We continue falling back, as per instructions," Kuhn growled. He jabbed a finger eastwards as he hefted his pistol. "Start moving."

Hennecke nodded in agreement. He hadn't been taught *much* about nuclear blasts, but - for a reason he had never been able to understand - it was better to keep moving rather than finding shelter at once. Kuhn kept snapping out orders as the stormtroopers staggered to their feet and started to move; Hennecke kept a wary eye on him, wondering how long it would be before Kuhn realised that only a handful of penal soldiers were still under his command. He might find the few survivors something worse to do.

The air blew hot and cold, seemingly at random, as they kept moving. Hennecke gritted his teeth, trying not to breath more than strictly necessary; he swallowed, hard, as the skies started to cloud over, as if the blast had triggered the onset of winter. He glanced back, every few minutes, watching as the mushroom cloud slowly started to break up. He'd seen too many horrors since joining the SS - and starting the march to Berlin - but there was something about the cloud that chilled him to the bone. It looked profoundly unnatural.

But it may have saved us from the rebels, he thought, as they marched into the next set of defensive lines. The stormtroopers on duty were drawing water from a well and washing down all the newcomers, despite the cold weather and colder water. *And yet, will we pay a price for having used it?*

He shivered, helplessly, as cold water splashed over his body. His uniform clung to his skin afterwards, mocking him as the temperature plummeted rapidly. Kuhn - of course - didn't give him any time to be miserable, instead pointing him in the direction of countless tasks that needed doing. Despite himself, Hennecke was almost grateful. The physical labour kept him from having time to brood. Some of the other stormtroopers looked as though they were too worn to get up, let alone fight if the enemy showed themselves.

And yet, as the wind picked up, he couldn't help wondering what it might be blowing in their direction…

…And what would happen, in the long term, to anyone who had been too close to the blasts?

CHAPTER NINETEEN

Washington DC/London, USA/UK
3 November 1985

"Ladies and gentlemen, the President of the United States."

President John Anderson kept his face impassive as he strode to the top of the table and sat down. He'd never liked the underground bunker, even though he knew it would keep him, his family and his staff alive if the *Reich* ever *did* start launching nuclear weapons at the United States. And he'd never really believed, despite the warnings of his predecessor, that the Third *Reich* was crazy enough to start a nuclear war. They would be completely annihilated by the American response...

Hell, he thought, sitting down. *They'd be crippled if they started a nuclear exchange with Britain.*

"There's little time for formality," he said. The Secret Service had yanked him out of the Oval Office as soon as the warning had come in from Cheyenne Mountain. "Did we have a genuine nuclear detonation?"

"Two of them," the Chairman of the Joint Chiefs of Staff said. "One north of Warsaw, one south; both precisely in place to blunt Berlin's offensive against Germanica."

"Preliminary analysis indicates that the devices were prepositioned," NSA added. "They must have kept it a closely-guarded secret. We didn't pick up any indications they were about to use nuclear weapons until the first detonation."

John nodded, curtly. "Can they fire the ballistic missiles?"

"I think we have to assume they can," NSA said. Beside him, the CIA Director nodded in grim agreement. "They certainly managed to detonate a pair of tactical nuclear warheads."

And Edward was right, John thought. *They are crazy.*

He studied the world map for a long moment, thinking hard. He'd been in his early twenties when Japan had bombed Pearl Harbour; he'd served in the army during the advance on Japan, then the long march to Tokyo that had ended the war. The Japanese had been odd…their soldiers had been fanatical, but many of their civilians had surrendered, once they realised it was *safe* to surrender. He still recalled, with a smile, a pretty young Japanese girl who had been his mistress during the occupation…

But the Germans? He'd thought they were fundamentally *rational*. They might be evil little shits - he loathed their government with a passion - but they weren't stupid. He'd assumed he'd be dealing with the Third *Reich* until his term ended, then his successor would be in the same boat. Instead, the *Reich* was tearing itself apart and threatening to drag the entire world into the fire.

From a coldly logical point of view, he'd been assured, there was something to be said for encouraging the Nazi Civil War to continue as long as possible. Whichever side won would be weakened - considerably weakened - by the fighting, allowing the various subject nations to slip out of their grasp without a fight. The world would be a safer place if the Third *Reich* was badly weakened. And yet, a nuclear exchange - even a relatively small nuclear exchange - would be devastating. Hell, two nukes had *already* been devastating.

"Right," he said, feeling out of his depth. "Do we know how much damage they did?"

"Nothing certain," CIA admitted, after a glance at NSA. "All we really have to go on is orbital imagery and radio intercepts."

"And very few of the latter," NSA warned. "We badly underestimated the effects of an EMP on their radio sets."

John nodded, curtly. There would be time for gloating - later - over just how far America had advanced over her mortal rival. Now, he needed to contain the situation and decide what to do before something worse happened.

"Understood," he said. "What do you know?"

"Basically, we think two of their panzer divisions - and infantry support - were destroyed," CIA said. "Other units probably took a beating too. We don't know - yet - just how *badly* they were hit, but I would be astonished if they can retake the offensive anytime soon."

"Particularly given how many corners they had to cut to launch the offensive before winter," the Chairman put in. "We should be worried by how quickly they threw the operation together."

CIA nodded. "Long-term, there will be major consequences," he added. "Anyone close to the blast zones would be at risk of radiation poisoning. Our weather forecasts suggest that the fallout might well be blown towards Berlin, threatening the entire population. There's no way to minimise the risk beyond what the Germans are already doing."

"Telling the entire population to stay indoors and keep all doors and windows closed," NSA said. "It might be enough to save them from the deadliest isotopes in the fallout."

"I hope so," John said.

He pressed his fingertips together. "Is there anything we can do to help?"

"We can ship supplies of medicine and protective gear to Berlin," CIA said. "But that will cause...problems."

John scowled. The risk of nuclear war hadn't been so high since the Missile Crisis. He hated to think what his political enemies would say, if they discovered that he'd shipped vast quantities of expensive medicine to the *Reich*. If a single warhead detonated on American soil, the medicine - and protective garb - would be needed at home. And even if it didn't, there were vast numbers of American voters who would be against providing any help to the Third *Reich*.

"Let me worry about that," he said, finally. "Is there anything else we can do?"

"Not unless we commit American forces directly," CIA said. "And that would be a nightmare."

"It would certainly be chancy," the Chairman agreed. "Mr. President, even getting a rapid reaction force over to Berlin would be tricky."

John met his eyes. "Is there anything we can do about the ballistic missiles?"

"I've had people considering possible options ever since the civil war broke out," the Chairman said. "They've looked at a number of ideas, but none of them guarantee success when there are just too many variables."

"I remember the briefing," John said. Getting American Special Forces to the Siberian Missile Fields would be hard enough, but destroying all the missiles before they could be launched would be harder. "We might wind up giving the ABM system its first real test."

He frowned. "What about stealth bombers? We could go nuclear ourselves."

"I don't know how Berlin would react," CIA said, "but we couldn't guarantee taking out all the warheads."

"Berlin would not be pleased," NSA warned. "And neither would London."

John nodded, shortly. The Third *Reich* had only a limited supply of missiles capable of reaching America, but literally thousands of missiles capable of reaching Britain. London would be less than pleased if John's decision unleashed a holocaust on Great Britain. And the Germanica Government could unleash hell on Berlin too…they'd just proved that they had no compunctions about deploying tactical atomic bombs against their fellow countrymen. *John* doubted that *he* could order a nuclear release if America split into two and started a second civil war…

But the Easterners have been moving away from the Westerners for a long time, John reminded himself. *They may not see each other as fellow countrymen any longer.*

It was a sobering thought. He'd just been entering politics when Truman had decided to smash racial segregation, once and for all. It hadn't been easy, even though Truman had been tough *and* he'd had a majority of the country behind him. Even now, there were parts of America that were purely white - and Japan, an American territory, had been used to resettle countless blacks. The political fight over Japanese statehood had been nasty; he dreaded to think what it would be like in the Third *Reich*, where the gulf between east and west had grown into an unbridgeable chasm…

A problem for my successor, he thought, dismissing the issue. *Right now, we need to contain the problem.*

"Assemble a collection of medicines and protective gear," he said. "We'll have to talk directly to Berlin."

"They may wish to retaliate," CIA warned. "Berlin *does* have atomic bombs too."

"They *will* retaliate," NSA said. "But against *what?*"

"They can decide that for themselves," John said. He doubted there was anything the US could offer to dissuade Berlin from retaliating. "But we do need to find a way to cripple the Germanica Government."

"Yes, Mr. President," CIA said. "However, our options are very limited."

"Short of nuking them and hoping they can't retaliate," the Chairman said. He gave CIA a challenging look. "I take it there's no reasonable hope of a covert operation?"

CIA reddened. "We never had very good sources in the east," he said. "Even before the civil war, Germany East always had much higher levels of security than Germany Prime. I don't think we can reasonably hope to do much of anything, Mr. President."

"Of course," the Chairman said.

John held up a hand. The constant rivalry between the Joint Chiefs of Staff and the CIA served a purpose, but right now it was a distraction. And a distraction was the last thing he needed.

"So we try to talk to Berlin," he said. "And otherwise…there's nothing we can do without an unacceptable level of risk? Does that sound accurate?"

"Yes, Mr. President," the Chairman said.

John scowled. "From a military point of view, what is likely to happen now?"

"I can't see the offensive being resumed until spring at the very earliest," the Chairman said, after a moment. "They'll need time to recover, time to decontaminate, time to rejuvenate and rebuild their forces. Winter *is* coming, after all. And that will give the SS time to rejuvenate its own forces."

"If it can," CIA said. "There are plenty of question marks over their industrial capability."

John sighed. He'd seen the projections - really, he'd seen too *many* projections. One set of analysts claimed that Germany East was well on its way to overtaking Germany Prime as the *Reich's* industrial heartland; a second, rather more pessimistically, had concluded that Germany East was likely to lose most of its industrial base if the civil war ground on for several more months. But none of them could be taken for granted. Too much about Germany East remained a mystery.

Even to the Germans themselves, John thought. The US Government was bloated and had a tendency towards stupidity, but the Third *Reich* far outdid it on both counts. *Their right hand didn't always know what the left was doing.*

"It has nukes," he said, tiredly. "And they might be enough to tip the balance in its favour once and for all."

———

Without false modesty, Prime Minister Margaret Hilda Thatcher knew she was an unusual woman. She'd actually been told, more than once, that she *wasn't* a woman, a charge hurled at her by Labour backbenchers who suspected she was letting down her gender during her term in office. But she *was* a woman and she took a certain pride in being the first female Head of Government in the modern world. And if the Nazis didn't take her seriously - and some of the backbenchers doubted her - she didn't care. Britain wasn't Nazi Germany - it had made her laugh when she found out that it had been a young *girl* who had founded the protest movement - but any woman in high office needed to be tougher than the men.

And she *was* tough, Margaret knew. She'd fought and won the Falklands War over the advice of some of her cabinet members, members who had been moved on shortly after that conflict had come to its bloody end; she'd taken on the might of the unions and crushed them so thoroughly that it would be decades before organised labour could undermine the country again. She regretted some of what she'd done, but she'd known there was no choice. The Third *Reich* lay on the far side of the English Channel, watching and waiting for an opportunity to launch a full-scale invasion. Britain could not afford to be weak when such a powerful foe was far too close to her borders.

The Nazis were monsters. Margaret had known that ever since she was a child, ever since she'd devoured the books written by men, women and children who'd managed to smuggle themselves out of Occupied Europe before it was too late. And nothing she'd seen since had managed to change her mind. Individual Germans could be good people, but collectively the Nazis were monsters. They had committed huge crimes, wiping out millions of people, in their rise to power; even now, with their power secure, they were still brutal, cruel and utterly untrustworthy. There was no one in Berlin, she'd thought a year ago, with whom she could do business. And there was certainly no hope of a genuine peace, only cold war.

She sat in her office, studying the wall-mounted display. It was a genuine marvel of technology, allowing her to see live reports from military bases around the country, but right now it underlined the dilemma facing Britain. The *Luftwaffe* wouldn't need more than a few minutes to launch from their bases in Occupied France and attack British airspace, if war broke out all of a sudden. And if the Germans decided to unleash their arsenal of cruise missiles, it would be even worse. Margaret couldn't escape the simple fact that nuclear war would be utterly unwinnable, with or without the Americans. A full-scale exchange would devastate Britain, even if Germany was thoroughly devastated in return.

And yet we have no choice, but to gamble, she thought, sourly. *To try to ensure that the next government in Germany is friendly to us.*

It was an unpleasant thought, but she faced it squarely. Britain had *always* had problems when one power dominated the European mainland, from Philip of Spain to Adolf Hitler and the Third *Reich*. A single bloc dominating Europe would always be a threat, even if relations were superficially friendly. But there was no way to break up the *Reich*, not without risking nuclear war. She doubted the French or any of the other subject nations could break free on their own…

…And even if they did, it would be decades before they could serve as counterbalances to German power.

She turned her head, gazing up towards the portrait of Sir Winston Churchill. The artist had depicted him in Ten Downing Street, although he'd clearly not bothered to look at any photographs of the office that might have been taken when Churchill had actually been Prime Minister. But that was of no account. Churchill had been forced out of office for wanting to continue the fight, after Russia fell; he'd warned, desperately, that it wouldn't be long before Hitler would seek to jump across the English Channel and take London. But no invasion had ever materialised.

What would you do, she asked the image silently, *if you faced the same choice as I?*

It was a conundrum, she admitted privately. Britain - and America - could support the Berlin Government, yet the Berlin Government might prove to be a menace in its own right. She had no illusions about the sheer power of the German military, although reports from the front lines suggested that some long-held beliefs had been grossly overstated. But a victory for the government in Germanica would unleash a nightmare. She'd never actually *met* Karl Holliston, but she'd heard enough about him to be sure that he was planning to purge everyone on the other side.

At best, Germany will be badly weakened, she thought, dryly. It wasn't much, but it was something. She intended to cling to it if she was ever called upon to justify her decisions. *But at worst, we'll unleash a nuclear holocaust.*

CHRISTOPHER G NUTTALL

It had not been easy for her to send the Royal Navy to the Falklands or to use the police and security services to break the miners. She'd known that people would get hurt - and while she was disinclined to care about enemy soldiers and communist subversives, she *did* worry about her own people. It was nearly seventy years since the Great War, but the British Government still remembered just how many young men had been killed. No government could hope to survive a callous approach to British casualties...

...And with nuclear weapons involved, the prospect of millions of people being killed was terrifyingly high.

But Holliston had stepped right across the line. He hadn't launched nuclear missiles at America or blown up a French city for defying him. He'd killed thousands of German soldiers and risked the lives of untold numbers of soldiers and civilians. Margaret had seen the projections. There was a very good chance that nuclear material would be blown over Berlin, sentencing the population to long lingering deaths. And Warsaw was even *closer* to the blasts...

And Warsaw was on his side, Margaret thought. *He sentenced thousands of his supporters to a hellish doom.*

She sighed as she stood. Something would have to be done, despite the risk. Karl Holliston had to be stopped. But what could they do? She'd already authorised the dispatch of antiaircraft missiles and other weapons to the Berlin Government, but even *that* was pushing the limits. Hell, what *were* the limits? SOE had long-since given up shipping weapons and supplies to Occupied France; now, all they could do was watch from the sidelines and hope.

We can offer help, she thought. *But it won't be enough to tip the balance. The Germans will have to do it for themselves.*

Churchill would not have understood, she suspected. He had been a man of action, always looking for ways to take the fight to the enemy. But Churchill - and Hitler - had lived during the last great period of conquest. *She* - and Karl Holliston - lived in a world overshadowed by atomic bombs. And those bombs had kept the peace for over forty years.

But now the genie is out of the bottle, she thought. *And who knows what will happen next?*

CHAPTER TWENTY

Germany East
3 November 1985

The snowstorm came out of nowhere.

Horst cursed savagely as he fought for control of the vehicle, wishing he'd thought to demand an ATV from the troops in Warsaw. But there had been no time. He wrestled with the steering wheel as the vehicle threatened to skid off the road, then somehow forced it to keep going as the temperature plummeted rapidly. By the time they finally reached the next set of settlements, he was ready to risk everything just to get his hands on a better vehicle. He'd hoped to reach Germanica before the storms hit.

"This is a bigger settlement," he said, as they stopped outside the gates. "Try not to sleep with any of the girls."

Kurt gave him a nasty look. Horst hadn't been able to resist teasing him lightly about Heidi, although he had to admit that Kurt had done well to resist her. *He* would have had problems if she'd come onto him like that, even though he was wearing a wedding ring. Hell, for all he knew, the ring had been the only thing *keeping* Heidi from trying to seduce him...he pushed the thought to the back of his mind as the guards appeared, their weapons at the ready as they walked towards the car. This settlement, clearly, was far more significant than the previous two they'd visited.

And if we could find another farm, Horst thought, *we would.*

The guard tapped on the window, meaningfully. Horst opened it, cursing the cold under his breath as he passed the guard their papers. The guard scanned them quickly, then waved at the gatekeepers. Horst braced himself as the gates opened, knowing they might be walking into a trap. If there was something wrong with their papers - if someone had checked with Germanica - they might be about to find out.

"Welcome," a grim-faced older man said, as they parked outside the main building. "It has been too long since we have had guests."

Horst nodded, clambering out of the car. "We are glad to be here," he said, truthfully. "Can you put us up for the night?"

The question was a formality. No settlement would turn away a German citizen, *whatever* his papers said. Trying to sleep out in the open would be a death sentence, with or without the threat of insurgent attacks. It was already bitterly cold and he knew, all too well, that it would get worse. He glanced around, taking in the guardposts and spotlights shining into the darkening sky, then hurried into the main building. Kurt followed him, already shivering helplessly. He simply wasn't used to the eastern cold.

Inside, it was warm and welcoming. Horst took off his coat with an effort and passed it to a young boy who gazed at him with admiring eyes. Horst felt an odd pang of disquiet at the obvious hero-worship in the youngster's eyes, remembering when he'd admired the black-clad men who'd visited his uncle. He'd *wanted* to wear the black uniform and the *Sigrunen* for himself, but he hadn't understood the price. He had been lucky - very lucky - that Gudrun hadn't tried to kill him, when she'd found out the truth.

And I was expected to betray her, he thought, as he followed the lady of the house into a large sitting room. *My superiors would have rewarded me if I'd betrayed her the day we first met.*

He felt a flicker of homesickness as he took a seat on the sofa. Germany East *believed* in extended families, believed in doing everything it could to encourage family ties; the sitting room was large enough to accommodate the entire adult population of the settlement, male and female alike. It was warm and comfortable and *welcoming* in a way Gudrun's home in Berlin had never been, reminding him of days playing chess and singing songs with his family...

...But there was an odd tinge of *something* in the air.

It wasn't suspicion, he thought, as he was passed a mug of warm chocolate. The guards didn't seem to have the slightest doubt about Horst and Kurt's credentials. But there was...*something*...hanging in the air, a tint of fear that bothered him more than he cared to admit, even to himself. This wasn't Germany Prime. The locals knew just how harsh and cold and bitterly unpleasant life could be. They wouldn't be scared by just *anything*.

He sipped his chocolate and waited, studying the handful of settlers who'd joined them. The girls looked young and pretty, yet still radiating the sense of *toughness* he'd missed so much in Germany Prime. Only a fool would take an Easterner girl lightly, no matter what the *Reich* had to say about the proper relationship between men and women. A farmwife had so much more to do than cook food and bear children. He would be surprised if the girls facing him, eying him with frank interest, were weaker than men from Germany Prime.

There were no men of military age in the room. The guards outside had clearly been of military age, but he suspected there wouldn't be many others in the settlement. There were four men in the room, yet three of them were clearly too old for military service and the fourth too young. But then, if the settlement came under attack, they would have to take up weapons to defend themselves.

The oldest man leaned forward, suddenly. "Have you heard the news?"

Horst and Kurt exchanged glances. "No," Horst said, finally. "We've been on the road all day."

He kept his face impassive with an effort. What news? Had someone assassinated Karl Holliston, and his successor had sued for peace? Or had the great offensive finally begun? Horst didn't know many details - there had been a very real risk he would fall into enemy hands - but he knew the offensive should have started by now. The battle might still be underway.

"The rebels used *atomic bombs*," the old man said. He looked as if he wanted to spit. "They've used atomic bombs on German soil!"

Horst stared at him in shock. Nukes? He couldn't imagine Volker Schulze authorising the use of nuclear weapons, not on German soil. No matter how they were used, large swathes of the fatherland would be contaminated indefinitely. Horst had even heard that the ruins of Jerusalem and Mecca were still radioactive, even thirty-five years after the blasts. But no one had been interested in rebuilding the destroyed cities...

"They couldn't have," Kurt said. He sounded as shocked as Horst felt. "Sir..."

"They might have done," Horst said, cutting him off. "What did they *do*?"

"They destroyed Warsaw," the old man said. "The city wouldn't surrender and they destroyed it."

Horst nodded slowly, keeping his face under *very* tight control. It was a lie. It *had* to be a lie. And yet, there was something about it that bothered him. Volker Schulze wouldn't use nuclear weapons, but Karl Holliston had already shown he was more than willing to devastate Germany from end to end if it was what it took to put him back in power. And there was no point in spreading such a story unless nuclear weapons *had* been used.

They want to get ahead of the rumours, Horst thought. *And so they're not denying that nuclear weapons were used, they're just lying about who used them.*

He considered the problem rapidly, hoping that Kurt would have the sense to keep his mouth shut. They couldn't be seen denying the official version of the story, even if it was utter nonsense. Germany East was vast. Rumours would spread, of course, but Holliston would have plenty of time to shape them. And no one would *want* to believe that their *Fuhrer* could unleash radioactive hell on German soil without a second thought.

And *Warsaw?*

Volker Schulze would *not* have authorised the destruction of an entire city, certainly not so quickly. Even *Himmler* hadn't made the decision so rapidly - and *Himmler* hadn't had to worry about targeting German civilians. Warsaw might have surrendered, once it was cut off from Germany East, or it might have been isolated and starved into submission. There was no need - there *hadn't* been a need - to destroy the entire city. And smashing Warsaw would damage the road and rail networks the *Heer* would need for its advance.

No, the story made no sense. But the only reason anyone would *spread* the story was to explain the use of nuclear bombs.

Holliston must have used them to stop the offensive in its tracks, he thought. *And that means our mission to Germany East is more necessary than ever.*

"That is horrific," he said, finally. "We saw the rebels commit many atrocities during the fighting, but using an atomic bomb on an innocent city is a whole new level of horror."

The small boy - Horst hadn't picked up his name - looked fascinated. "Is it true the rebel *Untermenschen* drank the blood of dead stormtroopers?"

"*Johan*," one of the older men snapped.

Horst bit down the response that came to mind. Johan - Gudrun had a brother called *Johan*, he recalled - was a child. Death and devastation were abstract concepts to him, even though he'd been raised in Germany East. He probably wasn't old enough to realise that death meant death, or that a war wound could destroy a person's life…or that civilians, caught up in the maelstrom of war, could suffer worst of all.

"I'll be going to war next year," Johan continued. "My tutor says I have the best shooting skills in my class."

"No, you won't," one of the girls snapped.

"You're just jealous," Johan said. "*You* don't get to go to war."

Horst rolled his eyes as Johan was marched out of the room. Had *he* been such an enthusiastic little shit when *he'd* been a boy? Probably - *he'd* certainly looked forward to the day he could join the *Waffen-SS*. Johan wouldn't be fighting next year, Horst hoped; he wouldn't be joining the SS unless Horst had vastly underestimated his age. But if the war raged forward and swept over the settlement, he feared that Johan would take his rifle and try to fight.

"His father is away at the front," one of the older men said. "I beg pardon for his conduct."

"It's quite all right," Horst said. "Your grandson?"

"Yes," the older man said. "And all three of my sons are away."

Horst felt a stab of pity that left him feeling numb. This was war; not glory, not conquest, but broken lives and dead bodies. Whoever won, countless families would be mourning their dead for decades to come. He knew women back in Berlin who had married their sweethearts before the men marched off to the front, only to discover that they were pregnant - and that their new husbands had been killed, long before their children were born. They wouldn't face the stigma of being unmarried mothers - they *had* been married - but they wouldn't have easy lives. Getting married again wouldn't be easy.

Polygamy is legal in Germany East, he thought. *But it isn't in Germany Prime.*

He shuddered as he peered into the future. Countless war widows, some with children, unable to support themselves as they struggled to bring up their families. Who would support them? The government had nearly bankrupted itself paying bonuses to women who won the *Mutterkreuz*. And that had been before the war…

Kurt elbowed him. He realised, suddenly, that the old man was still talking.

"I'm sorry," Horst said. "I lost my train of thought."

"I was wondering what you made of it," the old man said. "And what you think we should do."

"I don't think this settlement will attract a nuke," Horst said, after a moment. "It's too small."

He shrugged. The Americans were supposed to have *millions* of nuclear bombs and missiles, according to the *Reich* Council, but that struck him as rather unlikely. That would be enough tonnage to reduce the entire planet to rubble. No, no one would waste a nuclear warhead on a tiny little settlement in the middle of nowhere. But what would happen when civilians started fleeing the front?

"I think you should tighten your guard," he added, after a moment. "People are going to start fleeing soon."

And dying, he added, silently. *Winter has arrived.*

He shook his head as a middle-aged woman - probably Johan's mother - carried a tray of bread and cheese into the room. The smells that followed her suggested that it was merely the first course. If the settlement was anything like the one Horst had grown up on, there would *always* be additional food for unexpected guests. But he couldn't help wondering just how long that would last. Winter had arrived…and it might not be long before hordes of refugees started battering at the doors.

It wasn't a pleasant thought. Travel within Germany East was tightly controlled - it was why he'd gone to so much trouble to forge their papers - but he doubted Holliston could spare many men for internal security. People concerned about radioactivity - or even the rebel advance - would flee their settlements, heading east. And many of them would be armed, presenting a whole new problem for any guards who tried to stop them. How long would the SS stormtroopers remain popular in Germany East if they started shooting refugees?

And it might trigger a civil war within the civil war, he thought. *And there will be nothing left but chaos.*

The conversation around the dinner table was gloomy, even though the meal was excellent and the beer superb. Horst listened as more and more exaggerated stories of radiation poisoning were told, ranging from everyone infected dying within seconds to long-term suffering that could only be ended by a mercy kill. He couldn't help wondering just what would happen, if such a staunchly loyal settlement was terrified of the future. And what they would do if they found out the truth.

If it is the truth, Horst reminded himself. *You don't know what really happened, not yet.*

"We'll continue on our way in the morning," he said, after dinner finally came to an end. "If you don't mind, we'd like to rest now."

"Of course," the old man said. "I have a bedroom ready for you."

You mean you asked one of the girls to make the beds up for us, Horst thought, rather sardonically. Women couldn't escape doing most of the household chores, not even in Germany East. *I wonder if one of the girls will try to crawl into Kurt's bed again.*

"Thank you," he said, out loud. "We appreciate it."

Kurt wasn't sure if he should be disappointed or relieved that, apart from a handful of flirtatious looks when their parents weren't watching, the girls made no move to invite him into their beds. He knew, intellectually, that he'd done the right thing when he'd declined Heidi's offer, but his body was reminding him that it had been a *very* long time since he'd slept with a girl. It was silly, yet part of him wanted to turn around and head back to Heidi's farm. But he knew it was impossible.

The bed was warm, but he felt cold as he contemplated the news. He couldn't discuss it with Horst - the room might well be bugged - yet he was *sure* that *his* side wouldn't have nuked an entire city. Destroying Warsaw would be nothing more than pointless spite - no, it would be worse, more like cutting off his nose to spite his face. The *Heer* needed control of Warsaw, not a ruined city and a destroyed reputation. He simply couldn't imagine anyone in Berlin issuing such an order.

He shivered, helplessly. The tactical devices *had* to have been used to stop the advance in its tracks - how many of his friends and former comrades were dead? He had no doubt that the Berlin Guard would have formed part of the spearhead, after its valiant service in the defence of Germany Prime. No one could argue that they were just play-soldiers after they'd bled the SS during the retreat to Berlin. And it would have gotten them killed...

...It would have gotten *him* killed, if he'd been there.

And father said he was going back to the war, Kurt remembered, suddenly. *What happened to him?*

The thought was truly horrific. His father had been strict, but fair. Kurt knew boys who had feared their fathers, boys who had dreaded going home each day, yet he'd never believed his father was a monster. He respected as well as loved the older man. It could have been a great deal worse, for him and his brothers - and his sister. No one would have said anything if Gudrun had been married off at sixteen, rather than being allowed to follow her dream...

...And his father might be dead. The man who had sired him, the man who had raised him, the man who had encouraged him and disciplined him... his father might be dead. How could there *be* a world without his father? He couldn't imagine it.

Kurt shifted his head to glare at Horst, snoring loudly as he slept. How *could* he sleep so soundly after the news? But his anger was mingled with envy, because he knew there was nothing either of them could do. Even if they turned around and drove straight back to the front lines, what could they do? What could they possibly hope to accomplish?

All we can do is carry on, Kurt told himself. He knew, all too well, that they were operating on a wing and a prayer. The slightest mistake, in the wrong place, could get them both killed - or worse. *And hope to hell we can make a difference when we finally arrive.*

CHAPTER TWENTY-ONE

Front Lines, Germany Prime
4 November 1985

The suit - American-designed, of course - was hot, heavy and thoroughly uncomfortable, but Volker knew better than to take it off. His Geiger counter was ticking menacingly, warning him that there was a dangerous level of radiation in the air. The American technicians who had helped him and his staff to assemble the suit had warned him not to stay in the danger zone for too long, but Volker had largely ignored them. He owed it to his conscience to take some risks.

He'd seen horror. He'd *thought* he'd seen horror. But this was worse than anything he'd ever seen, even in his worst imaginations. The landscape had been utterly devastated; countless trees burned to ash, the remnants of humanity's presence utterly swept away by the blast. He turned slowly, feeling his skin crawl as the counter ticked louder. The winds were blowing to the south, thankfully, but he could still *feel* the radiation touching his skin, no matter how hard he tried to tell himself that he was imagining it. He *knew* he was imagining it…

…But he didn't believe it.

A lone panzer was positioned nearby, two more lying on their sides; the blast had picked them up and tossed them over as casually as a man might pick up and toss a pebble. He'd been warned not to go near them, even though they were probably salvageable. The vehicles themselves had survived, but their armour would have trapped the radiation and ensured that the crews died quickly. Or something. He wasn't sure he *understood* the explanation, but it didn't matter. All that mattered was that he didn't go near the vehicles.

He turned, peering east. Flames and smoke were rising up from the direction of Warsaw, reminding him that an entire city had been far too close to the blasts. The flash of superheated air had set fire to everything flammable, according to the recon flights; everyone caught in the open had been burned, blinded or simply killed by the blast wave. And then there was the fallout... Warsaw might survive, once the flames burned themselves out, but countless innocent civilians were doomed to long lingering deaths. It was no surprise that utter anarchy had gripped the city.

Holliston was willing to sacrifice Warsaw just to stop our offensive, Volker thought. He was too tired to feel anything beyond numb horror. *Why didn't we see it coming?*

But he already knew the answer. Using the atomic bomb on German soil - so close to so many cities - was horrific beyond words. No one had imagined, even in their darkest nightmares, that Karl Holliston would unleash nuclear fire on pureblood Germans. But he had...and now thousands of soldiers were dead, with thousands more dying slowly from blast wounds and radiation poisoning. The Americans and British had already started shipping in medical supplies, but it was pathetically inadequate to cope with the sheer scale of the problem. He didn't even *want* to imagine how many people would die in the next few weeks.

We knew he was a monster, he thought, as he turned and walked back towards the armoured vehicle waiting for him. *But we didn't realise just how much of a monster he was.*

The doors opened as he approached, readying the decontamination procedure. Volker stepped inside, closing his eyes instinctively as water washed down and over the protective suit. He'd been assured that the whole process was safe, that it offered the greatest chance of avoiding contamination, but part of him found it hard to accept. A handful of irradiated dust could cause all sorts of problems if he took it back to Berlin.

He stepped into the next compartment as the vehicle lurched to life. He'd practiced several times before heading out to the blast zone; he removed the suit and his undergarments, then stepped into the *third* compartment and straight into the shower. Warm water splashed down, washing his naked body clear of any contamination. An orderly met him outside the shower and passed him a bathrobe, then led him into the driving compartment. The

RAGNAROK

vehicle itself would have to be decontaminated before the crew - and Volker - could disembark.

And then I have to go straight back to Berlin, he told himself, firmly. *There's no time to waste here.*

The roads were jammed, he discovered, as he climbed into the official car and started the journey back home. Countless ambulances and buses had been pressed into service, rushing wounded men back from the front lines. Volker had seen some of the wounded and, despite himself, knew he never wanted to see such sights again. Far too many of the injured men were beyond all help, no matter what medicine arrived from America. He'd nearly punched the doctor who had suggested it would be better if the wounded were simply given mercy kills, even though cold logic insisted the *swinehund* had a point. There was nothing his government could do to save their lives.

And I'm the one who gave the orders that sent them back to the war, Volker thought. *But what choice did I have?*

He closed his eyes in bitter pain. Everything he'd done had seemed so *logical,* so *right.* And yet, countless men were now dead - or worse than dead - because they'd followed his orders and gone to war. He'd never imagined that Holliston would use nuclear weapons on his fellow Germans, let alone contaminate German land for years.

He's mad, Volker thought. *And we have to stop him.*

Berlin was practically a ghost town, he noted, as the vehicle drove through the barricades and into the city. The streets were empty, save for a handful of men wearing protective gear and carrying Geiger counters. Even the *prostitutes* were following orders and staying indoors, even though it would cost them money. But they had no choice. The level of radiation in Berlin had risen sharply in the last day, while the wind might shift at any moment, blowing radioactive fallout towards the city. Keeping the population indoors while the worst of the contamination faded away was the only way to keep them alive.

And it might not be enough, Volker thought. *We'll be dealing with the consequences for generations to come.*

He passed through the security barriers outside the *Reichstag,* then walked down to the bunker. If Holliston was mad enough to use those horrific weapons, he might decide to destroy Berlin as a show of power. And what would happen then?

We'll have to fire back, he thought, as he stepped into the briefing room. *And then he'll launch another bomb…and another…*

He'd glanced at a handful of nuclear war simulations, back when he'd found himself Chancellor. They hadn't seemed important at the time, not with a brewing civil war and a hundred smaller problems that had to be addressed. But the briefing papers hadn't made pleasant reading. Some of them had asserted that there would be a single savage nuclear exchange between the *Reich* and the North Atlantic Alliance, others that two or three missiles would fly at a time and that the agony would be prolonged indefinitely.

"Be seated," he said, grimly. "Do we have an updated report?"

"Over five thousand men confirmed dead or missing, believed dead," Luther Stresemann said. The Head of the Economic Intelligence Service sounded stunned, as if he didn't quite believe his own words. "Approximately ten thousand soldiers and civilians badly wounded - so far. The count is nowhere near complete."

"And vast amounts of direct and indirect economic damage," Hans Krueger added. "I…"

"To hell with the economy," Voss snapped. "We have worse problems at hand!"

Volker tapped the table. He doubted that any of them had slept in the last day or two, not after the offensive had begun. Now…they were all short-tempered, wanting to fight each other rather than calming down and deciding what to do coldly and rationally. But what *could* they do?

"The situation is dire," he said. "It may take us weeks to come to grips with it…"

"The situation is disastrous," Voss corrected. "*Herr* Chancellor, there is *no* hope of resuming the offensive before spring."

"And if that's the case," Volker said, "we may have no hope of resuming the offensive *at all.*"

"Yes, *Herr* Chancellor," Krueger said. "The impact of those nuclear detonations might have been enough to tip our economy right over the edge. Workers have stayed home over the last twenty-four hours, even outside the red zone. I'd say we'll be looking at complete collapse within the next few weeks."

Volker met his eyes. "And then...*what?*"

Krueger stared back at him. "There will be a cascade of failures as factories and other industrial plants shut down, each closure starting the *next* closure," he said. "Workers will be dismissed, placing more pressure on our social security networks at the worst possible time; money will run short, making it impossible to convince farmers to ship food into the cities as we won't be able to pay them. We can paper over the cracks for a while, *Herr* Chancellor, but I doubt we can make it last until spring."

He swallowed hard. "It will be just like 1919 and 1932," he added. "Only a great deal worse."

Volker rubbed his eyes. He wasn't old enough to remember the Great Depression, but he'd heard the stories of deprivation...and how the *Volk*, desperate for a saviour, had turned to Adolf Hitler. How long would the Provisional Government last if another Hitler arose on the streets and demanded power? And what could he do to stop it?

"That's a long-term problem," Voss said. "Right now, we have to retaliate."

Krueger coughed. "You would sentence countless *Germans* to death?"

"Right now, Holliston thinks he's scared us," Voss snapped. "He thinks we're too scared of his nuclear arsenal to resume the offensive."

"We *are* too scared of his arsenal," Admiral Wilhelm Riess said, dryly.

"It will not be long before he gets the impression he can simply use those weapons to force us into submission," Voss insisted. "We have to strike back, hard. Pick a target and annihilate it!"

"And what happens," Krueger asked, "when he blasts another target in response? Do we blast a second target in Germany East?"

"If necessary," Voss said. "He doesn't have the power to devastate Germany Prime."

"He *does* have the power to fire on America," Volker said.

"If he's managed to get the ballistic missiles unlocked," Voss said.

"I think we've just seen proof that he *has* managed to unlock and detonate some of the tactical devices," Riess said. "We cannot take the risk of assuming he *can't* fire the ballistic missiles."

"This is madness," Krueger said. "If we strike a military target, we make matters harder for us; if we strike a civilian target, we butcher thousands of our own people."

"And if we don't," Voss said, his voice rising sharply, "Holliston will butcher more of *our* people."

"They are *all* our people," Krueger said. "Field Marshal…"

"*Enough*," Volker snapped. He slapped the table, loudly. "Is there any other way to deter Karl Holliston from unleashing more of his tactical nuclear weapons?"

"We could try to come to terms with him," Riess suggested. "He can have Germany East, as long as the Easterners are prepared to put up with him…"

"And then we see him launching another invasion in the spring," Voss said.

"I would be surprised if he could," Krueger mused. "Replacing all of the lost or damaged pieces of war materiel will take years."

"You don't know that," Voss said.

Volker held up a hand before the argument could get out of hand again. "Let me pose a question," he said. "Can we resume the offensive before spring?"

"No, *Herr* Chancellor," Voss said. "We lost too many men and machines in the blasts. I think the best we can hope for is some raiding of enemy lines - and now that winter is approaching rapidly, even that will have to be curtailed. The offensive will have to be delayed until spring."

"And it may not be possible even then," Krueger put in.

Volker barely heard him. He'd hoped for a quick victory, despite the certain knowledge that his government would pay a hellish price for it. But Holliston had trumped him, using nuclear weapons to ensure that the war couldn't be won quickly - if at all. He was fairly sure that Holliston *couldn't* devastate Germany Prime - most of the SS's cruise missiles had been fired during the invasion of Germany Prime - but the price would still be horrendous. *Could* Germany East be invaded without so much death and devastation that the victory wouldn't be worth the candle?

And if I irradiate a military target in my path, he thought, *I'll simply make life harder for my own men.*

He didn't *like* the idea of using atom bombs. Voss was right, Holliston had to be deterred; Krueger was right, Holliston might just launch a *third* nuclear device in response. And who knew what would happen *then?* The tit-for-tat missile exchanges predicted by the briefing notes depended on the commanders on both sides being fundamentally rational. What happened when one or both of the commanders was *not* rational?

And how many Germans am I prepared to kill, he asked himself, *in what might be a vain attempt to deter a madman?*

There was always the Germanica Option, he admitted silently. It wouldn't be *that* hard to get a nuclear warhead to Germanica, to destroy the city. And it *might* destroy Holliston's Government too.

And who knows, he mused, *what will happen then?*

He had no answer. Holliston wasn't the type of person to appoint a successor, not when his successor might be ambitious enough to stick a knife in Holliston's back. It was possible that Germany East would come apart, but also possible that someone more rational would take control...or that the remaining weapons would be launched in one final spasm of violence before the *Reich* disintegrated. There were too many variables for him to take the risk.

And there's no guarantee of killing Holliston, he thought. *The bastard might survive long enough to order a full-scale nuclear strike.*

He cleared his throat. "Find a target - a *military* target - somewhere within Germany East," he said, slowly. "Make sure it's somewhere that won't cause us problems, when - if - we resume the offensive. That target will be destroyed with one of our atomic bombs."

"I must protest," Krueger said, stiffly.

"I understand," Volker said. "But we *cannot* allow Holliston to believe that we will just bend over for him."

"There's a large SS training centre," Voss mused. "It might make an ideal target."

"Or the docks near Valhalla," *Grossadmiral* Cajus Bekker offered. "They'd be close enough to Germanica for the civilians to see the flash."

Volker shook his head. He understood Bekker's concerns - the SS controlled the docks near Valhalla, at the eastern edge of the Gulf of Finland, and it had captured a number of warships during the chaotic early days of the uprising - but the target was too close to Valhalla. The city would be devastated by the blast, even if it wasn't targeted directly. No, better to target a training centre. If nothing else, it might show everyone else in Germany East just how far matters had gone downhill.

"The training centre will do," he said, shaking his head slowly. A year ago, he had never even *imagined* that he would be making such decisions. And now, part of him had quietly accepted the deed and moved on. "Prepare the weapon and the delivery system."

"*Jawohl*," Voss said.

Volker looked from face to face. They all looked tired, tired and worn. He didn't really blame them, either. They all bore some responsibility for the nuclear holocaust, even if it had been Karl Holliston who'd pushed the trigger. And they all knew that they were helpless to put an end to the war.

Horst is still on his way east, Volker thought. *Maybe he can find allies in the east.*

He pushed the thought aside and leaned forward. "We'll continue to repair our defences, raid their positions and generally make their lives miserable," he said. "And we will do our best to ensure that the wounded are well treated."

"We can't," Krueger said, flatly. "Our health system was on the brink for years. It was breaking down even before *this* catastrophe."

"We will try," Volker said. He was *not* going to order the mass execution of countless soldiers, even if it would be a mercy kill. "We owe it to men who fought for us."

Krueger met his eyes. "At what cost?"

"Whatever we have to pay," Volker snarled. The surge of anger surprised him. If Konrad had lived, would his son now be dying of radiation poisoning? No, the uprising would never have taken place. But what would have happened instead? "We *owe* them."

He caught himself. "And I want everyone in this room to get some sleep," he added, knowing it wouldn't be easy. He was tempted to uncork the bottle of wine in his quarters and have a stiff drink before he went to bed. His wife would have a fit, but he found it hard to care. "We are not in any fit state to face the world."

Sitting back, he watched as his cabinet slowly left the room. None of them looked happy; Voss was shooting nasty looks at Krueger's back, while Krueger himself was mulling over the costs of coping with the nuclear blasts and rebuilding the economy. Even if the war came to an end tomorrow, it wouldn't be easy. The *Reich* was *very* short of hard cash. Volker knew - all too well - that there would be many hard years to come.

And it doesn't matter, he thought, numbly. *I've just sentenced hundreds of men to death.*

CHAPTER TWENTY-TWO

Germanica (Moscow), Germany East
4 November 1985

Something was in the air.

Gudrun could feel it as the orderlies entered her cell, two of them glaring at her as if they expected her to spring to life and attack them, the third carrying a long set of chains that she recognised from the last time she'd been taken out of the underground complex. She offered no resistance as they hauled her to her feet, searched her roughly - she honestly couldn't understand how they thought she could obtain and conceal a weapon when it was blatantly obvious that she was being watched continuously - and then shackled her hands behind her back so tightly that she winced in pain.

"Forward," the leader grunted.

It wasn't easy to walk while shackled, but Gudrun had had plenty of practice. She inched forward, delaying as much as she dared; the guards, for once, didn't seem inclined to either slap her to force her to move quicker or pick her up and carry her. It was funny how she didn't feel concerned about the prospect any longer, but she'd been a prisoner for too long. The first time she'd had fingers poking and prodding at her most intimate places had been humiliating, yet it had lost its horror after the seventh or eighth time they'd done it. It was just something else to be endured.

She shuffled down the corridor, feeling the odd sensation in the air growing stronger as she passed a couple of black-clad men. They didn't seem to be interested in her, neither leering at her naked body nor treating her as a potential threat; they seemed distracted, instead, by some greater thought. Gudrun puzzled it over as she was pushed into a white-walled room and marched over to a solid metal chair. The guards forced her to sit, snapped extra cuffs around her wrists and ankles, then marched off leaving her alone. Gudrun rolled her eyes at the cameras, trying to pack as much defiance as she could into an expression that had always annoyed her mother. Did they seriously believe that a woman - or a man - could hope to escape so many chains?

The door opened. She turned her head, just in time to see Doctor Muller stepping into the room.

Gudrun kept her face as expressionless as possible, drawing on her experience at school to keep from showing him a *hint* of fear. Doctor Muller was a sadist, as bad - no, worse - as any of the BDM matrons. And there was no one else in the room, no one who could take the brunt of his feelings. Gudrun had never been alone with any of the matrons, but she'd heard plenty of rumours about what happened to girls - and boys - who had. She hoped that none of them were true…

…But given how much she'd uncovered, after the uprising, she rather suspected they were understated.

"Gudrun," Doctor Muller said. He walked around to face her, his eyes leaving trails of slime all over her body. "I have some questions and you *are* going to answer them."

"You're finally going to ask me questions," Gudrun said. She forced herself to giggle, although she doubted she'd fooled anyone. "You've had me as a prisoner for weeks and you're *finally* getting around to asking me some questions."

"You've been in this complex for months," Doctor Muller said, calmly. "And there was no *need* to ask you questions before."

No, I haven't, Gudrun thought. Her period was approaching rapidly. She could *feel* the first pains in her womb. *I can't have been here for more than two weeks at most.*

"I don't know anything you can use," she said, instead.

"You were on the rebel council," Doctor Muller said. "You were sent to France and Italy to speak with their treacherous rulers. I don't think you were *unimportant.*"

He reached out and twisted her nipple, hard. "You were *important,* weren't you?"

Gudrun gritted her teeth to keep from yelping in pain. Her trip to France had been secret - and she'd never been to Italy. And yet the SS knew she'd been to France...how? A spy in Berlin, a spy in Vichy...she cursed, mentally. She'd probably never know.

"I was just a girl," she said. It hurt her pride, but it was probably better to let him underestimate her. "They didn't tell me anything *important*."

Doctor Muller slapped her, hard. Gudrun felt her head snap to one side, tasting blood in her mouth as he stared down at her. She bit her lip, hard, to keep from screaming, forcing herself to lower her eyes instead of showing defiance. If she knew sadists - and she'd met too many BDM matrons - submission was the only thing that would save her from a beating. But as she felt blood dripping from her mouth and splashing on her legs, she knew it wouldn't be enough to save her.

Something has changed, she thought. *But what?*

"You *were* important," Doctor Muller said. "And smart too, smart enough to understand what I've told you."

He caught her hair and pulled it, forcing her to look up at him. "You *do* understand what I've told you, don't you?"

Gudrun nodded, wordlessly. He'd told her that he *knew* she'd been to France, although his knowledge clearly wasn't *perfect*. And *that* meant that he might catch her in a lie, giving him all the excuse he needed to give her a proper beating. Something had *definitely* changed if the SS had abandoned mind games, if they'd decided they no longer needed her looking unharmed. But what?

"Very good," Doctor Muller said. He let go of her hair and stepped backwards. "Who is in charge of the nuclear weapons in Berlin?"

"Not me," Gudrun said. Her jaw hurt. "I..."

"I *think* we know that," Doctor Muller said. "Who *is* in charge?"

Gudrun swallowed, hard. She knew the answer - did she dare lie? Would he know if she did? Or would he just keep piling on the pressure until she confessed to a lie? Or...

"The codes were shared out," she temporised. "I don't know..."

"Yes, you *do*," Doctor Muller said. "Who has the codes?"

Gudrun sighed. "The Chancellor, the Field Marshal and the Finance Minister," she said, reluctantly. "It takes two of them to unlock a warhead."

"They basically kept the same security protocol the *Reich* Council used," Doctor Muller mused. "Under what conditions would they use the weapons?"

"I don't know," Gudrun said.

Doctor Muller reached out and pinched her nipple, again. "Under what conditions would they use the bombs?"

"I don't know," Gudrun repeated. "It was never discussed!"

"It should have been discussed," Doctor Muller said. "I think you're lying."

Gudrun forced herself to think, even as he started pinching her, running his fingers over her body. The nuclear codes...why would they want to know about the nuclear codes? Had someone actually used one of the bombs? Was *that* what was different? She couldn't imagine the Provisional Government using the weapons, but...what if they had? Or what if Holliston was planning to use atomic bombs himself?

She shivered as a thought struck her. *What if he already has?*

"Doctor," she said. "Has Holliston used an atomic bomb?"

Doctor Muller slapped her, again. "You will address him by his title, you little bitch," he snarled, as her head started to spin. She felt sick; she had to fight to keep from opening her mouth and throwing up. "He is the *Fuhrer*."

He punched her shoulder, hard. "Why will they use nuclear warheads?"

Gudrun gritted her teeth. "I don't know..."

She screamed as Doctor Muller hit her, again and again. She'd never imagined such pain, never imagined that a hail of punches and kicks could leave her begging for mercy. Nothing, not even the tender mercies of the matrons, had been so painful. But she didn't *know* the answer to his question. She didn't know if *anyone* knew the answer to his question.

"Answer me," Doctor Muller said. She was dimly aware of him pausing, his hands gripping her bleeding jaw. Her position had shifted, somehow, until she was leaning forward helplessly. "Answer the question."

Gudrun braced herself, then closed her eyes. Perhaps it would be quick.

———

Katherine was no stranger to casual violence. She'd grown up on a settlement where beating *Gastarbeiters* was common, even before she'd joined the SS. She knew there were plenty of times when violence was the answer, the *only* answer; she had no compunctions about hurting someone who questioned her post or her value to the *Reich*. But she also had her orders from the *Fuhrer*, orders she couldn't disobey. And those orders specifically forbade allowing any serious harm to come to her prisoner.

She snapped a command at the guards, then hurried out of the security room and down to the interrogation chamber. Gudrun's screams echoed down the corridor, fading as her strength faded. Katherine braced herself, then strode into the chamber. Gudrun was kneeling, trapped in a restraint chair, while Doctor Muller stood behind her, unzipping his pants. He was going to rape her…

"Get away from her," Katherine snarled. Her eyes flickered over Gudrun. She was bleeding, blood dripping to the white floor, but the damage looked mostly cosmetic. Doctor Muller was an expert at hurting someone without inflicting lasting damage. "Now!"

Doctor Muller turned to look at her, his hand on his fly. "I have orders…"

Katherine grabbed him, yanked him forward and slammed him into the wall. "And *I* have orders to make sure she survives," she snapped. "*You* are going to kill her."

She wanted to scream her disgust at him, perhaps knock his head into the wall several times, but she suspected it would be pointless. Doctor Muller didn't seem inclined to fight - like most of his ilk, he was a coward at heart - but she frog-marched him to the door anyway, shoving him out into the corridor. He'd probably go whining to the *Fuhrer*, rather than sneak back or do something else stupid. Katherine gritted her teeth, then turned to hurry back to Gudrun. The restraint chair wasn't *designed* to hold someone in that uncomfortable position indefinitely.

No, it can hold them, Katherine reminded herself as she inspected the chair. *But people can't endure it indefinitely*.

Doctor Muller was *definitely* a coward, she noted. Gudrun had been beaten half to death, yet he'd *still* kept her restrained while he prepared to rape her. Katherine silently promised herself a shot at the doctor's back, then undid the cuffs around Gudrun's ankles, allowing her to slip forward. The girl twisted her head, slightly, as Katherine released her wrists, holding Gudrun close to keep her from falling. A moment later, she had Gudrun lying on the ground, her blue eyes staring up at nothing.

"Remain still," Katherine said, as gently as possible. Gudrun would be in pain, considerable pain. And *she* didn't have two years of intensive training to draw on to help her survive. "Let me help."

She ran her hands up and down Gudrun's body, checking for breaks. It didn't *feel* as though anything was broken, but she couldn't help noticing how Gudrun flinched away at her gentle touch. She'd heard stories from the east, stories about women who had been beaten and raped by insurgents, stories about how they'd never been the same afterwards. Katherine had sneered at such women - weakness could not be tolerated - yet she had to admit that she'd never been raped. Perhaps, just perhaps, it was easier to understand afterwards. Those women had lost control of their own bodies, just as Gudrun had lost control of hers.

"There's no real damage," she said, as reassuringly as she could. "I know it feels bad, but it could have been worse."

Gudrun shifted, uncomfortably. Katherine sat back and studied her for a long moment. Her pale skin - the very image of ideal German womanhood - was covered in nasty bruises, including both of her breasts and between her legs. Blood was still dripping from her jaw, although Katherine knew it looked worse than it actually was. She put out a helping hand as Gudrun tried to sit up, only to have her hand brushed away. Gudrun would be sensitive to physical touch for months - perhaps years - to come.

And she's married, Katherine thought. Horst Albrecht was a traitor, a traitor most foul. She would shed no tears for him when he was hung from meathooks below the *Reichstag*, the customary punishment for traitors. And yet, she couldn't help feeling an odd twinge of...*something*. Gudrun had been far more impressive than she'd had any right to be. *What will happen to her when she's released?*

She told herself not to be stupid, angrily. Gudrun would never be released.

"I don't know," Gudrun said, slowly. Her voice was so weak that Katherine feared she had finally broken. "I don't know the answers."

"So it would seem," Katherine said, dryly.

Gudrun twisted her head. One of her eyes was already turning black, suggesting that Doctor Muller had struck her there. Katherine cursed under her breath. She was no stranger to physical pain - her training had left her bruised and bleeding more than once - but there were limits. Doctor Muller had beaten Gudrun out of sheer sadism.

And out of a desire to please his master, Katherine thought, coldly. *I wonder if he was authorised to ask questions about nuclear weapons.*

"What..." Gudrun coughed and started again. "What *happened?*"

"Nuclear weapons were used," Katherine said. There was no point in trying to conceal it, not from a girl as smart as Gudrun. Besides, the only way she could ever be rescued would be through a direct assault on the *Reichstag* itself. The war would be lost. "Your offensive failed."

Gudrun let out a bitter sound, a cross between a gasp and a sob. She'd probably known people who would have fought on the front lines, Katherine thought. Her older brother was a soldier, according to her file; her younger brother was pushing the edge of military age. He might have been enlisted already, if the rebels were desperate for manpower. Somehow, she found it hard to imagine Gudrun using her position to ensure that her relatives were sent to safety while others stood and fought.

"I don't know what will happen," Katherine added. "But we should be safe down here."

She sighed as she helped Gudrun to her feet. The bunker under the Germanica *Reichstag* was heavily protected, easily the most secure place in the city. If the city was hit with atomic weapons, she'd been assured, the bunker would be perfectly safe. She had her doubts - there was no such thing as perfect safety, in her experience - but she had a great deal of faith in the *Reich's* engineers. If Germanica was nuked, Karl Holliston and his government would survive to carry on the fight.

And the hell of it, she conceded reluctantly, was that she was no longer sure if that was a good thing.

Gudrun leaned against her, her body frail. It was easy to forget that she was only three or so years younger that Katherine herself, that she'd done well in the BDM. Two weeks of captivity, fed starvation rations and drugged repeatedly, had done her no favours. Doctor Muller might have been told he couldn't feed Gudrun some of his more...*interesting*...concoctions, but what he *had* slipped her had been more than bad enough. Katherine would have been surprised if Gudrun had a clear grip on *anything*.

"You're being nice to me," Gudrun managed. "Are you planning to ask me questions too?"

"I do not have orders to ask you questions," Katherine said, truthfully. She'd heard of using two interrogators - one nice, one nasty - to break down a suspect, but the *Reich* had rarely considered it a worthwhile technique. "I'm going to make sure you get some proper medical attention."

Gudrun flinched. Too late, Katherine remembered what Gudrun's *last* medical exam had been like. Doctor Muller and his goons had poked and prodded every last orifice, doing everything in their power to make it clear that Gudrun was no longer in control of her own body. And while Gudrun had put up a brave show, it was clear that she was coming to the end of her tether. The SS got everyone in the end, eventually.

They do, a voice said at the back of her mind. *And you have to decide how you feel about that.*

She half-carried Gudrun down the corridor and into the infirmary. The doctor - she didn't know his name or reputation - looked surprised to see them, but took Gudrun and guided her to a bed. Katherine suspected that Gudrun would have preferred a female doctor, yet there were none to be found in the *Reichstag*. Even the *nurses* were male. One might have to be called in from the city above, if necessary.

A stern-faced stormtrooper appeared at the door. "*Herr Hauptsturmfuehrer,*" he said, quietly ignoring Katherine's obvious femininity. "The *Fuhrer* demands your immediate presence. I am to escort you to him."

Katherine nodded. Doctor Muller had *definitely* gone whining to the *Fuhrer.* But she was only following orders, *Holliston's* orders. She had a feeling the doctor was in for a nasty surprise.

"One moment," she said.

She looked at the doctor. "Take *very* good care of her," she ordered, nodding to Gudrun. "If there is any cause for complaint afterwards, you will suffer for it."

"*Jawohl,*" the doctor said.

Katherine eyed him for a long moment - a doctor who worked in an interrogation chamber would have questionable morals, if nothing else - and then followed the stormtrooper through the door. Gudrun would be safe, for the moment...

...But with nuclear weapons being launched, Katherine had no idea how long that would last.

CHAPTER TWENTY-THREE

Germanica (Moscow), Germany East
4 November 1985

"The reports from the front make it clear," Karl said, "that the enemy offensive has been stopped."

He looked at Ruengeler. "This is correct?"

"Yes, *Mein Fuhrer*," Ruengeler said. His face was pale, his hands sweaty. "The offensive has been stopped."

"Exactly," Karl said. He looked at the assembled *Gauleiters*. "Victory is within our grasp."

The *Gauleiters* didn't look impressed, but none of them seemed willing to challenge him openly. Karl wasn't surprised. None of them would have the nerve to challenge him unless the war went badly - and the nuclear blasts had stopped the offensive in its tracks. That would change, he was sure, but for the moment they would be quiet. It would give him time to move to the next stage of his plan.

Gauleiter Emil Forster cleared his throat. "Our forces were far too close to the blasts," he said, smoothly. "Did they escape the worst of the fallout?"

"Yes," Karl said, flatly. "Our defence lines are currently being rebuilt east of Warsaw. The onset of winter will make it harder for the enemy to resume the offensive before spring."

Forster looked unconvinced. Karl scowled, inwardly. He'd known that Forster would be trouble, but without the support of his fellows there was nothing the older man could do to unseat his *Fuhrer*. And besides, Karl still controlled most of the military *and* all of the atomic bombs.

"But that raises another question," Forster said. "What of Warsaw itself?"

Karl allowed his face to darken. "The city was partly evacuated before the enemy offensive began," he said. It was true enough, but only a small fraction of the population had been relocated. "The remainder of the population were warned to take cover once the fighting actually began."

"But they were still too close to the blasts," Forster said. "How many of our citizens were killed or wounded - or blinded - by the bombs? And how many have been sentenced to death by radiation poisoning?"

"There are sacrifices that must be made for the greater good," Karl said. He had no idea how many civilians had been killed, but it hardly mattered. All that *really* mattered was preserving Germany East. "The population of Warsaw is a small price to pay for the salvation of the Third *Reich*."

"Undoubtedly," *Gauleiter* Hugo Jury said. "It is a *honour* to die for the Greater German *Reich*!"

"Those men and women were not soldiers," Forster said, coldly. "They were *civilians*."

He looked around the room, his eyes flickering from face to face. "The damage to the city is bad enough," he said. "Rebuilding it is beyond our resources. But the long-term damage to the *Volk* may be worse."

Karl allowed himself a moment of anger. Forster was smart, too smart - and too independent-minded. Jury could be counted upon to support the *Reich* and Innsbruck was too weak to oppose anyone, but Forster was dangerous. And yet...

"They will retaliate," Innsbruck said. "They will use nuclear weapons on *our* territory."

"They would not *dare*," Jury hissed. "They *know* we will retaliate..."

"And then what?" Forster asked. "Do we keep exchanging nukes until the entire *Reich* is destroyed?"

"No," Karl said. Germany East didn't *have* enough working bombs to destroy Germany Prime, not yet. The engineers were working as fast as they could to unlock the remaining warheads, but it was slow going. "I do not believe they would have the nerve to strike one of our cities."

"Particularly as Warsaw *is* one of our cities," Forster said, dryly.

Karl ignored him. "We will take advantage of this pause in the storm to demand their surrender," he said. "I doubt they have the willingness to continue their advance in the face of nuclear attack."

180

"And General Winter," Jury added.

"Quite," Karl said. He looked up. "We beat an offensive the enemy threw together in a hurry. It will take them months to ready another offensive - months we can use to prepare our own forces for our return to Berlin, months we can use to further subvert their positions by reminding their people of how good life was before the rebellion. And then we will re-establish the Third *Reich* and purge the subversives who nearly brought us to our knees."

He smiled, careful to keep his *real* emotions hidden. Using the atomic bombs had been a calculated risk - and, so far, it seemed to have paid off - but he knew it would be a long time before his forces could begin the second advance on Berlin. Who knew what would happen in the five or six months it would take to ready the offensive?

"Perhaps it would be better to come to terms with them," Forster said. "Split the *Reich* into two."

Karl blinked in surprise. "You would allow the rebels to go unpunished? You would allow the *Reich* to fragment?"

Forster stared back at him evenly. "Your original offensive assumed that Germany Prime could be recaptured in a quick campaign," he said. "You believed that we could go on the offensive and win before the enemy had a chance to recover from the damage to its command network and mobilise the resources at its command. That offensive failed - the enemy not only failed to submit, but also managed to move enough forces eastward to allow a counter-offensive of their own."

"Which has now failed," Karl snapped. "The enemy is gravely weakened."

"Which has failed," Forster agreed. "But our own forces are weakened too." He took a breath. "Do we *want* Germany Prime?

"*Mein Fuhrer*, Germany Prime has been infected with liberalism for decades," he continued. "Men and women have forgotten their roles in life; parents are neglectful of their children, children are disrespectful to their parents. The influx of American products has weakened the heart and soul of the *Reich*. Do we really *want* to win the war and spend years purging every last trace of weakness from the body politic?"

Karl took a moment to compose his reply. Forster's argument was completely wrong-headed, yet it would have a certain resonance in Germany East. Contempt for the weaklings of the west would eventually - inevitably - lead to people asking why they *needed* to regain control over Germany Prime. And most of the obvious counter-arguments were not ones that would impress the Easterners...

"Regardless of any other concerns," he said finally, "the border between east and west is too long to be patrolled and sealed. We would need to fear sedition from the west, even if we washed our hands of them..."

"But why?" Forster added. "What is the *appeal* of blue jeans and hip-hop music to boys and girls raised in Germany East?"

He snorted, rudely. "Let them sink into degeneration, *Mein Fuhrer,*" he said. "Let them wallow in a cauldron of miscegenation and depravity. Let them watch their American videos and slake their lusts on one another like the animals they are. Our purity will allow us to rise above them, setting an example that they will inevitably come to emulate. We will welcome them back to us when the time is right - and they will come willingly."

Karl silently promised himself that he'd have Forster killed, the moment he had an opportunity to strike without triggering a civil war. The man was right, damn him; Germany East had built-in protections against subversion that Germany Prime had long-since lost. There was a...*vigour* to life in the east, an awareness of community - and danger - that had started to decay in Germany Prime. And a respect for one's elders that ensured that rebellion was impossible. That too had been lost in Germany Prime.

"They are our fellow Germans," he said, finally. "We cannot allow them to sink into depravity without making some attempt to stop it."

Forster snorted. "And fighting a war that will hand the Americans mastery of the world?"

"They do not have the will to power," Jury sneered. "Let them think us weakened, if they wish. We will teach them different soon enough."

"Of course," Karl said. He smiled, rather darkly. "They will not be ready for us when we rise from the ashes."

"Let us hope so," Forster said. "We may find that we have paid too great a price to reunify the *Reich.*"

———

Katherine wasn't too surprised to discover that the regular complement of guards around the *Fuhrer's* office and living quarters had been doubled overnight. Karl Holliston had always been a paranoid man and, with a civil war underway, had excellent reason to be worried about his own safety. She handed her pistol over to the guards at the checkpoint without protest, then submitted to a surprisingly professional pat-down before they allowed her into the waiting room. The guards, it seemed, were more focused on security than exploiting their authority.

And that makes them better than the men downstairs, she thought, grimly. *They wouldn't hesitate to grope anyone who entered their domain.*

The thought made her feel sick. She hoped that Gudrun would be safe - she doubted Doctor Muller would dare return to torment his prisoner - but she knew it wouldn't last. Safe? What safety *was* there below the *Reichstag?* Gudrun could be taken out of her cell and shot - or worse - at any moment and she knew it. And, despite her determination, she was on the verge of breaking completely. Katherine had no trouble reading her. She *was* about to snap.

She looked up as three men walked through the room. *Gauleiter* Hugo Jury looked proud as he strode through the outer door; *Gauleiter* Emil Forster and *Gauleiter* Staff Innsbruck both looked oddly worried. Indeed, they were standing so close together that she would have unhesitatingly declared them to be lovers, if one of them happened to be female. Clearly, they were planning *something.* Perhaps they were intent on remaining united in the face of the *Fuhrer…*

"You may enter," Marie said.

Katherine nodded, rose and walked through the inner door. She hadn't seen the *Fuhrer* for several days and she was shocked by the change in him. He looked as if he hadn't slept for several days, his unshaven face covered in dark stubble. And his blonde hair was shading to grey…she wondered, suddenly, if he'd been dying his hair for the last few years. Blonde hair was considered a mark of good breeding, even though neither Hitler nor Himmler had been blonde. She'd heard that the vast majority of girls in Germany Prime dyed their hair every few days, just to make sure they appeared blonde.

Idiots, she thought. *There are far more important things in life than hair colour.*

"*Mein Fuhrer,*" she said, snapping out a perfect salute. "*Heil Holliston!*"

"Katherine," Holliston said. He sounded oddly relieved to see her, even though she thought she was in trouble. Doctor Muller had probably told the *Fuhrer* that Katherine had beaten him to death. "It is good to see you."

Katherine frowned, inwardly. Holliston sounded...*wrong*. Not lecherous, not fearful...she couldn't put her finger on it. But something was wrong. She looked down at his desk and had to fight to keep her face impassive when she saw the photographs. Scorched buildings, shattered lives...the men in the photographs looked as though they'd been through hell. And perhaps they had...

"Thank you, *Mein Fuhrer*," she said.

It struck her, suddenly, that Holliston had good reason to be paranoid. Not *everyone* would approve of his decision to use nuclear weapons. If a protest movement had started - and eventually overthrown the government in Berlin - because the government had covered up the deaths of German soldiers, who knew what would happen after word of Warsaw started to spread freely. Rumours grew in the telling...

...And not everyone would believe that the *rebels* had been the ones who'd detonated the warheads.

"Doctor Muller whines that you beat him up," Holliston said. A ghost of a smile flickered across his face. "Is that actually true?"

"I threw him out of the room," Katherine said, briskly. "He was on the verge of raping your...*special*...prisoner."

Holliston lifted an eyebrow. "And is that a bad thing?"

"You gave me orders to ensure that Gudrun suffered no long-term harm," Katherine said, firmly. "I submit to you, *Mein Fuhrer*, that the beating he gave her was quite bad enough. It will be days, at best, before her face clears. Raping her would only push her *completely* over the edge."

She paused for a long moment before pushing onwards. "I don't believe that interrogating her offers anything of value," she added. "She simply doesn't know anything significant, not now."

"We had her in our hands, only a couple of months ago," Holliston said. His tone was so...distracted that Katherine honestly wasn't sure if he'd heard a word she'd said. "If we'd known who she was at the time...we could have stopped *everything*."

"Yes, *Mein Fuhrer*," Katherine said.

Holliston's voice was beginning to worry her. He sounded as though he'd lost track of reality, as if he were refighting battles that were over and done with rather than rolling with the blows and looking to the future. She studied the *Fuhrer* as carefully as she could, drawing on all her training to ensure he didn't notice her scrutiny. She was no honey trapper, no woman trained in all the arts of seduction, but she knew enough to keep her interest concealed. And she also knew what to look for.

He's not eating enough, she thought. Lack of sleep was bad enough - Holliston was hardly a young man any longer - but lack of food *and* sleep was worse. *And he isn't drinking enough either.*

"There were traitors everywhere," Holliston added. "We could have stopped everything if the traitors hadn't intervened."

That, Katherine knew, was true. Horst Albrecht could have betrayed Gudrun at any moment; instead, he'd sided with her despite the risks. And Katherine found it hard to blame him after meeting Gudrun. She'd thought that Horst was driven by lust, allowing his hormones to override his common sense, but there was something about Gudrun that appealed to Katherine too. What would Gudrun have become, Katherine wondered, if she'd grown up in Germany East? Would her…determination have been beaten out of her? Or would she have changed the world?

"Something must be done," Holliston said. "She must be broken."

"She is on the way to breaking," Katherine said. She hesitated, then took the plunge. "I believe if I were to show her affection and support now, it would push her over the edge."

Holliston seemed to snap back to reality. "And you think that would help?"

"Yes, *Mein Fuhrer*," Katherine said. "There is a point where punishment - harsh punishment - just hardens the soul. Gudrun may turn unbreakable - or she may die - if more beatings are handed out. But varying her treatment will undermine her resistance."

She kept her face impassive, wondering if Holliston would take the bait. She'd known a teenage boy, back in school, who'd been stubbornly defiant to the last, despite regular beatings, forced marches and public humiliations. He would have been excellent material for the commandos, Katherine thought in retrospect, if he hadn't disappeared during her sixteenth year. She had no idea what had happened to him…

…But she'd admired his ability to just keep going, whatever the teachers threw at him.

"Very well," Holliston said. "You may do as you please."

"Thank you, *Mein Fuhrer*," Katherine said.

She carefully kept her face impassive. She'd expected to have to search for a loophole, but Holliston had rendered it immaterial. Do as she pleased…she *would* do as she pleased. And Doctor Muller wouldn't be able to say a word about it.

"I'll return to the cells at once," she said. "I'm sure Doctor Muller will be happy to hear the news."

Holliston smirked. "You may give it to him personally," he said. "And you can *also* remind him that my orders are *not* to be broken."

"*Jawohl, Mein Fuhrer*," Katherine said.

She saluted again as he dismissed her, then wheeled about and walked out of the giant chamber. Holliston was clearly in a bad way, even though the enemy offensive *had* been halted before it could do serious damage. She couldn't help fearing for the future. She'd been taught that the men at the top were cold dispassionate thinkers, ruthlessly putting their feelings aside to serve the *Reich*. But Holliston was nothing of the sort…

And if that isn't true, she asked herself, *what else isn't true?*

She mulled it over as she walked back down to the cells, passed through the security checkpoint and peered into Doctor Muller's office. He hadn't dared return to the cells, let alone his office. Katherine checked on Gudrun, just in case, but there was still no sign of Doctor Muller. She had no doubt he was amusing himself somewhere else in the underground complex while trying to work up the nerve to face her. And she was looking forward to that meeting…

But what do I do, she asked herself, *if everything I've been taught is a lie?*

She stepped back into the security office, dismissed the two guards on duty and sat down in front of the monitors. Gudrun was sleeping in the medical chamber, sedated. The doctor had cuffed her hand to the bed, but otherwise left her largely alone. Katherine was more relieved than she cared to admit. If she'd had to threaten a second doctor - and she knew she might have had no choice - it would have raised eyebrows.

And what would you do, she asked the sleeping form, *if you discovered the truth?*

But, deep inside, she already knew the answer.

No, she told herself. *I know what you did.*

CHAPTER TWENTY-FOUR

front Lines, Germany Prime
4/5 November 1985

Hennecke felt sick.

He had no idea what was wrong with him, but he wasn't the only man in the trenches to be suffering. He'd thrown up everything in his stomach shortly after the nuclear blasts, then dry-heaved several times through the night; his head hurt, his body felt dizzy and he'd had real problems just getting up after an uncomfortable night's sleep. There was no food or drink in the trenches, save for snow they'd collected and melted for drinking water. It hadn't made them feel any better.

"Get up," a voice snarled. "Now!"

Hennecke glared, but slowly stumbled to his feet. The speaker was a young officer, too young to have seen any real combat. He looked so perfect, as if he'd stepped off a recruiting poster, that Hennecke hated him with an intensity that surprised him. It was all he could do not to stagger forward and try to vomit on the newcomer. But he barely had the energy to stand upright.

"Help the others to stand," the officer barked. Each word sent a shock of pain through Hennecke's aching head. "See who can't stand under their own power."

His head spinning, Hennecke did his best to obey orders. A couple of dozen men looked as though they could walk, although only two of them looked coordinated enough to march in unison. The others were either too ill to move - he felt a chill running down his spine as he saw them shaking with fever, despite the bitter cold - or dead. He couldn't help feeling sick himself as he saw a big soldier, a man so large he could practically pass for a gorilla, screaming like a baby as he shuddered violently, then fell silent. By the time Hennecke checked him, he was dead.

He froze in horror as he stumbled across *Scharfuehrer* Kuhn. The man was lying on the ground, his hair falling out...he stared up at Hennecke, his eyes silently begging for life...or death. Hennecke could do nothing. He'd honestly believed that Kuhn was too tough to be wounded. But now he was dying, poisoned by...what? He didn't want to *think* about what happened to those too close to nuclear explosions, but it seemed as though he had no choice.

The water, he thought, feeling a flicker of horror. *We collected poisoned water and drank it.*

But there was nothing he could do, either for Kuhn or himself. Tottering forward, he carefully removed Kuhn's pistol and strapped it to his belt, pocketing the two ammunition clips Kuhn had kept in his belt. Kuhn made no protest, something that frightened Hennecke more than one of his savage rages - and beatings. The man he'd seen knock a rowdy stormtrooper down with a single punch was now as weak as a kitten...and dying. Hennecke was torn between giving Kuhn a mercy kill and leaving him to die. What should he do?

"Strip the corpses," the officer barked. "And then strip anyone too weak to walk!"

Hennecke swallowed hard as he realised the truth. Whatever had poisoned them - radiation or not - those orders made it clear what was about to happen. Soldiers who were beyond salvation were to be left to die - including him, if he collapsed. Gritting his teeth, fighting to make his hands work despite his pounding headache, he forced himself to stagger over to the nearest corpse and start to undress it. But it was nearly impossible to strip the body...

It felt like hours before a team of newcomers showed up, wearing baggy protective outfits that he hadn't seen - or used - outside training exercises that felt as though they'd taken place a millennia ago. They had radiation poisoning then, he realised; he hadn't wanted to accept it, but there was no choice. The *Fuhrer's* nuclear weapons had poisoned their own men...

"Get some food," the officer snarled. The handful of walking men hurried over to the food cart, passing a trio of stormtroopers on the way. "And make sure you get back here to continue the work."

Hennecke was too tired to say or do anything, but sip the broth they'd been provided. It was warm, crammed with pieces of meat and vegetables, yet he couldn't help thinking that it tasted of manure. Perhaps their food, too, had been poisoned by the sleet of radiation. He wished, suddenly, that he knew more about radiation poisoning, although what he *did* know was more than enough to make his hair want to fall out. But now, with far too many men losing their hair - or worse - it wasn't anything like as funny as it seemed. He still giggled helplessly as he finished his broth. Thankfully, the dry-retching had come to an end.

He heard a shot and glanced back, sharply. The stormtroopers were moving from body to body, systematically shooting each and every one of the wounded in the head. Hennecke knew just how ruthless the SS could be - he'd been there when an entire village had been slaughtered for harbouring rebels - but killing their own men so casually was a whole new dimension of ruthlessness. He watched in utter horror as a stormtrooper shot Kuhn, leaving the man's body to lie on the ground, then forced himself to look away.

They sent us here to die, he thought. *And then they killed us.*

He found himself torn between the urge to laugh and the urge to start crying. He'd thought he was serving the *Reich*, but the *Reich* had turned on him. No rebel had killed him, no rebel had even come *close* to killing him... he'd been killed by his own side. He didn't know enough about radiation poisoning to be sure, but he thought it was always fatal. Did he have a hope of surviving long enough to get medical treatments? Would he even be *given* medical treatments?

I have to get better, he told himself, numbly. *But how?*

The men were pushed back to work as soon as they finished their scanty meal, digging a large pit and burying their former comrades. Hennecke had plenty of experience digging mass graves, but without the proper tools the job was nightmarish. The newcomers didn't do anything to help, either. They just killed two men who collapsed on the job and couldn't even *begin* to get up. Hennecke thought about drawing his stolen pistol and shooting them - or at least the damned officer - but his hands were too weak. He wouldn't have a hope in hell of shooting even *one* of them before they shot him down.

There was no rest even after the mass grave was dug. The remainder of the corpses were stripped and buried, then covered with a thin layer of earth.

Hennecke doubted they'd *remain* buried for very long - there were plenty of animals who'd dig them up even if the rebels didn't come to see who'd been buried in the grave - but it seemed to be enough for the officer, who ordered them to follow him east. His legs still felt weak as he walked, yet the thought of being killed if he dropped out of line kept him going. The officer didn't seem to care.

He was probably well away from the blasts, Hennecke thought, savagely. *Or perhaps he was just out of training when the war began.*

The landscape had been utterly devastated by the blasts. Hennecke had travelled down the roads during the build-up for the first offensive - they'd been typical roads at the time - but now they were badly damaged, bridges knocked down and pavement torn up, leaving them impassable to anything short of a panzer. The trees by the side of the roads had been incinerated or knocked down; a number of burned-out vehicles bore mute witness to the deaths of a number of unfortunate civilians - or soldiers - caught in the open. He wondered, numbly, if the cars had belonged to higher-ups in Warsaw fleeing the war, although he had to admit it was more likely that the vehicles had been commandeered by the military. But he clung to the former thought anyway as bitter resentment gnawed at his soul. It was all that kept him going.

He tried to remember what little he'd been taught about nuclear weapons during basic training, but very little of what he could recall was actually *helpful.* His instructors had talked about blast effects in some detail, yet they'd said next to nothing about radiation poisoning and nuclear fallout. He wasn't even sure what they *were.* But then, no one had seriously expected the Americans to launch a nuclear strike on the *Reich.* Everyone had known the Americans didn't have the stomach to start a nuclear exchange...

And they didn't, he told himself. He had no doubt of it. *We dropped the bombs on ourselves.*

The small party came to a halt - it felt as if they'd been walking for hours - near a camp by the roadside. Hennecke felt a flicker of relief, mixed with concern, as he saw a set of armed stormtroopers standing by the gates, wearing the same protective gear as the others. He kept inching forward anyway, even though part of him kept insisting that he was going to die in the next few moments. The stormtroopers might have orders to gun them down...

Cold water came out of nowhere, drenching them to the bone. Hennecke barely had a moment to turn his head and see men holding hoses before they were drenched again, water soaking through their uniforms and leaving them shivering helplessly. He saw a man drop to the ground like a sack of potatoes, just as the gates were opened and they were ordered forward, into the camp. Behind him, he heard a single shot.

"You'll remain in this tent," the officer said, as he led the way towards a large tent. "Do *not* attempt to leave without permission."

Hennecke scowled at his back. The other officers and soldiers in the camp were staring at them, as if they weren't quite sure what to make of twenty-five stormtroopers dripping water as they marched. They were being isolated, Hennecke saw, and he wasn't quite sure why. He was feeling better, wasn't he? But not all of the men looked better. He stepped into the tent, cursing under his breath as he realised there was nothing there beyond a pile of looted blankets. They'd need to undress before they could even *think* of taking a nap.

His head started to pound again as he struggled to undo his battledress. His fingers refused to cooperate; he started to shiver, helplessly, as he finally managed to get undressed and take one of the blankets to dry himself. He wasn't the only one to manage it, he saw, but several of the others had just collapsed, either through tiredness or radiation damage. Gritting his teeth, he lay down and closed his eyes. His head was spinning helplessly…

…He started awake, hours later. The tent was dark, the only light coming from a lantern mounted over the flap. And it stank, of shit and piss and vomit and blood. He heard a faint moaning, the sound so close that he wasn't sure *who* was moaning. It might have been him…he just didn't know. His head was pounding like a drum, his body so utterly dehydrated that it was hard, so hard, to roll over and crawl naked towards the tent flap. He needed water, desperately. He'd been told to stay in the tent, but he *couldn't* stay in the tent, not if he wanted to live.

Outside, it was dark; rain and snow lashing down around the camp, mocking him. What was the snow bringing, but death? It was hard to see the shape of any other tents, even though he knew they were there. The cold gripped him, slicing into his naked body…he was torn between staying where he was and freezing to death or trying to make his way back into the tent. Surely there should be a guard, someone who could help? But there was no one…

"Hey," a female voice said. "What are you doing outside?"

Hennecke turned his head and stared. His vision seemed to have blurred…an angel was standing there, wearing a white uniform. And it was tight in all the right places, revealing curves a man could stroke and fondle to his heart's content. A surge of lust flashed through him, only to fade just as quickly. She wasn't a nurse, he was sure. There was no *way* she was a nurse. She was probably an officer's lover…the shithead had brought her with him while his men suffered and died…

"Water," he croaked. His head was a mess. Part of him wanted to grab her and make love to her, part of him wanted to snap her neck just for daring to exist. It was hard, so hard, to sort out right from wrong. "Please…"

"I'll bring you water," the girl promised. She had a voice he would have found reassuring, under other circumstances. Now, he merely found it annoying. "Stay inside."

Hennecke stumbled back inside and crouched by the tent flap, feeling utterly helpless. He couldn't even *walk*. If the girl was an officer's lover, rather than a nurse…his head kept spinning, tossing up hundreds of possibilities that faded almost before he could get a grip on them. But he was dependent on her now…his body twitched, as if he wanted to cough but couldn't muster the energy. If she wasn't a nurse, he knew he wouldn't live through the night and see morning. Not again…

The tent flap opened. Hennecke looked up as the girl, looking even more angelic than before, stepped inside, carrying a small glass of water in one hand. She knelt in front of him and held the glass to his lips, as if she were feeding a baby. Hennecke sipped gratefully, unable to keep his eyes off the rise and fall of her breasts. His feelings were so conflicted that he couldn't even keep track of them himself. He wanted her, yet he knew he couldn't muster the energy to have her. And his head was still pounding.

"Stay still," the girl advised. "You've been through hell."

Hennecke grunted. It was hard, too hard, to form actual *words*. He *had* been through hell for the *Reich*, risking life and limb so that Karl Holliston could march back into Berlin and sit down in Adolf Hitler's chair. And then the offensive had failed and he'd found himself penalised, even though the failure hadn't been his fault. He'd worked as a penal soldier, only to be drenched in radiation by his own side and probably condemned to a long, lingering death.

And it just wasn't fair!

The bitterness became rage. He stumbled back, thinking of the pistol concealed within his wet clothes. It would be easy to take it and start killing officers, to kill and kill until he was killed himself, but he knew he didn't have the strength. He looked up at the girl and felt another surge of rage, the desire to throw her down and just *take* her mingling with the urge to kill her. Here she was, young and pretty, utterly unaware of what he'd done in her name - and in the name of German womanhood everywhere...

"You will recover," the girl said, quietly.

Hennecke reached out with sudden strength and grabbed her wrist. She gasped in pain, but - even weakened as he was - she couldn't pull free. He yanked her forward, honestly unsure himself what he intended to do. Force her down or snap her neck? The girl opened her mouth to scream; he clamped his other hand over it, slamming her lips together. She tried to bite him, but it was futile...

"Recover?" He asked. Savage hatred welled up within him. How *dare* she stand next to him in her clean uniform and mouth such platitudes? "Do you really think I will recover?"

He let go of her wrist and caught hold of her throat. It felt strange to the touch, strong and weak at the same time; he tightened his grip, pulling her closer and closer to him. Her eyes started to flutter helplessly; he felt a surge of sudden power, as if he was draining her strength into his, as she weakened. She couldn't fight him, she couldn't stop him, she was utterly in his power.

It was an intoxicating sensation. He'd never known true power in his life; he'd certainly never known true *freedom*. He could use his uniform to bully civilians - he'd certainly done it - but that wasn't true power. There had always been others who could break him with a single word, while even *civilians* could complain if he was too brutal. But now, there was a girl - perhaps an officer's whore - completely at his mercy. He could do anything he liked to her. There were just too many possibilities...

And then his strength failed him and he fell back to the ground, letting go of her. The girl scrambled backwards, rubbing her throat. There were dark marks on her pale skin, easily visible in the semi-darkness. She let out an odd sound - half-gasping, half-choking - and then jumped to her feet and practically *ran* out of the tent. Hennecke found himself giggling helplessly, despite the throbbing pain - and the grim awareness that he might be in deep shit, if the girl made a report. The officers might just have him killed...

...And the hell of it, he decided as he crawled back to his blanket, was that it might be a relief.

CHAPTER TWENTY-FIVE

Berlin, Germany Prime
5 November 1985

It had been nearly thirty years, Volker recalled, since he'd set foot on the SS Training Centre at Kursk. He'd been part of an opposition force, teaching young SS recruits what they could expect when they put on the black uniforms and went to war. The base had been immense, graduating tens of thousands of stormtroopers every year. Wewelsburg Castle might still be the single most *prestigious* place for a stormtrooper to train, but Kursk might have overtaken it in a few years.

But now Kursk was gone.

Volker had debated endlessly, with himself and others, over the wisdom of using a atomic bomb of his own. And it had been his decision. Destroying Kursk was safer than blasting a whole city - or somewhere that was likely to cause problems for the *Heer* - but there was no way to *know* how Holliston would react. Would he accept the retaliation without demur or would he lash out himself, in response? The would-be *Fuhrer* was becoming dangerously unpredictable.

He didn't want to look at the photographs, but he forced himself to study them anyway. The first set showed the training base he remembered; barracks, training grounds and airfields designed to ensure that the prospective stormtroopers received the widest-possible education before they actually went to war. The second showed what was left, after the nuke had detonated: flattened buildings, ruined training grounds and burning aircraft. Volker had ordered an airburst, in the hopes of limiting fallout, but he knew it would still be a problem for the clean-up crews. But Holliston was not short of slave labourers who could be sent in to do the dirty work...

And we can't get to the blast zone near Warsaw, he thought, grimly. *They're on their own.*

He braced himself, then looked up at Ambassador Turtledove. The American looked older too, somehow, even though his country wasn't *officially* involved in the war. But Volker knew that Karl Holliston had crossed a line when he'd deployed tactical nuclear weapons near Warsaw. If he'd been willing to unleash radioactive hell on his own people, why would he hesitate to fire on the United States? And there was no way to know if he *could* fire on the United States.

"My country would prefer that no more nuclear weapons were used," Turtledove said.

Volker snorted. "My country would prefer the same," he said, sarcastically. "How do you intend to convince *Holliston* not to use more nuclear weapons?"

He didn't blame the Americans for being cautious. If the long-predicted American Civil War - their *second* civil war - had actually taken place, the *Reich* would have been careful too. But the Americans could afford to be dispassionate, to limit what help they offered to minimise their exposure. Volker - and every citizen in the *Reich* - had no such luxury, not with a man like Karl Holliston on the other side. It was fight or surrender. There was no middle ground.

"My analysts believe that Holliston will not risk a general exchange," Turtledove said. He had the indefinable tone of a man who didn't quite believe what he was saying. "They think he'll understand the warning and back off."

"I have never known him to back off," Volker said.

He'd never spoken to Karl Holliston, but he'd studied the man's career. Holliston had been almost *disturbingly* ambitious, even at a young age; he'd served as Himmler's aide for nearly seven years, giving him plenty of time to learn where the skeletons were buried and considerable understanding of the use and abuse of power. He'd been making a long-term power play even before the *Reich* Council had collapsed; now, as self-appointed *Fuhrer*, he had no choice but to keep pressing the offensive. He couldn't afford to have his image called into question.

He nodded at the message that had been passed through Finland. The Finns had been trying hard to remain neutral as the *Reich* tore itself apart, not out of love for the Germans - Volker was sure - but the grim awareness that, if they backed the wrong side, the winner would take a terrible revenge. Holliston hadn't pushed the issue, somewhat to Volker's surprise. The Finns didn't have nuclear weapons or modern aircraft, but they *did* have a formidable army and plenty of shipping they could use to attack Germany Prime.

"He wants us to surrender," he said, tapping the note. "And we will *not* surrender."

"No," Ambassador Turtledove said. "But can you win the war?"

Volker snorted. *Victory* in the Battle of Warsaw - as it was already being called - would have bought him some time, but defeat - and such a catastrophic defeat - had been disastrous. It would take weeks, perhaps months, for the economy to recover…if it ever did. Too many people had fled their homes out of fear of radiation poisoning, not trusting the official government broadcasts that reassured them that they were perfectly safe. And Volker had to admit, privately, that *he* wouldn't have trusted the official broadcasts either. The *Reich* Council had lied so often that its successor was rarely believed.

"Perhaps," he said, finally.

He sighed as he turned to look at the map. There was no silver bullet, no way to win quickly; they *had* to march all the way to Germanica and remove Holliston from power. But he doubted Germany had the capability, any longer, to put together the force necessary to do that, even without nuclear weapons. *With* atomic bombs…Holliston might be quite safe in his fortress. He might even start thinking about pushing westwards again.

If we could be sure of dealing openly with him, he thought, *we might try to come to terms.*

Ambassador Turtledove cleared his throat. "My government is prepared to step up the aid program," he said. "Will that make any difference?"

"I wish I knew," Volker said. He'd been a stormtrooper - and a factory foreman - long enough to know that confessing weakness was a dangerous mistake, but he was too tired to care. "Even if you committed American troops to the war, you'd still have to get them to Germanica."

"The President will not make that move," Ambassador Turtledove told him.

"Of course not," Volker agreed, dryly.

It was what he would have done, he suspected, if the positions were reversed. The risk of a madman like Holliston firing on America was not one to be taken lightly. No one really knew how good the American ABM system actually was or how it would fare in a genuine shooting war. And besides, it would take years for the Americans to build up the logistics they'd need to support troops in Eastern Europe. They *couldn't* have positioned enough stockpiles in Britain to make it happen in a hurry.

He shrugged, as if it was meaningless. "What *can* you do?"

"We can send you more medicine and food supplies," Ambassador Turtledove said. "But there are limits to what we can do. Certain...*factions*... within the voting populace insist on trying to get concessions out of you first."

Volker sighed. Most of the intelligence networks within the United States had been run by the SS, but the Economic Intelligence Service had operated enough agents - overt and covert - for him to have a good idea of the ebb and flow of American politics. The Polish vote shouldn't, logically, have been important, but there *was* an election coming and the President needed to appease them. And the Poles wanted their motherland back, a motherland that few of them had seen, a motherland that no longer existed...

"There's something you should bear in mind," he said, bluntly. "Would you rather deal with us - or *Fuhrer* Holliston?"

"That's not an argument that will appeal back home," Ambassador Turtledove said.

"Then it should," Volker said.

He understood the value of giving one's populace as much freedom as possible. God knew he intended to ensure that the first elections to the *Reichstag* were as free and fair as he could make them. But there was something utterly absurd about allowing a tiny minority of people - most of whom were no longer truly *part* of that minority - to dictate foreign policy. What sort of idiot believed he could run a foreign policy based on wishful thinking? Poland was gone, as completely as the American civilisations that existed before Columbus...it was high time they accepted it and moved on.

And yet they cling to it, he thought. *Do they really think they'll be able to go home one day?*

"We cannot launch a second offensive until late spring at the earliest," he said, bluntly. "By then, our economy might have shattered completely. And if *that* happens, any further operations will be postponed indefinitely. I cannot run a war *and* deal with a starving desperate population, a population who may start to *listen* to Holliston's claims."

"I understand your problems," Ambassador Turtledove said.

"Then I suggest you start considering the implications," Volker said, flatly. "Because I am *not* going to destroy the *Reich* in order to save it."

Ambassador Turtledove looked at him, sharply. "Are you planning to make peace?"

"I don't know," Volker said. "Right now, we *cannot* make peace with Karl Holliston. But if there was an alternative, we would have to take it."

He looked back at the American. "Would Lincoln have fought the civil war to the bitter end if the survivors would wind up envying the dead?"

"I do not know," Ambassador Turtledove said. "But I will do everything in my power to ensure that your government gets the aid and support it needs."

Volker sighed, inwardly, as the American rose and left the office. The Americans *were* trying to help, he had to admit, but it wasn't enough. It *couldn't* be enough. Even sending American troops to reinforce the front lines and spearhead the offensive wouldn't be enough, not when Holliston had nuclear weapons and he was willing to use them. But Holliston couldn't be trusted…

And if he thinks he's lost, he thought, *he might just try to take the entire world down with him.*

———

"Make sure you keep taking your pills," the nurse said. "If you get any symptoms at all, inform me at once."

"Thank you, *Fräulein,*" Herman said.

His unit had been well away from the blasts, but they'd still been in danger. Thankfully, he'd had the wit to order them to take shelter as soon as it began to rain, yet getting back to the front lines had been a nightmare. Luckily, the soldiers at the rear had been ready for them; they'd been quarantined, given a list of symptoms to watch for and then ordered to remain in a tent and wait to see what happened. It hadn't been pleasant - Herman had had to break up a couple of nasty fights - but they seemed to have missed the worst of the danger.

He opened the pill box he'd been given - neatly marked with the stars and stripes - and took one of the pills. They'd been assured that the pills did something to boost their immune systems against radiation, but Herman hadn't understood the explanation. Medicine had never been his forte. He knew how to do some battlefield medicine and that was about it, even during his later career as a police officer. But the doctors and nurses seemed confident when they handed out the pills.

And it keeps us from feeling abandoned, he thought, as he swallowed the pill. The first one he'd taken had tasted foul; now, he just tried to get them down as quickly as possible. *And wondering just what's going to happen to us.*

It wasn't a reassuring thought. He'd seen men throwing up helplessly, others shaking with fever in the middle of a snowstorm. And they'd been closer to the blast…what would happen if the wind changed, blowing the radiation towards them? Or towards Berlin? He wished, suddenly, that he'd asserted himself enough to send his wife westwards. She'd always wanted to go to Paris and she would have been well out of the way of any nuclear cloud. But instead she was still in Berlin.

He shook his head, slowly. Adelinde was the mother of a member of the Provisional Government. She would have been in the bunker - and even if she hadn't been in the bunker, she would have been *taken* to the bunker as soon as the warheads detonated. She'd be amongst the safest people in Berlin, with an escape tunnel she could use to get out of the city if it was turned into radioactive rubble. She would hate being carried out of the city, he knew, but at least she'd be alive.

But what, he asked himself, *are we going to do?*

He shook his head, again. He didn't know. If the offensive had been pushed forward in line with tactical doctrine - and tactical doctrine hadn't changed since he was a paratrooper - the blasts might have wiped out hundreds of panzers and thousands of soldiers. And thousands more would be injured, sick or dying from radiation poisoning. Calling the offensive off had really been nothing more than a formality. Everyone had *known* that it was doomed to failure after the nuclear blasts…

…And now the snows were falling to the east.

He shuddered, bitterly. He'd heard plenty of horror stories about fighting in the ice and snow, legends from the days Germany had invaded Russia and crushed the Communists in a series of savage battles. Could the offensive be resumed before spring? He doubted it. And could the *Reich* hold together long enough to resume the offensive?

Herman cursed under his breath. He might never know.

———

The tent was crammed with the dead or dying.

Field Marshal Gunter Voss gritted his teeth as he took in the horrific sight. The *Heer* had worked hard to care for battlefield wounded, but there were so many injured after the nukes that the system had broken down completely. Dead bodies occupied beds while men, their faces blackened and burnt, lay on the hard earthen floor, struggling desperately to keep breathing. The handful of doctors and nurses - and a number of volunteers from Berlin - were completely overwhelmed, running from bed to bed in hopes of finding someone they could help before it was too late.

He cursed as he heard a man calling for his mother; no, *several* men calling for their mothers, as if they knew - on some level - that they were about to die. It wasn't uncommon, he knew from bitter experience, but he had never grown used to it. Dying men should be allowed to retain some of their dignity, not lose everything in a desperate cry for help that would never come. A young nurse, tears running down her face, tended to a man who couldn't have been more than a year or two older than her, his eyes hidden behind a makeshift cloth wrap. He would have been blinded, perhaps, simply by being unlucky enough to be looking in the wrong direction when one of the weapons detonated. There was nothing anyone could do for him, Gunter knew. Even before the civil war, the blind had quietly been encouraged to go into isolated nursing homes, their ties with their families broken before they were moved to the camps and killed. Now...

I'm sorry, he thought.

It would take weeks, perhaps, to impose order on the chaos, weeks they didn't have. He'd been told that the enemy were in just as bad a state; he hoped - prayed - that that was actually true. His forces were in no condition to resist an offensive, even though they'd hastily re-manned the defences around Berlin and summoned reinforcements from further west. If the enemy *did* manage to mount an attack there would be a bloody slaughter.

He didn't want to spend any time in the tent, but he forced himself to move from bed to bed, saying a few words to each of the wounded men. It was a duty, he'd learned during his training, that senior officers had to assume… but no one, not even in the worst stages of the South African War, had had to visit so many wounded. There hadn't been casualty figures so high since the Second World War, when battles had gone on for days or weeks on end. Now…he didn't even know how many men were dead. The figure kept rising all the time, mocking his dreams of ending the war quickly and cleanly. God alone knew when - or ever - they would be able to resume the offensive.

A nurse gave him a nasty look as he promised a young man he'd get better, knowing it was a lie. Even the best medical treatment in the *Reich* wouldn't be able to repair his body or replace his missing legs. Gunter felt a stab of guilt as he took the hint and walked out of the tent, catching sight of a crying nurse being comforted by an older woman. He didn't really blame her for breaking down. No one had really expected so many casualties in one battle.

And what are we going to do, he asked himself, *when the supplies run out?*

He knew the answer, even though he didn't want to admit it. Supplies had to be reserved for the lightly wounded, the ones most likely to recover. It was logical, but it was cold and harsh and thoroughly unpleasant. And who knew if some of the wounded would have a chance, if they received proper care? But there was no time to give them proper care.

His fingers touched the pistol at his belt. It was tempting, so very tempting…

…But he knew his duty. He couldn't give up, not now. But, in all honesty, he didn't know what else they could do.

CHAPTER TWENTY-SIX

Autobahn #34, Germany East
6 November 1985

"I think we have a problem," Kurt muttered.

Horst nodded in agreement. The snowstorms had stopped for the last two days, much to his relief, but travel was no safer. They'd been warned, several times, that bandit attacks were on the rise; now, a large checkpoint was blocking the road, forcing all vehicles to slow down and wait to be inspected. And, with nearly forty armed stormtroopers within view, it was unlikely that anyone would try to drive straight through the checkpoint.

"Looks that way," he said. There was no way to reverse course, even if it wouldn't have tipped off the stormtroopers that they had *something* to hide. "We'll just have to go through it."

Kurt frowned. "Is this normal here?"

"Sometimes," Horst said.

He scowled. The radio broadcasts hadn't been very informative - the official story had changed several times - but it was clear that civilians were being ordered to stay in their homes and avoid travel. Normally, Germanica would have been obeyed without question; now, with the threat of nuclear war hanging over their heads, it was quite possible that people were voting with their feet and heading east. And anyone caught in a checkpoint would be in deep shit. They'd probably be marched off to the labour camps before anyone could protest.

"We'll just have to hope our papers still pass inspection," he said, as they inched closer to the checkpoint. "There's no way out now."

The stormtroopers were doing more than inspecting papers, he noted; they were searching cars and trucks thoroughly, while keeping a sharp eye on the uneasy passengers. It wasn't *uncommon* for people moving from *Gau* to *Gau* to carry items for the black market - he had a feeling that they weren't the only ones who had something to hide. A pair of young men were marched off under armed guard, their vehicle driven through the checkpoint and dumped on the far side of the barricade. Deserters? Smugglers? Or merely people trying to head east without a permit? There was no way to know.

"They're depressingly professional," Kurt said. "Is that a bad thing?"

"Probably," Horst grunted.

He scowled at the thought. Someone more interested in groping young women than inspecting papers would be useful, but Kurt was right. The stormtroopers ahead of them were clearly professional. He glanced back, silently calculating the odds of making a dramatic escape, but it was still hopeless. Even if they weren't shot trying to escape, the entire country would be roused against them. They'd have to be abandon the car and make their way east on foot, which would be a death sentence when the snow started to fall again.

"Don't do *anything* that might attract their attention," he warned, as the car in front of them moved into the inspection zone. A small family - an old man, two middle-aged women and a trio of young children - clambered out as soon as their vehicle came to a halt. "Let them see us as completely harmless."

He winced helplessly as he watched the family get searched, followed by their car. He'd often praised life in Germany East, yet the downside was right in front of him. Authority was arbitrary all over the *Reich* - and corruption a fact of life - but it was worst in Germany East, where bandit attacks were depressingly regular. Gudrun's protest movement would never have gotten off the ground in Germany East, no matter how difficult it had been to gain traction in Germany Prime. She would have been lucky if she'd *only* been marched east and married to a farmer along the unsettled zone.

"Here we go," he muttered. "Be careful."

The stormtroopers looked alert as he climbed out of the car, but it didn't *look* as though they were suspicious. He passed his papers to the leader without comment, then waited patiently as the car was searched from end to end. There was no danger of them finding anything, he knew; there was nothing there to find, save for their picnic lunch and several flasks of hot coffee. Their uniforms were getting alarmingly rank by now, even though he'd had them washed and dried at one of the settlements.

He felt his heart sink as the leader took their papers into a small building. He'd check the seals and watermarks, of course, but would he call Germanica? The papers were genuine - he'd used the SS's own equipment to produce them - yet there would be no records of their existence in Germanica. How could there be? And now, with Berlin no longer in the business of issuing SS papers…

The stormtroopers still didn't look concerned. Horst kept his expression blank, silently cursing the SS's mania for bureaucratic excess. Paperwork wasn't just duplicated and stored at two separate locations; it was copied and distributed around the *Reich*. One simply could *not* escape paperwork. Their papers, if they had been genuine, would have at least a dozen copies scattered around Germany East. And it was unlikely they'd just allow them to walk through if there was even a *hint* of suspicion.

He tensed, covertly studying the nearest stormtroopers. He was good - he *knew* - he was good - but even Otto Skorzeny would have had problems taking out twelve stormtroopers without being battered into a bloody pulp. And there were other stormtroopers who would come running when they heard the fight. No, they'd walked right into a trap. They'd just have to hope that the jaws weren't about to spring shut.

The leader strode back, his hands dancing in a pattern Horst knew all too well. He tensed as the stormtroopers lifted their weapons, silently praying desperately that Kurt wouldn't do anything stupid. Their papers *hadn't* passed…and they were in deep shit…but they might just be able to talk their way out of it. And if they couldn't…

"There's some confusion over your papers," the leader said. "Germanica is requesting additional details."

"We have strict orders to report to the *Fuhrer* personally," Horst said. He forced his tone to become as unbending as possible, as if *he* was the one holding the guns. "We do not have time to delay."

"We need to take your fingerprints," the leader said. He didn't seem inclined to budge. But then, he'd probably run into hundreds of local bigshots who'd tried to bluster their way through the checkpoints. "Once they're checked against the records, you will be permitted to proceed."

Horst cursed under his breath as the leader indicated that they should walk towards the nearest building. He had no idea what *Kurt's* fingerprints would do, but *his* would set off red flags. It struck him, suddenly, that they'd outsmarted themselves. If they'd been *real Reich* Inspectors, it would have been their duty to report *any* failings to their superiors. The checkpoint guards *had* to give them the full treatment, even though they were badly outranked. They were *definitely* in deep shit.

Or perhaps they were already suspicious, he thought, as the stormtroopers fanned out behind them. *If someone filed a report...*

He glanced at Kurt, desperately trying to think of a plan. But there was nothing. They were outnumbered and outgunned; they'd be shot down before they could get their pistols out of their holsters. Could they try to *bribe* their way out of trouble? He doubted it - even if the guards had been as venal as a French soldier in North Africa, there were just too many of them to bribe. And besides, they didn't have *anything* they could use to bribe the guards...

Kurt looked...*concerned.* Horst cursed mentally, again. Kurt was a good man, but he didn't have any real experience in practiced deception - certainly nothing more than the average German citizen. He might break at any moment, getting them both killed...

The stormtroopers grabbed them as soon as they passed through the door. Horst kicked out automatically, but it was too late. His hands were yanked firmly behind his back and held in place while the guards removed his pistol, his dagger and anything else that could be used as a weapon. Beside him, Kurt was getting the same treatment. Horst gritted his teeth as he felt cold metal cuffs being snapped around his wrists and ankles, rendering him helpless. They were trapped.

We should have avoided the autobahns, he thought, numbly. *But that would have led to questions we couldn't answer.*

"On your feet," the leader snarled. "Now!"

Horst tried, but standing upright while cuffed and shackled was impossible. The guards hauled him to his feet and slammed him against the stone fall, their hands poking and prodding at his clothes to ensure that he wasn't hiding anything. Kurt tried to kick the guards as they lifted him up, which earned him a punch in the belly that left him choking as they pushed him up, next to Horst.

The leader glared at Horst, then at Kurt. "Who are you?"

"Inspectors Johann Peltzer and Fritz Hanstein," Horst said. Could they still bluff their way through? It didn't seem likely, but he had to try. "This…"

"We checked the numbers on your papers against the records in Germanica," the leader snapped, angrily. "They don't exist. So why do *you* exist?"

"We report directly to the *Fuhrer*," Horst bluffed. "Our records are sealed."

"There would be a number," the leader said, dryly. "Even if it was attached to a classified file, there would be a number."

He nodded to one of his men, who stepped forward and slammed a haymaker into Horst's jaw. Horst moved backwards automatically, but it was too late. The blow cracked his head against the stone wall. Beside him, Kurt took another punch to the chest, leaving him retching helplessly. Absolute despair threatened to overcome him as the guards picked up their batons, clearly preparing to hand out a savage beating. They'd failed. There was no hope of reaching Germanica now, certainly not as prisoners. And if they'd found his *real* records, they'd be very careful not to give him even the *slightest* chance to escape.

"You have no records," the leader mused. "And yet, your paperwork is nearly perfect."

His voice hardened. "You're from the rebels."

Horst said nothing. His training had taught him not to tell his captors anything, even when it was clear that his captors already knew. Weakening once - even slightly - could open a crack in his armour, a crack that could eventually be used to break his resistance completely. But he knew, deep inside, that he had lost. They'd be taken to Germanica and executed, no matter what they said or did. Holliston would certainly want to make sure that Horst, a man who had betrayed the SS, would be brutally punished. The only consolation was that it probably wouldn't be public.

The guards closed in, bringing their batons down time and time again. Horst fought to keep from screaming, silently grateful that his training had taught him how to take punches and handle pain. Indeed, the beating wasn't anything like as bad as some of the hammerings he'd taken during unarmed combat training. The guards were trained in inflicting pain, but they shied away from anything that might cause permanent damage. And yet…

"You'll be shipped to Germanica," the leader said. His voice sounded as though it was coming from a very far distance. "They'll decide your fate there."

Horst bit down a curse as he was hauled to his feet - he hadn't even realised he'd fallen to the ground - and half-carried out of the building. It was hard, so hard, to think clearly, but he had no choice. The guards pushed them into another building - a small prison - and chained them to the wall, then strode off, slamming the iron door behind them. Horst wasn't fool enough to assume that they were unwatched. There would be cameras hidden somewhere in the chamber.

He glanced at Kurt. There was a nasty scar on his face and blood was dripping from his nose, but most of the damage looked superficial. He hadn't broken either. Horst had always been taught that the SS's training was far more intensive than anyone else's - but Kurt had handled himself well. And yet, they were still prisoners. He tested the cuffs carefully, hoping - desperately - that their captors had made a mistake. But he found nothing.

Of course not, he thought, angrily. *The one thing they're good at is taking prisoners.*

He met Kurt's eyes, silently willing him to stay quiet. There would be microphones in the cell as well as cameras. Kurt looked worried, but said nothing. Horst was silently relieved, even though he doubted they could get in worse trouble. They'd already been pegged as infiltrators from Germany Prime. He supposed they should be grateful that they hadn't simply been marched outside and shot.

But they'll want to know who we are and what we want, he told himself. *We might wind up wishing that we'd been shot out of hand.*

He sighed, looking down at the stone floor. They'd failed. There was no way they could find Gudrun now, let alone try *something* in Germanica. All of his plans had come to naught…he knew, as he tasted utter despair, that he would never see Gudrun again, that she'd be broken by the SS and then, eventually, executed. And with nuclear weapons being used, it was possible that her dreams of a better world would also come to nothing.

Would it have been different, he asked himself, *if I'd done my duty?*

It was a bitter thought. He'd known, right from the start, that he was risking a truly awful death by siding with Gudrun and her group. He could have betrayed them, easily; Gudrun and the girls would have been exiled east, the boys would have been shipped to labour camps and worked to death. And he would have been feted as a hero, the brave little SS operator who'd revealed a plot against the entire *Reich*.

But he had never been able to hide from himself. Gudrun had been right. The SS *had* cruelly betrayed its own people. Horst had no doubt, now or ever, that if Konrad and he had swapped places, it would have been *him* who would have been crippled for life, if he'd survived at all. And it would have been *his* uncle who'd been lied to by the SS…

And besides, he thought. *I would never have known Gudrun.*

He couldn't have turned away, he told himself. He'd accepted the risks when, in truth, they were far greater. He wouldn't have been caught - now - if he hadn't driven into Germany East with forged papers. And he was damned if he was giving up now, even though it looked hopeless. Who knew what the future would bring?

It felt like hours before the guards returned, released them from the chains and unceremoniously marched them out of the cell. Darkness was falling over the autobahn, but there was still a long line of vehicles waiting to pass through the checkpoint. Horst wondered, absently, just how many delays the checkpoint had caused, although he knew they were unlikely to be fatal. The guards said nothing as they were pushed towards a large truck and carried up into the rear. Inside, it was decked out to carry prisoners.

"Remain silent," the guard ordered, as they were cuffed to the railings. "And enjoy the ride."

Horst glared at him. He'd ridden in prisoner transports before, although as a guard rather than a passenger. They seemed *designed* to give their riders as uncomfortable a journey as possible. He still shuddered at the memory of supervising a trio of slave girls as they washed out the transport after a bunch of prisoners were transported to the mines. The vehicle had been *littered* with vomit and piss. He took a breath and regretted it instantly. Their vehicle was surprisingly clean, but the smell still lingered.

The door slammed closed. Moments later, the engine started. Horst caught a sniff of the engine fumes and felt sick. He'd seen transports that had begun the journey with live prisoners and ended with a bunch of twitching corpses. He didn't *think* anyone wanted to kill them immediately - they could have been shot or had their throats cut if someone thought it was necessary - but accidents happened. It was unlikely that anyone would give much of a damn if they expired on the way to Germanica.

They'll want to interrogate us, he told himself. *Surely.*

He shuddered as the vehicle lurched violently, then started to move. The smell grew worse, but the air still seemed breathable. Even so...He'd calculated that it would take at least four more days to reach Germanica in a car, assuming everything went as planned; logically, it would take at least a week for the truck to reach the city. The thought of spending so long in the cramped confines was appalling. But he doubted they had a choice.

"Try to get some sleep," he advised. Kurt was bearing up well, but he would have to be watched. His basic training was nowhere near intense enough to prepare him for what was coming. "We don't know what will happen when we get there."

Kurt nodded, soberly.

Horst shook his head, rattling his chains mournfully. He *did* have a good idea what awaited them. If he'd been able to commit suicide, he might have considered it. There was nothing he could *tell* the SS, certainly nothing useful, but he doubted they would believe it. They'd assume he had a head full of secrets they could force him to spill.

And when they finish trying to get secrets out of us, he thought soberly, *we'll be killed.*

And, try as he might, he couldn't think of a way to escape.

CHAPTER TWENTY-SEVEN

Germanica, Germany East
7 November 1985

Gudrun honestly wasn't sure if she should be relieved or worried.

Doctor Muller had beaten her - and come very close to raping her - only to be stopped by Katherine, who had apparently taken over responsibility for Gudrun's safety. Gudrun was grateful beyond words to the older woman, yet she was also all too aware that the whole scene might have been staged to *make* her grateful to Katherine. The possibility of being raped had lingered over her ever since she'd been captured, yet it hadn't happened...

She rubbed her aching jaw as she sat on the bed, cursing under her breath. It had been easier when she'd *known* everyone was against her, even though it had also meant she didn't have a hope in hell of escaping. But if Katherine genuinely *was* on her side, what did it mean? Did she want Gudrun to escape...or did she merely want Gudrun to be broken properly? And if she asked, would she be putting Katherine's life in danger?

Of course, she thought, looking up at the cameras. *Everything I say in here is probably recorded and studied.*

It wasn't a pleasant thought. Part of her was tempted to start singing - very few people had told her she was a good singer - just to force her unseen watchers to listen to her; part of her felt that singing would be a risk, even with Katherine watching over her. The beating had left her shaking for hours afterwards. Who knew what would happen if Doctor Muller - or someone else - decided to have another go? She was grimly determined to keep from breaking as long as possible, but she was terrifyingly aware that she had come far too close to snapping...

…And she wasn't sure how long she could continue to hold out.

She gazed around the cell, finally understanding why her father had insisted that his prisoners preferred to go to the work camps rather than go to jail. There was something to *do* in the work camps, even if the stories she'd heard ranged from horrible to truly horrific. Here, all she could do was sit on the bed and wait to be tortured - or worse. There was simply nothing else to do. And, for someone who had always enjoyed doing *something*, it was agony.

Boredom is a worse threat than anything else, she thought, crossly. It was frustrating as hell just to sit in the cell, even though she *knew* it could be worse. *By the time they come for me, I'll have driven myself mad.*

She shook her head as she rose to her feet, pushing her aching body through a series of exercises she'd been taught in the BDM. Her matrons would probably have laughed at her, but it kept her body healthy and her mind off dwelling on what could happen to her. And yet, her body was no longer hers. Part of her had accepted, she realised, that she was naked, that she would always be naked…and the fact she wasn't horrified about that worried her more than she cared to admit. Slowly - but surely - she was breaking.

And there's nothing I can do about it, she thought, sourly.

She ground her teeth in frustration as she finished the exercises. What did Holliston *want* with her? Did he seriously imagine she could convince the Provisional Government to surrender? She hadn't really been in control of events from the moment everything had started to move - and a good thing too or her arrest might have blown the whole movement out of the water. He had nothing to gain by keeping her prisoner, save satisfaction. And even that had to have its limits.

The door rattled. Gudrun straightened up as it opened, allowing Katherine to step into the room. She was carrying a pair of handcuffs, suggesting that Gudrun was going to get a chance to walk out of the cell. Gudrun sighed inwardly as Katherine motioned for her to turn around, but submitted quietly. Oddly, the simple fact that she was *always* handcuffed or chained when she was out of the cell gave her heart. It suggested her captors were surprisingly nervous about her.

She met Katherine's eyes as the older woman opened the inner door. "Where are we going?"

"The *Fuhrer* wants to see you," Katherine said. Unlike some of the other guards, she didn't bother to search Gudrun's body before helping her out of the cell. "I suggest that you put on your best behaviour."

Gudrun frowned. Katherine sounded normal, but there was a...*hint*... in her tone that she was preoccupied with an infinitely greater thought. She was tempted to pry as she was marched down the corridors and through a series of security checkpoints, yet she didn't dare risk the uneasy rapport she'd developed with the older woman. Instead, she concentrated on memorising the layout of the Germanica *Reichstag* as much as possible. It was surprisingly deserted, even on the upper levels. The handful of men she saw - no women - barely glanced at her before scurrying away.

Something's gone wrong, she thought, worried. *But what?*

A nasty thought occurred to her and she froze. If Holliston had used nuclear weapons - and Doctor Muller had practically admitted as much, during the beating - the Provisional Government might have retaliated. No, it *would* have retaliated. She knew little about nuclear weapons, but she *did* know that *not* retaliating would merely have encouraged the first user to do it again. There would have been retaliation...

...But against what?

Germanica is still standing, she thought, although it occurred to her that that might not be true. The engineers in Berlin had bragged that their bunkers could survive direct nuclear hits and ride out nuclear wars. She couldn't imagine the SS accepting anything lesser for Germanica, a city that was practically a second capital. Might the city have been nuked? She found it hard to imagine that she wouldn't have felt *something*...but it was impossible to be sure. *I might be trapped under a nuclear wasteland.*

It was a relief, two minutes later, to step out of the elevator into an antechamber. A giant window dominated the near wall, allowing her to peer out over Germanica. She couldn't help thinking that it looked like Berlin, only bigger, but it was definitely intact. The city hadn't been blasted to rubble by a nuclear weapon.

Two guards poked and prodded at her for a long moment before allowing her to enter Holliston's office. She tensed, half-expecting to be on public display again, but the giant room was empty, save for Holliston himself. The would-be *Fuhrer* was sitting behind a desk large enough to pass for a dining table, larger than the one she remembered from her last headmaster's office. He'd had an immense ego too.

"Gudrun," Holliston said. He sounded surprisingly normal. "Please. Come forward."

Gudrun felt her skin crawl as Katherine walked her forward until she was standing in front of the desk. There was something about the way he was looking at her that creeped her out, even though it didn't seem overtly sexual. She wasn't a pretty girl to him, she realised; she wasn't even an attractive piece of meat. To him, she was something he could *use*; no more, no less. It was a chilling thought.

Holliston smiled at her. "Have you no words of greeting?"

"*Guten Morgen, Herr* Holliston," Gudrun said. She was damned if she was calling him '*Mein Fuhrer*'. He was certainly not *her Fuhrer*. "How are you?"

His expression darkened. "You will address me as *Mein Fuhrer*."

Gudrun hesitated. If she refused...what would he do? But she already knew the answer. A beating, perhaps, or worse. She was in no state to defend herself. She'd loathed her last headmaster - she didn't know anyone who'd *liked* the brute - but she'd known better than to deny him the respect he'd thought he was due.

"As you wish, *Mein Fuhrer*," she said.

Holliston seemed amused by her submission. "I believe that fool Muller told you that nuclear weapons have been deployed?"

"Yes, *Mein Fuhrer*," Gudrun said. It felt odd to call *anyone* by that title. She'd never actually *met* the previous *Fuhrer*, even after he'd lost his position and been exiled to the countryside. He'd been a figurehead, nothing more. No one had thought him worth the bother of executing. "He was very definite about it."

"A third has now been used," Holliston said. "A minor training base at Kursk was destroyed."

Gudrun didn't believe him, not completely. Why would anyone drop a nuclear warhead on a minor training base? If the nuclear budget had been a major drain on the *Reich's* economy - and she knew it had been - why would an expensive weapon be wasted on a minor target? It made no sense. Logically, Kursk had to have been a far *bigger* target - and Holliston was trying to minimise the impact. But she found it hard to care.

"If you used nuclear weapons, *Mein Fuhrer,*" she said, "the Provisional Government would certainly retaliate in kind."

"Quite," Holliston said. "This war will destroy both sides."

He cocked his head. "What were you *thinking* when you took up arms against the *Reich?*"

Gudrun stared back at him, evenly. "I was thinking that the *Reich* had betrayed its soldiers," she said, flatly. "I *told* you that…*Mein Fuhrer.*"

Holliston ignored the implicit disrespect. "A young girl like you should be married and bringing up children by now," he said. "What was your father thinking when he allowed you to go to the university?"

"I believe he was thinking I should follow my dreams and actually put my intelligence to some use," Gudrun said. "I wanted to be more than just a housewife."

"You appear to have succeeded," Holliston said. He smirked, rather unpleasantly. "What would Konrad Schulze have thought of it?"

Gudrun flinched, then told herself not to be stupid. She'd mentioned Konrad's name a *lot*, after the *Reich* Council had been broken. The SS wouldn't have had any difficulty tracking him down, even if his father *hadn't* become the Provisional Government's leader. Hell, they'd probably made the connection between Konrad and herself a long time before they'd realised that she'd *started* the protest movement.

"Yes," Holliston said. "What *would* he have thought of it?"

"I think he would have approved, *Mein Fuhrer,*" Gudrun said.

She shrugged. In truth, she had *no* idea what Konrad would have thought of it. He'd been an SS stormtrooper, a loyalist…would he have joined her, like Horst, or would he have reported her to his superiors? Or would he have married her and then insisted on her remaining in the home, rather than getting involved with politics? He would probably have told himself that he was doing the right thing, keeping her from doing something that could get her killed…

"His file suggests otherwise," Holliston said. "He was marked down for early promotion."

Gudrun felt her temper flare. "Before or after he was wounded?"

"He would have been one of the youngest officers in the service," Holliston said. "I think he would have gone on to great things."

"You betrayed him," Gudrun said. Her temper snapped. "You didn't even let his family know he was injured."

She fought back tears of rage and bitter helplessness as her voice rose. "And what does it matter now? He'd dead! I can't change what I did, even if I wanted to! And you can't change it either!"

Holliston rose. "Do you not regret what you did?"

Gudrun sensed - vaguely - that she had crossed a line, but she found it hard to care. "I hated it," she said. "I hated growing up, knowing I had to watch my words all the time. I hated being scared of unexpected knocks on the door. I hated going to school, knowing that asking the wrong question would earn me a beating - or worse. I hated being told that I would bear the next generation of children while the boys had all the fun..."

She shook her head slowly, feeling her hair brushing against her bare shoulders. "This is no way to live," she added. She knew he wouldn't understand. "Your *Reich* is nothing more than a prison camp and a mass grave."

"We did what was necessary," Holliston said, stiffly. "*You* are the one who betrayed the *Reich*."

He reached out and poked her in the chest, sharply. "You, a young girl of the highest of bloodlines, had a duty to the *Reich*," he snapped. "And instead you forsook that duty and tore the *Reich* down."

Gudrun stared back at him, defiantly. "The *Reich* does not deserve to live!"

Holliston slapped her, hard. She stumbled backwards and fell, landing on her bottom. He loomed over her, fists clenched; she braced herself, expecting it to end. Katherine wouldn't save her from the *Fuhrer*. Just for a second, it dawned on her that she'd finally managed to get Holliston to see her as a *person*. And then it struck her that that was no longer a good thing.

"You have no idea what it was like," he hissed. "You...you *child*...you imprudent *brat*...you have no idea what it was like, back before the *Reich*. You..."

He made a visible attempt to calm himself down. "There were entire families starving because the French and the British had blockaded Germany," he said. "Jewish-Communist subversives were worming their way into everything. The bankers were steadily bringing us under their control, weakening the *Volk*...we would have been crushed, eternally enslaved to the Jewish filth, if the *Fuhrer* had not taken control. And you, you...you stand here and dare to tell me the *Reich* does not deserve to exist?"

"You murdered countless millions of innocent people," Gudrun said. Uncle Frank had drunk, heavily, to forget what he'd done. As horrible as the old man had been, she thanked him now for showing her what lay behind the facade. "And you crushed hundreds of countries..."

"They would have destroyed us," Holliston said. "They were the masters of the world..."

Gudrun met his eyes. "And if they were the masters of the world," she said, "how come they were *always* the first to get the blame when everything went wrong?"

Holliston lifted his fist, then stopped himself. "The world is not *genteel*," he told her, sharply. "It is red, red in tooth and claw, full of enemies who will drag you down and kill you if they scent weakness. We did what was necessary to establish the *Reich*, to prove that we were the strong, that we *deserved* to rule. And the weak have no choice, but to bow their heads."

He reached down, caught hold of her hair and hauled her to her feet, then thrust her forward until she was bent over the table. "You are weak," he snarled. He slapped her bare buttocks, hard. "I can take you right now and *no one* will stop me. Do you understand me? I can do anything to you, because I am strong and you are weak! The only thing that keeps you from being raped is my decision not to rape you!"

Gudrun grunted in pain. "How brave," she managed. Perhaps he'd kill her for it, perhaps not. "Deciding *not* to rape a handcuffed and naked girl."

Holliston thumped her back, hard. "Your safety was bought at a cost," he snapped, as she gasped for breath. "The *Reich* protected you from the true nature of the world and all it asked, in return, was your loyalty. And you didn't even bother to do *that*.

"I sent men like your boyfriend south to uphold civilisation," he added, his fingers clawing at her flesh. "And you betray their sacrifice by turning on the *Reich*. His service served the *Reich*; you betrayed it. How *could* you?"

He let go of her, turning to stalk around the room. "I should never have agreed to let Krueger establish the university," he snapped. He sounded as though he was talking to himself. "And it was a mistake to let women enter as students. Women...

"Krueger, the rat bastard, claimed we needed to make better use of female labour," he added, darkly. "But what better use is there than turning out the next generation of Germans?"

"A woman doesn't have to be nothing more than a mother," Gudrun said. "She could be a mother and something else..."

"Be silent," Holliston snarled.

"You know nothing. You have been safe for so long that you are not even aware of the depths of your own ignorance. The nightmare you have unleashed on the *Volk* will consume hundreds of millions of lives...just because you were *feeling* instead of *thinking*. Your boyfriend's death was necessary..."

"You lied," Gudrun said. "He was crippled, yet you lied to his family."

Holliston ignored her. "The Provisional Government is doomed," he said. "Too many problems, too many people with their own agendas...they're doomed. *We* are strong, *we* are united, we will triumph."

He turned to face her, his eyes shining with an unholy glee. "I shall return to Berlin and take control, once again," he said. "By the time I arrive, the battered population will greet me as a saviour. But you...you will never see it."

Gudrun closed her eyes. This was it.

"You'll be sent east," Holliston said. "There are settlements there in *desperate* need of young women, desperate enough to overlook a few...*irregularities* in their pasts. I'm sure you'll fit in *quite* nicely."

He laughed. "And if you cause trouble," he added, "I'm sure they won't hesitate to hobble you. Or something."

Gudrun felt her heart sink. "But..."

"But nothing," Holliston said. "I'm sure this punishment will be worse than being executed."

And the hell of it, Gudrun realised as a silent Katherine marched her back to her cell, was that he was right.

CHAPTER TWENTY-EIGHT

Near Germanica, Germany East
9 November 1985

Horst started awake when he heard the truck grind to a halt.

It hadn't been a pleasant trip. He'd hoped, despite himself, that their captors might have been concerned that they'd made a mistake, but the hope had faded as their treatment worsened over two days of captivity. They'd been half-starved, washed by hoses and generally kicked or beaten for even the most minor - or imagined - offences. It wasn't quite as bad as the dreaded SS counter-interrogation course - Horst had privately resolved to thank his instructors if he ever saw them again - but it was definitely taking a toll. They might be too weak to escape when the time came.

If it ever does, he thought, as he heard voices shouting outside. *We're still chained up all the time.*

He stretched, as best as he could. His wrists and ankles hurt badly, reminding him that being cuffed up for several days might inflict permanent damage. One of his aunties had made a habit of chaining her Slavic maid up overnight, as if she were a dog who couldn't be trusted while her masters slept; the poor girl had wound up with permanent bruises on her neck and a broken voice. He couldn't recall what had happened to her, but he doubted it had been anything good. There was no such thing as a happy retirement for a slave girl in Germany East.

The voices outside were getting louder. It sounded as though one of them was demanding that the driver open the rear compartment, while the driver was trying hard to argue that the compartment should be left unopened. Horst didn't blame him. Two days - perhaps more - had left the compartment smelly as hell. But if they'd run into another checkpoint…he smiled, rather dryly at the thought, then tensed as he heard gunshots. Someone was *shooting* out there.

Kurt looked up. "What?"

Horst shrugged. They were chained to the rails. There was nothing they could do, but wait and see what happened. He heard a final gunshot, then someone rattling at the rear door and trying to get it open. Kurt started to say something, but stopped as the door crashed open, revealing two men in green uniforms. Horst stared in disbelief. Local *Volkssturm*?

"Get them out," a voice barked. "Hurry!"

The men hurried forward, found the keys to release Horst and Kurt from the railings and then carried them out of the truck. It was cold outside, bitterly cold; Horst stared up at the grey sky, knowing that another snowstorm was on the way. Their new captors marched them towards an unmarked van; he glanced back, just in time to see the bodies of their previous set of captors hurled into the truck. And then a grenade was tossed into the vehicle, which went up in a colossal fireball.

They'll think we died in the fire, Horst thought, as they were shoved into the van. *But is that actually a good thing?*

He shrugged. The van was clearly not designed to take prisoners. They were parked against the wall and told to stay still, rather than cuffed to railings or anything else that might have left them completely immobile. Horst exchanged a glance with Kurt, then shrugged. He had no idea who'd grabbed them - or why - but it had to be better than being shipped all the way to Germanica. He forced himself to relax as the van lurched to life. They'd find out where they were going soon enough.

He'd always had a good sense of time and direction, but he found himself losing track of both as the vehicle turned time and time again, seemingly at random. The driver was clearly worried about pursuit, unsurprisingly. Whoever they were, whoever had issued the orders, they'd just attacked an SS convoy and recovered two prisoners. Karl Holliston was unlikely to be in a forgiving mood when he found out.

They can't be bandits, he thought. *Bandits would have killed us with the others.*

The vehicle came to a halt, hours later. Horst allowed himself a moment of relief as the doors opened, revealing that they'd parked in an underground garage. A pair of guards searched them gently, then pointed them through an armoured door. Inside, there was a small welcoming room…and a man, standing at the far end, waiting for them.

"Horst," he said. His voice was rather amused. "I was *most* offended when you failed to invite me to your wedding."

Horst stared. "Uncle Emil?"

"Ah, so you *do* remember me," his uncle said. "I was starting to think I'd been forgotten."

"Never," Horst said. Uncle Emil - *Gauleiter* Emil Forster - *had* been on the list of people he'd intended to contact, but he'd intended to do it on his own terms. A *Gauleiter*, even the one who had practically raised him after his father died, would always have his own agenda. "I would have contacted you once we arrived at Germanica."

Kurt coughed. "Horst…who is this person?"

"This is my uncle, *Gauleiter* Forster," Horst said. He rattled his cuffs. "Are we still prisoners, uncle?"

"No," Forster said. He wrinkled his nose. "I'll have the men free you, then you can have a shower and change into something clean. And then we can talk."

Forster was as good as his word. Horst had always *liked* being clean, yet after spending two days in the truck it felt utterly marvellous to just stand underneath the spigot and allow the water to flow down his body. Their uniforms had been taken away - probably for burning - but his uncle's staff had provided replacements, albeit one without rank badges or any other sort of markings. And, most importantly of all, they'd been offered pistols and ammunition, a sign they were genuinely trusted. Horst checked the weapon and bullets, just in case, but found nothing wrong. His uncle was making a very definite statement.

"He's a *Gauleiter*," Kurt whispered, carefully leaving the shower on to make it harder for anyone to spy on them. "Can he be trusted?"

"He's sane," Horst said. "But he has his own agenda."

He took a deep breath as they were shown directly into his uncle's study, remembering the times he'd been marched into the study to explain himself. His uncle had been strict, but fair; he'd never hated Horst - or any of the other children - purely for being children. And while he never relaxed enough to play with them, he'd never been distant from them either.

221

"Please, take a seat," Forster said. "I'll have some food sent in for the three of us."

Kurt sat, gingerly. "How did you find us?"

"I had a theory that the Berlin government would send *someone* into Germany East," Forster said, after a moment. "When your papers - perfect and yet unrecorded - appeared, I *knew* I was looking at potential allies. And so I arranged for your transport to be ambushed."

"You took a hell of a risk," Horst said. He rubbed his wrists meditatively. "What if you'd been wrong?"

"I could have covered myself," Forster assured him. "It being *you* was a stroke of luck, of course. I *had* hoped you'd make contact, but…"

"Contacting you would be a gamble," Horst said. He felt the question welling up inside him, even though asking would reveal a potential weakness. "Where is my wife?"

"Alive, for the moment," Forster said. He smiled, lightly. "Although I *should* question the legality of a marriage that took place without your guardian's consent."

Horst barely heard him. Gudrun was *alive*! He'd hoped - desperately - that Holliston would keep her alive, but he'd feared that she might simply have been shot out of hand. Gudrun was useless to him. It was possible, all too possible, that Holliston would simply have ordered her death. And he'd vowed that, if his wife was killed, he would make damn certain that Holliston died too.

And if it cost me my life, he thought, *I would be reunited with her at the end.*

"We are married," he said, finally. "You can't separate us."

"I wouldn't dare to try," his uncle said. He sounded amused. "She is a very formidable young lady."

Kurt blinked. "You've *met* her?"

"We'll discuss that later," Forster said. "There are other matters to discuss."

"True," Horst agreed. He leaned forward. "Are you switching sides, uncle?"

Forster looked pained. "Direct as ever, my boy?"

"Yes," Horst said.

The door opened before Forster could answer, revealing three maids carrying trays of food and steaming mugs of hot coffee. Horst and Kurt tucked in gratefully; Forster, seated behind his desk, nibbled at his platter. Horst would have liked to concentrate on the food, but he knew - deep inside - that they didn't have time. He needed to know what was going on.

"Uncle," he said, once the first hunger pangs had been quelled. "Are you switching sides?"

Forster looked back at him, evenly. "There are...*some*...of us who believe that prolonging this war will only result in mutual destruction."

"They are correct," Horst said. "If nukes are being used..."

"Three nukes," Forster said. "The training base at Kursk - I believe you know it - was destroyed a few days ago."

Horst and Kurt exchanged glances. They'd heard nothing about it, neither on the radio nor at any of the settlements they'd passed through. The radio had chattered endlessly about how horrible the rebels were to use nuclear weapons, but it had seemed focused on the explosions near Warsaw. A *third* nuclear detonation?

"To be precise, Holliston deployed two nuclear weapons near Warsaw," Forster clarified, carefully. "Your government retaliated by destroying the training centre with a nuclear warhead."

"I see," Horst said. "And you plan to switch sides?"

"Let's just say that...*we*...would like a negotiated solution," Forster said. "We cannot bring you to heel and you cannot bring *us* to heel. Further conflict will merely weaken the *Reich* to the point that whoever wins will actually lose. We believe that a parting of the ways may be the best possible solution to the problem."

Kurt snorted. "And Holliston?"

"Is insane," Forster said. "He needs to be removed."

"Good," Horst said.

Forster held up a hand. "Is your government prepared to talk?"

Horst hesitated. "We do have some authority to make promises," he said. "But it would depend on what you were prepared to offer."

"And it would be contingent on Berlin's approval," Kurt added.

"I do understand," Forster assured him. "And seeing that I'm not a diplomat either, I shall be blunt."

He cleared his throat. "Germany East formally separates from Germany Prime," he said, firmly. "There is a formal amnesty for anyone within Germany Prime - or the *Reich* as a whole - who served the *Reich* Council in any role.

Anyone you find unbearable - or merely wants to stay with the *Reich* - gets to emigrate to Germany East, no questions asked. The same goes for the other parts of the *Reich*."

Horst lifted an eyebrow. "You don't want to keep control of Germany Arabia? Or Germany South?"

"I suspect the former will stay with you," his uncle said. "And the latter is too far away to be ruled effectively."

"Yeah," Horst agreed. "Plenty of people living there with impure pedigrees."

His uncle ignored the remark. "You will not interfere in the internal affairs of Germany East; we will not interfere in the affairs of Germany Prime. You can reshape the west to suit yourselves - who knows? You might come up with a new way to live."

"It would be more accurate to say that *your* way of life is killing us," Kurt said, stiffly.

"Your sister said much the same," Forster said. "Although she did *seem* to put her former boyfriend on a pedestal."

Horst felt his cheeks heat. "She was engaged to him for months, uncle," he said. "Even after she *knew* they would never be together, it still hurt her to leave."

His uncle lifted his eyebrows. "And that doesn't bother you?"

"I grew up here, *Uncle*," Horst said, sharply. "Women remarrying - or several women marrying the same man - is not uncommon here. I choose not to worry about it."

"Nor should you," Forster said. "Do you find our terms acceptable?"

"We would want to put the nukes under tight control," Horst said. He doubted his uncle would agree to simply *surrender* the weapons. If nothing else, their mere presence would keep Berlin from resuming the war at a later date. "Can that be done?"

His uncle frowned. "Holliston is the only person who has access to the launch codes," he said. "Whatever we do will have to make sure he doesn't have a chance to send a command to the launchers."

Horst nodded. Whatever the state of the ICBMs, the SS would have no trouble shooting tactical nuclear warheads from long-range guns. The entire front line could be bathed in nuclear fire. Hell, smuggling nukes west into Berlin - and the other cities - would be relatively straightforward. If Holliston decided he wanted to take everyone else down with him, he had the tools at his disposal. Keeping the warheads from being detonated would be the first priority, superseding everything else.

Really? A voice asked, at the back of his mind. *Even Gudrun's life?*

He pushed the voice out of his head. "I believe the Provisional Government would accept your terms," he said, carefully. "If you can send them a message, I can give you the codes you need to have it accepted."

"Of course," his uncle said. "Do you have a plan?"

"Not yet," Horst said. He considered the possibilities for a long moment. "I assume you don't have any control over the forces in Germanica?"

His uncle nodded. "They're controlled directly from the *Reichstag*," he said. "I don't have any influence over them at all. A few of the officers are my clients, but I'm not sure which way they'd jump."

Horst nodded. *He'd* jumped too.

But it would definitely make life tricky. Getting *into* Germanica had never been easy, even before the war. The city was encircled by a protective wall, the gates heavily-guarded; everything moving in and out of the city was carefully inspected before it was allowed to proceed. Getting an entire army into the city would be impossible. He might be able to get a small strike team into the city, particularly if they had the right paperwork, but they'd be surrounded by thousands of stormtroopers.

And Holliston will run into his bunker and hide if the shit hits the fan, he thought. *He doesn't have the stomach to come out and fight.*

It was the bunker that would pose the *real* problem, he knew. If it was anything like the bunker in Berlin, there would be an escape tunnel - perhaps more than one - and a direct link to a high-power radio transmitter. Taking out that transmitter might be the only way to keep the missiles from flying, but where *was* it? And where was *Gudrun*?

He looked up at his uncle. "Where is my wife?"

"Under the *Reichstag*," his uncle said. "I believe Holliston intends to ship her east."

Horst shuddered. Beside him, Kurt swore.

"No," he said, simply. "That will not happen."

"It will, unless you can stop him," Forster said. "How do you plan to proceed?"

Horst sighed. "What sort of forces do you have under your direct command?"

"Very few," Forster admitted. "Just two battalions of *Volkssturm*. The remainder were folded into the *Waffen-SS* and sent to the front."

"I see," Horst said. Holliston hadn't made a bad call. The *Volkssturm* were often more attached to their communities - and to their *Gauleiters* - than they were to the *Reich*. And in Germany East, the *Volkssturm* were often quite well armed. "We'll need reinforcements, then."

"It looks that way," his uncle said. "It might be possible to subvert a few of his officers."

Horst frowned. The more people involved, the greater the chance of a leak - and certain failure. He'd been forced to study two operations during his training that had both failed because the target had been warned, in advance, that the operation was underway. And if it happened here, in Germanica, the consequences were likely to be a great deal worse.

"I'd prefer to avoid it, if possible," he said, biting his lip. "Uncle, this is going to take far too long."

"You don't *have* very long," Forster said. "Holliston is already insane. What's he going to do next?"

He sighed. "I'll sweeten the pill," he added. "I know the name of the spy on the Provisional Government."

Horst straightened. "You are *sure?*"

"I believe so," Forster said. "It was not easy to track him down, but I have a contact in the *Reichstag* records department. I don't believe it was a coincidence, given how much power the SS was accumulating before your wife came along. And *someone* definitely warned Holliston that your people were planning an invasion."

"Shit," Kurt said. "Who is he?"

"Admiral Wilhelm Riess, head of the *Abwehr*," Forster said, simply.

"Impossible," Kurt said.

Horst frowned. He barely knew Riess - he certainly hadn't met the man socially - but the *Abwehr* had been losing ground to the SS for years. It was possible, quite possible, that he'd been working for Holliston a *long* time before the civil war. And, by openly declaring for the Provisional Government, he'd put himself in place to gather all sorts of intelligence for his true master. No *wonder* the offensive had failed so badly.

He took a breath. "Very well," he said. "We'll get in touch with Berlin. And they can decide how to proceed."

"Good," Forster said. "But, like I said, time is running out."

"I know," Horst said. "Give us everything you know. We'll try to put together a provisional plan."

CHAPTER TWENTY-NINE

Berlin, Germany Prime
9 November 1985

"If this is true," Voss said, quietly. "If this is true..."

He sounded stunned. Volker didn't blame him. Everyone *knew* that the *Abwehr* and the SS were deadly enemies. They'd been competitors ever since the Third *Reich* had risen from the ashes to dominate the world. The thought of Admiral Riess choosing to side with the SS was bizarre. If Holliston won the war, Riess would be lucky if he was allowed to take his pension and retire quietly. The *Abwehr* itself would be folded into the SS.

"It makes no sense," Volker said. "And yet...someone betrayed us."

"Maybe," Voss said. "We don't *know* we were betrayed."

Volker shrugged. It was impossible to be *sure*, but the two nuclear blasts that had stopped the offensive dead in its tracks had almost certainly been ground-bursts. The weapons had been prepositioned and detonated on cue, not dropped from aircraft or fired from long-range guns. And *that* suggested that the *Waffen-SS* had known the direction of attack from the start, allowing them to position the tactical nuclear weapons for maximum effect.

And if it *was* Riess who had betrayed them...

He contemplated it for a long moment. The *Abwehr* had every reason to distrust the SS, but their leader might have more reason to distrust the Provisional Government. Who knew what would happen to the *Abwehr* after the war was won? It certainly wouldn't enjoy the unrestricted powers it had gained under the *Reich* Council. And besides, Riess might be loyal to the Third *Reich*. He might have joined the Provisional Government with the intention of betraying them to Holliston.

Or it might be a trick of some kind, Volker thought.

He rubbed his forehead, wishing for the simplicity of a battlefield. If Riess was a traitor, why *was* he a traitor and how could it be exploited? And if he *wasn't* a traitor, why had he been *fingered* as a traitor? What did the enemy hope to achieve? It wasn't as if he'd trusted Riess even before the man had become the prime suspect. No spymaster could be trusted completely, certainly not in the *Reich*. The position simply offered too many opportunities for advancement at the expense of other, more deserving candidates.

"I don't see what they have to gain," he mused. "This offer…this is what we want, isn't it?"

"Some of us would prefer to reunite the *Reich*," Voss reminded him.

Volker shook his head. There was no way the *Reich* could be reunited, not now. The nukes had seen to that. Even if Germany Prime managed to hold together long enough to launch a second invasion, there was too great a chance of nuclear weapons being used again. And even if they weren't, the hatred between the two sides was too great. He doubted east and west would ever cooperate happily again.

Which means that this offer is the best we're going to get, he thought, morbidly. Horst had done a good job - if everything could be taken at face value. Germany East would get its independence - taking with it everyone who couldn't fit into the new world order. *But it will only work if Holliston is removed.*

He had no trouble in believing that a *Gauleiter* - perhaps more than one - would side against Karl Holliston. The prospect of a nuclear war had probably concentrated more than a few minds in Germany East, particularly after the Provisional Government had retaliated. And even if they *didn't* fear nuclear war, they'd certainly fear Holliston gaining undisputed control over the *Reich*. Their powers would be cut back sharply as Holliston tightened his grip over the *Reich*. They'd be worried even if Holliston remained confined to Germany East.

And we might be carving a rod for our own backs, he thought.

It was a frustrating problem. Holliston was going insane, if he wasn't already mad. But the *Gauleiters* were presumably sane. *They* might be able to turn Germany East into a long-term threat. And yet, right now, Holliston was the *real* problem. He *had* to be stopped, whatever the cost. His madness might eventually lead to all-out nuclear war.

"This plan," he mused. "Is it workable?"

"Perhaps," Voss said. "Long-range airmobile operations were practiced, time and time again, during the wars in Arabia and South Africa. We have the aircraft on hand to insert troops several hundred kilometres from their airbases. But I'd be reluctant to risk it without knowing more about the situation on the ground. It would have a very low probability of success."

Volker scowled. Karl Holliston must have faced the same dilemma, shortly after the *Reich* Council had fallen…but Holliston was demonstrably more ruthless than any of his opponents. Sending an airborne commando unit to Berlin had been a low-risk, high-reward strategy as far as he'd been concerned. If he won, he got to retake Berlin without a fight; if he lost, it didn't significantly weaken his position. But it was different for the Provisional Government. Losing hundreds of men on a *very* high-risk mission might bring his government toppling down.

"Start planning for it, anyway," he ordered. "Compartmentalise *everything*. Make damn sure *nothing* gets out."

"I'll draw up a training program," Voss said. "We can call the whole operation a training program."

"And we'll make it clear that we won't be taking the offensive until spring," Volker added, shortly. He'd planned to discuss the operation in council, but there was no way to prevent Riess from taking his seat without tipping him off. "As far as anyone apart from the two of us know, there will be no further military operations until then."

"My briefing will make that clear," Volker assured him. He smiled. "It wasn't as if we were planning anything, anyway."

Volker nodded, shortly. The combination of snowstorms and radioactive contamination had *definitely* halted all offensive operations. His forces were currently digging in, ready to repel attack…if, of course, the *Waffen-SS* was in any state to take the offensive. The enemy seemed to be patrolling the lines aggressively, but intelligence suggested that the *Waffen-SS* had taken a beating too. Voss had suggested, quite seriously, throwing in a second attack just to see if the enemy lines crumbled. Volker had been tempted, but there was too great a danger of nuclear attack.

If Horst is right, he thought, *we stand to win everything. But if this is a trap…*

He shook his head. They'd just have to roll the dice one last time...

...And hope to hell they came out ahead.

"And so we are currently establishing three successive defensive lines west of the combat zone," Voss droned. "Four panzer divisions, held in reserve, will move at once to intercept any enemy force that threatens to break through the defence lines. Forward scouts and air patrols should give us more than enough warning of any major offensive to put the men on alert..."

Admiral Wilhelm Riess kept his face impassive as Voss droned on and on. It was a shame Field Marshal Justus Stoffregen hadn't stayed in his post as Head of the OKW - *he'd* understood the importance of putting the *Reich* ahead of their petty rivalries - but Stoffregen had chosen to resign, rather than serve the Provisional Government. Wilhelm understood the man's feelings, which made his sense of betrayal all the more acute. A man who could be *trusted* in his post would have been very useful.

It was a bitter thought. The *Abwehr* and the SS were natural enemies, their rivalry exploited by the *Reich* Council to keep the intelligence services from forming an alliance that would catapult their leaders into power. Normally, Wilhelm would not have hesitated to do the SS a bad turn, particularly if it would do nothing more than embarrass his hated rival. And he knew the *Reichsführer-SS* would not have hesitated to do the same to him. But now, with the New Order under threat, he had no choice but to work with the SS. Holliston, damn him, was the only hope of preserving *anything* of Adolf Hitler's legacy.

Wilhelm had no illusions about the *Reich*. It was a brutal state, founded on brutality and maintained by brutality. Gudrun and her ilk had absolutely *no* comprehension of just how brutally the *Reich* controlled its subjects or of how many lives had been lost in building the *Reich* and establishing its control over Europe. The whole thought was truly distasteful; indeed, he didn't understand how Holliston and *his* ilk could come to enjoy all the horrific things they did to keep the *Reich* in power. There was no *reason* to enjoy it...

But the *Reich* was necessary. The world was divided into the strong and the weak, but the strong could easily become the weak if they lost sight of the true nature of the world. He might recoil in horror at what the *Reich* did, yet he saw no alternative. Easing off on the French tomorrow might see a French army, champing at the bit for bloody revenge, crossing the Rhine in ten years. The world could be either crushed under the *Reich's* heel or at the *Reich's* throat. There was no middle ground.

And that means talking to the enemy, he thought. *And that means accepting the risk of being destroyed myself.*

Kruger leaned forward. "Do you believe the enemy intends to take the offensive?"

"The weather is growing rapidly worse," Voss said. "They would be foolish to try before the spring. I do not expect to see anything more than a few raiding parties."

Wilhelm nodded in agreement. He wasn't an infantryman or a panzer driver, but he understood the dangers of launching an offensive during winter. They'd hashed them out, time and again, while planning the thrust against Warsaw. And that thrust had failed spectacularly. It was unlikely, he assured himself, that Karl Holliston would repeat the same mistake.

"We will also continue evacuating the towns and settlements that may come under long-range fire," Volker Schulze said, changing the subject. "The population wants to flee. We cannot stop them, but we can try to manage the flow."

Wilhelm shuddered, cursing Gudrun and her Valkyries under his breath. Evacuating millions of people would put an immense strain on the nation's resources at the worst possible time, but there was no choice. The thought of those people freezing to death as the weather got colder - or being forced to struggle to find food and shelter - was appalling. And yet, Volker Schulze was right. There was no way the population would stay still with the threat of nuclear war looming over their heads.

And we don't have the manpower to keep them in place, he thought, sourly. *It isn't going to be easy to stop them.*

"We will be very short on food, even with the…emergency shipments," Kruger said. "But we will do our best to keep them alive."

Wilhelm kept his face impassive with an effort. The fact that those shipments came from Britain and America was an open secret. Indeed, he doubted that Holliston had *needed* him to tell him that the Americans were aiding the rebels. And why not? The *Reich* would happily have aided any American faction intent on tearing the United States apart, knowing that crushing the victor would be a great deal easier. Hell, the Americans might be satisfied merely to pry France, Italy, Spain and Turkey out of the *Reich's* orbit. It would give them a chance to establish a powerful armoured force in Europe for the first time since 1919.

And cut us off from all sorts of resources, he thought, darkly. *They have to be stopped.*

The meeting seemed to take forever. It was a relief when Volker Schulze finally called it to a halt, noting that they all had to go home to their wives. Wilhelm rose and hurried out of the room, heading to the tunnels that would take him back to the *Abwehr's* headquarters, right next to the OKW. Holliston would be delighted to know, he was sure, that there would be no further offences until spring. It would give him time to prepare his own counterstroke.

He nodded to his secretary as he reached his office, then poured himself a stiff drink. The Provisional Government's counter-intelligence services were woefully lacking, but betraying them was still a risk. *Someone* might figure out that there was a mole at the very highest levels and it wouldn't take them long to start looking at men known for their loyalty to the Third *Reich*. But the risk had to be borne. Germany demanded it…

And if we win, we may still lose, he thought, sourly. *Holliston will ensure that we are no longer an independent service.*

But that, too, had to be borne.

———

"You believe this to be true?"

"I'm not privy to *all* of their high-level discussions," Andrew Barton said, as he sipped his coffee gratefully. He'd only just returned from the front and his bones *still* felt cold as ice. "But I don't believe they are planning an offensive in the next few days."

"That's…awkward," Ambassador Turtledove said.

"For us, perhaps," Andrew agreed. "But the logistics of waging war as winter falls over the *Reich* are…are very poor."

He scowled at the thought. The Germans had been happy to detail the horrors of waging war in winter, ranging from vehicles refusing to start to guns refusing to fire because the oil had frozen solid. They *did* have plenty of experience in waging war in the winter, he knew, but most of it involved small-unit operations. Moving an entire army through the winter snows was appallingly risky, even if the enemy didn't put up a fight.

And they would, he thought. *Everything we're hearing from Germany East makes it clear that they're preparing to fight.*

"So the war will literally freeze until spring," Ambassador Turtledove said.

"It looks that way," Andrew said. "I *would* expect a number of skirmishes up and down the defence lines, Mr. Ambassador, but nothing more serious. Both sides are going to need to replenish their losses after the recent battles."

"If they can afford to keep fighting," Ambassador Turtledove said. "The Provisional Government has already requested a loan."

"They could do with it," Andrew said. "What did Washington say?"

"They're still arguing," Ambassador Turtledove told him. "The President seems to be in favour of propping up the Provisional Government, but factions in Congress want to insist on some ironclad guarantees before releasing the purse strings. And none of them seem to agree on what they want from the *Reich*."

Andrew sighed. "They can't agree on *anything?*"

"The Polish vote wants a free Poland," Ambassador Turtledove said. "Jewish voters want some kind of apology and recompense for the Holocaust. Others want to ensure that the *Reich* surrenders political control over the subject nations..."

"It's not going to be easy," Andrew said. "The Germans are a prideful people. They're not going to bend the knee to us so easily."

"I understand that," Ambassador Turtledove said. "But the average congressman does not."

Andrew nodded, crossly. Once again, domestic politics in America were interfering with foreign policy. He had no illusions about the *Reich* - nor about the Provisional Government - but they had to deal with the world they had, not the one they wanted. Pushing the Provisional Government too hard might cause it to tumble - or come to terms with Germanica, rather than surrender to the United States. And, in either case, the US would end up with a far worse problem on the other side of the Atlantic.

"They see it as a chance to make speeches and look good," Turtledove added. "It isn't *them* who will bear the blame for any failures."

"There's no way we can re-establish the world of 1938," Andrew said, quietly. "Poland is gone; Czechoslovakia is gone; Greece is gone; France, Italy, Hungary and Romania are shadows of their former selves…nothing can restore the destroyed nations or bring the countless dead back to life. The President cannot sign some papers and reshape the world."

He shook his head. "All the mistakes Chamberlain and Roosevelt made cannot be undone," he added. "The *Reich* is gravely weakened, but it isn't dead. And while they may be grateful to us for our help, they won't forget their own interests. Trying to push them may undo everything we've done over the last few months."

He'd studied history extensively. There had been plenty of opportunities, in hindsight, to stop the *Reich* long before it built a colossal empire, but most of those opportunities had been missed. What would have happened if Churchill had been Prime Minister in 1938? Or Truman President in 1941? Might the *Reich* have been stopped? The thought of a war on such a horrific scale was terrifying, but would it really have been worse than the *Reich's* unchallenged dominance over Europe?

Perhaps, he thought. *They might have been able to produce enough nuclear bombs to make a difference.*

"I know," the Ambassador said. "But try telling that to someone back home."

Andrew nodded. America was the most powerful nation on Earth, even if it hadn't truly *believed* it until recently. The *Reich* wasn't a paper tiger, but it wasn't the formidable force everyone had taken it for either. There was no way, he knew now, that the *Reich* could win a conventional war against America, with or without the NAA. But it had nukes and a proven willingness to use them. There were limits to how far America could push the *Reich* into making reforms.

"I'm pushing for us to keep supporting the Provisional Government," Ambassador Turtledove said. "But limited military action…it doesn't seem so urgent."

"Washington is likely to regret it," Andrew warned. "We have a unique opportunity to forge ties with the most powerful successor state. Missing it will cost us dearly."

CHAPTER THIRTY

Germanica, Germany East
10 November 1985

"So," *Gauleiter* Emil Forster said. "Do they meet with your approval?"

Oberstgruppenfuehrer Alfred Ruengeler bit down the response that came to mind as he watched the young men exercising on the drill field. They were *painfully* young, ranging from fourteen to sixteen...even in Germany East, they would normally have been considered too young to join the military. They should have been working the fields, playing games with the Hitler Youth, making the first tentative steps towards relationships with the opposite sex...not joining the military.

But we are desperate for manpower, he told himself, sharply. *And recruiting these young men early may be our only hope.*

"They look healthy," he said, finally. "And the Hitler Youth has prepared them well."

He kept his expression blank with an effort as the young men - boys, really - were put through their paces by training officers. He hadn't *wanted* to visit a training base near Germanica, let alone play nice with the *Gauleiters*. He'd *wanted* to go west to inspect the new defence lines - and visit the wounded - but Holliston had said no. The entire front had been declared off-limits to just about everyone, something that hadn't kept nasty rumours from spreading through Germany East. Even Alfred, the commander of the *Waffen-SS*, wasn't allowed to go.

"One would hope so," Forster said. "They may be young, but some of them have seen the elephant."

"Not a *real* elephant," Alfred said, tartly. "Being in the military isn't *quite* like being in the Hitler Youth."

He fought down a surge of despair that threatened to overwhelm him. Didn't the *Gauleiter* understand? These young men were the hope of the future, yet they were going to be squandered in a hopeless war, their lives tossed away like paper. And yet, the bastard was *proud*. He wouldn't be laughing after the young men died in the fighting, never to return home. Or maybe they would, their bodies torn and broken...

No, he thought. *They would never be allowed to return home in such a state.*

"I need a drink," the *Gauleiter* said, suddenly. "Please, join me in a toast."

He turned and led the way towards a nearby building without bothering to wait for Alfred's response. Alfred tried to think of an excuse - the last thing he wanted was to spend time with a particularly smug *Gauleiter* - but nothing came to mind. There was no way he could just refuse, not when a *Gauleiter* controlled enough land and resources to make even Karl Holliston nervous. He had to be polite...

Damn him, he thought. He took one last look at the young men, then turned and followed the *Gauleiter*. *Damn all of them to hell.*

The building - or at least the room they entered - was clearly designed for senior officers and politicians. Luxury dripped from every wall, suggesting that more *Reichmarks* had been spent on the decorations alone than on training up the next generation of officers. Alfred hated it on sight, even though he had no idea who'd actually ordered it. He had no particular dislike of luxury, but it should very definitely be excluded from a military base. It ruined young officers for life.

"I'm particularly fond of Scotch," Forster said, as he removed a bottle from a fridge and poured them both a glass. "I had this sent to me before the war began."

"Quite," Alfred agreed, stiffly. Scotch wasn't exactly banned - along with anything else from outside the *Reich* - but it was taxed so heavily that only the very wealthy or well-connected could hope to obtain it. "The Scots do make good whiskey, I suppose."

The *Gauleiter* smiled. "Would you have preferred something produced in an illicit still?"

Alfred didn't bother to rise to the bait. Soldiers producing their own alcohol was technically against regulations, but smart officers turned a blind eye

RAGNAROK

as long as the men didn't drink while on duty. Besides, battle-alcohol could be used as an antiseptic if there was nothing else available. But it was rare to taste something made in an illicit still that didn't threaten to ruin his teeth.

"I have a question for you," Forster said, as he waved Alfred into a comfortable armchair and sat down facing him. His eyes were suddenly very hard. "Do you believe the war can be won?"

Alfred hesitated. "Why do you ask?"

"You are the field commander of the *Waffen-SS*," Forster said. If he knew how empty the title was, he showed no sign of it. "Your opinion is presumably very well informed."

"It is," Alfred said, flatly. Was this some test of his loyalty? Karl Holliston's paranoia seemed to be growing by leaps and bounds, particularly as he didn't have any real *outlet* for his feelings. The people he suspected of plotting against him were the people he couldn't move against without risking another civil war. "Why do you ask?"

Forster met his eyes. "Because Holliston is insane," he said, flatly. "And because this war needs to end."

Alfred tensed, bracing himself. If this was a test of loyalty, sharing his true opinion would probably lead rapidly and inevitably to his execution. But would Holliston take the risk? Would he even *need* to take the risk? Alfred knew, without false modesty, that he was far from irreplaceable. There was no shortage of officers who could be promoted into his shoes, if necessary.

"Let me tell you how *I* see it," Forster said, when Alfred said nothing. "The *Waffen-SS* has been gravely weakened, first by the ill-fated offensive against Berlin and then by the enemy's counteroffensive, a problem made worse by our own nuclear weapons. We are desperately short of everything from panzers and assault rifles to training cadre, which is why we are calling up men who shouldn't be going into the army for at least another two years. Our air force has been effectively destroyed and we have no naval forces to speak of - and they wouldn't be particularly important anyway, if we did.

"Our economy is a mess, our internal security system is falling apart and rumours are spreading like...like water after it breaks through a dam. In short, we are on the verge of losing the war. The only thing we have that might deter the enemy from resuming the offensive in spring is a handful of nuclear weapons, which are controlled by a madman. Do you agree with my assessment?"

Alfred took the plunge. "I do."

Oddly, he felt almost liberated. Perhaps it *was* a trap. Perhaps he'd just ensured that he'd end his days hanging from meathooks below the *Reichstag*. But he still felt liberated by saying the words out loud. And yet…

His mind raced. The *Gauleiter* wouldn't have dared to approach him, not like this, if the building wasn't secure…and if he didn't have a way to deal with Alfred, if Alfred proved unreceptive to his advance. Chances were that the guards, hanging around outside the building, owed their loyalty to their *Gauleiter* rather than the *Reich*. And *that* meant that he was seriously considering doing something about Holliston.

"I see," Forster said. He studied Alfred for a long moment. "Is our position salvageable?"

"I do not believe so," Alfred admitted. "Quite apart from shortages in nearly every category, we have far too much territory to defend with far too small a force. I do not know how many tactical nukes are available, but I doubt they would make a difference. There's just too much territory to defend."

He grimaced. "But the enemy is unlikely to just let us go," he added. "They *need* us."

"They are willing to agree to a permanent split," Forster said. "But they need us to remove Holliston."

Alfred frowned. He'd grown to loathe Holliston. It wouldn't bother him in the slightest if some kindly soul put a bullet through his head. But Holliston was perhaps the only person with a solid claim to rule Germany East and there was no clear successor. Who knew what would happen after he was dead? He had a feeling that the man in front of him had a very clear idea.

He smiled, humourlessly. "And then…what?"

"The *Reich* Council will be re-established," Forster said. "We can offer you a seat on it, if you desire."

Alfred felt his frown deepen. *We*…who was this *we*? How many of the *Gauleiters* were involved in the plot? There were twenty-one *Gauleiters* in all - they couldn't *all* be involved, not when he knew at least two of them were fanatical Nazis. They'd support Holliston until the bitter end. But the offer was tempting, if it came with *real* power. He'd always suspected that the previous *Fuhrer* hadn't been the only figurehead on the *Reich* Council.

"A very tempting offer," he said, slowly. "Who *else* would be on this council?"

"The *Gauleiters*," Forster said. "And perhaps a few other military figures."

Alfred frowned. Rule by committee was notoriously inefficient. Some of the problems facing the *Reich* probably owed their origins to rule by committee. But it was better than piling unchecked authority and power on one man. No one, not even Hitler, had been able to grasp the full immensity of the *Reich*.

"Very well," he said. Knowing there were others out there who thought as he did was reassuring. They might still be caught - he had no illusions about the sheer number of spies within Germany East - but at least they weren't alone. "What do you want from me?"

"Help in getting into the *Reichstag*," Forster said. "We have to find and kill Holliston before he can trigger a nuclear war."

Alfred took a breath. "That won't be easy," he warned. "Even I don't control everything."

"I know," Forster said. "But you can help us get through the outer defences."

"Maybe not even that," Alfred said. "You'd need to get your forces into the city itself."

"We have half a plan," Forster said. "Let us see how it works out, shall we?"

———

"Horst," Kurt said. "Why didn't you tell Gudrun that your uncle is a *Gauleiter*?"

Horst took a moment to consider his answer. He would have been astonished if Gudrun had told Kurt *anything* about their relationship, even though it was clear that Kurt was less stuffy - and controlling - than the average brother. He'd accompanied Gudrun to the hospital at considerable personal risk. But even so, Gudrun probably wouldn't have told him much about their relationship. Kurt might have felt obliged to start a fight if he *knew* Gudrun and Horst had been sleeping together before their wedding night.

But he *hadn't* told Gudrun about his uncle...

"I wanted to make a name for myself," he said, finally. It was why he hadn't changed his name to Forster, even though he *had* been effectively adopted. "I didn't want to be promoted merely because of my relatives."

Kurt nodded, slowly. He'd probably faced the same temptation, although he'd been promoted rapidly anyway. No one had questioned it as far as Horst knew, probably because Kurt had done an extremely good job when the *Reich* was dangerously short on good officers. And besides, asking his *sister* for a promotion would be embarrassing as hell to the average German male. The whole affair seemed calculated to cause all sorts of problems.

"But it could have helped us earlier," Kurt pointed out. "If we'd known…"

"It would have only upset people," Horst said. *He* knew he'd changed sides, when he'd found out the truth, but hardly anyone else would have accepted it without at least *some* suspicion. Even *Gudrun* would have had her concerns. Turning on the SS was one thing, turning on one's family was a great deal harder. "And besides, it isn't as if I'm in line to inherit anything."

He scowled at the thought. Technically, *Gauleiters* were appointed by the *Reichsführer-SS*, but there was always a great deal of political manipulation behind the scenes. A person who rose to become a *Gauleiter* would be in a very good position to solidify his family's position within the *Reich*, making sure that no one - not even the *Reichsführer* - could ignore them without consequences. And Emil Forster had been a past master at the art. He'd had enough connections to ensure that Horst had a chance to enter advanced training well ahead of schedule.

And he might have seen me as a tool too, Horst thought. *The higher I rose in the ranks, the more useful I was to him.*

"I suppose not," Kurt said. "I don't suppose Holliston is your father, is he?"

Horst grimaced. "My father died when I was six," he said, curtly. "I was told he died a hero, fighting in the wars. Now…I wonder what really happened."

He shook his head. That, more than anything else, had been why he'd changed sides. If the *Reich* had been happy to lie about Konrad Schulze, a stormtrooper whose father had *also* been a stormtrooper, were they prepared to lie about a man who'd been closely linked to a *Gauleiter*? Had his father been killed in honest combat…

…Or had he been wounded and left to die?

Kurt shrugged. "Can we trust Ruengeler?"

Horst shrugged back. *Oberstgruppenfuehrer* Alfred Ruengeler had a good reputation, but he'd never met the man in person. He might easily be one of Holliston's supporters, playing along with Forster until he was in position to have all of them arrested. And yet, Horst had watched the man, from a distance, as he was shown around the training ground. Ruengeler was distinctly unhappy, his expression suggesting he would rather be somewhere - anywhere - else. Perhaps he could be trusted...

And if he can't be trusted, his own thoughts mocked, *we're all about to die.*

His uncle had assured him that they *should* get word, if Ruengeler went straight to Holliston and betrayed the entire plan. He had a couple of his clients in the *Reichstag* and several more in the *Waffen-SS.* But Horst had his doubts. *He'd* switched sides, after all. His uncle's clients might decide that Holliston, rather than Forster, was the better bet. Or they might just tell themselves they owed their allegiance to the *Reich...*

"It's a gamble," he said. He still shivered when he recalled just how close they'd come to complete disaster. "But I don't think we have a choice."

He looked up as the door opened. His uncle stepped into the room, looking remarkably dapper in a *Volkssturm* uniform that had clearly been specially tailored for him. Horst felt a flicker of the old contempt for the *Volkssturm,* even though he knew his uncle had been a soldier before *his* father had called him home and put him to work. And he'd had a promising career too.

"The *Oberstgruppenfuehrer* appears to be willing to cooperate," Forster said, sitting down in one of the hard chairs. "I feel he can be trusted, at least for the moment."

Kurt looked doubtful. "Did he supply any useful information?"

"Enough," Forster said. He gritted his teeth. "We may be stuck with the original plan."

Horst scowled. He'd hoped they could get enough papers to get an assault force into the *Reichstag* itself, but his uncle had pointed out that there were too many security departments charged with protecting Germanica for them *all* to be subverted. Karl Holliston's paranoia would cause all sorts of problems, if Germanica came under conventional attack, yet...for the moment, it seemed to be working out for him. Any attempt to move more than a handful of men into Germanica would trigger an alarm...

...And getting the papers to actually get *into* the *Reichstag* was impossible.

"Then we have to make it work," he said. "Do you have a solid lead on the transmitter?"

"There's two," Forster said. "One in the *Reichstag* itself - that can be taken out fairly easily - and another, located in a hidden base near the city. We might be better off cutting the cable rather than trying to take out the base itself."

"If we *can* cut the cable," Horst pointed out. "It will be underground."

"Getting down to it may pose a problem," Forster agreed. "But if we attack the base itself…"

He allowed his voice to trail off, suggestively. Horst understood. Any attack plan that *depended* on everything going right - particularly when there were more than two or three moving parts - was a recipe for disaster. Attacking the base ahead of time would alert Holliston; leaving it intact, when the *Reichstag* itself came under attack, would run the risk of Holliston managing to send the launch commands before it was too late. But there was no choice. They were running short of time.

And if the reports from the Reichstag are accurate, he thought, *Holliston might be jumping right off the slippery slope.*

It was impossible to tell how many of the reports were accurate or simply nothing more than rumours - or wishful thinking - but it was clear that Holliston was losing his grip. His rages had already become the stuff of legends, while his long speeches on the subject of his inevitable victory were worrying his subordinates. And he'd had a private discussion with Gudrun without witnesses, something that bothered Horst more than he cared to admit. If Holliston had taken his frustrations out on Horst's wife…

I'm coming, he promised Gudrun, silently. His imagination offered too many possibilities for what could have been done to her. *And if you've been hurt, I'll make sure he's hurt worse.*

"I know the risks," he said, out loud. "And, once we know more about what's going on, we can probably mitigate them."

"Let us hope so," his uncle said. "Too much is at stake for any mistakes."

CHAPTER THIRTY-ONE

Front Lines, Germany Prime
12 November 1985

The ground felt like solid rock.

Hennecke Schwerk cursed inwardly as he lifted the shovel and brought it down, trying to push it into the soil deep enough to start digging a hole. The ground resisted him, forcing him to push harder and harder just to make a hole large enough to bury a grenade. His strength seemed to fail a moment later, leaving him leaning helplessly on the shovel as he fought for breath. Whatever had happened to him - and the doctors had been no help whatsoever - clearly wasn't over yet.

And to think I'm one of the lucky ones, he thought, bitterly. It was hard, so hard, to care enough to keep going. *Others went to sleep and never woke up.*

He gritted his teeth as he forced the shovel back into the ground. He'd been ordered to dig a trench large enough to bury the next set of dead soldiers, but alone...he doubted he could actually do it. His skin hurt, his head was pounding like a drum...he had the nasty feeling that he'd dig the grave, then become its first victim. It was all he could do, at times, to remain standing. Walking was almost completely beyond him.

Pointless, he told himself. *Just...pointless.*

He glanced up as he heard the sound of an aircraft flying overhead. A rebel aircraft, no doubt, the pilot looking down and sneering at the storm-troopers as they struggled to survive the cold. Part of him hoped that bombs would fall, putting him out of his misery, but nothing happened. He ran his hand through his hair - cursing as he saw more strands start to come loose and drift to the ground - then turned back to his work. The officers - damn their black souls - had made it clear that he wouldn't be fed if he didn't work. They were determined to get as much work as they could out of the injured before it was too late.

An impossible task, he thought. *They really hate me.*

It felt like hours before the trench was deep enough to qualify as a grave. He sat down, wishing for a cigarette or a drink or *something* to keep him going. His entire body felt hot and sweaty, despite the cold. He wasn't sure what it meant if he was sweating in cold weather, but he doubted it was anything good. And the surges of fever that threatened to overcome him *couldn't* be a good sign.

He was tempted just to stay sitting down, staring into the grave until one of the officers - or the cold - put him out of his misery. His world had shrunk to nothing more than a constant struggle to remain alive and breathing, despite the throbbing headaches and bouts of sweaty fever. He no longer cared about the *Reich*, or about his remaining comrades, or about teaching the rebels a lesson. All that mattered was remaining alive one more day...

...And even that was starting to pall.

Somehow, feeling as if he was watching his own body from a far distance, he pulled himself to his feet and stumbled back towards the camp. It was really nothing more than a mass of tents for the wounded, surrounded by a handful of heavily-armed stormtroopers. He'd been told that there were other defensive lines further east, but he had no idea if it was actually true. He hoped, for the sake of what little family he had left, that it *was* true. The idea of his camp being able to offer more than token resistance when the enemy launched a second offensive was laughable.

The guard wrinkled his nose as Hennecke staggered past. There had been a time when Hennecke would have taken it personally, demanding satisfaction with his fists if nothing else, but now he hardly cared. His makeshift uniform was stained and soiled, a disgrace to the *Waffen-SS*, yet he was hardly the only soldier who looked as if he had been swimming in a septic tank. Even the guards were no longer their dapper selves. Hennecke couldn't help wondering if they had been sentenced to death too.

He scowled at a pair of nurses as he walked up to the tent. Neither of them seemed to recognise him, but they both flinched back anyway. God alone knew what they were doing in the camp - it was no place for young women - yet it was clear they couldn't leave. They'd probably volunteered to tend the wounded, he thought with a bitter snigger; they'd found themselves trapped near the front lines, far too close to whatever radioactive contamination lingered in the air.

And if they don't catch radiation poisoning, he thought, *they might catch something else instead.*

Sanitation - battlefield sanitation - had been hammered into his head from the day he'd joined the Hitler Youth. His superiors hadn't hesitated to hand out savage beatings to any men foolish enough to soil their own nest. Even prisoners in concentration camps had been ordered to remain clean, on pain of death. And yet, the tent's interior was so foul that he was glad of the semi-darkness. He didn't want to *see* what was causing the smell.

He sat down hard on his bed - really, just a pile of blankets - and tried to gather his thoughts before he was put back to work. But it was hard, so hard, to keep focused. He kept rubbing at his hands, trying to get rid of the sunburned feeling he knew *wouldn't* fade until he died; his head, pounding savagely, only seemed to grow worse as he struggled to breathe. The air was so foul that he didn't know if he *could* breathe. Were the other men in the tent dead?

The shock yanked him awake, pulling him back into the world of moaning men waiting to die. He'd been asleep and dreaming and he hadn't even *realised* it. Gritting his teeth, he forced himself to stand, trying not to peer at any of the other men. But it was impossible to avoid seeing that a man, someone he vaguely recognised, had died sometime in the last hour or so. There was no one to carry out the body…

They'll probably burn the entire tent, he thought, as he staggered out into the open air. It was still bitterly cold, but the skies had cleared enough to allow the sun to pour its rays onto the camp. Hennecke would have been grateful if he hadn't already had a nasty burning sensation covering his body. *And then they'll burn the entire camp.*

Another nurse - one who looked vaguely familiar - was serving food outside a mobile canteen that looked to have seen better days. Hennecke stumbled up to her - she looked alarmed to see him, fear clearly visible in her eyes - and took a plate of stew. It tasted like it had passed through the digestive system of a cow - he didn't want to *think* about where the meat might have come from - but he was too far gone to care. He wolfed it down and managed to get his hands on a second serving before the trumpets blew, summoning every able-bodied man to the command tent. Licking his fingers to make sure he ate every last scrap, Hennecke made his way slowly to the tent. The only thing marking it out from the other tents was a large flag, hanging limply in the wind in front of the flap.

Not the only limp thing around here, Hennecke thought, sourly. He started to giggle, helplessly. The thought just wouldn't go away. *The commander…*

Someone smacked the side of his head, hard. "Pay attention," a *Scharfuehrer* snarled, angrily. "The commander is talking."

Kuhn, Hennecke thought.

But Kuhn was dead, wasn't he? It was growing increasingly difficult to be certain of *anything*. Had he seen Kuhn die or was it merely a dream, a happy fantasy he'd used to keep himself warm? He felt the pistol concealed within his belt and allowed himself a tight smile. He might be on penal duty, where he wasn't supposed to have any weapons without special permission, but he was still armed.

The commander was new, he noted, as the man perched himself on a bucket so he could be seen by the entire group. He wondered, absently, what had happened to the last one, then decided he didn't want to know. He'd been so out of it that there could have been a dozen changes of command in the last couple of days and he probably wouldn't have noticed. He felt a sudden flare of anger as he saw the commander's pristine uniform for the first time. It was perfect, even in the midst of utter hell. He looked down at his sodden trousers and shuddered.

"The war goes on," the commander said. "And we have not forsaken our duty."

Maybe he'd introduced himself. Hennecke hadn't heard. There was no point in caring, anyway. He'd lost quite a few commanders during the brief, but savage war. God alone knew what had happened to the men under his command, before he'd been stripped of his rank and sent to a penal unit. *He certainly didn't want to know.*

The group shuffled restlessly. They should have given a rousing cheer, Hennecke knew, but they were too ill, too tired or simply too bitter to care. *Heil Holliston?* He had no doubt that the entire camp would go over to the rebels if they thought there was a genuine chance they would be treated like human beings, instead of monsters. Even the promise of a good meal before they were shot would probably win them over.

"The *Reich* is wounded," the commander continued, "but the Fatherland is not yet broken!"

Hah, Hennecke thought. Judging from the faint snickers that ran through the group, he wasn't the only one who thought that way. *The Reich might be alive, but what about us?*

The commander turned an interesting shade of purple, but seemed perplexed. Men who thought they were doomed to die whatever they did - rightly or wrongly - couldn't be threatened with the camps. What sort of punishment could be worse than their current condition? And a beating, no matter how carefully controlled, would probably push some of the men over the edge and into death.

"We have orders," the commander said. He looked nervous. Hennecke didn't fail to take note. Showing weakness in front of junior officers and enlisted men could be fatal. "We will be raiding the outer edge of the enemy's defences!"

A low ripple of anger ran through the group. Raiding the enemy lines was standard doctrine, particularly when the SS didn't have the manpower to launch a full offensive, but there wasn't a single man in the camp healthy enough to carry out the mission. Hitting the enemy, even with the advantage of surprise, would be a suicide mission. The commander was trying to get them all killed, no doubt with an eye to saving bullets.

"We can take the enemy lines and hurt them," the commander snapped. "I..."

"*Nein*," someone said. "We want to go *home!*"

"Home," someone else shouted. "Home!"

"This is *mutiny*," the commander said. Hennecke could hear the hint of panic in his voice and knew that others would hear it too. What good was discipline applied to men who *knew* they were on the verge of death? "This is..."

The chant grew louder. "*Home, home, home...*"

"Damn it," the commander shouted. Hennecke saw him unbuckling his holster. "You..."

Hennecke drew his pistol and shot the commander neatly through the eyes. He toppled backwards as Hennecke moved the pistol to his next target, shooting the stormtrooper before he could fire more than a single burst into the air. The crowd roared and threw itself forward on the remaining two stormtroopers, knocking them down, stamping them into the ground, kicking the very *life* out of them. Hennecke looked around for more targets, then started to laugh helplessly as he saw the remaining guards high-tailing it out of the camp.

Cowards, he thought. Given everything he'd gone through since the war began, he found it hard to have any sympathy for the well-dressed stormtroopers. *And if that idiot* - he glanced towards the commander's body as it was stripped of weapons - *had kept his fat mouth shut, he could have just let the shouting burn itself out.*

He staggered, then led the way towards the storage tents. There were several boxes of rations inside, as well as a crate of fancy wine someone had liberated. He took a bottle for himself, then started to pass the rations out to the men. There was barely enough to feed everyone in the camp for two days, he saw, but it was hard to care about the long-term. Besides, they'd just mutinied against their legitimate commanders. The shitheads in Germanica would shit themselves so badly - the SS was renowned for its loyalty - that they'd probably drop a nuclear warhead on the camp.

They won't let us get away with this, he thought. Weapons were already being handed round, but a few dozen assault rifles and ammunition wouldn't stop the panzers when they came to crush the mutiny. *Of course they won't let us get away with this.*

He laughed at the thought. Whatever comforting lies the nurses had tried to sell him, he'd *known* he'd been sentenced to death the moment he realised he had radiation poisoning. They'd use him as long as they could make him work, but they had no intention of curing him. They *couldn't* cure him. He would have been killed the moment he got too weak to work. And the nurses...

A thought struck him. Taking a long drink from his bottle, he turned and strode towards the cabin - the sole true building in the campsite - that had been assigned to the nurses. A handful of men were already outside, eying the locked building with the look of lean and hungry wolves. Hennecke would have thought the nurses would flee, but evidently they hadn't realised what was happening until it was too late. No one, but no one, harassed a nurse in the military. But discipline was a joke.

"Break the door down," he ordered.

He laughed as four men threw themselves against the door, smashing it down. The nurses should have learned a lesson from what *he'd* done, a few days ago. Or had it all been a dream? No one had come to teach him a lesson for frightening one of the bitches, even though it was what *would* have happened in a normal camp. A soldier who harassed a nurse would be beaten senseless by his own comrades. But now…

Laughing and joking, they ran into the building. He heard screams as the nurses were captured and dragged out, beaten bloody when they tried to resist. Their clothes were torn from their bodies, leaving them exposed and shivering in the cold. Once, he would have felt shame and pity for putting German girls through such an ordeal; now, he only felt anger, hatred and a surge of lust so powerful that it overwhelmed him. The nurses started to scream as the men closed in, unbuttoning their pants as they surrounding the girls. Hennecke caught one - a little dark-haired woman, barely younger than himself - and forced his lips down on hers. His hands caught hold of her breasts and squeezed, hard.

She bit him, desperately. He yelped, then slapped her so hard she fell to the ground, screaming in pain. Hennecke laughed as he landed on top of her, rolling her over and holding her down as he forced his way into her. Her screams grew louder, but he ignored them. He no longer cared about anything, save for himself.

Afterwards, he walked away, heedless of her bitter sobs. Other men were already lining up for their own go at her, discipline utterly forgotten in the wake of the mutiny. Hennecke knew, at some level, that they'd gone too far, but it simply didn't matter. They were dead men walking. If they weren't killed by their own leaders, or by the rebels, or by the surviving nurses if they managed to get their hands on some weapons…the radiation poisoning would kill them. Survival simply wasn't in the cards.

He sat down, feeling the pistol's comforting presence in his hands. They'd come for him, of course, and he'd fight. He'd try to take down one or two of the bastards before the remainder overwhelmed him. And then…

Death, of course. He doubted he'd be allowed to survive long enough to stand trial - if, of course, the SS bothered with a trial. It wasn't as if there would be any doubt of their crimes, not after the stormtroopers had fled. And then…who knew?

He'd never been a particularly religious man. Religion - Christianity, at least - had never been encouraged in Germany East, although all the attempts to reintroduce the Old Gods had sunk without trace. And yet, the thought of an afterlife called to him, even though he knew he was probably destined for Hell. But, really, what did he deserve? His crimes stretched back months. Mutiny, murdering senior officers, gang-raping nurses...they were merely the tip of the iceberg. Perhaps they'd been right, after all, when they'd condemned him to the penal unit. He'd failed the men placed under his command.

And that had been the worst crime of all.

He shook his head, ignoring the screams as they echoed behind him. His head was starting to pound again, mocking him. All he could do now was wait...

...And see what tomorrow would bring.

CHAPTER THIRTY-TWO

Germanica, Germany East
12 November 1985

There had been a time, *Oberstgruppenfuehrer* Alfred Ruengeler had thought, when giving bad news to Karl Holliston had been a relatively safe occupation. Clearly, that wasn't true any longer.

"There's been a mutiny?"

"Yes, *Mein Fuhrer*," the unlucky reporter said. "And it's spreading."

Alfred took a breath as Holliston's face purpled. A mutiny among the *Waffen-SS*? It was unprecedented. The SS did *not* mutiny. Ever. But it had…

"The SS *cannot* have mutinied," Holliston snarled. "It *cannot*."

The reporter took a very visible breath. "*Mein Fuhrer*, a number of forward bases have mutinied," he said. "Senior officers have been shot or forced to flee; junior and enlisted men are in control. Stores have been looted, prisoners have been killed out of hand…there are even reports of entire units just breaking up and heading west. The entire front line may be on the verge of breaking up."

"Get out," Holliston snarled.

The messenger turned and retreated as fast as he could without actually running. Alfred took a moment to think. The reports from Holliston's spy - still sitting comfortably within the rebel government - had made it clear that the rebels had no intention of taking the offensive until spring. But a mutiny - one that threatened to weaken or destroy the front lines - might cause them to change their minds. Launching an offensive into the driving snow would be nightmarish, but it might just pay off for them. Even if it didn't…

He shuddered. The *Waffen-SS* had been through hell over the last few months. They were trained and conditioned to fight *Untermenschen*, not their fellow Germans. He'd already been keeping track of a series of disturbing incidents - suicides, in particular - that had suggested that discipline was breaking down, but now...? A mutiny was unprecedented, yet the seeds had been sown over the last few weeks. The retreat from Berlin, the breakdown in supplies, the nuclear contamination...yes, he could see soldiers turning on their officers and shooting them down. It had happened before, during the final days of Stalin's Russia.

And back at the end of the Second Reich, he thought, numbly. *Are we doomed to be defeated again?*

"It cannot have happened," Holliston said. He sounded shaken, so badly shaken that Alfred almost felt sorry for him. "The SS *cannot* mutiny."

"The report would not have been passed up the chain to Germanica if it hadn't been verified," Alfred said. He doubted *anyone* would be keen to report a mutiny. The officers on the ground, if they hadn't already been killed, would be sent to the camps after the mutiny was crushed. If, of course, the mutiny *was* crushed. "*Mein Fuhrer*, we need to take action."

Holliston didn't seem to hear him. "They swore to be always faithful," he said. "They cannot have turned on me."

He looked up, sharply. "How bad is it?"

"I don't know, *Mein Fuhrer*," Alfred said. He hated confessing to ignorance at the best of times; now, with Holliston clearly losing his grip, he had the feeling it might prove fatal. "I will attempt to garner more information, if you wish."

He sighed, inwardly. The command and control network was already in tatters, thanks to the chaos caused by the civil war. Radio links to the forward bases were unreliable, if the bases hadn't already been overrun by the mutineers. He found it hard to imagine the *entire* front line disintegrating into mutiny, but if the command network went down completely it would be hard to restore any kind of control. Each unit would be cut off from its fellows, so completely isolated that it could mutiny - or be overwhelmed by the rebels - and no one would be any the wiser.

We never planned for civil war, he thought. *The possibility was never considered.*

"Do it," Holliston ordered. "And then prepare to move troops from Germanica to crush the rebels."

Alfred blinked. Holliston wanted him to move troops *away* from Germanica? Now, more than ever before, the troops protecting the city were the only ones Holliston could *rely* on. But perhaps that was the point. The other units - particularly the *Volkssturm* - might not be reliable when it came to crushing mutineers. They might side with the mutineers and turn their guns on their officers instead.

And weakening the defences of Germanica can only help us, he told himself.

"I shall see to it at once, *Mein Fuhrer*," he said. "At least we know the rebels are not planning an offensive."

Holliston gave him a ghost of a smile. "They are too scared of our nuclear weapons to risk taking advantage of the mutiny," he said. "Perhaps we should use them to destroy the mutineers."

Alfred hesitated. "Let me see how bad the situation is, *Mein Fuhrer*," he said. Bathing the mutineers in radioactive fire might satisfy Holliston, but it might also force the rebels in Berlin to take action. "Perhaps it can be handled relatively quickly."

But it wouldn't be, he knew, as he saluted and left the giant office. The mutiny - whatever had actually happened - was too good an opportunity to let pass. He'd do as he'd promised, he'd send troops to the west, then he'd make sure Forster knew that he'd have a window of opportunity. But he wasn't sure if there was time to get anything organised. There were simply too many loyalists in Germanica.

And too many others who have nowhere else to go, he thought, grimly. *They'll be doomed if the entire government shatters.*

He swallowed, hard. The *Reich* had never known defeat. Sure, there had been setbacks, but no real *defeats*. They had grown used to a reputation for invincibility, even though they'd won their victories against inferior foes. The French, the Russians…the British would have been crushed, too, if they hadn't been able to retreat behind the English Channel. Every time they'd matched their army against the *Reich* they'd lost - and lost badly, even when the odds had been in their favour. Rommel had practically driven them all the way to India by the time Britain and Germany finally made peace.

But now there *had* been a defeat, a shattering defeat. And it had come hard on the heels of the chilling realisation that the *Reich* was not united behind the *Fuhrer*.

He composed himself as he strode into the war room. The staff were already hard at work, trying to track the progress of the mutiny. A glance at the map told him that the situation wasn't as bad as he had feared. Several forward bases had been lost completely, but most of them were either reserved for the walking dead - men suffering from radiation poisoning - or penal units. There had been incidents further east, but none of them had turned into full-fledged mutinies.

Yet, he told himself. A number of bases were definitely out of contact. Bad weather…or mutiny? *The situation is still developing.*

"The *Fuhrer* has ordered us to move reinforcements from Germanica to the front," he said, as his staff assembled. "I want orders to be sent within the next hour."

He kept his face impassive as he started to thumb through the list of available units. The *Fuhrer* would probably smell a rat if *all* of the loyalist units were dispatched, but a number could be shipped west without arousing suspicions. And, with a little effort, they could be kept out of touch even if the *Fuhrer* changed his mind. And then…

We may be about to find out, he thought, grimly. *And if Forster can't mobilise his forces, we're all about to die.*

———

Karl Holliston sat in his office and brooded.

He had been raised on stories of loyalty. He'd been told there was no one more faithful to the *Reich* than the SS, in any of its incarnations. And he'd thought it was true. SS stormtroopers threw themselves into battle, time and time again, to defend the *Reich*; SS *Einsatzgruppen* purged entire camps of *Untermenschen*, dissidents and other enemies of the state, just to make sure that they could not rise from the ashes and threaten the *Reich* anew. Himmler had crafted a force - the most formidable fighting force on the planet - that was pledged to defend the *Reich*.

And he'd trusted them. He'd trusted them even after the uprising, even after much of the *Heer*, *Kriegsmarine* and *Luftwaffe* had switched sides and joined the rebels. The *Waffen-SS* had obeyed his orders to march west to Berlin, terrorising the rebels as they marched; the *Waffen-SS* had held the line at Warsaw, fighting to lure the rebels into the nuclear trap. But now that loyalty seemed a joke. Old certainties were falling everywhere. Was the loyalty of the SS just another certainty that was about to break?

He couldn't understand it. The *Waffen-SS* had fought countless battles for the *Reich*. They'd dominated the Russian steppes, crushed the Greek resistance, slaughtered hundreds of thousands of rebels in Arabia and Germany South...they'd purged countless thousands of Germans who had family ties to rebels, traitors, dissidents and people who'd been in Holliston's way. Surely, they would not betray him now...

...But they had.

He reached for the nuclear briefcase, positioned by his chair. The launch codes were calling to him, urging him to burn mutineers off the face of the planet. He could, he knew. The nuclear formations were the most intensely conditioned soldiers in the *Reich*. They'd obey orders, if he issued them, to fire nuclear-tipped shells towards the mutinying camps.

Or would they? Could they be trusted? Could *anyone* be trusted? He felt the pistol at his belt, wondering if his closest friends and allies would turn on him now. Germany East was already unstable. One good push would be more than enough to bring the entire edifice crashing down. It couldn't end like this, he told himself. Adolf Hitler's dream of a reborn *Volk* dominating the world couldn't end with a whimper. But it could...

He rose, picking up the briefcase as he strode through the door, into the outer office. Maria took one look at his face and clearly thought better of what she was about to say. Probably another appointment with some political aristocrat who needed his hand held or his head patted. It wasn't important, not now. The mutineers would probably hang all of the aristocratic fatheads he'd been lumbered with, when he'd taken power. He couldn't help smiling at the thought as he stepped into the corridor. His bodyguard fell in around him as he headed straight to the lift.

Could *they* be trusted? He found himself glancing at them, out of the corner of his eye, as they walked into the lift and headed down into the bunker. They were the best of the best, survivors of some of the most intensive training programs - and combat - the *Reich* could offer. Once, he'd had no doubt that they would put their bodies between him and a bullet, if necessary. Now...now he couldn't help wondering where their loyalties actually lay. Might they be leading him straight into a trap?

Hauptsturmfuehrer Katharine Milch rose as Karl stepped into the security room, hastily snapping out a salute. Karl had no doubt of *her* loyalty, if only because she'd faced a far harder set of challenges than almost everyone else in the SS. Women could be spies, women could be secretaries...but commandos? Katherine was one of the handful of women who'd made it, passing one of the hardest training programs in Germany East. She would have given up years ago if she'd had the slightest doubt of her vocation.

"*Mein Fuhrer*," Katherine said.

"I need to see your prisoner," Karl said. "Open the cell door, then turn off the bugs."

Katherine looked unsure. "*Mein Fuhrer*, she isn't cuffed or shackled..."

"She's still behind bars, isn't she?" Karl asked. "I'm sure I will be safe."

"*Jawohl, Mein Fuhrer*," Katherine said.

Karl motioned to his bodyguards to stay behind as he stepped through the metal door and into the cell. It was larger than he recalled from his time as an interrogator, the room utterly devoid of fittings, save for a single bed firmly locked to the wall. Gudrun lay on the bed, staring up at the featureless ceiling. The nasty part of his mind noted that she was still completely naked. But it didn't seem to bother her any longer.

He stepped up to the bars as Gudrun sat upright. She was beautiful, he had to admit; long blonde hair splashing down to brush against her breasts, muscular arms - a legacy of the BDM - covered in flawless pale skin. Konrad Schulze had been a lucky man, Karl noted, or perhaps he'd had a lucky escape. A woman who could bring down an entire government - who *had* brought down an entire government - was unlikely to be cowed by her husband's fists. And anyone who did try to beat her into submission would be very unwise to fall asleep beside her afterwards.

And she betrayed her entire country, he reminded himself, sharply. He stared at her for a long moment, feeling a strange mixture of emotions. Opposition from outsiders - Americans, British, Russians, Chinese - he understood, but not Gudrun. She had been born into a world that had given her every advantage and asked for very little in return. *Sending her east is too good for her.*

"*Mein Fuhrer*," Gudrun said. He couldn't tell if she was mocking him or not. "What can I do for you?"

Karl met her eyes. "Why did you do it?"

"I think I already answered that question," Gudrun said, coolly. She didn't seem bothered by his presence - or his stare. She certainly made no move to cover her nakedness. "Why are you here?"

"Your...influence has spread," Karl said. Perhaps it was unwise to talk to her, but who *else* could he talk to? "An SS unit has mutinied."

Gudrun smiled, just for a second. "Perhaps you pushed them too far."

Karl reminded himself, sharply, that Gudrun had been in the cell for nearly a month. She couldn't have done *anything* to influence the mutineers, one way or the other. And she couldn't have added to the discontent spreading through Germany East either. Displaying her naked might have been a mistake, but it hadn't been *her* mistake. She was more important as a symbol than as a living, breathing person.

"They knew the job was dangerous when they took it," Karl said, dismissively. "Your *boyfriend* knew the same."

Gudrun nodded, once. Her father had been in the military, Karl recalled; her brother was *still* in the military, unless he'd been killed in the fighting. And the remainder of her siblings would be called up too, in time. She *knew* that death could come to a soldier...

"He didn't expect to be betrayed," she said, quietly. "And neither did his family..."

"It doesn't matter," Karl snapped. "Soldiers exist to serve the *Reich*; nothing more, nothing less. It is their *job* to fight and die in defence of the fatherland..."

"They're *people*," Gudrun said. "They have thoughts and feelings, lives and loves...you had to earn and keep their loyalty, not treat them as disposable pieces of shit."

"The *Reich* demands sacrifices," Karl said. He fought to keep his tone even. "Surely even *you* understand that!"

Gudrun met his eyes. There was no hint of fear, as far as he could tell. Gudrun hadn't broken during her imprisonment, she'd hardened. Karl would have been impressed if she hadn't been on the other side. As it was, the sooner she was shipped east the better.

"I understand," she said. "Do you?"

Karl glared. "What do you mean?"

"I read your file," Gudrun said. "You have never been in combat. You have never even been in real danger. Your entire career was spent in internal security. You never joined the *Waffen-SS*, you never even served alongside its fighting men. You have no wife, no children…"

"Shut up," Karl snapped. He hadn't mourned his wife after her death. Himmler had arranged the match, pointing out that a senior SS official could not be unmarried. It hadn't been a successful marriage. There hadn't even been children. "*You* have no children."

Gudrun ignored him. "You have no conception of war," she said. "To you, soldiers are nothing more than *numbers*. You don't understand them, any more than you understand me, because you have never lived their life. And *your* life has never been in any real danger."

"You didn't live their life either," Karl said.

"No," Gudrun agreed. "But I was engaged to one. And I would have married him, if he'd returned alive and well. I know the cost of war, *Mein Fuhrer*. You *don't*. And now your grip on power is weakening because you've pushed your men too far…"

Karl clenched his fists. If she'd been a man - and if they'd been in public - he would have had to punch her for her words. There would have been no way to avoid it. She'd practically called him a coward! Her words were fighting words. And yet, they weren't in public…

He cocked his head. "A woman can say what she likes and escape punishment," he said, lightly. "Aren't you lucky?"

Gudrun shrugged, as if she were bored. "My father never knew *that*," she said. "He was always strict with me."

"A shame he wasn't stricter," Karl said. "He might have saved you from a gruesome fate."

He cleared his throat. "Enjoy the rest of your time in the cell," he added. "You'll be heading east in four days."

Gudrun looked pale. "Is that all you came to tell me?"

"I suggest you learn to behave yourself," Karl added. "Or you'll find the east absolute hell."

"Really," Gudrun said. "And to think that *you* are already in hell."

CHAPTER THIRTY-THREE

𝔊ermanica, 𝔊erman𝔶 𝔈ast
12 𝔑ovember 1985

Katherine had never contemplated treason before.

It just wasn't something she'd ever done. She'd never had any *reason* to contemplate treason against the *Reich*. The *Reich* had been good to her. Certainly, it had pushed her hard to see if she *really* wanted to serve in the military - rather than one of the handful of roles open to women who *didn't* want to be solely mothers, daughters and wives - but it had accepted her, once she had proved herself. She'd thought little of the protests, when they'd sprung up for the first time; she'd thought even less of the Provisional Government, when it had taken control of Berlin.

And yet, the *Reich* was coming apart at the seams.

She listened to the bodyguards and knew, without a doubt, that the end was approaching rapidly. Mutiny in the *Waffen-SS* was unknown. It almost certainly spelt the end of the *Reich*, at least in the east. The trust and loyalty that bound Germany East together had broken, raising the spectre of a second civil war while the bandits and insurgents started to reclaim the land they'd lost. And that meant…and that meant what?

The end, she thought, morbidly.

She had no illusions about the world, none of the blinders that westerners like Gudrun wore before they came face to face with reality. Holliston, whatever his flaws, had been correct when he'd called the world red in tooth and claw. The Third *Reich* had been established by force, was maintained by force and would collapse when the force holding it together could no longer do the job. And that force had now broken.

Part of her wanted to hate Gudrun for her role in bringing down the *Reich*. But the rest of her had to admit that the flaws had always been there, the fault lines just waiting for someone to exploit them. Gudrun might have been the leader, the first person to stand up and question the *Reich*...but if it hadn't been her, it would have been someone else. Gudrun, for all of her intelligence and bravery, wouldn't have managed to do more than get herself arrested if others hadn't supported her.

She watched, warily, as Karl Holliston confronted Gudrun. Gudrun was putting on a good show, but it was easy to tell that she was frightened. Katherine didn't blame her. The *Fuhrer's* instability had only grown stronger since their last face-to-face meeting. It would be easy, chillingly easy, for him to order her tortured or raped or murdered. Or to do it himself...and if he did, Katherine would be unable to save her. Katherine knew she was good, but she wasn't good enough to take down five bodyguards and kill the *Fuhrer*. Even Otto Skorzeny would have found it a challenge.

I need to get her out of here, she thought, grimly. *But how?*

She was fairly sure she could get Gudrun out of the cell. Now the *Fuhrer* had pronounced her fate, Gudrun was under far less supervision. Katherine had even been able to get her some exercise, although the *Fuhrer's* benevolence hadn't reached far enough to give her some clothes. And she could see his point. A naked girl running through the corridors would be instantly noticeable. But realistically, Gudrun couldn't hope to break out of her cell and escape without help. Even Skorzeny would have found that impossible.

Katherine sighed as she watched the *Fuhrer* turn and storm out of the cell. His bodyguards fanned out around him, again, as he headed down the corridor towards the lift. He was definitely insecure, Katherine noted. The man who had once strode around the *Reichstag* as if he were a common secretary was now escorted by armed guards at all times. She couldn't help wondering if they followed him into the toilet.

She smirked at the thought, then returned to her contemplations. Getting out of the bunker was tricky, but doable; getting out of the city itself would be a great deal harder. She thought, briefly, about finding an apartment and just staying there, but she knew it wouldn't last. There were too many watching eyes in Germanica, too many people who would be happy to report anything...the moment the alarm was sounded, people would be on the alert for them. No, she had to get Gudrun out of the city...

...And she had to do it before the alarm was raised.

She checked the monitors - Gudrun was seated on the bed, crying silently - then turned back to her files. Gudrun didn't seem to have any family within the city, no relatives at all. There was certainly no one who could be counted upon to help, not when it ran the risk of crossing the *Fuhrer* himself. Katherine's own family were hundreds of miles away...and, in all honesty, she knew they probably wouldn't help either. They hadn't been very supportive of her dreams, back when she'd been a child.

Shaking her head, she started to dig into Horst Albrecht's file for the sixth time. She'd read it very carefully, back when she'd taken the risk of contacting him after the *Reich* Council had fallen; she honestly hadn't seen any reason why he might have turned on the *Reich*. But after meeting Gudrun she'd known the answer. Horst Albrecht's father had died on active service, under mysterious circumstances. He might have wondered if his father's death - and the bland notification they'd received - had come after he'd been crippled, just like Gudrun's boyfriend. And now they were married...

Katherine pursed her lips in irritation. Horst Albrecht had two sisters, both of whom lived in Germanica West...there was no sign they'd been arrested, let alone purged for daring to be related to a traitor. It puzzled her more than she cared to admit. There might have been some doubt over Horst's true role in the uprising, shortly after it had taken place, but there was no longer any doubt *now*. Both girls should have been arrested shortly after Katherine had made her report.

The report might be out of date, she thought. It didn't seem very likely. The *Reich* had a fetish for bureaucratic efficiency. If the girls had been arrested after Katherine's return from Berlin it would have been included in the file. *Or was there a reason they weren't arrested?*

She worked her way through the file, growing increasingly puzzled. One of the girls was married, but her husband was a mere stormtrooper. He might be on the front lines - or dead - yet he didn't seem important enough to dissuade the SS from arresting his wife. Hell, he'd probably be arrested too. And the other sister was unmarried, which was odd for a girl of twenty-two. Was there something wrong with her? *Katherine* wasn't married, but *she* was a soldier. She doubted the other girl was a soldier too...

Her father died before he could arrange a match, she mused. *But surely someone else would have stepped in...*

She worked her way through the girl's file and struck gold. *Impossible!*

Katherine had been warned during her training, time and time again, that anything that looked too good to be true probably wasn't. And yet, the connection was right in front of her. Horst Albrecht's father had been no one of any real consequence, but his maternal uncle was a *Gauleiter*! She supposed that explained some of the oddities in his file. His early acceptance into the training program *might* have had something to do with his need to appear *young*, but it might also be because his uncle pulled strings on his behalf...

Bastard, she thought. *She'd* had to work her ass off to get into the program. Horst had had it handed to him on a silver platter. And yet, his marks had been excellent. *They won't have graduated him if they didn't think he passed.*

She felt her smile widen as she worked her way through the file. Clearly, *Gauleiter* Forster had done a great deal more than *just* pull strings on Horst's behalf. He'd somehow concealed his connection to Horst from the *Fuhrer* himself. And if he'd done that, he could certainly assist Katherine in getting Gudrun out of the city. Hell, with Gudrun married to Horst, he'd have an *obligation* to help her.

And if I do it properly, she thought, *he'll have no choice but to help me.*

———

It had been nearly seven years since Horst had set foot in Germanica, back when he'd been a schoolboy visiting the giant city for a week. The immense buildings, each one designed to make him feel like a midget, had awed him, even though he and a couple of friends had managed to get into trouble by sneaking out one night to the bars. He'd even considered moving to the city, even though migration in and out of Germanica was heavily restricted. It had impressed him beyond words. Now...

The city had changed, he noted, as they strode through the streets. Or perhaps *he* had changed, more than he cared to admit. The giant buildings no longer seemed so marvellous; the population scurried from place to place, their faces hidden under heavy winter coats and clothing. Dozens of storm-troopers lined the streets, their eyes flickering from place to place as if they expected to be attacked at any moment. There was almost no threat, as far as Horst knew - the Provisional Government had made the decision not to bomb Germanica even after Berlin itself had been attacked - but the guards were still on alert. They'd been asked for their papers four times already.

Thankfully, Uncle Emil was able to get us into the city, he thought. *But he can't get us into the Reichstag itself.*

From a distance, the Germanica *Reichstag* looked largely identical to the Berlin *Reichstag,* only larger. A towering blocky building, surrounded by Nazi flags and stone eagles…he couldn't help thinking that there was something *wrong* about it, although he couldn't put his finger on it. And yet, as he walked closer, the sense of *oddness* only grew stronger. The guards standing by the barricades looked like mites guarding the home of a giant. Whatever the builders had done messed with his head, as if his perceptions were somehow out of alignment. It made him dizzy just thinking about it.

"Papers," a harsh voice snapped.

Horst handed over his ID card at once. The guard examined it briefly, then glanced at Kurt's before waving them both on. Horst had no trouble recognising a uniformed bully, the type of man who *lived* to make others feel small and worthless. And yet, like all such men, he was a coward at heart. He certainly didn't have the nerve to harass them after seeing where their cards had been issued. Who knew? He might have landed in *real* trouble.

Bastard, Horst thought, darkly. The man was clearly too *much* of a coward to actually head west and *fight.* But then, if some of the rumours spreading through the city were accurate, the entire front line was crumbling. *No stomach to do anything but bully people.*

He kept his face expressionless as they walked back towards his uncle's residence. A trio of vans had parked outside a housing block, a dozen stormtroopers watching as an entire family was marched out of the building and into the vans. It was impossible to tell what they'd done, but Horst could guess. Rumour-mongering, according to the wireless, was now a capital offense. Someone had said something indiscreet…

He shuddered as he saw four children, the oldest probably no older than ten. Perhaps the SS would be merciful and send them to a farm in the east as a group…no, *mercy* was one thing the SS never showed. The entire family would be turned into a gruesome example of what happened to people who spread rumours. They'd be split up, the two boys sent to orphanages and boarding schools while the girls were sent to the farms. Their names would be changed, they'd be beaten every time they talked about their families…

…And they'd never see each other again.

There's nothing we can do, he thought, sourly. *Not yet.*

They walked the rest of the way in silence, passing two *Volkssturm* guards as they walked through the guards and into the residence. A *Gauleiter* was entitled to a mansion in Germanica, although Horst had a nasty feeling it wasn't quite as secure as his uncle might have hoped. The SS would certainly have tried to get a spy into his household staff or suborn one of his trusted subordinates…

And if he's wrong about who can be trusted, Horst thought morbidly, *we'll all wind up hanging from meathooks under the Reichstag.*

"Ah, Horst," Forster said. His uncle sounded remarkably cheerful for someone who was plotting a revolution. "We have a rather unusual visitor."

He nodded towards the lounge. Horst exchanged glances with Kurt, then stepped into the room. A young man was seated on the sofa…no, a young *woman*. Horst straightened, one hand dropping to the pistol at his belt, as he *recognised* her. And judging by the way her eyes went wide, she recognised *him*.

"You…"

Horst drew his pistol, ignoring his uncle's warning. "You took her!"

Katherine held up her hands. "Yes, I did," she said, bluntly. "And I was wrong."

"Katherine has a proposition for us," his uncle said. "She'll be in the bunker when the balloon goes up."

Horst glanced at him, sharply. "She's a *loyalist*…"

"I am loyal to the *Reich*," Katherine said, tartly. "And the *Reich* cannot survive with Holliston at the helm."

"Oh," Horst said.

He carefully returned his pistol to the holster, unsure if he should laugh or cry. Katherine had been in *command* of the SS squad in Berlin. A position like that wasn't handed out like beer at Oktoberfest. And a woman…she wouldn't have reached such a position *without* being better than the men - and probably more fanatical too.

And Uncle Emil's recruited her, he thought, numbly. *Is he out of his mind?*

It wasn't a pleasant thought. There were plenty of people who'd switched sides - Uncle Emil, Volker Schulze, Hans Krueger...hell, Horst himself. But Katherine...could she be trusted? How had she even known to find them?

"Your wife is still alive," Katherine said. "The *Fuhrer* plans to send her east in a few days."

Horst swallowed, hard. East...even if they won the war, Gudrun would never be the same again. A dozen questions came to his lips, but he wasn't sure he wanted the answers. She...

He took a breath. "How is she?"

"Bearing up very well," Katherine said. "I believe the *Fuhrer* regrets some of his early decisions concerning her. She is alive and well, if a little bored."

Horst wasn't sure he believed her. He knew too much about the SS. Gudrun was a special prisoner, but it was unlikely they'd refrain from torturing her. And yet...

"You knew to come here," he said, flatly. "How?"

"I worked my way through the records, looking for someone who might be willing to help," Katherine said, slowly. "I uncovered the connection between you and your uncle" - she nodded to Forster - "and decided he might be able to help me smuggle Gudrun out of the city."

Horst shook his head slowly. "And you came here?"

Katherine, for the first time, showed a hint of annoyance. "I made sure to have an excuse," she said, bluntly. "No one will question my visit."

"If you're in touch with Gudrun," Kurt said suddenly, "you can ask her a question from us, can't you?"

"Perhaps," Katherine said. "But I have to be very careful when I speak to her."

Oddly, Horst found that a little reassuring. He *knew* how 'special' prisoners were treated, even the ones who had to be treated gently. Gudrun would be under constant observation, her every last word and action scrutinised for hidden meaning. But Katherine would have no trouble speaking to her if her superiors *knew* she was in contact with the underground...

"Very well," Kurt said. "I want you to ask her about what happened after the winter fire."

Horst blinked. "The winter fire?"

"She'll understand," Kurt said.

"As you wish," Katherine said. She took a breath. "You have heard the news?"

"There have been mutinies on the front line," Forster said, when Horst looked puzzled. "*Bad* mutinies, depending on who you ask."

Horst frowned. Was there such a thing as a *good* mutiny? And yet, had there ever *been* a genuine mutiny in the *Waffen-SS*? He couldn't recall one... but then, *he* had technically mutinied too. And now Katherine was joining him in treachery...

Unless she's conning us, he thought.

He shook his head. If Holliston had known about his presence, he would have had the residence surrounded and stormed. No one would have quibbled after Holliston displayed the body of Horst Albrecht, arch-traitor. Even the remaining *Gauleiters* would have kept their mouths firmly shut.

"We'll discuss that later," he said. How would Holliston react? He doubted it would be pleasant. "For the moment, get us the answer to the question. After that, we can discuss how to proceed."

Katherine rose. "Understood," she said, briskly.

She met his eyes. "I know that you have no reason to trust me," she added. "But what I do now, I do for the *Reich*. This war must end."

"Quickly," Forster added. "Because if the front line is coming apart, Holliston is likely to do something desperate."

"Or try to burn the world," Horst said. He watched Katherine leave, wondering if they hadn't just signed their death warrants. "Kurt, what happened after the winter fire?"

Kurt looked rather shamefaced. "It's a long story," he said. "But it's not one she will ever forget."

CHAPTER THIRTY-FOUR

front Lines, Germany Prime
14 November 1985

Obergruppenfuehrer Felix Kortig was caught on the horns of a dilemma.

The mutiny hadn't spread as far as he'd feared, in the last two days, but he was uneasily aware that his men were wavering. Rumours were spreading like wildfire, ranging from grim stories of atrocities to suggestions that the entire army had been poisoned by the radioactive fallout. The more intact units, the ones that had been spared the brunt of the retreat, were largely free of mutineers, but he knew better than to take it for granted.

And I can't wait for reinforcements either, he thought. *I have to move now.*

It wasn't a pleasant thought. The brief encounters along the front lines had stopped, but that wouldn't last. If the enemy realised that his entire force was in disarray, they'd throw in a general attack that would shatter his remaining defences and open the road to Germanica. They probably wouldn't *make* it to Germanica - the roads were already becoming impassable because of the heavy snowfall - but they'd certainly be able to take up positions that would make it easier to reach the city when the snow melted.

He cursed, savagely, as he paced the tent. It had been a mistake, a bad mistake, to risk everything on one throw of the dice. And the mistake had been compounded by how poorly the wounded had been treated, after the nuclear blasts. It was hard to blame the mutineers for rising up against their superior officers, even though they'd signed their own death warrants - it wasn't as if they had much to lose. The ones who had been contaminated with radiation poisoning would probably be *grateful* if they were shot.

And now the Fuhrer commands that I put down the mutinies as quickly as possible, he reminded himself. *But can it be done without weakening the forces I have left?*

It was…frustrating. No, *worse* than frustrating. He'd never doubted his men before, even during the bloodiest battles in South Africa. The *Waffen-SS* was always faithful, always loyal. But now that loyalty was a joke. He didn't dare show weakness in front of the stormtroopers, yet everything he did to safeguard his position and prevent another mutiny was a show of weakness. And if his men doubted him, who *knew* what they would do?

Jumped-up spymaster, he thought, in the privacy of his own head. It wasn't something he could say out loud. He had no doubt that *someone* would report him if he said something unpleasant about the *Fuhrer. He has no understanding of the military realities.*

But orders were orders. He couldn't delay any longer, not without being branded a mutineer himself. Holliston wouldn't listen to any excuses, no matter how firmly they were rooted in military realities. To him, obstacles like rivers and mountains and snowfalls were just lines on a map. And little things like morale meant nothing to him.

And the hell of it, Felix reluctantly conceded, was that Holliston had a point.

The mutineers were desperate. They *had* to be desperate. And if they were desperate, they might just take themselves - and their equipment, and everything they knew - across the lines and straight into the rebel's welcoming arms. Felix didn't want to *think* about what would happen if the rebels started sweet-talking his men. The war had turned so sour that far too many of them would probably surrender, if they thought they wouldn't be shot out of hand.

He turned as the flap opened. "*Herr Obergruppenfuehrer,*" *Sturmbannfuehrer* Friedemann Weineck said. "The infantry divisions have been readied for their task."

"Good," Felix said. It was hard to keep the annoyance out of his voice. Weineck sounded depressingly enthusiastic. Infantrymen shouldn't be given such a task, one more suitable for butchers like the *Einsatzgruppen* than stormtroopers. "Order them to proceed as planned."

"*Jawohl.*"

Felix shrugged as he turned back to the map. Crushing the mutineers shouldn't take too long, assuming they didn't turn and flee. But it wouldn't stop the *Fuhrer* from sending reinforcements, men who would probably trigger off the *next* set of mutinies. And then…

Briefly, very briefly, he considered just leaving and strolling across the front lines himself. It wasn't as if he couldn't do it - and he knew enough to convince the rebels that he should be left alive. But he'd sworn loyalty to the SS - and to the *Reich* - and he wasn't going to break his oath so easily. He was an officer in the *Waffen-SS* and he would *remain* an officer in the *Waffen-SS* until he died.

I hope you flee, he thought, as he studied the map. He didn't really *hate* the mutineers, even though they'd caused him a great deal of trouble. *You don't want to be there when the infantry arrive.*

———

Hennecke honestly wasn't sure what to do.

The mutiny - and everything that had come afterwards - had blunted his thinking for a couple of days. Eating rations, drinking alcohol, having fun with the nurses…he simply hadn't had *time* to think about the future. But now, as the alcohol began to run out, he found himself irritatingly sober as the first light of dawn started to glimmer over the dark sky.

He still didn't feel well, although he wasn't sure if that was because of the radiation or the binge-eating. Rations were barely designed for human consumption in any case. His head hurt, although it was a vast improvement over the headache he'd had two days ago; his body throbbed, leaving him feeling as though he had a fever. And to think he was one of the healthiest people in the camp! Even *after* the guards had been shot or driven away, the wounded continued to die.

Of course they did, he thought, darkly. *We are all going to die.*

He'd sat one of the nurses down, midway through the second day, and interrogated her about radiation poisoning. Nothing she'd said, after he'd provided proper encouragement, had been reassuring. There was nothing that could be done, she'd explained; no magical cure that would save their lives. Even if they survived the first bout of radiation sickness - and that was unlikely - they'd be walking wounded for the rest of their lives.

He gripped his rifle as he rose, nodding towards the guards at the edge of the camp. Getting them out there had been one hell of a struggle, now that authority had broken down completely; he'd had to point out, as if he was talking to children, *precisely* what would happen if they were caught by surprise. Some of his mutineers had deserted, heading west to the rebels or east back to their homes, but he knew it was going to end badly. The rebels would kill them for their conduct in Germany Prime, the loyalists would hang them for mutiny.

And yet, here we are, all exposed, he thought.

He peered into the distance, half-expecting to see an armoured force advancing towards him as the day grew brighter. But there was nothing. There hadn't even been any aircraft flying overhead. It was tempting to believe that they were completely alone, that they were completely cut off from both sides, but he knew better. By now, word had probably spread all the way to Germanica. He knew the *Fuhrer* would not let their mutiny pass without a harsh response.

A scream echoed on the air, coming from one of the smaller tents. Hennecke shrugged, unconcerned. The nurses had known they were going to die, known right from the start that there was nothing that could be done for any of the wounded. He found it hard to care about their treatment, even if they *were* decent German girls. Besides, it wasn't as if the mutineers could be executed more than once. The *Fuhrer* would have some problems trying to fit all the charges on a single execution warrant, assuming there *was* an execution warrant.

Stupid bitch, he thought, as the screaming abruptly stopped. *No one cares about you.*

He shrugged as he started to walk from tent to tent, checking on the wounded. Three more men had died in their sleep, relatively comfortably. He sighed as he called a couple of other men to help drag the bodies out, strip them of anything useful and then dump them away from the camp. They really should dig a grave, he told himself, but he didn't have the energy to do anything more than leave the bodies in the snow. He and the rest of the mutineers would be dead long before decomposing bodies became a real problem.

His hands started to ache as he turned and strode back towards the command tent. The nurse hadn't been too clear on the *why* and *how*, but she'd been insistent that his aches and pains would only get worse. Unless he was very lucky…and even then, the damage had still been done. He had nothing to look forward to, save for a life of increasing pain and eventual death.

A tent opened. A stormtrooper emerged, buttoning up his fly. Behind him, Hennecke could hear whimpering from inside the tent. It should bother him to pass the women around from mutineer to mutineer, allowing them to slake their lusts before they died, but he had long since lost the ability to care. Death was coming for them, no matter what they did. They might as well have some fun before they died.

"Get some food, then join the guards," he ordered. "Hurry."

He turned…and then stopped as he heard a roar in the distance. Engines…coming from the east. He barked a command, then pulled a whistle from his belt and blew it as loudly as he could. The tents opened, revealing all the men who were fit to fight. Hennecke felt his heart sink as he took in the sight - twenty-seven men, half of them barely strong enough to walk - and then he started to bark orders. Any objections were rapidly buried by the sound of approaching engines…

"Get into position," he snapped. He had no illusions about their ability to defend the camp against an armoured thrust, but at least they could hurt the stormtroopers before they were crushed. "Hurry!"

He groaned, inwardly, as the men stumbled into position. They'd never had a chance to plan out a defence before the mutiny; afterwards, they'd been too busy enjoying themselves to do anything about their defences. In hindsight, it had been a mistake…

…But there was no point in worrying about it, not now. The radiation would kill them even if the bullets didn't.

He sucked in his breath as the first vehicle - an armoured fighting vehicle - came into view, a squad of black-clad infantry surrounding it. Their paranoia was almost laughable. Bandits and insurgents might do everything in their power to slow the vehicles down - rigging bombs and mines - but his men hadn't done anything of the sort. They hadn't even had the weapons and equipment to *try*. Two more armoured fighting vehicles appeared, grinding forward…

"Take aim," he ordered. The enemy could probably see them - and if they couldn't see them, they could certainly *smell* them. "Fire on my command."

A scattered volley of shots rang out. Hennecke had barely a second to realise that some of his men had fired without orders before the approaching vehicles returned fire. Machine gun bullets tore through the air, slashing through tents as though they were made of paper; three of his men jumped to their feet, only to be torn apart by the hail of bullets. They'd wanted to die, Hennecke realised, as he started to shoot himself, picking off two stormtroopers before the others took cover. There wasn't anything to live for…

He turned and crawled away as the shooting grew louder. The entire camp had been devastated in the blink of an eye. He snickered as he thought of the nurses, killed by their would-be saviours, then kept moving until he was right across the camp and heading into the woods. Behind him, the roar of engines grew louder as the enemy took possession of the camp. He smirked as he picked himself up and started to run, despite the throbbing pain in his head. Taking the camp wouldn't do them any good, unless they *wanted* to have a few hundred dead bodies.

There was no sign of pursuit, but he kept moving until he was sure he was lost in the cold forest. His body felt feverish as he stopped long enough to lean against a tree and catch his breath, despite the snow around him. Despite himself, he started to giggle helplessly. The stormtroopers had attacked, they'd killed everyone…but him. He'd survived the war, he'd survived the radiation, he'd survived brutal labour that was meant to kill him…

The skies were darkening rapidly. He looked up, sharply, as it started to snow. There was no way he could stay still, not if he wanted to remain alive. And yet, where could he go? He gritted his teeth as he started to stumble through the snow, his body starting to shiver despite the fever. And yet, the snowfall only grew worse. It was so intense that he could barely see…

He stumbled, then fell to the ground. It was so cold that he could barely move, the cold seeping into his body as if it were a living thing. He tried to summon up some determination, the same determination that had kept him alive after the nuclear blasts and radiation poisoning, but it was gone. There was nowhere to go. Who would help him? Who would take him in…?

Stupid bastards, he thought. He thought he understood the rebels a little better now, as he hovered on the brink of death. He'd thought the stories about betrayal were lies, enemy propaganda, until he'd been betrayed himself. *We could have won the war if they'd just thought…*

The darkness reached up and swallowed him. And then there was nothing.

———

"Do you think they can be trusted?"

Herman shrugged. Seven enemy deserters sat in the tent, their hands tied behind their backs while the army tried to figure out what to do with them. Their story - that they had deserted from the *Waffen-SS* - didn't *sound* believable, but he'd been a policeman. People had tried to lie to him all the time and he'd gotten very good at spotting it.

But these goons came from the SS, he thought, darkly. *They're probably very good liars.*

"Have them sent to a detention camp," he suggested, finally. "And make sure they're kept separate from the other prisoners."

He scowled as the prisoners were marched out of the camp. The entire offensive had been called off, leaving him feeling rather exposed after most of the remaining panzers had been recalled and repositioned behind the front lines. He understood the logic, but he wasn't too pleased about it. His unit would take the brunt of any enemy blow, allowing the front-line units time to get ready to meet and repel the offensive.

But at least we're not stuck guarding POWs, he thought. *Or…*

He turned as he heard the sound of running footsteps behind him. A young man - barely old enough to shave - was running up to him, his face flushed with excitement. Herman couldn't help feeling a stab of guilt and shame at seeing the young soldier, a boy no older than his middle son, in the midst of a battlefield. There was no way he had enough training to do more than point and shoot, even if he *had* been in the Hitler Youth.

"*Herr Leutnant,*" the young man managed, as he came to a halt. "I…you have been called back to Berlin, immediately."

He turned and hurried off. Herman would have rebuked him, if he'd still been a paratrooper, but he doubted there was any point. He'd need to be *very* harsh - and it would probably kill the young man's determination to do well.

The thought made him scowl as he turned and headed towards the gate. Johan was already in training. If he thought there was someone his age fighting on the front line, he'd probably sneak out of the training centre and head east.

And that would get him killed, Herman thought, morbidly.

He'd been terrified when Kurt had headed off to the Berlin Guard, even though he'd hidden it behind a facade of enthusiasm and pride. The thought of losing his firstborn son had been horrific. And *Johan* was much younger. It was always the ones who had never been to war who spoke of glory. War was hell, no matter what the songs said; war was blood and suffering and death. War should never be the first choice.

But there were times when the alternative was worse, when fighting was the only alternative to submission. And the Provisional Government had no choice but to fight. Everyone involved in the government - including Herman himself - would be purged in the aftermath, if Holliston won the war. And that would only be the beginning of the nightmare...

He sighed as he saw the van, waiting by the gates. There was no way to know why he'd been summoned. He'd find out soon enough. Berlin might have something in mind for him - or he might just be told he was needed back on the streets. He climbed into the van, spoke briefly to the driver and then sat down and closed his eyes. Whatever was coming, he had the feeling he needed to be alert.

And if the enemy is starting to leak deserters, he thought, *we might just be on the verge of ending the war.*

CHAPTER THIRTY-FIVE

Germanica, Germany East
15 November 1985

"I need to ask you a question," Katherine said, as she half-pushed Gudrun into the washroom and turned on the water. "What happened after the winter fire?"

Gudrun froze. There was no way *anyone* outside her family knew about the winter fire. How could *Katherine* have learned of it? How…?

"I need to know," Katherine hissed. "What happened?"

"I have a cousin - Fritz," Gudrun said. She felt a sudden surge of hope. Katherine wouldn't have known to *ask* unless she was in contact with someone from her family. Kurt? Or her father? Or…"He told me that I wouldn't be anything other than a housewife. I punched him."

"Good for you," Katherine said.

Gudrun had to smile, despite her conflicting feelings. "He fell over backwards, his nose bleeding," she added. "Father was very unhappy and Kurt took the blame."

"Oh dear," Katherine said. "Was that all?"

Gudrun shrugged. She didn't know - she'd *never* known - if her father had seen through the lie or not. He'd never been easy to lie to, but he'd given Kurt a thrashing instead of asking questions that would have unravelled the whole deception. *Fritz* had certainly never told the truth, although if the truth *had* come out everyone would have laughed at him. He'd had his nose bloodied by a girl!

She didn't feel too sorry for him. Fritz had been a little creep when he'd been a child and he hadn't improved as he'd grown into a teenager. Gudrun had caught him ogling her more than once, even though they were cousins. He'd bragged of his grand plans to join the SS, but she had no idea if he actually *had*. She hadn't seen him since the day she'd bloodied his nose.

He was probably snapped up at once, she thought, nastily. *He had the right mindset to spy on everyone.*

"We didn't see him afterwards," she said. "He never came round again."

She smirked. Fritz wouldn't have suffered if Kurt *had* punched him - at least, he wouldn't have been a laughing stock - but he wouldn't have wanted to risk being smacked by Gudrun again. If Kurt hadn't lied…Gudrun had never quite understood *why* Kurt had lied. It wasn't as if Gudrun had been in any real danger. Her father might have laughed at Fritz himself rather than punishing Gudrun.

"I see," Katherine said. "Thank you."

Gudrun looked at her. "Why…?"

"Not a word," Katherine said. "And *don't* speak of it outside this room."

She pushed Gudrun under the water before Gudrun could say a word. Water ran down her body, washing away the dirt and grime from the cell. She rubbed at her hair, wishing for some shampoo, as she began to think. The only way Katherine could have found out about the whole affair was from Gudrun's family…no, it had to be Kurt. No one *else* knew the full story.

And that meant…hope warred with fear in her breast. Katherine had taken care of her over the last few days - and she'd saved Gudrun from Doctor Muller - but it might all be a trick, a plot to get her to let down her guard. And yet, Holliston had been very clear that Gudrun was going to be sent east. There was no *need* to try to break down her defences any longer, no need to force her to talk. And besides, she honestly didn't know anything of value.

They probably thought I wasn't at the table for any military decisions, she thought. She'd punched Fritz for his casual assumption that she'd never be anything other than a housewife, but she had to admit that most women in Germany never *were* anything more than housewives. It galled her to know that such casual misogyny had provided her with a degree of protection. *And even if I had been, anything I knew would be out of date.*

She scowled at the thought. If she'd been a man, she would probably be dead by now. No, there was no *probably* about it. There was no other reason to keep her alive, now that Holliston had apparently abandoned the plan to use her to somehow break the Provisional Government. She would have ended her life hanging from a meat hook under the *Reichstag* if she hadn't been a girl. Instead…

I'll be sent east if he has his way, she thought, morbidly. *And that will be the end.*

It wasn't a pleasant thought. She'd heard enough horror stories - mainly from Horst - to know she *didn't* want to go to the east. Conditions were terrible, she'd been told; it was hard, nearly impossible, to find women who were *willing* to go. The *Reich* preferred to send its female prisoners east because it was cheaper than keeping them in the camps - and because it let the *Reich* get some use out of them. And if the women objected to their new roles as housewives and mothers, there were plenty of ways to keep them in line.

She looked at Katherine as she stepped out of the shower. Could she be trusted? Gudrun had no idea, but she knew she didn't dare ask. Katherine had taken an immense risk asking her the question, even with the running water making it hard - if not impossible - for the audio pick-ups to hear her. And yet, was it all a trap? There was no way to know.

Occam's Razor, she reminded herself. *The simplest solution is normally the correct one.*

There was no *need* to get her to incriminate herself further. She was the founder of the protest movement that had overthrown the *Reich* Council. Holliston didn't *need* any more of an excuse to dispose of her, even if he did have to send her east in a mocking display of clemency for the misguided - and foolish - female. And there was no point in trying to use it to entrap Kurt. If Katherine was in contact with him, she'd know where to find him.

She glanced at Katherine. "Can I get some clothes?"

"Not yet," Katherine said. She sounded regretful. "Orders."

Gudrun nodded, crossly. Walking around naked now felt quite natural, although she suspected she'd change her mind if she had to leave the building. Hell, she'd change her mind if she had to face Holliston again. The would-be *Fuhrer* was going mad. How long would it be, she wondered, before he decided to hurt her himself? Katherine couldn't stop *him* from doing whatever the hell he wanted.

And it's probably cold outside, she thought, darkly. She couldn't have been in the cell for longer than a month, if that. Winter was probably already sweeping over Germanica. *If I walk out like this I'll freeze to death.*

———

"She's alive," Kurt said.

The relief he felt was overwhelmingly powerful. He'd been tormented for weeks by the thought that it was *his* fault that Gudrun had been captured, even though she'd made her own decisions. If he'd refused to go to the hospital with her - or even reported her plans to their father - the world would be a very different place. But his sister was alive! He wanted to go to her right now...he shook his head, forcing himself to calm down. Rash action now, in the middle of the enemy camp, would be utterly disastrous.

Katherine eyed him, quizzically. "Why did you take the blame?"

Kurt shuddered. Fritz...had been a thoroughly unpleasant person. Kurt had caught him staring at Gudrun dozens of times, his eyes crawling over her breasts or buttocks and then looking away hastily when she turned her head. And he had a feeling that Fritz would have spied on Gudrun in her bedroom, if he'd had the chance. He'd been on the verge of punching the little bastard a dozen times before Gudrun had slammed her fist into his nose. Watching Fritz fall, whimpering in pain, was one of the few decent memories of his cousin.

But he'd known, even then, that Fritz would never forgive Gudrun if the world *knew* it was her who'd flattened him. God alone knew what he would do, in retaliation, but it wouldn't be pleasant. Fritz was a born coward and sneak, someone who should have been kicked out of the Hitler Youth; Kurt honestly didn't understand why he *hadn't* been given the boot a long time ago. But he'd stepped forward, when his father had demanded answers; he'd told his father that *he'd* punched Fritz.

"Because Fritz would have sought revenge," he said, finally. Someone like Fritz would *never* let it go. He'd wallow in hatred and resentment until he did something very stupid - and destroyed a life. "Gudrun's life could have been ruined if he'd reported her for something."

Katherine cocked her head. "You didn't think Gudrun could handle it herself?"

"I'm her brother," Kurt said. "It's my job to protect her."

He ignored Horst's snicker and Katherine's look of indignation. Fritz had never visited their home again, thankfully. Perhaps it was out of a misplaced sense of gratitude - or perhaps he was simply afraid of another encounter with Gudrun's fist. But if he had…Kurt had no illusions. The right word in the right place could have utterly destroyed Gudrun's hopes and dreams for a different future. And if he'd simply attacked her instead…

He wouldn't have tried to rape her, he tried to tell himself. *Fritz is too much of a coward to try.*

Horst glanced at him. "What happened to the bastard?"

"He joined the SS," Kurt said. He'd worried, for a while, that Fritz intended to do something to take revenge, but nothing had ever materialised. "I don't know what happened to him afterwards."

"Perhaps he got purged for being related to Gudrun," Horst said.

Kurt shrugged. "Maybe," he said. It *was* a pleasant thought. "Or maybe he's still out there, somewhere."

He cleared his throat, then looked at Horst. "Are you satisfied?"

"Mostly," Horst said. "Are *you?*"

"I think so," Kurt said. There was no one alive, save for Gudrun and himself, who knew the full story. Their *father* didn't know…although Kurt had often wondered if the old man had noticed that he didn't have blood on his knuckles. "She's alive and well and we have an ally."

Horst nodded, reluctantly. He'd expressed his concerns quite loudly, after Katherine had departed earlier, but they were running short of options. The possibility of being betrayed would have to be factored into their plans, along with all the other variables. And besides, if everything went well, they should be able to cope with a last-minute betrayal.

And if we can't, we die, Kurt thought.

Katherine looked at him. "I can smuggle Gudrun out of the *Reichstag* in two days," she said, bluntly. "You'll have to get her out of the city before the alarm is raised."

"No," Horst said. "We're going to attack the *Reichstag* tomorrow."

Katherine started. "How many men do you have?"

"Enough," Horst said. "You're in the bunker, are you not? If Holliston gets into the bunker before we arrive, I want you to catch him."

Kurt saw Katherine stiffen, just for a second. "You *do* realise he'll be escorted by his bodyguards?"

"Yes," Horst said. "But if he gets into the bunker and seals himself in, the entire plan will fail."

Kurt winced. They'd learned far too much about the *Reichstag* in the last couple of days to be comfortable with *anything*. Shutting down radio transmissions would be easy enough, thankfully, but there were underground communications cables leading directly to SS bases outside the city. And there was a tunnel Holliston and his cronies could use to escape, if they were lucky. Given a chance to rally resistance, Holliston could plunge Germany East into a civil war.

"I understand," Katherine said, stiffly. "Does Gudrun know how to shoot a rifle?"

"I taught her," Horst said.

"Pathetic westerners," Katherine said. She gave Kurt a dark look. "Do you refrain from training your women so they'll be helpless?"

Kurt smiled. "I don't think *Gudrun* is helpless."

"And yet you felt the urge to look after her," Katherine pointed out.

"Yes," Kurt said. "Because I'm her brother and that's what brothers *do*."

He scowled. A rumour - even a relatively harmless rumour - could do endless damage to a young lady's reputation. Konrad had loved Gudrun - Kurt was sure of that - but would his family have approved the match if Gudrun had acquired a reputation for sleeping around? It wouldn't matter if the rumour was true or false, not if it had spread too far to be easily countered. Konrad would have been told, in no uncertain terms, that marrying Gudrun would cost him the rest of his family…

And no one would have cared if Konrad had slept around, he thought, grimly. *Because girls have to be virgins while men…*

"We can track down and kill Fritz later," Horst said. His attitude made it clear that he wasn't joking. "For the moment, we need to concentrate on the plan."

Katherine gave him a sidelong look. "You do not care about your wife?"

"I care a great deal about my wife," Horst said. "And the only way to save her is to bring this regime crashing down."

"Good," Katherine said. Kurt couldn't help thinking that she and Horst would make a good match. There was something…*cold*…*distant*…in both of them. But then, Gudrun had probably warmed Horst up a little. "I'll be ready when the time comes."

"I can't give you a specific time," Horst said, as Katherine rose. "But it will come."

Katherine nodded and strode out of the room. Kurt watched her go, unable to keep from noticing just how *mannish* she was. She even *walked* like a man. Kurt doubted Gudrun could pose as a man so effectively, even if she'd worn male clothes. There was something about Katherine that shouted out *man* to him. Even knowing the truth, he found it hard to see her as just another female…

…And yet, there was something about her he liked.

"You're staring," Horst said, quietly.

Kurt flushed. "Sorry."

"Yeah," Horst said. He shrugged. "Can you handle your part of the mission?"

"Yes," Kurt said, flatly. He would have preferred to be on the ground, with Horst, but it couldn't be helped. "Can your uncle handle *his* side of the plan?"

"If he can't, we're in trouble," Horst said.

Kurt nodded. He wasn't keen on the idea of trusting a *Gauleiter*, but he had to admit that Emil Forster had had ample opportunity to betray them after making contact. Hell, he hadn't had to do *anything*. Kurt and Horst would have been executed as soon as they reached Germanica and the *Gauleiter's* secret - his inconvenient relations - would be thoroughly buried.

And there are too many others involved, he thought, grimly. *The longer we delay, the greater the chance that one of them will get cold feet.*

"I'll be on my way this afternoon, then," Kurt said. "See you on the other side."

"Victory or death," Horst agreed.

Kurt winced. The plan was a desperate gamble. If it succeeded, the war would end; if it failed, they'd be trapped in Germanica, hundreds of miles from support. And while they *would* do immense damage to the city, it wouldn't be enough to unseat Holliston.

"Victory or death," he agreed.

———

Germanica looked quiet.

Karl Holliston stood in front of the window and peered out over the city. Darkness was descending rapidly, but he could still make out the guards watching carefully as the streets were swept clean of snow. Bringing the *Untermenschen* cleaners into the city was a risk, particularly now that half of the garrison had been dispatched west, yet it was one that had to be borne. It was important, *very* important, that life in Germanica remain as close to normal as possible.

He took a sip of his drink, tasting the alcohol as it slid down his throat. The original group of mutineers had been crushed, save for a handful of survivors who had fled into the snow to die. And the others would be crushed too, given time. And many senior officers who hadn't shown enough fortitude, in the early hours of the mutiny, would be purged.

And the rebels haven't tried to take advantage of the chaos, he thought, feeling a grim flicker of satisfaction. His spy was *still* reporting that everything was quiet in Berlin, that the enemy was going into winter quarters. By the time the rebels were ready to resume the offensive, his forces would be ready to meet them. *They don't even know we had a mutiny.*

He smiled, rather coldly. The *Gauleiters* were meeting, plotting against him...did they think he hadn't noticed? But they couldn't overthrow him. A *Fuhrer* could not be removed from office, save by force...

...And their forces had been sent west to confront the rebels or east to protect the settlements.

They will be purged too, he promised himself. There were just too many *Gauleiters* who were disloyal to him. The entire position needed to be rethought, perhaps replaced by men who would do his bidding and nothing else. *Once the rebels are defeated, I will reshape the Reich so I can lead it into a glorious future.*

He took another sip, enjoying the taste. His position was secure. Gudrun, for all her defiance, could do nothing to save herself; the Provisional Government, hundreds of miles away, would fall apart as it struggled to build a new order; the *Gauleiters*, ambitious bastards to a man, were powerless. And while there had been some setbacks, the future was bright and full of promise. The inevitable American collapse would allow the *Reich* to finally realise its destiny of ruling and reshaping the entire world.

And soon, he promised the city silently, *the entire world will look like you.*

CHAPTER THIRTY-SIX

Emergency Airfield, Germany East
16 November 1985

Unterscharfuehrer Edwin Telkamp cursed under his breath as the dawn rose, cursing his commanding officer under his breath. There had been no bandit attacks this close to Germanica for years - and they were hundreds of miles from the war front - but the asshole insisted on Edwin and his men standing guard in front of the gates at all hours. Edwin would have obeyed orders - happily - as a young man, but as an older man it seemed remarkably pointless. He'd been recalled to the military and assigned to guard an airfield in the middle of nowhere, rather than defending his farm…he had no idea what his wife and daughters were going to do in the coming year. His three sons had *also* been called up…

He gritted his teeth. The cold was seeping into his bones more than usual, but the CO didn't give a damn. It was alright for him, Edwin supposed; the bastard had spent the night in a cot, not standing in the bitter cold staring into the darkness. Edwin had wound up keeping his men moving in and out of the guardhouse all night, catching some heat before they walked back out into the cold. He didn't know if it was any good, but without the tiny heater in the guardhouse he had a feeling they would all have frozen to death before the sun rose.

Bastards, he thought, crossly. *They could have just forgotten about me.*

He scowled at the thought. He'd *done* his service, hadn't he? He'd put in fifteen years as a stormtrooper, patrolling the settlements to the east and hunting down bandits and other threats to the *Volk*. His long tour on the Chinese border had been particularly gruelling, which was why he'd retired and returned to the family farm to raise his family. But now he was back in the uniform, patrolling an airfield built for a war that had never come…

…And then he heard the engines.

He tensed as a line of armoured patrol vehicles came into view, heading straight towards the airfield. They *looked* normal, flying standard pennants in the morning sun, but the bandits were known for being devious. And yet, he found it hard to believe that nine patrollers could have been captured and put to work. Most of the bandits simply didn't know how to drive!

The lead vehicle came to a halt outside the gate. Its hatches opened a moment later, disgorging a dozen men in *Volkssturm* uniforms. They looked younger than he'd expected…he felt a flicker of anger as he realised that most of the soldiers would have gone into the *Volkssturm* to escape service on the eastern front. But the joke was on them now, he knew; a number of *Volkssturm* units had been dispatched west to confront the rebels. He stepped forward…

…And froze as a rifle was jabbed into his chest.

"Make a sound, any sound, and you're dead," his captor growled.

Edwin stared in utter shock as his men were rounded up, searched and then cuffed while two of the intruders opened the gates. Who *were* they? There was no way that they were bandits, not when they were clearly Germans. And yet…he gritted his teeth as the *Volkssturm* drove up to the control tower and stormed it, probably capturing everyone before they could get a message out. If it was a security inspection - and it *was* a possibility - he had to admit that they'd just failed. The commander was probably going to be reassigned to the eastern front after losing so badly…

…But there was something about the way they moved that suggested otherwise.

"On your feet," a voice growled. "March."

Edwin tested the cuffs lightly as they were frog-marched towards the nearest hangar. They were tight, almost certainly unbreakable. The tricks he knew for escaping his bonds were probably worthless. There was no way out, no way to pass the test - or escape to warn their superiors if it *wasn't* a test. Whatever happened, they had lost…

…And he had no idea what would happen next.

———

Kurt allowed himself a moment of relief as it became clear that the airfield guards hadn't had a chance to transmit a warning message before they were overwhelmed and captured. They hadn't been very alert at all, despite being in the middle of Germany East. But then, most of the guards were old enough to be his father and their commander didn't seem to take his job very seriously. They were a *long* way from any actual *threat*.

The airfield itself was really nothing more than a back-up for other airfields, located to the north or the east. Kurt had been on several airfields in his career, but he had to admit that the emergency airfield was easily the least impressive of them all, really nothing more than a pair of runways designed for heavy bombers, a couple of empty hangars and a single mid-sized control tower. He was surprised that Germanica thought the airfield was worth the trouble of guarding. But the radar network covering Germany East had been taking a battering ever since the civil war began - and hadn't been designed to track aircraft coming from the west in any case - so he supposed the radar station had needed *some* protection.

But not enough, he thought, as he searched the control tower to make sure that no one had been missed during the first sweep. *We practically walked in and took the place.*

He shrugged. The airfield had been practically abandoned for months, perhaps years. There were no signs of individuality in the handful of rooms, save for a pornographic magazine someone had dumped on the floor before leaving. Nearly all of the supplies, save for a medical kit, had been cleaned out as well. Kurt was surprised the fuel dump had been left intact - he could think of some other uses for aviation fuel - but he knew better than to question their good fortune. It was about time something went their way.

"The base is secure, *Herr Hauptmann,*" one of the soldiers said.

"Very good," Kurt said. He sucked in a breath. "Send the signal. Tell them we are ready for them."

"*Jawohl.*"

"And then check the runways," Kurt added. "We want them completely free of ice."

———

I'm too old for this shit, Herman thought.

He'd been a paratrooper, true, but it had been over ten years since he'd last jumped out of a plane. It wasn't something he'd had to do as a policeman. But everyone with paratrooper training - save for the handful who were too old or infirm to make the jump safely - had been called to a secret airbase, told they were being prepped for a mission and then warned that they weren't allowed to leave on pain of death. If there hadn't been nearly a hundred young men - with far more recent experience - included he might have seriously considered trying to get out of the mission.

He shuddered awake as the plane started to descend. Nothing had changed, it seemed, in the last ten years. The planes were still uncomfortable, the pilots were still crazy, and the racket was just barely short of unbearable. He'd been told that the planes were *designed* to encourage the paratroopers to jump as quickly as possible, but he'd dismissed it as obvious nonsense. Even if someone wanted to ensure that the paratroopers jumped out without hesitation, the pilots would still be in the planes. Unless something went spectacularly wrong, of course.

The entire airframe shook, violently. He cursed under his breath, reminding himself sharply that turbulence just had to be endured. He'd never been entirely comfortable flying through heavy turbulence, even though the pilots had often reassured him that turbulence was largely harmless. He liked to be in control and being in a plane, one that felt as though it was being tossed around the sky by an angry god, was the exact opposite of being in control.

They should have recalled more young men from South Africa, he thought, as the plane hit the ground and bounced. *They'd have more experience in landing on top of an enemy position.*

He gritted his teeth as the plane came down for a second time and landed properly, skidding along the runway as if there was nothing slowing it down. The engines whined loudly as they went into reverse, the plane careening from side to side before finally slowing down enough to turn right and get off the runway. Herman sighed in relief - the other aircraft would be landing within a very tight window - and forced himself to relax. They'd landed safely, no matter how unnatural it felt…

"You'll have ten minutes to walk around and stretch your legs," the CO said, briskly. "But don't go beyond the fence."

Herman nodded as he joined the line of soldiers hurrying towards the rear doors and scrambling down to the ground. The air was bitterly cold, the ground coated in grit designed to keep the runaway from icing over. It looked deserted, save for a handful of armoured vehicles sitting near the control tower. A low roar echoed through the air as the remaining aircraft landed, one by one. Thankfully, they all made it down safely.

Maybe not so old after all, Herman thought. He hadn't realised how much he'd missed the life until he returned to it. There was something about being in the military, even during a civil war, that was more honest than being a police-man. *It feels almost like coming home.*

He pinched a cigarette from one of the younger men and lit it, taking a deep breath. His wife would disapprove of him smoking - particularly on an airfield - but he needed something to help calm his nerves. Besides, there was a very good chance they wouldn't be returning. The briefing had made it clear that they either had to win completely or die. And if they lost, no one would remember their names.

"Father," a voice said.

Herman spun around. Kurt was standing there, wearing a *Volkssturm* uniform that looked to have been sewn for a man two or three sizes bigger than him. Herman stared, then reached out and gave his son a tight hug. It had been too long since he'd seen Kurt...

"She's alive," Kurt said, as he led Herman away from the others. "Father, she's alive!"

"Thank God," Herman breathed. "Are you sure?"

"I asked...our contact to ask her something only she would know," Kurt said. "And the correct answer came back."

"Good," Herman said. He trusted Kurt to get it right. He'd always been close to Gudrun, closer than Herman had ever been to his own sisters. But then, Gudrun and Kurt weren't *that* far apart in age. "I hope you're *sure.*"

"I am," Kurt said.

Herman hoped he was right. His children would have been horrified by just how much their father knew about them, even though he had to admit that he'd missed the signs that Gudrun was involved with the protest move-ment. Secrets weren't always secrets in small households, no matter how closely they were kept. But Kurt and Gudrun probably had some shared memories that no one else knew. He just hoped they weren't being set up for a nasty fall.

Kurt met his eyes. "How is mother? And the brats?"

"Your younger *brothers* are fine," Herman said, sternly. He'd hoped that Kurt would be a decent older brother to Johan and Siegfried, but they were really too far apart in age for genuine friendship. Johan and Siegfried looked up to Kurt, he knew, and that was about the best anyone could hope for. "Your mother is…is still politicking, I'm afraid."

"Oh," Kurt said. "I'm sure she'll do well."

Herman shrugged. Really, he was too old to care about what others thought of him. Or at least he should be. *And* he'd survived the occasional snide remark about his daughter smoothing out his career path. But the part of him that was too stubborn to change was reluctant to accept that his wife had changed. He didn't know if he'd ever get used to it.

"The world is changing," he said. "And some of the changes are better than others."

He looked back towards the aircraft. There was no way he'd be allowed to stay in the military after the war, no matter what happened. And he doubted he would be able to return to the police force. But perhaps he could join the *Volkssturm*…

A whistle blew. It was time to go.

"I'm coming too," Kurt said, as they walked back towards the plane. "I'll see you on the far side."

Herman flinched. It was uncommon for fathers and sons to serve together - hell, it was rare for *brothers* to serve together - and there were good reasons for it. But the whole operation had been thrown together in a tearing hurry anyway. Reading between the lines, Herman had a nasty feeling the entire force had been deemed expendable if all hell broke loose. It might explain why his superiors had authorised him - and the other older men - to join the mission.

"Very well," he said, finally. There was no way he could say no. Kurt was a man now - he'd been a man since he'd joined the Berlin Guard - and was no longer subject to his father's edicts. And really, what sort of man would Kurt have become if he still allowed his father to rule his life. "Just make sure you survive or I'll kill you personally."

Kurt shot him a deadpan look. "I'll try my best."

Herman smiled as they climbed into the aircraft. He was proud of Kurt. He was proud of *all* his children. And Gudrun...he shook his head, torn between a multitude of feelings. She might have been a girl, but she'd changed the entire world. He was proud of her, more proud than he could ever say, yet he was also fearful for her life. *Gudrun* meant more to him, in some ways, than any of his sons. He'd always tried to protect her more than anyone else...

...*And how much of that,* he asked himself, *was because she was my daughter?*

He mulled it over, covering his ears as the aircraft engines came to life. He'd always seen his sons as *needing* to learn some lessons on their own, even if those lessons came with a price. Their bumps and bruises would teach harder lessons than his words. But he'd always been protective of his daughter. In an ideal world, she would have been safe for the rest of her life.

But it wasn't what she wanted, he thought. The aircraft lurched into the sky, shaking backwards and forwards as it grabbed for air. *And I may have been wrong.*

He was honest enough to admit that he might have been wrong, despite his fears. If he'd forbidden her from going to the university, he could have made it stick. Gudrun was in *his* charge until she married. But she wouldn't have been *happy*, he saw now. She would have seen him as a monster, even though he would only have her best interests at heart. And she might have been right.

The world is changing, he reminded himself. All the stories young children read featured women as housewives or mothers or sisters. Young girls just didn't *have* adventures. But Gudrun had written a whole new story, changing the entire world. *And I no longer belong.*

———

"*Herr Oberstgruppenfuehrer?*"

Alfred turned. It had been a tense night, ever since Forster had warned him that the attack was due to begin the following morning. The prospect of being caught had never been so high. And yet, part of him was almost relieved. Hurry up and wait had been a part of military life ever since the first caveman had bashed his enemy's head in with a rock. The prospect of action, no matter how risky, was always to be welcomed.

"Yes?"

"*Herr Oberstgruppenfuehrer*, radar has detected a flight of aircraft moving towards Germanica," the operator said. "Their IFF signals don't match anything in our records."

"They're holding a drill," Alfred said. "The *Fuhrer* wants you to track them carefully, but take no action."

The operator saluted, hastily. Alfred allowed himself a tight smile as the younger man turned away. A smart operator would have questioned allowing a dozen heavy aircraft to fly over the city, particularly now the nuclear genie had been let out of the bottle, but Karl Holliston had ensured that *no one* wanted to ask questions. He'd purged several senior officers in the last two days for questioning some of his more…extreme…orders. And so the aircraft would fly over Germanica with no one doing anything to stop them.

Not that we can, he thought, sourly. The city's antiaircraft defences had been formidable, but half the weapons had been stripped out and sent to the front. And they'd been of very limited value in a war zone. *As long as the pilots are lucky, they'll get in without a fight.*

————

"Outboard personnel, stand up," the jumpmaster barked. "We're crossing the city limits now."

Herman stood, feeling his heart starting to race as the jumpmaster ordered them through the entire routine. They'd studied the city extensively, during the flight, but a single misstep could put them several miles from their target. The skies were clear, according to the pilot, yet that would change very quickly. Surely, *someone* would notice that a dozen giant aircraft hadn't been cleared to fly over the city…

But their radar system is a mess, Herman thought. He checked his equipment for the final time. *And they're not ready for us.*

"Go," the jumpmaster barked.

One by one, the paratroopers made their way to the hatch and plunged down towards the streets below.

CHAPTER THIRTY-SEVEN

Germanica, Germany East
16 November 1985

"Go," Horst snapped.

Panic was already spreading through the streets as the squadron of heavy aircraft roared overhead, paratroopers spilling from their hatches and plunging downwards. Horst knew that Kurt would be amongst them, but he didn't have time to worry about his brother-in-law as he led his squad towards the *Reichstag*. Dressed in SS uniforms, carrying papers that marked them out as *Einsatzgruppen*, no one should bat an eyelid as they passed, not when the skies were darkening with paratroopers. A loud explosion echoed over the city as one of the radio transmitters blew, taken out by a *Volkssturm* team. They'd probably wanted some revenge for all the sneering they had to endure from the SS.

Armed soldiers were running to the *Reichstag* from all directions, some trying to take up positions on the barricades while others were hurrying towards the gates. Horst joined the latter, knowing that the guards would wave them through in silent contempt. Hardly anyone liked the *Einsatzgruppen*, save for Holliston and his cronies. The *Waffen-SS* saw them as cowards who only shot unarmed people; the bureaucrats and intelligence officials saw them as butchers who made it harder to exploit conquered populations. They'd be beneath suspicion.

The gates were rattling closed as they approached, but they managed to get through into the antechamber before it was too late. He heard shooting outside - the first wave of paratroopers would have landed already - but it was dulled as the secondary gates slammed shut. The *Reichstag* was a fortress, to all intents and purposes. It would be some time before the paratroopers managed to get into the building and by then everything would be finished, one way or the other.

An officer was barking orders, trying to organise fallback defensive positions for when - if - the gates were breached. Horst lifted his rifle and shot him, his squad opening fire a second later, sweeping the antechamber with bullets. Men fell in all directions, too shocked to return fire; Horst checked the nearest man, then led the way up the stairs. There was no point in trying to be stealthy, not now. They *had* to get to the *Fuhrer's* office before it was too late.

Ruengeler said he was always in his office at this time, he thought, grimly. Sweat ran down his back as he ran up the stairs, throwing a grenade down each of the hallways as he passed. *And unless we get to him quickly, he'll have a chance to make his escape.*

———

"They're dropping paratroopers," the operator said, horrified. "*Herr Oberstgruppenfuehrer...*"

Alfred drew his pistol in one smooth motion and shot the operator in the head, then shot the remaining five men in the operations room before they could react. Some of them would probably have joined him, he knew, as alarms howled through the *Reichstag*. But there was no time to try to convince them to join him, not now. He hit the emergency switch, closing and locking the doors, then sat down in front of the radio set. Reports were coming in from all over the city.

I suppose the enemy did have a plan, he thought. *Dropping so many paratroopers into Germanica will hide the real threat.*

Calmly, he started to issue false orders. The units that had been sent away from Germanica shouldn't be able to return in a hurry, but the others - closer to the city - had to be kept out of the fight. It was unlikely that everyone would obey - they'd probably think that Alfred was mounting a coup - yet there should be enough confusion to keep most of the men out of the fighting. Alfred certainly *hoped* that was true. Too many good men had died in the last few months for him to be comfortable sending more to their deaths.

And then the entire building shook, violently.

Let us hope it ends quickly, he told himself. *Because we will all die soon.*

———

Herman hit the ground hard enough to hurt, rolling over, discarding his para-chute and bringing up his weapon in one smooth motion. The shooting had already started, black-clad men pouring fire towards the paratroopers from the barricades as the fighter-bomber escorts roared overhead, seeking out targets of opportunity on the ground. Herman took cover as officers barked orders, forming the paratroopers up into rows for the assault on the *Reichstag*. He lifted his rifle as a bullet *pinged* off the masonry, scanning the building until he saw the sniper in the window and returning fire. The sniper fell back-wards and vanished from sight.

And I don't know if he's dead or alive, Herman thought, grimly. He turned as he heard engines approaching from the north. *Here they come…*

The SS stormtroopers moved forward with fanatical determination, trying to assault the paratroopers in the rear. They didn't seem to be so interested in taking cover, he noted; their vehicles were armoured against small arms, but their infantry weren't even *trying* to seek protection. He couldn't tell if they were desperate or merely poorly-trained - the best stormtroopers would have been sent west, surely - yet it hardly mattered. The paratroopers had antitank weapons designed to take out far heavier vehicles. One by one, the SS vehicles were wiped out.

"Take them out," he shouted, as the stormtroopers hit the ground, but kept crawling forward, shooting as they came. "Now!"

The ground shook, again, as bombs fell over part of the city. Herman barely noticed as he hurled a pair of grenades towards the enemy, then ran forward - followed by several of his men - as the grenades exploded. The stormtroop-ers had no time to react before they were finished off, just as a *second* line of vehicles charged around the corner, guns blazing as they blasted streams of bul-lets towards the paratroopers. Herman hit the deck; Kurt, behind him, rolled a grenade forward and underneath the vehicle. It exploded into a fireball, giving the paratroopers time to slip back under covering fire from their comrades.

"Good work," Herman grunted.

"Thank you, father," Kurt said. "I…"

Herman saw the stormtrooper appear from nowhere, behind Kurt. He was taking *aim* at Kurt...he shoved Kurt down, trying to get him out of the line of fire before it was too late. The stormtrooper fired...and Herman gasped in pain, four hammer-blows slamming into his chest. He saw, through a haze of pain, the stormtrooper falling backwards, shot by *someone*, but it was suddenly very hard to think. The world seemed to be fading away...

"*Father*," Kurt shouted. Herman could *feel* his son tearing at his uniform, trying to open the jacket so he could try to stanch the bleeding, but he knew it was too late. "Medic!"

Herman tried to speak, but the words refused to come. He wanted to tell his son that he loved him, that he loved all of his children, yet...yet his mouth would not cooperate. He couldn't say a word. He wished, suddenly, that he'd had a chance to make love to his wife one final time, to hug his daughter, to tell his sons that he was proud of them...

...And then the darkness reached up and pulled him down.

———

Kurt had barely had a second to realise that there was someone behind him when his father, still immensely strong for a man his age, shoved him to the ground. He'd rolled over automatically, bringing up his weapon to shoot the stormtrooper dead...

...And then he realised his father had been mortally wounded.

He stared down at the old man's body for a long moment, shaking his head in bitter grief and rage. There had been few better fathers, not in his experience. He'd known boys with fathers who let them do whatever they pleased and boys with fathers who beat them for the slightest mistake, but *his* father had been a mix of firm and fair. He hadn't deserved to die saving his son...

...*But it was how he would have wanted to go*, Kurt thought. *He was always looking out for us.*

Gritting his teeth, he turned back to the battle. There would be time to mourn later...

...If any of them were left alive.

———

296

Karl Holliston had been reading paperwork when the aircraft flew overhead and the alarms went off, falling silent a second later. The building shook a moment later, causing him to dive under the desk and draw his pistol, ready to fight for his life. He nearly shot his own bodyguard when the man came running in, almost pulling the trigger before realising who he was seeing. If his bodyguard had turned on him, all was lost.

"*Mein Fuhrer,*" the bodyguard snapped. "We've lost all contact with anyone outside the building!"

Karl swore under his breath as he crawled out from under the desk and hurried over to the large painting of Adolf Hitler on the far wall. A touch of a hidden button revealed a concealed communications set, linked directly to a high-power radio transmitter nearby. But when he tried using it, all he got in return was a screech of static that nearly deafened him. If he couldn't make contact with his supporters, what good was he? And what could he do with the nuclear codes if he couldn't pass them on?

"I can't get through," he snapped. He wished, suddenly, that he'd spent more time learning how to use the system. The basics were simple enough, but even tiny repairs were completely beyond him. He flipped through options that should have linked him with a dozen rooms in the *Reichstag*, but no one answered. Even the War Room was silent. "It's not working."

Cold ice ran through his veins. If he was isolated so completely that he couldn't even get a single message out…

His bodyguard grabbed his arm, shocking him out of his daze. "We have to get out of here!"

"Down to the bunker," Karl said. He gathered himself, as best as he could. He wasn't sure *quite* what was going on, but the *Reichstag* was definitely under attack. One of the *Gauleiters* was mounting a coup, perhaps. The rebels would have had real trouble projecting force so far from the front lines. "We need to get in touch with the rest of the country."

He scooped up the nuclear briefcase as the bodyguards opened the rear door and peered through carefully, before motioning him to follow them down the corridor. Karl did as he was told, silently promising himself that he'd make whoever was responsible for this atrocity very sorry indeed. He had the nuclear codes, he had a communications network built under the bunker that was practically indestructible…all he needed to know was who was attacking him. Or maybe he'd just fire on Germany Prime instead. Let the bastards burn.

Or fire on America instead, he thought. The sound of shooting echoed through the building, growing closer and closer. *Let the entire world burn.*

He gritted his teeth in rage as they slipped down a flight of stairs. He'd been so close to total victory, so close to stamping his will on the entire planet…he still would, once he made contact with his allies. No one, not even the *Gauleiters*, could subvert *everyone*. The loyalist units outside the *Reichstag* could quash the coup with brutal efficiency, then teach the *Gauleiters* a lesson by laying waste to their lands. And then he'd crush the rest of them, just to make sure that no one could get in his way ever again.

His bodyguard stopped, holding up a hand. The sound of shooting was definitely getting closer. Karl took a tighter grip on his pistol, silently cursing under his breath as he recalled they were completely out of touch with the rest of the *Reich*. If he died, here and now, the nukes would never fly. And Germany East would collapse into chaos if the coup-plotters failed to take control quickly enough to ward off challenges.

"Down this way," the bodyguard said. "Hurry!"

———

Horst wasn't surprised when the *Fuhrer's* door turned out to be defended with fanatical enthusiasm. No one was allowed to join a personal protective detachment unless they were ready and able to give up their lives to protect their charge. And yet, he didn't have *time* to deal with them. He snapped orders, then hurled a whole string of grenades down the corridor. The explosions were deafening in the confined space, the walls solid enough to ensure that the guards took the brunt of the blasts. Horst ran over their shattered bodies and straight into the outer office. A middle-aged woman with a formidable face took one look at them and fainted. He gave her a kick, just to be sure she wasn't faking it, then ran into the inner office. It was deserted.

He swore, feeling numb horror running down his chest. The radio set looked to be working, but the faint background noise from the speaker suggested that it couldn't reach anyone in or outside the *Reichstag*. Horst hoped, desperately, that was true, even as the building shook once again. If Holliston had already sent orders for the nuclear silos to launch their missiles, all hell was already breaking out...

It isn't over yet, he thought. *If he can't get a message out, he'll go to the bunker.*

Another explosion shook the building. Gritting his teeth, he forced himself to recall the plans Uncle Emil had located for them. The *Reichstag* had plenty of back passages that could be used to get a lone man down to the bunker, probably including some that didn't appear on the plans. But if *he* was trying to get someone downstairs without being spotted...

"This way," he ordered. "Quickly."

A protective detail wouldn't *want* to pick a fight, not if it could be avoided. He'd never considered such work for himself, but he'd covered the basics in training. It was better to sneak through enemy territory, rather than run the risk of losing the person they were supposed to protect. And if there *were* hidden passages running through the *Reichstag*, he'd expect them to be used too.

And there are hidden passages in Berlin, he thought. He'd gone through the Berlin *Reichstag* with a fine-toothed comb, after the uprising. There had been at least seven passageways that hadn't been on any of the diagrams and, if he was forced to be honest, he had never been quite sure that he'd found *all* of the passages. *Why can't they have them in Germanica too?*

He pushed the thought aside as they hurried down the stairs. They had to hurry. Time was very definitely not on their side.

———

Karl almost wet himself when the shooting started, two of his bodyguards firing down towards the ambushers while the remainder covered him, their weapons searching constantly for targets. He'd never been in danger before, not really; even the escape from Berlin, a hair-raising moment, hadn't been *that* bad. But now...

He cringed as the building shook time and time again. Whatever was happening outside, it sounded as though the building was being stormed. He nearly jumped out of his skin when one of his bodyguards caught hold and yanked him down the corridor, running past a trio of bodies in green *Heer* uniforms. Karl felt his head churning in absolute shock. The rebels? It couldn't be the rebels! How could they even have managed to get so far east?

Someone betrayed me, he thought, numbly.

It was the only answer that made sense, he told himself, as another burst of shooting rattled out behind him. The rebels *couldn't* have gotten into the *Reichstag* without help. He knew the radar network was a mess - in hindsight, it had been a mistake not extending the defence chain to cover aircraft heading east from Germany Prime - but it wasn't that bad. *Someone* had to have made certain that no warning was passed up the chain. And that meant...

He looked down at the nuclear briefcase and smiled. It didn't matter. He could send the orders as soon as he entered the bunker, orders that would burn the entire world. The *Reich* would pay for betraying him and his dream.

"Go forward," his bodyguard snapped, as the sound of running footsteps above them grew louder. "And don't stop for anything."

Karl gritted his teeth and ran. The bunker doors loomed up in front of him, guarded by two grim-looking stormtroopers. He ran through, snapping a command at the two guards. The doors slammed shut a moment later, sealing the bunker off from the remainder of the building. And the inner doors would start closing in a few seconds...

He smiled. They wouldn't get to him now.

———

Horst threw himself to one side as a stream of bullets nearly took off his head, then hurled his last two grenades down the stairs. The explosion shook the building, sending plaster dripping down from the ceiling as he hurried to the bottom of the stairs...

...and swore out loud as he realised they were too late.

The bunker doors were firmly closed. He stepped forward, his fingers pressing against the solid metal. He'd seen the diagrams. Even if they somehow broke through the first layer, there were enough inner layers to make it impossible to get down into the bunker, certainly not before the end of next year. Holliston could just walk through the escape tunnel to an SS base. And even if the escape tunnel was blocked, he could still launch the nuclear missiles and go out in a blaze of fire.

He sagged, shaking his head in bitter frustration. They'd failed…

…And there was nothing he could do, now or ever, that would retrieve the situation.

CHAPTER THIRTY-EIGHT

Germanica, Germany East
16 November 1985

Doctor Muller eyed Katherine sourly as she stepped into the security room. "She's still in her cell," he said, nodding towards the monitors. "Did you think she'd be somewhere else?"

Katherine shrugged, trying to keep the distaste off her face. The *Fuhrer* had ordered Doctor Muller to leave Gudrun alone, but she wouldn't have put it past the doctor, now that Gudrun had been sentenced to exile, to try to have some fun with the poor girl. But instead he was merely watching Gudrun through the cameras. Thankfully, Gudrun knew she was being watched at all times.

"The *Fuhrer* will be arranging her departure tomorrow," Katherine said, ignoring the question. She had no idea when all hell was going to break loose - Horst hadn't been too clear - but she couldn't afford to seem deficient in her duties. Too many familiar faces had vanished already as Holliston's paranoia began to bite. "Until then, let her get some rest."

"As you wish," Muller said. He leaned towards the monitors, drinking in the scene. "The farmers would prefer her to be intact, I am sure."

Katherine silently measured his back for the knife. It was easy, chillingly easy, to imagine the young Muller peeking at girls in changing rooms, slowly growing up into a monstrous pervert. No *wonder* the SS had recruited him. A man who *enjoyed* his work would be far more reliable than a man who saw it as a duty. And Muller would hardly be the first monster who had been offered a choice between service or going straight into the gas chambers.

"I am sure," Katherine said.

"They'll know she's not a virgin, of course," Muller added. "But I doubt they'll care."

Katherine touched the hilt of her dagger, resisting - barely - the urge to stab him there and then. She was no stranger to doing horrific things for the *Reich*, but she had never *enjoyed* them. Muller…did. He had nothing to gain from spying on Gudrun now, particularly after he'd been ordered to leave her alone, yet he was *still* watching the girl. And to think he had plenty of other victims at his disposal.

Bastard, she thought, nastily.

The alarms went off. She looked up, sharply, as red lights began to flash. The city was under attack! No, the *Reichstag* was under attack. She had no idea what Horst had done - he hadn't been remotely clear on the details - but it was clear that he had done *something*. Three different alarm tones - air attack, ground attack, security breach - were sounding, blending together into a terrifying cacophony. She couldn't help wondering, as she drew her dagger, if someone had deliberately set off the wrong alarms.

Muller glanced at her, his face suddenly fearful. She saw his eyes go wide as he noticed the dagger and realised what it meant. He stumbled backwards, but it was far too late. Katherine couldn't help feeling a flicker of contempt as she lunged forward and sliced the dagger across his throat. His body crumpled to the ground, bleeding like a stuck pig. The stench of piss rose to her nostrils, making her smile. In life as well as death, Doctor Muller had been a coward.

She stepped over the body and peered down at the console as the alarms faded to a dull background noise. Dozens of voices were shouting over the intercom, despite the best efforts of the emergency controllers. God alone knew what was happening on the surface…she pushed the thought to the back of her mind as she triggered a pair of security protocols, then opened the locker and removed two rifles and a pistol. Gudrun could shoot, she knew; she'd seen her using a pistol. She could still help even if she couldn't fire a rifle.

A low hum echoed through the bunker, followed by a voice babbling about lockdowns and sealed hatches. Katherine winced - there was no hope of simply taking Gudrun and sneaking out now - and then headed for the inner doors. They would have been sealed, of course, the moment the alarms went off, but they were easy to open from the outside. She'd just have to make damn sure the locking mechanism was jammed or she'd wind up trapped in the complex herself.

The two guards standing outside Gudrun's cell looked relieved, then astonished, to see her. Katherine shot them both before they could react, feeling a twinge of guilt as their bodies collapsed. *They* hadn't been nasty, unlike Doctor Muller. They'd done their duty as best as they could, instead of taking advantage of the situation. Hell, they'd even respected her as a fellow soldier. But there had been no time to try to talk them into surrender, even if she'd thought they *would* surrender. She'd had no choice.

She opened Gudrun's cell and peered inside. Gudrun was seated on the bed, her arms crossed over her breasts. She looked resigned, rather than eager. Katherine blinked in surprise, then recalled that Doctor Muller had told Gudrun that she'd be killed if the bunker ever came under attack. There *were* procedures in place to kill all the prisoners before they could be rescued. But the planners had never anticipated betrayal from the inside…

"On your feet," she snapped, as she opened the inner door. "Can you shoot a rifle?"

Gudrun shook her head. Katherine rolled her eyes. The BDM in the west was clearly useless. A girl who couldn't defend herself was a girl who was utterly dependent on men for her safety. Perhaps that was the point. Gudrun had practically *admitted* that she'd been dependent on her brother and father. Katherine shoved the pistol and two spare clips of ammunition at Gudrun, then motioned for her to get out of the cell. The remaining alarms cut off a second later.

"Your husband is attacking the *Reichstag*," Katherine said. She thought fast, trying to remember the emergency procedures. If the alarms had cut off, lockdown procedures had been completed. And *that* meant that Holliston was in the bunker. "And we need to cut off the *Fuhrer*."

She groaned, inwardly, as she led the way out of the cell. Holliston wouldn't have *many* guards with him, but the ones he *did* have would be fanatical. And she'd have to kill them all just to get to him. Unless there was another way…

…But what?

"The bunker has been sealed," she added, as she struggled with the outer door. "Everyone you will meet is an enemy. Kill him before he kills you."

She glanced back at Gudrun. She looked pale, but determined. Katherine prayed, silently, that she survived and escaped - or, if she was caught, that she died quickly. There weren't *that* many men in the bunker, but they'd be trapped underground for weeks and Gudrun would be the only available woman. Karl Holliston, his mind already snapping, would probably order them to rape her in succession until she died. He no longer needed to worry about anyone else's opinion.

"Here we go," she said, turning back to the door. "Don't stop for anything."

———

"Send half the operators out," Karl ordered, as he stepped into the communications room. "They are to go back to their bunks until further notice."

"*Jawohl, Mein Fuhrer,*" the commander said.

Karl sat down in front of the console and opened the briefcase, perching it on the table beside him. Radio transmissions could be jammed - if the transmitters weren't simply destroyed - but no one could do anything about the buried cables. The Americans had grown so good at intercepting and deciphering the *Reich's* communications that almost anything sensitive was sent over the wire, instead of through the air. And the rebels - and their treacherous allies - wouldn't be able to stop him from unleashing hell.

He sucked in his breath as he removed the small device and plugged it into the radio transmitter, then started to work his way through the paperwork. It was depressingly primitive, compared to some of the other systems he had used, but it was impossible to tamper with it. Or so he had been told. The authorisation code for each and every nuclear weapon in Germany East was included within the briefcase, with different codes for unlocking the warheads themselves and launching the missiles. And...

...And there was no way to know if all of the missiles would actually fly.

"Open the channel," he ordered.

He cursed the rebels, savagely. His men *thought* they had unlocked all of the warheads - and the missiles - but they didn't *know*. The only way to know would be to launch the missiles...and if it failed, the security devices would render the missiles useless. In hindsight, it had been a grievous mistake to allow the *Reich* Council sole control over the nuclear arsenal. But it had been the only way to prevent civil war.

Sorting through the papers, he found the plan for a two-fold nuclear offensive. The missiles would be launched at American cities, aimed at causing maximum carnage rather than destroying the American military machine. It was inefficient, he recalled from the briefings, but it would cripple the United States. The *Reich* might be mortally wounded, but it would take its enemy down too. And the tactical warheads would be hurled into Germany Prime.

The Americans may not destroy the rebels, he thought. *But we will.*

He allowed himself a moment to savour the thought as he produced the first set of coded signals. The rebels had no idea of the hell he was planning to unleash. But it was what they deserved. They'd betrayed him, they'd betrayed the *Reich*, they'd betrayed everything Adolf Hitler and his successors had done for the *Volk*. It was a shame he'd never get his chance to wring their necks personally, but it wasn't necessary. All that mattered was taking his revenge.

And we might survive down here, he thought. *We can recover control after the war.*

———

"Get onto the radio," Horst snapped. "Send the emergency code to the bombers."

"*Jawohl*," the operator said.

Horst cursed as he stared at the bunker doors. There was no hope, absolutely none, of getting through in time to make a difference. It was time for one last roll of the dice.

———

Gudrun shivered the moment she stepped through the door and into the main bunker complex. The cell hadn't been particularly warm, but it was colder here, deep below the ground. She couldn't help feeling horrifically exposed as Katherine led the way down the corridor, her nakedness bothering her for the first time in weeks. If they were caught, if they were shot, she had absolutely no protection. But then, that would have been true even if she was wearing an ugly uniform.

She clutched the pistol tightly, feeling her hands grow moist with sweat. Horst had taught her how to use it, but he'd never thought she'd have to fight her way through a bunker of stormtroopers. It sounded like something out a bad novel, perhaps one of the *SS Adventures* that Kurt had devoured as a young man. But she had no choice. She lifted her pistol as they rounded the corner and came face to face with two young men, both of whom stared at her in shock. Katherine shot them both down before they could say a word.

Gudrun swallowed, hard. She understood the logic, she understood the importance of not giving them time to sound the alert, but she still found it shocking. And yet, she knew there was no choice.

"This way," Katherine muttered.

She led the way into a room and opened fire, picking off five men before they had a chance to react. Gudrun followed her in, pistol at the ready, but it was already too late. Five men were dead, the sixth was staring up at Katherine in disbelief and terror. They didn't *look* like stormtroopers, Gudrun thought; they looked more like students. Who *were* they?

"We can do this the easy way or the hard way," Katherine said. She held a pistol to the young man's head as she drew her knife from her belt, holding it against his crotch. "I need you to answer some questions. If you lie to me, I'll turn you into a girl. Do you understand me?"

The man nodded, frantically.

"Good," Katherine said. "Where is the *Fuhrer*?"

———

"We have our orders," *Hauptmann* Walther Johannesson said. "Prepare to deploy the bomb."

He gritted his teeth as the bomber turned and headed east. Their training had assumed that they'd face massed antiaircraft fire as well as jet-powered interceptors, but so far Germany East hadn't been able to muster any real resistance to their incursion. Getting to Germanica had been so easy that he'd honestly wondered if it was a trap of some kind. But it seemed otherwise…

"The bomb is ready," his co-pilot said. "On three…"

Walther nodded, hastily tapping his arming code into the device when the co-pilot reached three. Down in the bomb bay, the weapons officer would be doing the same. It took three codes, entered within a minute of one another, to arm the weapon for detonation. And if they made a single mistake, the bomb wouldn't detonate at all…

"Code accepted," the co-pilot said. "Bomb away."

Walther nodded, pushing the engines forward as hard as he could. They'd *practiced* outrunning the blast before, but no one had ever *tried* until the war. The world seemed to flare white as the bomb detonated, a massive shockwave striking the aircraft seconds later, the airframe groaning in protest as it struggled to cope. He fought desperately to maintain control, but the shockwave was too strong…

An instant later, the bomber started to break up and fall from the sky.

————

Karl Holliston felt the ground shake and glanced up, sharply.

It shouldn't have happened. They were so far below the ground that nothing, not even a direct nuclear strike, should have affected the bunker. And yet he'd felt…*something*. Had the rebels invented a weapon that could break through the doors? Or had they purchased something from the Americans? Or…

The communicator failed. He poked it, puzzled, then looked at the technician. The young man scurried forward, fear written in every part of his bearing as he went to work. Karl glared at his back, silently willing him to work faster. He hadn't even managed to get the first set of command strings out before the line had failed.

"*Mein Fuhrer,*" the technician said. "The communicator is working, but there's nothing on the far end."

It took Karl a moment to process what he'd been told. There was an entire SS base on the far end, commanded and staffed by loyalists. The base couldn't be *gone*. But he'd felt something…had the base been *nuked*? The rebels had nuclear weapons and they'd certainly proven themselves willing to use them.

And how *else* could they take out the entire base before the nuclear codes were sent to their final destination?

His blood ran cold. If the base was gone - and if Germanica was in enemy hands - he was trapped. They might not be able to get down to him, but he couldn't escape either. And that meant…

Cold hatred congealed in his heart. "Bring me the bitch," he snarled. "Now!"

The technician hastily saluted and practically *ran* out of the room.

———

Katherine gritted her teeth as she ran down the corridor, cursing under her breath. She couldn't leave Holliston in the communications room, not when he could be using the radio and landlines to summon reinforcements or launch the nukes. But getting into the room might be tricky. She barely noticed two men as she shot them down, intent on her destination.

"In there," she said, as she slowed to a halt. The door was solid metal. She couldn't get through without a grenade. "We need to…"

The door opened. A young man ran out, his eyes going wide when he saw Gudrun. He started to say something incoherent, but Katherine shot him before he had a chance to finish whatever he was trying to say. And then she led the way into the room.

———

Karl heard the shot and jumped, picking up his pistol and bracing himself. Treachery! Even in his bunker, there was treachery! His eyes opened wide as he saw Katherine, of all people, running into the room, followed by Gudrun. The bitch was still naked…his head spun as he realised she'd subverted Katherine, of all people. Was he the only one immune to her charms?

But there was no time to worry about that, not now. He lifted his gun and fired.

———

Gudrun recoiled in shock as Katherine grunted in pain, then remembered herself and fired back. Holliston's eyes seemed to meet hers, just for a second, as he crumbled backwards, blood leaking from his chest. She saw utter madness and hatred staring back at her just for a second, then he fell to the ground. And yet, she kept pulling the trigger until she realised that the gun was clicking uselessly...She'd run out of ammunition.

She reloaded, then stepped forward, holding her pistol pointed directly at his head. But it was clear that he was dead.

It's over, she thought. She turned to look at Katherine and winced. Her left arm was hanging limp, blood dripping through the sleeve and down to the floor. *Shit...*

"It's a flesh wound," Katherine said, irritated. "Pass me that medical kit, then get in touch with the guards at the gate. Tell them to open the hatches."

Gudrun looked at her. "Will they listen?"

Katherine barked a harsh laugh. "The war is over," she said. She opened the medical kit with one hand and removed a bandage, wrapping it around her arm. "And they now have the choice between surrendering or staying down here until they die."

Gudrun nodded, then went to work.

CHAPTER THIRTY-NINE

Berlin, Germany Prime
27 November 1985

"The treaty will make everyone mad," *Gauleiter* Emil Forster predicted, cheerfully. "That is the mark of a good compromise."

Volker nodded in agreement. It had taken nearly two weeks - after Karl Holliston had been confirmed dead - for the *Gauleiters* to secure control of Germany East and then start the work of hashing out a peace treaty. Negotiations had been relatively simple - it helped that both sides wanted pretty much the same things - but there had been more than a few hiccups along the way. And yet, the urgent need to end the war as quickly as possible had helped paper over the cracks. The Berlin Treaty - the *first* Berlin Treaty - wasn't perfect, but it would have to do.

"You and your *Reich* Council will have Germany East all to yourselves," he said. "How many people do you think will desert you?"

Forster smirked. "How many people do you think will desert *you?*"

Volker shrugged. One of the provisions - perhaps the most controversial - had been a general amnesty for everyone involved in the pre-war regime and the war itself. It galled him to think that Karl Holliston would have gotten away with it, if he'd survived, but he had to admit that a general amnesty was the only way to end the war. Countless thousands would probably head east - or west - to escape their crimes, yet there would be no official prosecution. The stormtroopers who had slaughtered their way across Germany Prime would never face justice.

And they won't be the only ones, he thought, grimly. Far too many people were taking advantage of the chaos to settle old scores. *How many citizens have good reason to flee?*

"We will see," he said, briskly.

He shook his head as they left the office and walked down to the ball-room. Countless dignitaries had gathered in the *Reichstag,* from civil servants and military officers to ambassadors from a dozen different nations. The French and Italian representatives would be signing the *second* Berlin Treaty in a day or two, once the final provisions were checked and approved by their governments. And after that, the British and Americans would sign a treaty intended to put an end to the cold war.

Not that we're in any state to continue the confrontation, he thought, grimly. *Rebuilding the damage caused by the civil war will take decades.*

It was a frustrating thought. He'd already given orders to pull the remaining troops out of South Africa - the *Waffen-SS* would be headed directly to Germany East - but it would take time and money to disentangle the *Reich* from the rest of the world. South Africa was already screaming about a betrayal, even though Germany East had offered settlement rights and citizenship to any Afrikaner who wanted to move to the *Reich.* Volker couldn't help feeling guilty about abandoning Pretoria, but there was no choice. The *Reich* simply couldn't afford to maintain its commitment to South Africa.

He sighed as he caught sight of Gudrun, standing next to her husband and brother on the far side of the room. She wore a long green dress, her blonde hair falling down around her shoulders, but there was a grim...*vulnerability* in her eyes he couldn't recall seeing from her before. A month in captivity wouldn't have done her any good at all, even if she *had* shot Karl Holliston personally. Volker just hoped she'd be able to cope with her demons and remain on the Provisional Government. She'd be needed in the months to come.

"Winning the war was easy," he mused. "But winning the peace...*that* will be hard."

"Quite so," Forster agreed, equally quietly. "There's a lot of work to do."

Volker nodded. The Economic Intelligence Service had quietly concluded that Germany East was in deep trouble. Their industrial base had always been tiny, meaning it would take decades to replace everything lost during the civil war. And they'd taken hideous losses during the fighting...holding the territories they'd already settled against a resurgent insurgency would be difficult, perhaps impossible. But the Easterners were tough. They might just hold on long enough to rebuild their lands.

And they have nuclear weapons, he thought, sourly. *They can defend themselves.*

He wasn't surprised that Germany East had refused to give up its atomic bombs, even though the Americans had put immense pressure on them to do just that. They had no other way to *guarantee* that the other powers would leave them alone. But it was worrying. If relations between Germany Prime and Germany East collapsed, it might mean another war, one that might destroy the *Reich* for good. And then...

"Thank you for your assistance," Forster said, bringing him out of his thoughts. "If you hadn't helped us..."

"We were helping ourselves," Volker said. "Holliston had to be stopped."

He looked across the ballroom, his gaze passing over Admiral Wilhelm Riess. The head of the *Abwehr* had confessed the moment he was confronted, admitting that he'd sided with Holliston because it was the only way to protect the *Reich*. Volker had wanted to hang him for his crimes, but the treaty had made it clear that Riess needed to be sent into exile in France instead. Germany East didn't *want* him.

And he could tell our enemies too much, Volker thought. *Perhaps he should never be allowed to leave Germany.*

"Too many people have died," he added, after a moment. "Let's put an end to it, shall we?"

But he knew it *wouldn't* end. No one knew for *sure* how many people had died in the fighting, but hundreds of thousands of people had been displaced, their homes destroyed by one side or the other. The economy was a mess, crime was on the rise, and discontent was spreading rapidly. Volker honestly had no idea when they'd be able to hold elections, nor of what would happen when they finally *did*. How long would it be, he asked himself, before new political parties started to form?

And what will happen, he asked himself, *when they start promising the voters everything, in exchange for being voted into power?*

He didn't regret what he'd done. He'd served the state loyally - first as a stormtrooper and then as a factory foreman - but the state had betrayed him.

The state had betrayed everyone, from the highest to the lowest. There had been no choice but to rise up and fight. And yet, now the fighting was done, he couldn't help feeling a little unsure of himself. The war had been bad, but the peace was going to be terrible.

But you have no choice, he told himself sternly. *Get to work.*

————

"I heard the French are insistent on recovering their lost territory," Ambassador Turtledove said, as he leaned over the balcony and peered down at the crowd. "Do you think they have a chance?"

Andrew shrugged. The last few months had exposed more cracks in the *Reich's* towering edifice than he'd ever thought possible. Entire *swathes* of the German system had weakened, or shattered, or simply vanished into nothingness. The *Kriegsmarine* was largely intact - naval brigades had done excellent work shipping food and supplies through Germany - but both the *Heer* and the *Luftwaffe* were badly weakened. It was possible, perhaps, that France *would* have a chance to recover her territories.

But the Germans still have nukes, he thought. *And they've proven themselves willing to use them.*

He scowled. The Provisional Government hadn't warned anyone, least of all the United States, before authorising and carrying out a second nuclear strike. Andrew understood the logic - the SS base had *needed* to be destroyed before it was too late - but it still set a worrying precedent. God alone knew what would happen if Berlin threatened Paris or Rome if either of the two nations tried to assert themselves. Somehow, he doubted Washington would risk nuclear war for the French.

"There's too much at risk, right now," he said. "They might be better served building up their economies instead."

It would be possible too, he knew. His sources in the Provisional Government had slipped him a draft copy of the second Berlin Treaty. The French - and the other subject nations - were forbidden from developing nuclear weapons or signing any form of military treaty with outside powers, but otherwise they had free rein. Given time - and the mess the *Reich* Council had made of the German economy - Andrew wouldn't be surprised if the

French managed to rapidly outpace the *Reich*. Of course, the French would have their own problems - they had an empire to support - but they might well overcome them faster than the Germans.

"Let us hope so," Ambassador Turtledove said.

Andrew felt a flicker of sympathy for the older man. There were too many dissatisfied factions in Washington who blamed the ambassador for their feelings, even though no one would have been able to do a better job. Turtledove would be lucky to see out the rest of the President's term in office, let alone remain in his job after the 1988 election. Hell, the midterm elections of 1986 would probably serve as a judgement on Turtledove - and President Anderson - for their work.

And neither of them had much power to steer events in the Reich, he thought, grimly. *All they could do was try to influence developments.*

"We'll find out," he said.

If there was one advantage to the war, it was that the *Reich* wasn't going to be threatening the North Atlantic Alliance any longer. America and her allies could plough resources into space-based technology and other fields that promised massive returns. There would be no need to maintain a giant standing army, although he hoped that Washington would have the sense not to make any major cuts until they *knew* the *Reich* was going to stay peaceful. And then...who knew? Statehood for Japan? A closer union with the rest of the Anglo world?

But he couldn't imagine America simply turning its back on the world.

Turtledove nodded, grimly. "Time will tell, I suppose," he said. He nodded towards the people on the dance floor. "Do you think those people know their world is built on a giant mass grave?"

Andrew gave him a sidelong look. Turtledove was of Jewish descent, a fact that the *Reich* had chosen to ignore - if, indeed, it had *known*. The Ambassador certainly didn't fit the horrific depictions of subhuman creatures shown in elementary school textbooks all over the *Reich*. But he had had family who'd lived in the *Reich*, before Hitler had taken power. He'd never heard anything from them since the Nazis had clamped down on emigration.

"I suspect some of them know," he said, finally. "But the others..."

He shook his head. The *Reich* had always seemed oddly divided on its crimes. There were times when it seemed to glory in the horrors it had committed to safeguard its power and times when it seemed intent on covering them up. Schoolchildren had been arrested and sent east - their parents shipped to the camps - for possessing illicit copies of *The Diary of a Young Girl*, yet those same schoolchildren had been given textbooks that gloated over the devastation the *Reich* had wreaked on the pre-war world. And on everyone it considered subhuman.

"They may never come to terms with it," he said. "And we probably shouldn't push them either."

Turtledove cocked an eyebrow. "Like the Indians?"

Andrew sighed. The American Indians - Native Americans, as they wanted to be called these days - had been pushed aside and largely eliminated by the Europeans when they started to settle America. But everyone involved in the whole affair was dead and buried, their descendants innocent of their crimes. The *Reich*…he wondered, looking down at the men below him, just how many of them had committed horrific crimes to preserve the *Reich*. It would not be easy to bring them to justice.

And they might trigger another civil war if they tried, he thought, numbly. *They wouldn't want to risk tearing themselves apart.*

"I think it will be a long time before they try to come to terms with what was done in their name," he said. Even now, there were Americans who believed that the Native Americans had deserved to die. The strong dominated or destroyed the weak, they said; it was the way of the world. They would have made good Nazis. "And they'll have to do it in their own time."

He sighed, again. "And we escaped the danger of a nuclear holocaust," he added. "That's something to celebrate, Mr. Ambassador."

"It doesn't end," Turtledove said. "History is an endlessly repetitive story. It never has a happy ending."

"No," Andrew agreed. "But if history teaches us one thing, it teaches us to take what you can get."

———

"Horst," Uncle Emil said. He looked surprisingly cheerful for a man who knew he was walking on thin ice. "Can I borrow you?"

Horst glanced at Gudrun, who nodded. He wondered, suddenly, if he *should* leave her, even if she was with her brother. She'd been oddly depressed over the last two weeks, ever since their reunion. Being a prisoner had left its scars.

"Of course, uncle," he said.

He followed his uncle through a side door and into a small conference room. It would have been swept for bugs repeatedly, but there were so many people - and so many factions - within the building that security couldn't be guaranteed. He shrugged, then sat down on the nearest chair and motioned for his uncle to take the other one. Uncle Emil closed and bolted the door before taking his seat.

"Horst," he said. "How are you coping with Germany Prime?"

"It has its moments," Horst said. Not *everyone* had taken the fact that he had powerful relations on the other side very well. If he hadn't been married to Gudrun - and taken the lead in a desperate rescue mission that had ended the war - he had a feeling it would have been a great deal worse. "And it can be very exciting."

His uncle nodded. "Have you thought about returning?"

Horst hesitated. There was - or there had been - a beautiful simplicity about life in Germany East. Buying a farm and raising a family would be easy, particularly now. But *Gudrun* wouldn't want to live there and, really, how could he blame her? *Her* memories of Germany East were far from pleasant.

"No," he said, finally. It wasn't entirely truthful, but it would have to do. "I'm staying here."

His uncle smiled. "I would urge you to reconsider," he said. "Germany East *needs* good men."

"Men who are related to you," Horst pointed out. "How stable *is* your *Reich* Council?"

"Unstable," his uncle admitted. "Not *all* of the *Gauleiters* are in agreement over how we should proceed."

"And they're planning a civil war," Horst finished.

"They *might* be planning a civil war," his uncle corrected. "There are plenty of other problems for us to tackle."

Horst snorted. He'd met a couple of the *Gauleiters* after the war, during the early scramble to put together a working government. Neither of them had struck him as being out for anything other than their own power, although that was true of his uncle too. The well-being of the *Reich* could go hang, he was sure, as long as the *Gauleiters* had their power. His uncle might be planning a civil war too.

Another civil war, he thought.

"I'm a married man," he said, flatly. "I need to stay with my wife."

"Bring her with you," his uncle suggested.

"I don't think you know Gudrun very well," Horst said. His uncle had admitted he'd spoken to Gudrun in private, but they hadn't had a chance to really get to know one another. "She wouldn't let me drag her off to the east."

He wondered, absently, if his uncle would suggest that he simply *drag* Gudrun eastwards with him. Last year, it would have been perfectly legal. But now...he shook his head, dismissing the thought. Gudrun would slit his throat while he slept if he tried to force her to accompany him. And he certainly didn't want to go *alone*.

His uncle lifted his eyebrows. Horst felt an odd shiver of remembered guilt - it was the same expression his uncle showed whenever Horst had tried to lie to him in the past.

"I intend to stay with her," he said, flatly. "And if she wants to stay here, I want to stay here too."

"It isn't normal for a husband to follow the wife," his uncle observed.

Horst smiled. "Ah, but my wife is special," he said. "And besides, protecting her is a challenge."

His uncle nodded, ruefully. "There will be times when I will contact you with messages that you can pass on to others," he said. "A private line of communications, perhaps. I trust that will be acceptable?"

"I can pass messages," Horst said. "But nothing else."

"You're a good man, Horst," his uncle said. "I'm proud I had a hand in raising you."

Horst shrugged. He had a feeling he wouldn't be particularly welcome in Germany East, whatever his uncle said. He'd betrayed the SS, after all. And while Holliston's particular branch of the SS was in disarray, the *Waffen-SS* was still strong. God alone knew what would happen in the future.

"Thank you," he said, instead. "And if you hadn't helped us, we would be dead now."

"And so would countless others," his uncle said. "But now they have a future."

He rose and left the room. Horst watched him go, pensively. So much had changed in the past few months that he no longer knew where he belonged…

No, he thought, as he rose himself. *I belong with her.*

CHAPTER FORTY

Berlin, Germany Prime
29 November 1985

It was bitterly cold in the cemetery.

Gudrun wrapped her arms around herself as she looked down at the grave, silently grateful that Horst had agreed to wait by the gate. The funeral had been too large for her to relax and say goodbye properly, not when everyone who was anyone - or thought they were anyone - had insisted on attending. Herman Wieland - paratrooper, policeman, father - had been given a funeral fit for a king.

She felt a bitter stab of guilt as she looked down at the grave. Her father had insisted, in his will, on nothing more than a simple headstone, even though sculptors from all over Berlin had offered to craft elegant memorials for him. They'd been disappointed, she thought, after their services had been rejected, but it wasn't what her father had wanted. *He'd* insisted on the simple grave and he'd got it.

And he'd died in her defence.

She dropped to her knees, feeling tears brimming in her eyes. Her father was hardly the first or last to die, but he was the one whose death had hit her the hardest. He'd been part of her life since the very moment she'd been born, a firm but fair figure looming over her as she grew up. Konrad had been her boyfriend, but he'd represented the future - *a* future. Perhaps she would have been happy as his wife, perhaps not…she knew she wouldn't have been happy without her father.

"I'm sorry," she said, quietly.

She'd broken down the moment she'd seen the body, despite all that Kurt and Horst could do to stop her from looking. It had been quick, Kurt had said. Three bullets in the chest had killed him so quickly, they'd assured him, that there wouldn't have been much pain. And yet…how did they know? No one had ever come back from the dead to report on the final moments of life. Her father had died…

He'd been a good father. She'd seen worse fathers - fathers who were permissive, fathers who were abusive - in her life. And yet, she couldn't help blaming herself for his death. If she hadn't been captured, if she hadn't started the protest movement…would he still be alive? Or would something else have killed him? He'd been a policeman on the streets for years, sometimes coming home with bruises covering his face. He might have been killed by a drunkard or a thug or…

"I'm sorry," she said, again.

They'd fought, more than once. He'd had an impression of the role played by daughters as they grew older, a role that Gudrun hadn't cared to assume. She'd rebelled against him, seeking out higher education and an eventual place at the university…it still surprised her, at times, that he'd actually let her go. A woman's place was in the home, he'd said; a daughter's place was to do what her father said, until she married and left his house. And yet, he'd let her study, even knowing it would make it harder for her to find a suitable husband…

He had been strict and he'd been fair and he'd been firm and he'd been kind…she remembered him bringing her soup and talking to her when she'd caught the flu, just as clearly as she recalled him telling her off after her teacher had sent home a note about her behaviour. And he'd protected her, more than she'd realised at the time. How much worse would her time in the BDM have been if she *hadn't* had a policeman for a father? Or even her time in school?

The question ran through her head, time and time again. Her father hadn't been perfect, but he'd tried. Yes, he'd *tried*. Maybe he had been reluctant to change, maybe he hadn't quite understood the new world…yet he'd let his children - and his wife - go. Gudrun knew there were men who would have seen it as a sign of weakness, but she knew better. It had been a sign of kindness from a man who'd never really understood his children.

And now he was dead.

She wished, bitterly, that she could talk to him one last time. She couldn't recall if she'd told him she loved him, the last time they'd spoken face to face. And when had he told her that he'd loved her? But he hadn't *had* to tell her, not after he'd flown all the way to Germanica to rescue her. And everything else he'd done…

He loved me, she thought. *And he died for me.*

She reached down and gently touched her abdomen. Her period was late, at least four days overdue. Katherine had warned her that the combination of near-starvation and constant stress might have delayed her period, but Gudrun had always been regular before. It was possible, just possible, that she was pregnant. Horst and she had certainly spent a *lot* of time in bed after Holliston's death, waiting to see what would happen in Germanica. If she was pregnant…

…Her father would never know his grandchild.

She closed her eyes in pain. She'd always assumed that she would have children of her own, one day. She'd been told so often - by her parents, by her teachers, by her potential boyfriends - that she would be a mother that she'd internalised it. And she was a married woman, even if she *did* have a career of her own. There was nothing stopping her from having a child…

…But her father would never see the baby. Never see him - or her - learn to crawl or take the first baby steps. Never watch his grandchild while his parents took a rest; never go to school to watch plays or recitations from *Mein Kampf*…never know the grandchild who would never have existed, if he hadn't given his life for his daughter.

"I'll name him for you," she promised, quietly. "If it's a boy I'll name him after you."

She wondered, as she stood, just how many of the other headstones in the graveyard marked someone who'd died in the war, the war she'd started. Konrad wasn't buried too far away, she knew; there were countless others who had been buried after the fighting had finally come to an end. Would they have lived if she'd just turned her gaze away? Would their friends and families have been relieved if they'd lived? If Gudrun had chosen to forget what she'd learned?

But the *Reich* had been dying for years.

If it hadn't been me, she thought, *it would have been someone else.*

But it *had* been her. And she was the one who would have to live with the guilt.

She turned, striding back towards the gate. There were people who loved her, who called her their saviour - and people who hated her for what she'd done. And, in truth, she couldn't blame them. She'd turned the entire world upside down, revealing truths the world would have preferred to forget…

…And unleashing a civil war that had nearly killed everyone.

Horst was waiting by the gate, but he wasn't alone. Kurt and Katherine stood beside him, standing just a *little* closer than she'd expected. She concealed her amusement with an effort as she approached, wondering what her father would have made of *that* relationship. There was no *way* he would have approved of Katherine, at least at first. And yet, perhaps he would have accepted her.

She wondered, absently, just what would happen in the future. Kurt wasn't the typical German male, but he might have different ideas about his wife. And yet, Katherine wasn't the typical female either. Gudrun had *seen* her slaughter men without the slightest *hint* of remorse. God alone knew what would happen if Kurt and Katherine fought in the future…

But she helped save my life, Gudrun thought. *She deserves some happiness.*

"Gudrun," Kurt said. "I spoke to mother."

Gudrun winced. Their mother had taken to her room shortly after the funeral and refused to emerge, even for dinner. Gudrun couldn't help feeling as though her mother blamed *her* for everything - and, if she did, she would have been right. Her mother had lost a husband in the war, like so many other women, yet her *daughter* had played a role in starting the war. It would take her a very long time to come to terms with it.

"She's a little better," Kurt added. "But she's still in a poor state."

"I know," Gudrun said. She was her mother's only daughter. She should go to her. But she didn't quite dare. "Did she say anything…?"

"Nothing," Kurt said. "She's upset."

Gudrun nodded. "I'm sorry."

"Go to her," Katherine said. "If she's angry with you, let her get it out of her system."

"I can try," Gudrun said. She looked at Horst. She hadn't told him she might be pregnant yet, although he might have noticed *something.* "Was there any update from the *Reichstag?*"

"Not over the radio," Horst said. "But you're not going to be needed until tomorrow."

Gudrun nodded. She'd won the post of Education Minister in the Provisional Government, although it would be several days before she actually started her new job. But she was looking forward to it. A number of truly awful teachers would be heading east within the month or she'd know the reason why. And with stricter regulations on corporal punishment - and the disbanding of the BDM - a number of sadistic bastards would follow them.

And if the east puts them to work on the farms, she thought, *I won't care at all.*

"Then we'd better go home," she said. She'd have to tell him that she might be pregnant in a few weeks, unless her period genuinely *was* delayed. "We have work to do."

EPILOGUE

Dover, United Kingdom
29 November 1985

Dover had once been a thriving seaside town, Margaret Thatcher had been told, but most of the population had moved further inland after the Third Reich started building a vast array of air and naval bases on the far side of the channel. The British Army had practically taken over the whole region, turning Dover and the Channel Ports into a series of fortresses intended to intercept and crush any German invasion. And the defences - and the threat of nuclear war - had been more than enough to deter the Germans from trying.

She watched, from her vantage point, as the long line of Frenchmen and women walked towards the ship. Most of them were old, either Free French fighters who'd refused to abandon the war or refugees from Occupied France. Britain had given them a home, but now they were trying to get back to France. Margaret wished them well, although she suspected that none of them would find a warm welcome on the other side of the English Channel. It had been years since any of them had set foot in France and far too much would have changed.

"They have hope," President Anderson said.

Margaret shrugged. *Hope* was not a strategy.

"They will have a chance," she said. "But they will be lucky to get home."

She looked up at her American counterpart. It had barely been two weeks since the end of the *Reich* Civil War, but the Americans were already talking about pulling out of their bases and heading home. Hell, Parliament too was talking about sweeping cuts to the military's budget, no matter how hard she fought to keep the matter from a formal debate. She had no doubt that half of

Britain's most famous regiments would be cut from the books if some of her political enemies had their way...

"This isn't the end," she said. "There's a whole new world in front of us."

"I know," Anderson said. "But Congress thinks otherwise."

Margaret nodded in sympathy. Polish voters in the United States had protested, strongly, the lack of freedom for Poland. She understood their feelings, but Poland no longer existed. The Nazis had destroyed it as thoroughly as they'd destroyed every other nation they'd occupied directly. Even Norway and Denmark, both under relatively light rule, had been changed beyond recognition.

And the world outside Europe was very different.

She shook her head, bitterly, as a cold gust of wind swept in from the sea. Some of her political enemies were already sharpening their knives, whispering - quietly - that the Iron Lady was starting to rust. She'd been a great war leader, they acknowledged, but now the Cold War was over. It was time for someone else to take the helm and steer Britain into a Golden Age of peace, prosperity and freedom.

And unlimited rice pudding too, she thought dryly.

But it wasn't time to leave, not yet. The chaos in Europe had yet to subside, while the chaos in Africa and the Middle East was growing steadily worse. Britain needed a strong hand at the helm as she navigated her way through suddenly-choppy seas and she, Margaret Thatcher, was that strong hand. None of her enemies had been tested, not like her. *They* had never sailed the ship of state, even in calm waters.

"Change is never easy," she said. The *Reich*, for all of its horror, had been a predictable menace. Whatever rose from the ashes of history would be very different. "But we have to be ready."

"This is not the end," Anderson agreed. "*History* never ends."

The End

AFTERWORD

After the uprising of the 17th of June,
The Secretary of the Writers' Union,
Had leaflets distributed in the Stalinallee,
Stating that the people,
Had forfeited the confidence of the government,
And could win it back only,
By redoubled efforts. Would it not be easier,
In that case for the government,
To dissolve the people,
And elect another?

\- Bertolt Brecht

In his stand-alone novel, *In The Presence of Mine Enemies*, Harry Turtledove postulated that the Third *Reich* would eventually face a Soviet-style crisis: economic collapse, a crisis of legitimacy and, eventually, a decline into near-irrelevance. This would, as it did in the Original TimeLine (OTL), spur a demand for political reform, a re-examination of the founding principles of the Third *Reich* and the abandonment of its principles. There would neither be a Third World War nor a civil war.

I was not so optimistic.

We were amazingly lucky that Gorbachev's attempts to reform the Soviet Union did not lead to a civil war. Hard-liners within the Communist Party and the KGB could not have welcomed the changes, even if they understood that something *had* to change. The levels of stored hatred they'd built up ever since the Communist Party took a firm grip on power could easily have led to a bloody slaughter. Indeed, they *did* try to mount a coup - only to lose when it became clear just how little support they really had. And it was their coup attempt that led to the inevitable breakup of the USSR.

Gorbachev simply did not - could not - control the pace of change. The first signs of weakness led to other challenges to Moscow's authority. Indeed, there was a strong feeling in many places - Poland, in particular - that the time had come to stand up or lose everything. Each successive problem led to more as Gorbachev veered between appeasement and repression, each failure weakening his own position. Once the ice began to melt, the changes were utterly unpredictable. There was no way to slow the pace of change.

The Third *Reich*, assuming it survived, might not cope anything like as well. It would have faced many of the same problems, yet it might have reached for very different solutions. And yet, no matter what happened to the protesters, they would be unable to hide from the underlying problems pervading the *Reich*. The coup plotters in Moscow, even if they *had* succeeded in turning the clock back by shooting everyone who assembled to stop them, would *still* have had to deal with a collapsing economy. It had simply fallen too far to be stopped.

But a different decision, at a different time, might have changed the course of history.

———

The problem facing repressive regimes - Hitler's Germany, Stalin's Russia (and the USSR after Stalin), Mao's China, Saddam's Iraq, Gaddafi's Libya, Kim's North Korea, etc - is that they tend to be very bad at coping with change. Power is organised in a pyramid structure, with the dictator and his cronies at the very top and everyone else in successive levels working their way down towards the common people at the bottom. It can be very hard for the dictator to truly understand what is going on at the bottom, even if he *doesn't* have to deal with his subordinates constantly lying to him.

It doesn't take long for the rot to set in. Each of the dictator's cronies will try to gather as much power to himself as he can, relying on a patronage network to both protect him from the other cronies and set the stage for eventually usurping the dictator. Even if there are pre-dictatorship power structures - the military, for example - they will eventually be corrupted and folded into the dictatorship. The dictator will become corrupted by the unlimited power at his disposal, while his cronies will eventually become outright criminals.

If the state is based on ideology - Nazi Germany and the USSR, in particular - and it has avoided the trap of being led by a single family, it may be possible to mask this reality for decades. But the blunt truth is that the tools used to impose the ideology eventually create the dictatorship, if it wasn't already present. In order to impose communism on Russia, Lenin created a system - spearheaded by the NKVD - that allowed Stalin to take control and gather all the levers of power into his hands.

[This should not have surprised anyone. Attempts to impose ideologies - anything from Communism to Radical Islam - will always meet opposition. The proponents will then have to decide if they want to abandon their plans or start *forcing* people to comply. Inevitably, they always choose the latter - and open the doors to a Stalin.]

Such a state's leadership, therefore, may be split between true believers and the more cynical (and sometimes criminal) opportunists. The true believers will react to any threat to their power with horror - like the fanatics they are, they see the needs of the state as twinned with their own needs. They will ignore any inconvenient realities - such as a looming economic collapse - secure in the belief that their good intentions will see them through. Anything is justified in the name of their ideology. The opportunists, on the other hand, may be more interested in their personal power bases, but also more inclined to understand that a state that doesn't bend - when the winds shift - may simply break.

This is not to say that these people - both groups and everything in-between - are not genuine patriots. They may believe that they truly do have the best interests of their country at heart (this was certainly true of the plotters in Moscow) and they may have good reason to fear for the future if the reformers (or rebels or whatever you want to call them) are allowed to run free. But these people always see the interests of the country, as I noted above, and their own interests as being identical. They are rarely able or willing to separate themselves from their country.

Their opposition, on the other hand, may be hopelessly disorganised. Rampaging mobs do not tend to lead to good - or any - governance. Dictators rarely leave any other power structures intact to allow their opponents a chance to build up overt support. Even if the opposition does manage to build up a common front, it may run into problems deciding what will happen *after* the dictatorship is defeated, allowing the dictator a chance to play divide and rule with his opponents.

The end of a dictatorship, therefore, tends to be a messy business. If living under iron control tends to breed bitter resentment, the collapse of that control tends to lead to madness. Iraq and Libya fell into civil war after their dictatorships were removed because there were no alternate power structures on a national scale. The Syrian Civil War continues to rage because the dictatorship has been able to play its opponents against one another, as well as summoning assistance from outside powers. There was no reason, in 1991, to assume that the collapse of the Soviet Union - and the Warsaw Pact - would be peaceful…

…And there is no reason to assume that the collapse of an alternate Third *Reich* would be peaceful too.

———

Democracies have - or should have - one great advantage over dictatorships. There are multiple levers of power, established to make it difficult - if not impossible - for a single person to collect and wield them all. Political parties share power, acting as both the representatives of the people *and* as brakes on the ambitions of the political class. A political leader can, if the votes are there, be challenged and unseated by his former supporters, if they see his actions as a threat to their ideals. The political leaders may not take those ideals as seriously as they should, but they do understand the importance of paying lip service in front of the voters.

And yet, across the West, democracy is under threat.

I write these words in September 2016. In two months, the United States will go to the polls, forced to choose between two deeply unsatisfactory candidates: Hillary Clinton, a woman whose behaviour is outright criminal, and Donald Trump, a man with a particularly filthy mouth. Yet this is merely the tip of the iceberg. The United States has seen the rise of a political class - an incestuous union between political families and the media - that has achieved a stranglehold on power and is now trying to reshape the country to suit itself. But this has provoked resistance from men and women bitterly determined not to surrender any more ground…

Let us make no mistake. A Hillary victory means criminality and corruption on an unprecedented scale. There are good reasons to believe that she rigged the nomination process that made her the Democratic Party's candidate for President. She will put her personal interests ahead of those of the country as a whole. But a Trump victory means his supporters wrecking vengeance on everyone they blame for their woes. And why should they not? Their enemies have not been remotely subtle in using their power to quash dissidence, suppress free speech and ride roughshod over the rest of the country. The PC Thought Police have fuelled a mania for revenge, savage undirected revenge.

And why did this happen?

It happened because the political class - the political elites - lost touch with the general mood of the country. Trump rose to prominence because he addressed the needs and fears - *legitimate* needs and fears - of vast numbers of people who felt ignored by their rulers. And Bernie Sanders came close to winning the Democratic nomination because he followed the same line. He too addressed the needs and fears of the people.

I am not sanguine about the future. Civil discourse has all but evaporated. It is impossible to hold a reasoned discussion about anything, nor is it possible to discuss one's politics without fearing savage retribution. Both sides are convinced that the other is out to get them, that the other will be utterly merciless if it takes power. And both sides may well be right.

Democracy, as Winston Churchill remarked, is the worst system in the world…apart from all the others. And he was right. I would not care to live under a dictatorship. But one cannot expect politicians - particularly those born to the political class - to work to uphold democracy when democracy gets in their way. Expect, instead, for them to try to subvert the will of the people. As far as they are concerned, their interests come first.

And if we let them have their way, we may wind up with shackles on our wrists - or forced to launch a revolution. But if we did launch a revolution, there would be no guarantee of a happy ending...

Christopher G. Nuttall

United Kingdom, 2016

APPENDIX: THE LIMITS OF NAZI GERMANY

[I originally wrote this as a post for the Alternate History Weekly Update blog. Reprinted here with kind permission.]

One thing that bedevilled me, as I worked on the outline for what would become *Twilight of the Gods*, was the question of just how far the *Reich* could realistically go without becoming a Nazi-Wank. This is not actually an easy question to answer. Very few people in 1939 would have believed that the French could be crushed so easily in 1940 - indeed, the Germans came alarmingly close to running out of ammunition during the Polish Campaign - and very few commenters in 1941 gave the Soviets more than six months before they too were crushed.

Post-war writers have added their own spin on matters. Books such as *The Man in the High Castle* and *In The Presence of Mine Enemies* assumed that an alternate *Reich* would invade and occupy America in the process of an inevitable rise to global supremacy. Others - including myself - predicted a resumption of the war between Germany and Britain (and America). But just how realistic are such scenarios?

The important point to bear in mind is that Hitler lived during what I believe to be the last great period of conquest. Hitler's armies were armed and trained to race forward, seeking out the weak points in enemy defences and smashing through opposing armies before their enemies could react to the threat. Advances on such a scale were simply not possible during the Great War. At the same time, the threat of nuclear annihilation simply did not exist.

The RAF could - and did - bomb Germany, but - even if chemical weapons had been deployed - their ability to bring Germany to its knees was practically non-existent. Defence planners believed that the bomber would always get through, yet…so what?

By the time the 1960s rolled around, the armies were far more powerful - but, at the same time, more constrained. A Russian drive westward would almost certainly have triggered a nuclear response, when - if - NATO was unable to handle it. Russia would have been devastated, along with Western Europe. It is one of the many ironies of the Cold War that the US, which had a considerable nuclear supremacy, spent most of the war believing that it was fighting to catch up.

One may assume, of course, that Hitler was mad enough to consider launching a full-scale nuclear war. It would certainly fit into a story! But, at the same time, Hitler was rather more rational than we prefer to believe. Certainly, most of his pre-1944 decisions were rational *based on what he knew at the time*. Marching to Stalingrad was disastrous - we are told in hindsight - but it wouldn't have looked like a certain failure in 1943.

The other two major limitations on the Third *Reich* lie in their army and air force. Hitler had a fairly modern battle fleet - but it was grossly outnumbered by the British. (Adding the Italian Navy to the *Reich* doesn't really tip the balance.) Hitler could - and did - threaten supply lines between Britain and her empire (and America) but he couldn't strike directly at Britain itself. Meanwhile, the *Luftwaffe* was largely a short-range striking force. The Germans never had a successful long-range heavy bomber, ensuring that large parts of Britain were immune to German attack (and America was completely out of range.) Any attempt to assess the limits of the Third *Reich* must take those factors into account.

So…how far *could* Hitler have gone?

To the west, Operation Sealion was pretty much a pipe dream. Some authors have speculated that the invasion might have been possible, but the Germans really had too many limitations - a shortage of shipping, among others - to make Sealion anything other than a very risky gamble. Hitler simply could not get across the English Channel.

For this to change, Hitler would need to reshape his air and naval forces radically, following a strategy that would have no viable purpose other than the invasion of Britain. Even if the Hitler of 1938 was prepared to make the investment, long before France was crushed in 1940 and Sealion became necessary, such programs would very definitely change the political situation during the run up to the war.

[The idea that Hitler could have invaded America is so absurd not to require further discussion.]

Hitler presumably has no need to occupy either Spain or Portugal. Neither power was inclined to challenge the Third Reich overtly. However, he may well want to pressure the Spanish to take Gibraltar and the Portuguese to break ties with Britain. Both steps could be taken, at considerable economic cost to both Spain or Portugal. In such an eventuality, one might see Hitler facing his own version of the Peninsula War.

To the south, the problem facing Hitler is logistics. The Germans might have been better than the British at desert warfare, but Rommel was always operating on a shoestring. Hitler always saw the desert war as a sideshow, rather than a potential way to bring the British to heel. And again, from his point of view, he was right. Nazi gains in the Middle East would always be tenuous as long as the British remained undefeated and Soviet Russia loomed to the east.

Taking Malta during 1940 would have been easy - even the Italians could probably have done it. (Indeed, a timeline where Germany invades Malta instead of Crete might lead to German dominance in the region.) Malta would serve as a giant airbase, allowing the Germans to drive the Royal Navy out of the region and ship additional supplies to Rommel. Thus reinforced, Rommel might have been able to push forward to Suez and drive into Palestine, creating a massive humanitarian crisis. Scenting British weakness, the Arabs would rise in revolt, enthusiastically supporting the Germans. As the British position crumbled, the Germans would probably be able to cow the Saudis (unless American forces arrived in time to dare Hitler to attack them.) They'd certainly have access to a great deal of oil

Depending on precisely when this happened, Turkey and Iran would both become very important. Turkey would have good reason to secure Northern Iraq before the Germans could arrive - a long-standing Turkish objective - while Iran would probably try to remain neutral or even join the Germans. (Iran was occupied in August 1941, but if the Germans pushed forward hard

Iran might rise in revolt.) At that point, the Germans might see value in Iran as a buffer state.

Logistics would remain a major headache for the Germans. Marching all the way into India would seem the ideal way to end the war, but their logistics would need to be built up heavily before they could make their move.

To the east, just how far could the Germans go?

Hitler did come very close to taking Moscow in 1941 (this has, obviously, been hotly debated.) Taking Moscow would not just have dealt a crippling blow to Russian morale, it would also have cost the Russians a large part of their transport infrastructure and the bureaucratic system that kept the USSR running. It's tempting to joke that shooting the bureaucrats would make the USSR more efficient, but it's wartime - they *need* that command economy. Worse, perhaps, large reserves of manpower would be lost. Stalin, assuming he survives the battle, would have to rely on troops drawn from more restive parts of the USSR, troops who might not be remotely trustworthy. And if the Germans make even the slightest attempt to treat the natives well, even as a tactical measure, they are likely to win hundreds of thousands of adherents.

This was, I suspect, Germany's last chance to win the war outright. Taking Stalingrad in 1942/43 would have certainly hurt the Russians, but it wouldn't have been enough to keep the Americans from bombing Germany heavily and continuing to supply the Russians with Lend Lease, even if there was no second front. By 1945, America would have atomic bombs - if only a handful. Dropping those bombs on Germany would do immense damage, possibly prompting the military to overthrow Hitler and order a surrender. At that point, the *Reich* would be doomed.

So...let us assume a *Reich* that reaches from the French coastline to the Urals and the border of Iran. How long can they actually *keep* it?

That is not, of course, an easy question to answer. Taking territory is one thing, but controlling it indefinitely is quite another. The Germans would be no less willing than the Soviet Union to exterminate vast numbers of people or forcibly relocate them to places well out of the way. On the other hand, controlling places like Greece and France would be difficult. Would the French go quiet if the Germans offered them a liveable peace? Or would the French resistance grow stronger as the German grip tightened?

The Germans would, I suspect, face a great deal of partisan warfare in both Russia and the Middle East, if only because they *won't* be offering the natives any sort of liveable peace. Hitler might have been happy to work with the Arabs - the Arabs would probably exterminate the Jews in Palestine for him - but he didn't see them as anything more than *Untermenschen*. I would expect the Nazi grip to tighten, just to make sure the oil keeps flowing to Germany, and eventually a bid to outright exterminate the locals.

Hitler would need to boost his population by any means necessary. On one hand, the Nazi plans to encourage a growing birth-rate would have time to bed in, probably giving Nazi Germany a baby-boom. On the other, large numbers of young men will have been killed during the war, probably forcing the Germans to use young women in industries rather than bringing up children. (The Nazis didn't want women to work outside the homes, but they may have to compromise if there is a major manpower shortage.) The kidnapping program - in which the Nazis took 'Aryan' children from their parents and gave them to good Germans to raise - would probably pick up speed. So too would attempts to convince 'Aryan' westerners - like Norwegians - that they were actually Germanic.

The German economy is an interesting question. Historically, despite waging war against most of the world, the Nazis didn't embrace a command economy until 1942, when Speer was appointed as Minister of Armaments. Speer consolidated power over the German economy despite bitter opposition. I've actually heard it speculated that Speer's reforms came six months too late to save Germany. Assuming that Speer's reforms are not seen as necessary in this timeline, what will happen to the German economy? I suspect it might well remain a fragmented mess of bailiwicks, controlled by the various German ministries, rather than a single organised whole.

Nazi German *was* constantly pushing the limits of technology - rockets and jet aircraft in particular - but I doubt the US will remain behind for long. The real question would be German mass production. Using slave labour in factories which require precision and adherence to detail is asking for trouble. Choosing to ignore 'Jewish' science would cripple the *Reich's* nuclear program. As technology advances, the Reich might well start falling behind.

Education, in fact, is likely to have a dangerous long-term effect on the *Reich*. Children were *not* taught to think for themselves and question authority.

The SS wouldn't see any difference between questioning orthodox science and questioning the *Reich* itself. Children were expected to join the Hitler Youth and excel in manly pursuits - creating a body of part-trained manpower for the military - rather than study science. Matters would not be helped by the *Reich's* triumph seemingly 'proving' Hitler's nuttier racial theories. Reasoning from incorrect - and absurd - premises would lead future scientists to incorrect conclusions.

Overall, just how long would the *Reich* actually *last*?

Hitler will die at some point, shortly after the war. His health was already failing before he killed himself in OTL. Unless he does something to create a long-term governing structure for the *Reich*, there is almost certainly going to be a major dispute over the succession, not least because Hitler liked playing his subordinates off against one another. Himmler would seem to be the heir presumptive, but there would be other candidates. Speer? Goering? Or someone who rose in power past the end of 1945? It's very tempting to imagine a civil war following the death of Hitler, as the SS attempts to take complete control and the other factions actively resist it.

The *Reich* would presumably have a handful of nuclear weapons by 1950, unless - for whatever reason - nukes are never used in this timeline. I suspect at that point global politics would effectively freeze, just as they did in OTL. The *Reich* would maintain its dominance over Europe, while America built a NATO-analogue or went back to sleep (assuming there was no Japanese War). Britain would want to try to maintain its empire, but it would be incredibly difficult to do anything of the sort.

A nightmare would have descended across the *Reich*. Even in Germany, Germans would not be safe from the SS - war-wounded veterans, amongst others, would be targeted for elimination. Entire populations deemed inferior would be exterminated. Millions upon millions would be ruthlessly slaughtered or enslaved. It would be the end of the world as they knew it.

But would this *Reich* last for a thousand years?

That, of course, is the question. I believe the answer is very definitely *no*, barring a considerable - and unlikely - degree of political reform. The economy would grow weaker and weaker - while the US moved ahead - while no application of military force would be able to hide the *Reich's* underlying weaknesses. Would there be a semi-peaceful collapse, as Harry Turtledove speculated, or my outright civil war?

Perhaps we should be grateful that we will never know.

APPENDIX: GERMAN WORDS AND PHRASES

Abwehr - German Military Intelligence

Bund Deutscher Mädel (BDM) - League of German Girls/Band of German Maidens, female wing of the Hitler Youth.

Einsatzgruppen - SS extermination squads

Gastarbeiter - Guest Worker

Gau - an administrative subdivision.

Gauleiter, the party leader of a regional branch of the Nazi Party; later, regional leader of a district.

Generalmajor - Major General

Germanica - Moscow, renamed after the war

Hauptsturmfuehrer - SS rank, roughly equal to Captain.

Heer - The German Army

Herrenvolk - Master Race

Junker, German nobleman

Kessel - 'caldron,' German military term for trapping an enemy formation.

Kinder, Küche, Kirche - Nazi slogan, roughly "children, kitchen, church."

Kriegsmarine - The German Navy

Lebensborn - literally 'font of life.' SS-run program for increasing the German population, including measures to encourage breeding and the kidnapping of 'Aryan' children from non-German families.

Lebensraum - 'Living Space.'

Luftwaffe - The German Air Force

Mausefalle - 'Mouse Trap'

Mutterkreuz - Mother's Cross

Oberfeldwebel - *Heer* rank, roughly equal to Master Sergeant

Oberkommando der Wehrmacht (OKW, 'Supreme Command of the Armed Forces') - The German General Staff.

Obergruppenfuehrer - SS rank, roughly equal to Lieutenant General.

Obersturmfuehrer - SS rank, roughly equal to First Lieutenant.

Ordnungspolizei - Order Police (regular police force)

Reichsführer-SS - Commander of the SS

Reichsgau - an administrative subdivision.

Reichssicherheitshauptamt (RSHA) - Reich Main Security Office

Sigrunen - SS insignia (lightning bolts)

Standartenfuehrer - SS rank, roughly equal to Colonel.

Sturmbannfuehrer - SS rank, roughly equal to Major.

Sturmann - SS rank, roughly equal to Private.

Strumscharfuehrer - SS rank, roughly equal to Master Sergeant.

Swinehund - German insult, literally 'pig dog.'

Untermensch - Subhuman.

Untermenschen - Subhumans, plural of *Untermensch*.

Unterscharfuehrer - SS rank, roughly equal to Second Lieutenant.

Vaterland - Fatherland.

Volk - The German People.

Volkssturm - German militia.

Wehrmacht - The German Military (often taken to represent just the army (*Heer*)).

EXCERPT FROM *ACTS OF WAR*
USURPER'S WAR VOLUME I

James Young
Available as Paperback and also Available as an audiobook.
Usurper War Collection I *On Seas So Crimson*…is also available.

Follow James Young at the Following
Blog: https://vergassy.com/
FB: https://www.facebook.com/ColfaxDen/
Twitter: @youngblai

H.M.S. Exeter
North Atlantic
1330 Local (1030 Eastern)
12 September
Whether or not Eric was all right was likely a matter of opinion. He wasn't flying anymore, as the weather conditions had started to become much worse since he'd left *Ranger's* deck that morning. The base of the clouds had once again descended, and he estimated that the ceiling was well under ten thousand feet. At sea level, visibility was under ten miles, and an approaching squall promised to make it less than that very soon.

I don't blame the Brit pilots for nixing the thought of flying reconnaissance in this, Eric thought. *Yet for some reason I'd still rather take my chances in that soup than be on this ship right now. She's definitely going into harm's way, and fast.*

The heavy cruiser's deck throbbed beneath his feet, and the smoke pouring from her stack and stiff wind blowing onto her bridge told him that *Exeter* had definitely picked up speed.

"Sir, I've brought *Leftenant* Cobb," Adlich said, causing Captain Gordon to turn around. *Exeter's* master had obviously been mollified by the worsening conditions, as he gave Eric a wry grin when the American officer stepped up beside him.

Whoa, it's cold out here, Eric thought. As if reading his mind, a petty officer handed him a jacket.

"We remove the windows when we're getting ready to go into action," the man said. "Lesson learned after River Plate."

"Thank you," Eric said. "I guess the windows would be a bit problematic in a fight."

The petty officer gave a wan smile, pointing to a scar down his cheek.

"Glass splinters are a bit sharp, yes."

"Your squadron commander was either a very brave man or a much better pilot than anyone I know," Gordon said solemnly from behind the ship's wheel.

Or alternatively, Commander Cobleigh was an idiot who didn't check with the meteorologist before we took off.

Eric was about to reply when the talker at the rear of the bridge interrupted him.

"Sir, *Hood* should be coming into visual range off of our port bow," the rating reported. "Range fifteen thousand yards."

"Thank you," Gordon replied. The captain then strode to the front of the bridge, stopping at a device that reminded Eric of the sightseeing binoculars atop the Empire State Building. Bending slightly, Gordon wiped down the eyepieces, then swiveled the binoculars to look through them.

"Officer of the deck," Gordon said after a moment.

"Yes, sir?" a Royal Navy lieutenant answered from Eric's right. Roughly Eric's height, the broad-shouldered man looked like he could probably snap a good-sized tree in half with his bare hands.

"Confirm with gunnery that the director's tracking *Hood's* bearing to be three one zero, estimated range fourteen thousand, seven hundred fifty yards."

"Aye aye, sir," the officer replied. Eric heard the RN officer repeating the information as Gordon stepped back from the sight and turned to look at him.

"Well, if you want to see how the other half lives, *Leftenant* Cobb, feel free to have a look."

Eric hoped he didn't look as eager as he felt walking forward towards the bridge windows. Bending a little further to look through the sight, he pressed his face up against the eyepieces. Swinging the glasses, he found himself looking at the H.M.S. *Hood*, flagship of the Royal Navy. With her square bridge, four turrets, and rakish lines, the battlecruiser was a large, beautiful vessel that displaced over four times the *Exeter*'s tonnage. Black smoke poured from her stack, and her massive bow wave told Eric that she was moving at good speed.

"You can change the magnification with the switch under your right hand," Gordon said, startling Eric slightly. He followed the British master's advice, continuing until he could see the entire approaching British force as it closed. Destroyers were roughly one thousand yards in front of and to either side of the *Hood*. Behind her at one-thousand-yard intervals were two large vessels, either battleships or battlecruisers, with another one starting to exit the mist like some sort of great beast stirring from its cave. After a moment, Eric recognized the distinctive silhouette as that of a *Nelson*-class battleship.

"That is the *King George V*, *Prince of Wales*, and *Nelson* behind her. *Warspite* should be next."

Eric nodded at Gordon's statement, continuing to watch as the final battleship made its appearance. A moment later, Gordon starting to give orders to the helmsman. *Exeter*'s bow began to swing around to port, causing Eric to step back from the sight with a puzzled expression.

"We'll be passing between the destroyer screen and the *Hood* to take our place in line," Gordon said. Eric turned back to the device, continuing to study the British battleline. A few moments later, there was the crackle of the loudspeaker.

"All hands, this is the captain speaking," Gordon began. "Shortly we will be passing by the *Hood*. All available hands are to turn out topside to give three cheers for His Majesty. That is all."

Eric stepped back from the sight, his face clearly radiating his shock. Gordon smiled as he came back up towards the front of the bridge with the officer of the deck.

"The *King* is going into battle?" he asked incredulously. "Isn't that a bit…"

"Dangerous?" Gordon finished for him. "Yes, but much like your situation, circumstances precluded His Majesty's transfer to another vessel."

"What? That doesn't make any…"

"His Majesty was apparently aboard the *Hood* receiving a briefing from the First Sea Lord when the *Queen Mary* was torpedoed," Gordon said, his voice cold. "We were not expecting the German surface units to be as close as they were, and it was considered imprudent to stop the *Hood* with at least two confirmed submarines close about. Is that sufficient explanation to you, or would you like to continue questioning our tactics?"

Eric could tell he was straining his host's civility, but the enormity of what was at risk made him feel he had to say something.

"I'm no expert at surface tactics…"

"That much is obvious," Gordon snapped.

"…but the *Hood* is a battlecruiser," Eric finished in a rush. "While I didn't get a great look at the Germans before they shot up me and my commander, Rawles saw at least two battleships."

"Your concern is noted, *Leftenant* Cobb, but I think that you will see the *Hood* is a bit hardier than a dive bomber."

Okay, I'm just going to shut up now, Eric said. *I may have slept through a lot of history, but I seem to recall the last time British battlecruisers met German heavy guns it didn't go so well. A quote about there being problems with your "bloody ships" or something similar comes to mind.* The Battle of Jutland hadn't been that long ago, as evidenced by the *Warspite* still being a front-line unit. Eric sincerely hoped Gordon's confidence was well-placed.

"Sir, we are almost on the *Hood*," the officer of the deck interrupted. Eric turned and realized that the lead destroyer was indeed almost abreast the *Exeter*, with the *Hood* now a looming presence just beyond.

"The *Hood*, after her refit, is the most powerful warship in the world," Gordon continued, his voice a little less frigid. "The *Bismark* and *Tirpitz* have only recently gone through refit, while the *Scharnhorst* and *Gneisenau* have not been in the open ocean for almost six months. There should not be any major danger."

If you're looking around the room and you can't find the mark, guess what? You're the mark. Eric's father's words, an admonishment to always be suspicious of any situation that seemed too good to be true, came back to him with a cold feeling in his stomach.

The Germans would **not** *be out here unless they had a plan,* Eric continued thinking. *Somehow I think that, much like the Royal Air Force, the Royal Navy is about to receive a rude shock.*

"All right lads, three cheers for His Majesty," The loudspeaker crackled. "Hip…hip…"

As the *Exeter's* crew yelled at the top of their lungs, Eric studied the *Hood* in passing. The two vessels were close enough that he could see a party of men in white uniforms standing on the battlecruiser's bridge and the extraordinarily large flag streaming from the *Hood's* yardarm. Picking up a pair of binoculars resting on a shelf near the bridge's front lip, he focused on the pennant.

"That's the Royal Standard," Gordon said after the last cheer rang out. The device consisted of four squares, two red with the other pair gold and blue, respectively. The two red were identical, forming the top left and bottom right portions of the flag. Looking closely, Eric could see elongated gold lions or griffins within the squares. The gold square had what looked like a standing red lion within a crimson square, while the blue had some sort of harp.

"What do the symbols mean, sir?" Eric asked. Gordon shook his head.

"*Leftenant*, I could probably remember if I thought hard enough about it, but I do not think that is very important right now."

Eric nodded, placing the binoculars back down as the *Exeter* continued to travel down the battleline. After *Warspite*, there were two more British heavy cruisers. At Gordon's command, the *Exeter* finished her turn, taking her place behind the other two CAs. Satisfied with his vessel's stationing, Gordon began dealing with the myriad tasks that a warship's captain was expected to perform before battle. Eric observed these with a sense of detachment, noting that the bridge crew operated like they had been there dozens of times. Mentally, he compared the men to those he had observed aboard the American heavy cruiser *Salt Lake City*.

Things are so similar, yet so different. You can tell these men have been at war for over three years, Eric thought, feeling strangely comforted by the obvious experience in front of him. The feeling was fleeting, however, as the talker at the rear of the bridge broke the routine.

"Sir, *Hood* reports multiple contacts, bearing oh three oh relative, range thirty thousand yards," the talker at the rear of the bridge said. It was if his words touched off a current of electricity around the entire compartment, as each man seemed to stiffen at his post.

"Well, glad to see that she's got better eyes than we do," Gordon muttered under his breath. "Pass the word to all stations."

Eric saw motion out of the corner of his eye and turned to see the *Exeter's* two forward turrets training out and elevating.

"Flag is directing a change in course to one seven zero true," the talker continued. "Vessels will turn in sequence. Destroyers are to form up for torpedo attack to our stern."

Gordon nodded in acknowledgment, and Eric could see the man was obviously in pensive thought. After their earlier exchange, Eric had no desire to attempt to discern what he was thinking. Judging from the look on the man's face, it was probably nothing good. Looking to port, Eric could see the British destroyers starting to steam past for their rendezvous astern of *Exeter*, a scene that was repeated a moment later on the starboard side.

Is it my imagination, or is it getting a little bit easier to see again? Eric thought. *If so, is that a good or a bad thing?*

"Enemy force is turning with us," the talker said quietly.

Now that is definitely a bad thing.

Eric had a very passing familiarity with radar, as he had been the target dummy for *Ranger's* fighter squadron to practice aerial intercepts. It was obvious, given the visibility, that the *Hood* hadn't sighted the enemy with the naked eye. Unless the Germans had a team of gypsies on their vessels, it appeared that they also had the ability to detect ships despite the murk.

Explains how they were able to shoot down Commander Cobleigh, Eric thought, feeling sick to his stomach. *My God, they probably knew we were there long before we came out of the cloudbank but wanted to make positive identification.*

The visibility was definitely starting to get better, at least at sea level. With only the distance of the British line to judge by, Eric guesstimated that visibility to the horizon was somewhere around twenty thousand yards.

Well within maximum range of everyone's guns, he thought. *I hope someone on this side knows what size force we're facing, as I doubt the Germans are idiots.*

"Sir, the *Hood* reports she is…"

With a roar and spout of black smoke from her side, the British flagship made the talker's report superfluous. The rest of the British battleline rapidly followed suit, the combined smoke from their guns floating backward like roiling, black thunderheads.

I can't see what in the hell they're shooting at, Eric thought, searching the horizon as he felt his stomach clench.

In truth, *Hood* and her counterparts had only a general idea of what they were engaging. Indeed, if the commander of the opposing force, Vice Admiral Erich Bey, had actually followed his orders to simply compel the Home Fleet to sail a relatively straight course while avoiding contact, there would have been no targets for them to engage. Instead, Bey had decided to close with the last known position of the Home Fleet in hopes of picking off the vessel or vessels the *Kriegsmarine*'s U-boats had allegedly crippled that morning. Regardless of his reasoning, Bey's aggressive nature had inadvertently led to his superiors' worst nightmare—the hastily organized Franco-German force being brought into contact with the far more experienced Royal Navy.

Admiral Bey, to his credit, played the hand he had dealt himself. Moments after *Hood*'s initial salvo landed short of his flagship, the KMS *Bismarck*, the German admiral began barking orders. The first was for the radar-equipped vessels in his fleet to return fire. The second was for the entire column to change course in order to sharpen the rate of closure and allow the Vichy French vessels, limited to visual acquisition, to also engage. The final directive was for a position report to be repeatedly sent without any encryption so that nearby U-boats could immediately set course in an attempt to pick off any stragglers.

"Well, looks like the other side is game," Captain Gordon drily observed as multiple waterspouts appeared amongst the British battleships. A moment later the distant sound of the explosions reached Eric's ears.

"Looks like they're over-concentrating on the front of the line though," Eric observed.

Gordon turned to look at the American pilot.

"Would you prefer they spread their fire more evenly so we can have a taste, *Leftenant?*"

"No sir, not with the shells that are being slung out there."

Gordon brought his binoculars back up.

"Still can't see the enemy yet, but that's why the boffins were aboard during our refit," Gordon said. The man turned to his talker, jaw clenched.

"Tell Guns they may fire when we have visual contact or the enemy reaches nineteen thousand yards, whichever comes first," Gordon said, his voice clipped. "Inform bridge of the eventual target's bearing so we may get a look."

"Aye aye, Captain."

Gordon turned back towards Eric and opened his mouth when he was interrupted by the sound of ripping canvas followed by the *smack!* of four shells landing between *Exeter* and the next British cruiser in front of her. A moment later, a bell began ringing at the rear of *Exeter*'s bridge. Eric was about to ask what the device signified when the heavy cruiser's forward turrets roared, the blast hitting him like a physical blow. The look of shock was obviously quite apparent, as Gordon gave Eric an apologetic smile.

"Sorry, guess I should have…"

Exeter's captain was again interrupted, except this time by two bright flashes aboard the cruiser forward of her the British battleline. The other vessel was visibly staggered by the blows, with a fire immediately starting astern.

"Looks like *Suffolk* has worse luck than we do," Gordon observed grimly. The British heavy cruiser's turrets replied back towards the enemy, but it was obvious, even to Eric, that their companion vessel was badly hit.

"Guns reports target is at bearing two nine zero, range twenty thousand yards…"

The bell ringing cut the rating off, as it was followed immediately by the *Exeter* unleashing a full broadside. Gordon had already begun to swing his sight around to the reported bearing, and bent to see what his guns were up to. Eric, looking past the captain, saw *Suffolk* receive another hit, this one causing debris to fly up from the vicinity of her bridge. He suddenly felt his mouth go dry.

Someone has the range, he thought grimly.

"Bloody good show Guns!" Gordon shouted into the voice tube near his sight. "Give that bastard another..."

The firing gong rang again, Exeter's gunnery officer apparently already ahead of Gordon. Eric braced himself, the roar of the naval rifles starting to cause a slight ringing in his ears. He turned to look towards the horizon, following the direction of Exeter's guns.

"These will help," the officer of the deck said from beside him, handing him a pair of binoculars.

"Thank you," Eric said, turning towards the officer only to see the man go pale.

"Oh bloody hell! Look at the Hood!"

Eric turned and looked down the British line, noting as he turned that the Suffolk was heeling to Exeter's starboard with flames shooting from her amidships and rear turret. Ignoring the heavily damaged heavy cruiser, he brought up his binoculars as he looked towards the front of the British line. In an instant, he could see why the officer of the deck had made his exclamation. The battlecruiser's guns appeared frozen in place, and oil was visibly gushing from her amidships. As Eric watched, another salvo splashed around her, with a sudden flare and billow of smoke from her stern indicating something serious had been hit.

"Captain, the Hood is signaling a power failure!" the officer of the deck shouted. Eric turned to see the man had acquired another set of eyeglasses and was also studying the flagship.

Gordon nodded, stepping back from his captain's sight and brought his own set of binoculars up to study the battlecruiser. Eric quickly handed his over before the OOD could react.

"It would appear that our Teutonic friends can shoot a bit better than we expected," Gordon said grimly.

Admiral Bey would have agreed with Gordon's assessment had he heard it, as he too was pleasantly surprised at how well his scratch fleet was performing. Unfortunately for the Germans, however, the British could shoot almost as well, their guns seemed to be doing far more damage, and they had much better fire distribution. The only British capital ships with major damage were the Hood, set ablaze and rendered powerless by the Tirpitz and Jean Bart, and Nelson due to hits from the Bismarck and Strasbourg. Among the cruisers, only the Suffolk had been hit, being thoroughly mauled by the KMS *Hipper* and *Lutzow*. In exchange, only the *Jean Bart*, *Gneisenau*, and *Bismarck* remained relatively unscathed among his battleline. Of the rest of his vessels, the French battlecruiser *Strasbourg* had been thoroughly holed by the H.M.S. *Warspite's* accurate shooting, *Tirpitz* was noticeably down by the bows, and *Scharnhorst* had received at least two hits from *Prince of Wales* in the first ten minutes of the fight.

Bey's escorts, consisting of the pocket battleship *Lutzow* and a force of German and Vichy French cruisers, had arranged themselves in an *ad hoc* screen to starboard. The fact that they outnumbered their British counterparts had not spared them from damage, albeit not as heavy as that suffered by the Franco-German battleline. Moreover, while *Exeter's* shooting had set the lead vessel, the French heavy cruiser *Colbert*, ablaze and slowed her, this was more than offset by the battering the *Suffolk* had received from the *Lutzow*, *Hipper*, and *Seydlitz*. As that vessel fell backward in the British formation, the remaining cruisers split their fire between the *Exeter*, *Norfolk*, and the destroyers beginning their attack approach.

Word of the British DDs' approach caused Bey some consternation. While it could be argued that his force was evenly matched with the British battleline, the approaching destroyers could swiftly change this equation if they got into torpedo range. Deciding that discretion was the better part of valor, Bey ordered all vessels to make smoke and disengage. It was just after the force began their simultaneous turn that disaster struck.

The KMS *Scharnhorst*, like the *Hood*, had begun life as a battlecruiser. While both she and her sister had been upgraded during the Armistice Period with 15-inch turrets, the *Kriegsmarine* had made the conscious decision not to upgrade her armor. The folly of this choice became readily apparent as the *Prince of Wales'* twentieth salvo placed a pair of 14-inch shells through her amidships belt. While neither shell fully detonated, their passage severed the steering controls between the light battleship's bridge and rudder.

The *Scharnhorst's* helmsman barely had time to inform the captain of this before the second half of *PoW's* staggered salvo arrived, clearing the battleship's bridge with one shell and and hitting *Scharnhorst* on the armored "turtle deck" right above her engineering spaces with a second. To many bystanders' horror, a visible gout of steam spewed from the vessel's side as all 38,000 tons of her staggered like a stunned bull. Only the fact that her 15-inch guns fired a ragged broadside back at the British line indicated that the vessel still had power, but it was obvious to all that she had been severely hurt.

One of those observers was the captain of the KMS *Gneisenau*, *Scharnhorst's* sister ship and the next battleship in line. Confronted with the heavily wounded *Scharnhorst* drifting back towards him, the man ordered the helm brought back hard to starboard. In one of the horrible vagaries of warfare, the *Gneisenau* simultaneously masked her sister ship from the *Prince of Wales'* fire and corrected the aim of her own assailant, the H.M.S. *Nelson*. No one would ever know how many 16-inch shells hit of the five that had been fired at the *Gneisenau*, as the only one that mattered was the one that found the German battleship's forward magazine. With a massive roar, bright flash, and volcanic outpouring of flame, the *Gneisenau's* bow disappeared. *Scharnhorst* and *Jean Bart's* horrified crews were subjected to the spectacle of the *Gneisenau's* stern whipping upwards, propellers still turning. The structures only glistened for a moment, as the battleship's momentum carried her aft end into the roiling black cloud serving as a tombstone for a 40,000-ton man-of-war and the 1,700 men who manned her.

"Holy shit! Holy shit!" Eric exclaimed, his expletives lost in the general pandemonium that was *Exeter's* bridge.

"Get yourselves together!" Gordon roared, waving his hands. As if to emphasize his point, there was the sound of ripping canvas, and a moment later, the *Exeter* found herself surrounded by large waterspouts.

"Port ten degrees!" Gordon barked, the bridge crew quickly returning to their tasks.

"Sir, *Nelson* is signaling that she is heaving to!"

"What in the bloody hell is the matter with her?!" Gordon muttered, a moment before *Exeter's* guns roared again.

"Guns reports we are engaging and being engaged by a pocket battleship. He believes it is the..." the talker reported.

Once again there was the sound of ripping canvas, this time far louder. Eric instinctively ducked just before the *Exeter* shuddered simultaneously with the loud *bang!* just above their heads. Dimly, he saw something fall out of the corner of his eye even as there was a sound like several wasps all around him. Coming back to his feet, Eric smelled the strong aroma of explosives for the second time that day, except this time there was a man screaming like a shot rabbit to accompany it.

"Damage report!" Gordon shouted. "Someone shut that man up!"

Feeling something wet on his face, Eric reached up to touch it and came away with blood. He frantically reached up to feel if he had a wound, and only came away with more blood. Looking around in horror, he suddenly realized that the blood was not his, but that of a British rating who was now missing half of his head, neck, and upper chest. Eric barely had time to register this before a litter crew came bursting into the bridge. The four men headed to the aft portion of the structure, obviously there for the man who had been screaming before a gag had been shoved in his mouth. Eric followed the litter team's path, then immediately wished he hadn't as his stomach lurched. The casualty's abdomen was laid open, and Eric saw the red and grey of intestine on the deck before turning back forward.

Oh God, he thought, then had another as he thought about the injured man's likely destination. *I hope Rawles is okay.*

"Hard a starboard!" Gordon barked. Eric braced himself as the *Exeter* heeled over, the vessel chasing the previous salvo as her guns roared back at the German pocket battleship. He noticed that the guns were starting to bear even further aft as the cruiser maneuvered to keep up with the remainder of the British battleline. Looking to starboard, Eric saw the battleship *Nelson* drifting past them on her starboard side. The vessel's forward-mounted triple turrets, still elevated to port, fired off a full salvo once *Exeter* was past, but it was clear that the battleship had suffered severe damage.

"Sir, we took one glancing hit to the bridge roof," the OOD reported, pointing at the hit that had sprayed splinters into the structure. Eric was amazed at the man's calm. "We took another hit aft, but it detonated in the galley."

"*King George V* signals commence torpedo attack with destroyers," the talker interrupted. "All ships with tubes to attack enemy cripples."

Six waterspouts impacted approximately three hundred yards to port, and Eric found himself questioning the wisdom of staying aboard the heavy cruiser after all.

"Well, looks like this ship will continue her tradition of picking on women bigger than her," Gordon observed drily. "Flank speed, port thirty degrees. Get me the torpedo flat."

Eric looked once again at the hole in the bridge roof.

A step either way and I'd probably be dead, he thought wildly. *Or worse, if that shell had it full on we'd all be gone.* Shaking his head, he turned to look off to port as the throb of *Exeter's* engines began to increase.

"You ever participate in a torpedo attack during your summer cruise, Mr. Cobb?" Gordon asked after barking several orders to the helm.

"No sir," Eric croaked, then swallowed to get a clearer voice. "Our cruisers don't have torpedoes. I'm familiar with how to do one theoretically…"

Exeter's guns banged out another salvo, even as the German pocket battleship's return fire landed where she would have been had the cruiser continued straight.

"Well, looks like you're about to get to apply some of that theoretical knowledge," Gordon said, bringing his binoculars up. The man scanned the opposing line.

"The three big battleships are turning away under cover of smoke along with the majority of the cruisers. That Frog battlecruiser looks about done for, and that pocket battleship and heavy cruiser will soon have more than enough to deal with when the destroyers catch up," Gordon said, pointing as he talked. *Exeter's* master turned to give his orders.

"Tell Lieutenant Commander Gannon his target is the pocket battleship! Guns are to…"

The crescendo of incoming shells drowned Gordon out, this time ending with the *Exeter* leaping out of the water and shuddering as she was hit. Once again the bridge wing was alive with fragments, and for the second time Eric felt a splash of wetness across his side. Looking down, he saw his entire left side was covered in blood and flesh. For a moment he believed it was his, until he blissfully realized that he felt no pain.

"Damage report!" Gordon shouted again. "Litter party!"

"Sir, I believe I am hit," the OOD gasped. Eric turned to see the man's arm missing from just below the elbow, blood spraying from the severed stump.

"Corpsman!" Gordon shouted angrily, stepping towards the lieutenant. The captain never made it, as the OOD toppled face forward, revealing jagged wounds in his back where splinters had blasted into his body.

"Helmsman! Zig zag pattern!" Gordon barked. "Someone get me a damage report! Midshipman Green, inform damage control that we need another talker and an OOD here!"

"Aye aye, Captain!"

"*Leftenant* Cobb!"

"Yes sir?" Eric asked, shaking himself out of stupor.

"It might be prudent for you to go to the conning tower," Gordon said.

"Sir, I'd prefer to be here than in some metal box," Eric said. "With the shells that bastard's tossing it won't make a lick of difference anyway."

"Too true," Gordon said. "Looks like the heavy cruisers and that pocket battleship are covering the bastards' retreat."

Gordon's supposition was only partially correct. In truth, the pocket battleship *Lutzow* had received damage from the *Exeter* and *Norfolk* that had somewhat reduced her maximum speed. This had prevented her from fleeing with the rest of the screen, their retirement encouraged by a few salvoes from the *Nelson*. Realizing that she could not escape the closing British destroyers, *Lutzow*'s captain had decided to turn and engage the smaller vessels in hopes of allowing *Scharnhorst* to open the distance between herself and the British. Unfortunately, *Lutzow* had failed to inform the heavy cruiser KMS *Hipper*, trailing in her wake, of her desire to self-sacrifice while ignoring Admiral Bey's signal to retire. Thus the latter vessel, her radio aerial knocked out by an over salvo from the *Nelson*'s secondary batteries, found herself committed to engaging the rapidly closing British destroyers along with the larger, crippled *Lutzow*.

The British destroyers, formed into two divisions under the experienced Commodore Philip Vian, first overtook the damaged French battlecruiser *Strasbourg*. Adrift, afire, and listing heavily to port, the *Strasbourg* wallowed helplessly as the British destroyers closed like hyenas on a paralyzed wildebeest. Just as Vian was beginning to order his group into their battle dispositions, flooding finally compromised the battlecruiser's stability. With a rumble and the scream of tortured metal, the *Strasbourg* rotated onto her starboard beam and slipped beneath the surface.

That left the crippled *Scharnhorst*, the *Lutzow*, and the hapless *Hipper*. Still receiving desultory fire from *Nelson* and *Warspite*, the trio of German vessels initially concentrated their fire on the charging *Exeter* and *Norfolk*. After five minutes of this, all three German captains realized Vian's approaching destroyers were a far greater threat. The *Lutzow* and *Hipper* turned to lay smoke across the retreating *Scharnhorst*'s stern, the maneuver also allowing both vessels to fire full broadsides at their smaller assailants. The *Hipper* had just gotten off her second salvo when she received a pair of 8-inch shells from the *Norfolk*. The first glanced off the heavy cruiser's armor belt and fell harmlessly into the sea. The second, however, impacted the main director, blowing the gunnery officer and most of the cruiser's gunnery department into disparate parts that splashed into the sea or onto the deck below. For two crucial minutes, the *Hipper's* main battery remained silent even as her secondaries began to take the approaching British destroyers under fire.

The respite from *Lutzow's* fire had arrived just in time for *Exeter*, as the pocket battleship had been consistently finding the range. Staggering to his feet after another exercise in throwing himself flat, Eric looked forward to see just where the heavy cruiser had been hit this time. His gaze fell upon the devastation that had been *Exeter's* "B" turret, where a cloud of acrid yellow was smoke pouring back from the structure's opened roof to pass around the heavy cruiser's bridge. Damage control crews were rushing forward to spray hoses upon the burning guns, even as water began to crash over the cruiser's lowering bow.

"Very well then, flood the magazine!" Gordon was shouting into the speaking tube. "Tell the *Norfolk* we shall follow her in as best we can."

Looking to starboard, Eric could see the aforementioned heavy cruiser starting to surge ahead of *Exeter*, smoke pouring from her triple stacks and her forward turrets firing another salvo towards the *Hipper*.

"We are only making twenty-three knots, sir," the helmsman reported.

"Damage control reports heavy flooding in the bow," the talker stated. "Lieutenant Ramses states we must slow our speed or we may lose another bulkhead."

Gordon's face set in a grim line.

"Torpedoes reports a solution on the pocket battleship," the talker reported after pausing or a moment.

"Range?!" Gordon barked.

"Ten thousand yards and closing."

"Tell me when we're at four thousand..."

The seas around the *Exeter* suddenly leaped upwards, the waterspouts clearing her mainmast.

"Enemy battleship is taking us under fire!"

Looking over at *Norfolk*, Eric saw an identical series of waterspouts appear several hundred yards ahead of their companion.

"Two enemy battleships engaging, range twenty-two thousand yards."

"Where's our battleline?" Gordon asked bitterly. "Report the news to the *King George V.*"

Another couple of minutes passed, the *Exeter* continuing to close with the turning *Lutzow*. Four more shells exploded around the *Exeter*.

"The *Nelson* is disengaging due to opening range," the talker replied. "The remaining ships are closing our position to take the enemy battleship under fire."

Again there was the sound of an incoming freight train, and the *Exeter* was straddled once more, splinters ringing off the opposite side of the bridge.

"Corpsman!" a lookout shouted from the crow's nest.

Okay, someone stop this ride, I want to get off, Eric thought, bile rising in his throat.

"Commodore Vian reports he is closing."

"Right then, continue to attack!" Gordon shouted. Eric winced, convinced he was going to die.

Unbeknownst to Eric, the *Bismarck* and *Tirpitz* had only returned to persuade the British battleline to not pursue the *Scharnhorst*. Finding the two British heavy cruisers attacking, Bey had decided some 15-inch fire was necessary to discourage their torpedo run as well. In the worsening seas the German battleships' gunnery left much to be desired, but still managed to force the *Exeter* and *Norfolk* to both intensify their zig zags.

Unfortunately for the Germans, the decision to concentrate on the heavy cruisers meant that Commodore Vian's destroyers had an almost undisturbed attack run. Vian, realizing that he would not be able to bypass the aggressively counterattacking *Hipper*, split his force into two parts. The lead division, led by himself in *Somali*, continued after the crippled *Scharnhorst*. The second, led by the destroyer *Echo*, he directed to attack the *Hipper* in hopes that the heavy cruiser would turn away.

The German heavy cruiser reacted as Vian had expected, switching all of her fire to the approaching *Echo* group. For their part, the British ships dodged as they closed, the *Echo's* commander making the decision to close the range so that the destroyers could launch their torpedoes with a higher speed setting. Seeing the German cruiser starting to turn, *Echo's* commander signaled for his own vessel, *Eclipse*, and *Encounter* to attempt to attack from her port side, while the *Faulknor* and *Electra* were to move up to attack from starboard.

Discerning the British destroyerman's plan, *Hipper's* captain immediately laid on his maximum speed while continuing his turn towards port. Ignoring those vessels attempting to move in on her starboard side, the German vessel turned her guns wholly on the trio of British destroyers that was now at barely seven thousand yards. With a combined closing speed of almost seventy knots, there was less than a minute before the British destroyers were at their preferred range. In this time, *Hipper* managed to get off two salvoes with her main guns and several rounds from her secondary guns. Her efforts were rewarded, the *Echo* being hit and stopped by two 8-inch and four secondary shell hits before she could fire her torpedoes. That still left the *Eclipse* and *Encounter*, both which fired their torpedoes at 4,000 yards before starting to turn away. The latter vessel had just concluded putting her eighth torpedo into the water when the *Hipper's* secondaries switched to her as a target, knocking out the destroyer's forward guns.

Pursuing the *Hipper* as the German cruiser continued to turn to port, the *Faulknor* and *Electra* initially had a far longer run than their compatriots. However, as the German cruiser came about to comb the *Echo* group's torpedoes, the opportunity arose for the two more nimble vessels to cut across her turn. Hitting the heavy cruiser with several 4.7-inch shells even as they zigzagged through the *Lutzow's* supporting fire, the two destroyers unleashed their sixteen torpedoes from the *Hipper's* port bow. Belatedly, the German captain realized that he had placed himself in a horrible position, as he could not turn to avoid the second group of torpedoes without presenting a perfect target to the first.

It was the *Eclipse* which administered the first blow. Coming in at a fine angle, one of the destroyer's torpedoes exploded just below the *Hipper's* port bow. The heavy cruiser's hull whipsawed from the impact, the explosion peeling twenty feet of her skin back to act as a massive brake. The shock traveled down the vessel's length, throwing circuit breakers out of their mounts in her generator room and rendering the *Hipper* powerless. Looking to starboard, the vessel's bridge crew could only helplessly watch as the British torpedoes approached from that side. In a fluke of fate, the braking effect from *Eclipse's* hit caused the heavy cruiser to lose so much headway the majority of the tin fish missed. The pair that impacted, however, could not have been better placed. With two roaring waterspouts in close succession, the *Hipper's* engineering spaces were opened to the sea. Disemboweled, the cruiser continued to slow even as she rolled to starboard. Realizing instantly her wounds were fatal, the *Hipper's* captain gave the order to abandon ship. The order came far too late for most of the crew, as the 12,000-ton man-o-war capsized and slid under the Atlantic in a matter of minutes.

"Well, the destroyers just put paid to that heavy cruiser! Let's see if we can get a kill of our own!" Gordon said, watching the drama unfolding roughly twelve thousand yards to his west. Another salvo of 15-inch shells landed to *Exeter's* starboard, this broadside somewhat more ragged due to the heavy cruiser's zig zagging advance.

"Battleships are returning to aid us."

"About bloody time!" Gordon snapped.

When the *Warspite's* first salvo landed just aft of *Jean Bart*, Admiral Bey had more than enough. Signaling rapidly, he ordered the *Scharnhorst* and *Lutzow* to cover the remainder of the force's retreat. Firing a few desultory broadsides, the Franco-German force reentered the mists.

Eric watched through his binoculars as *Lutzow* gamely attempted to follow Bey's orders, slowly coming about so she could continue to engage the destroyers closing with *Scharnhorst*. Barely making fifteen knots, the pocket battleship was listing slightly to port and down by the bows. Just as *Lutzow* finished her turn, several shells landed close astern of the German vessel.

"*King George V* is engaging the pocket battleship."

"Good. Maybe she can slow that witch down so we can catch her."

"*Warspite* and *Prince of Wales* are switching to the closest battleship."

Gordon nodded his assent, continuing to watch as *Lutzow* attempted to begin a zig zag pattern.

"Destroyers are running the gauntlet," Gordon observed drily, pointing to where the *Lutzow* was engaging the five destroyers passing barely eight thousand yards in front of her. Eric nodded grimly, then brought his attention back to *Lutzow* just in time to see the *King George V*'s next salvo arrive. Two of the British 14-inch shells slashed into the pocket battleship's stern, while a third impacted on the vessel's aft turret with devastating effect. Eric was glad that *Exeter* was still far enough away that he could not identify the contents of the debris that flew upwards from the gunhouse in the gout of smoke and flame, as the young American was sure some of the dark spots were bodies.

"Looks like you got your wish, sir," Eric observed as the *Lutzow* began to continue a lazy circle to port. There was a sharp crack as the *Exeter's* secondary batteries began to engage the pocket battleship, leading to a disgusted look from Gordon.

"Tell Guns we may need that ammunition later," he snapped. "I'm not sure those guns will do any damage, plus she's almost finished."

I was wondering what good 4-inch guns would do to a pocket battleship, Eric thought. *Especially when* **Norfolk** *is pounding away with her main battery and a battleship has her under fire.*

"*King George V* is inquiring if we can finish her with torpedoes?"

Gordon looked at the pocket battleship, now coming to a stop with fires clearly spreading.

"Report that yes, we will close and finish her with torpedoes, she may assist in bringing that battleship to bay," *Exeter's* master stated.

"*Norfolk* is firing torpedoes," the talker reported.

Eric brought up his binoculars, focusing on the clearly crippled *Lutzow*. As he watched, one of the German's secondary turrets fired a defiant shot at *Norfolk*. Scanning the vessel from bow to stern, Eric wondered if the gun was the sole thing left operational, as the pocket battleship's upper decks were a complete shambles. Looking closely at the *Lutzow's* forward turret, he could see two jagged holes in its rear where *Norfolk's* broadsides had impacted. The bridge was similarly damaged, with wisps of smoke pouring from the shattered windows, and the German vessel's entire amidships was ablaze. The vessel's list appeared to have lessened, but she was clearly much lower in the water.

"Should be any time now," Gordon said, briefly looking at his watch. "Tell guns to belay my last, we're not wasting any more fish on her than necessary."

Eric turned back to watching the *Lutzow*, observing as *Norfolk* hit the vessel with another point blank salvo an instant before her torpedoes arrived. Given that the *Lutzow* was a stationary target, Eric was surprised to see *Norfolk's* torpedo spread produce only a pair of hits. It was still enough, as with an audible groan the *Lutzow's* already battered hull split just aft of her destroyed turret. Five minutes later, as *Exeter* drew within five hundred yards and Eric could see German sailors jumping into the sea, the *Lutzow* gave a final shuddering metallic rattle then slipped stern first into the depths.

"Stand by to rescue survivors," Gordon said, dropping his binoculars. "How are the destroyers doing with that battleship?"

The answer to Gordon's question could be summed up with two words: very well. The *Scharnhorst* had briefly managed to work up to sixteen knots, and had *Lutzow's* fire been somewhat more accurate, may have managed to escape the pursuing destroyers. However, as with the *Hipper*, Vian's destroyers split into two groups even as *Scharnhorst's* secondaries increased their fire. Another pair of hits from *Prince of Wales* slowed the German light battleship even further, and at that point the handful of tin cans set upon her like a school of sharks on a lamed blue whale.

Like that large creature, however, even a crippled the *Scharnhorst* still had means to defend herself. As the *Punjabi* closed in from starboard, the battleship's Caesar turret scored with a single 15-inch shell. The effects were devastating, the destroyer being converted from man-of-war to charnel house forward of her bridge. Amazingly, *Punjabi's* powerplant was undamaged by the blast, and the destroyer was able to continue closing the distance between herself and the larger German vessel. The timely arrival of a salvo from *Warspite* sufficiently distracted the *Scharnhorst's* gunnery officer, preventing him from getting the range again until after both groups of destroyers were close enough to launch torpedoes.

Severely damaged, *Scharnhorst* still attempted to ruin the destroyers' fire control problem at the last moment. To Commodore Vian's intense frustration, the battleship's captain timed his maneuver perfectly, evading twelve British torpedoes simply by good seamanship. Had *Scharnhorst* had her full maneuvering ability, she may have then been able to pull off the maneuver *Hipper* had attempted by reversing course. Whereas geometry and numbers had failed the German heavy cruiser, simple physics served to put the water-logged battleship in front of three torpedoes. Even then, her luck remained as the first hit, far forward, was a dud. Then, proving Fate was indeed fickle, two fish from the damaged *Punjabi* ran deep and hit the vessel just below her armored belt. Finishing the damage done by *Prince of Wales'* hits earlier, the torpedoes knocked out the German capital ship's remaining power and opened even more of her hull to the sea. Realizing she was doomed, her captain ordered the crew to set scuttling charges and abandon ship.

"*King George V* is inquiring if any vessels have torpedoes remaining."

Gordon gave the talker a questioning look.

"I thought Commodore Vian just reported that the enemy battleship appears to be sinking?" Gordon said, his voice weary. "No matter, inform *King George V* that we have all of our fish remaining."

Wonder what in the hell that is about? Eric thought. Looking down, he realized his hands were starting to shake. Taking a deep breath, he attempted to calm himself.

Well, this has been a rather...interesting day. I just wish someone would have told me I'd get shot down, see my squadron leader killed, and participate in a major sea battle when I got up at 0300 this morning.

"*Leftenant* Cobb, are you all right?" Gordon asked, concerned.

Eric choked back the urge to laugh at the question.

"I'm fine sir, just a little cold," he said, lying through his teeth. The talker saved him from further inquisition.

"*King George V* is ordering us to come about and close with her. She is also ordering Commodore Vian to rescue survivors from *Punjabi* then scuttle her if she is unable to get under way. *Norfolk* is being ordered to stand by to assist *Nelson*."

"What about the Germans?" Gordon asked.

"Flag has ordered that all other recovery operations are to cease."

There was dead silence on *Exeter's* bridge.

"Very well then, guess the Germans will have to come back for their own. Let's go see what *King George V* has for us," Gordon said.

Eric was struck by just how far the running fight had ranged as the *Exeter* reversed course. From the first salvo to the current position, the vessels had covered at least thirty miles. The *King George V* was a distant dot to the south, with her sister ship and *Warspite* further behind.

No one is going to find any of those survivors, Eric thought. *Especially with this weather starting to get worse.* He could smell imminent rain on the wind, and even with *Exeter's* considerable size he could feel the ocean's movement starting to change.

"I hope this isn't about to become too bad of a blow," Gordon observed, looking worriedly out at the lowering sky. "Not with the flooding we have forward."

"If you don't mind, sir, I'd like to avoid going swimming again today," Eric quipped.

"Wouldn't be a swim lad. If we catch a big wave wrong, she would plow right under," Gordon replied grimly. "What has got *King George V* in such a tussy? She's coming at us full speed."

Eric looked up and saw that the battleship was indeed closing as rapidly as possible. As she hove into visual range several minutes later, the *King George V's* signaling searchlight began flashing rapidly.

DO YOU READ THIS MESSAGE? DO YOU READ THIS MESSAGE?

"Acknowledge," Gordon said. A few moments later Eric could hear the heavy cruiser's signal crew employing the bridge lamp to respond to the *King George V.*

YOU WILL PROCEED TO *HOOD.* ONCE ALL SURVIVORS ARE OFFBOARD, YOU ARE TO SCUTTLE.

"What in the bloody hell is that idiot talking about?" Gordon exploded. He did not have time to send a counter message, as the *King George V* continued after a short pause.

YOU HAVE TWENTY-FIVE MINUTES TO REJOIN. FORCE WILL PROCEED WITHOUT YOU IF NOT COMPLETE. TOVEY SENDS GOD SAVE THE QUEEN

"God save the...*oh my God!*" Gordon said.

Eric looked at the *Exeter*'s captain with some concern as the man staggered backward, his face looking as if he had been personally stricken.

"Ask," Gordon began, the word nearly coming out as a sob before he regained his composure. "Ask if I may inform the ship's company of our task?"

Three minutes later, the *King George V* replied.

AFFIRMATIVE. EXPEDITE. HER MAJESTY'S SAFETY IS
THIS COMMAND'S PRIMARY GOAL.

"Acknowledge. Hand me the loudspeaker," Gordon said, his voice incredibly weary. Eric could see tears welling in the man's eyes.

This is not good, Eric thought. *This is not good at all.* Although he was far from an expert on British government, he dimly remembered seeing a newsreel when *Ranger* had been in port where the Royal Family had been discussed. He felt his stomach starting to drop as he began to process what the *King George V* had just stated.

"All hands, this is the captain speaking," Gordon began. "This vessel is proceeding to stand by the *Hood* to rescue survivors. It appears that His Majesty has been killed."

Holy shit, Eric thought. *Isn't Princess...no, **Queen** Elizabeth barely sixteen?*

Eric looked around the bridge as the captain broke the news to the *Exeter*'s crew. The reactions ranged from shock to, surprisingly, rage. As *Exeter*'s master finished, the young American had the feeling he was seeing the start of something very, very ugly for the Germans.

I would hate to be someone who got dragged out of the water today, he thought. *That is, if **any** Germans get saved.* Eric's father had fought as a Marine at Belleau Wood. In the weeks before Eric had left for the academy, his father had made sure that his son understood just what might be required of him in the Republic's service. One of the stories had involved what had befallen an unfortunate German machine gun crew when the men tried to surrender after killing several members of the elder Cobb's platoon. Realizing the parallels to his current situation given the news he had just heard, Eric fought the urge to scowl.

Looks like you don't need a rope for a lynch mob, Eric thought as he reflected on the "necessity" of leaving the German and French sailors to drown. He was suddenly shaken out of his reverie by the sound of singing coming from below the bridge.

"*Happy and glorious...long to reign over us...*"

The men on the bridge began taking up the song, their tone somber and remorseful.

"*GOD SAAAAVEEE THE QUEEEEENN!!*"

Almost a half hour later, the *Exeter* sat one thousand yards off of the *Hood*'s starboard side, the heavy cruiser's torpedo tubes trained on her larger consort. The *Hood*'s wounds were obvious, her bridge and conning tower a horribly twisted flower of shattered steel. Flames licked from the vessel's X turret, and it appeared that the structure had taken a heavy shell to its roof. Further casting a pall on the scene was the dense black smoke pouring from the *Hood*'s burning bunkerage, a dull glow at the base of the cloud indicating an out of control fire. The battlecruiser's stern looked almost awash, her bow almost coming out of the water with each swell, and as Eric watched there was an explosion of ready ammunition near her anti-aircraft guns.

Might be a waste of good torpedoes at this point, Eric thought. He realized he was starting to pass into mental shock from all the carnage he had seen that day.

"I'm the last man, sir," a dazed-looking commander with round features, black hair, and green eyes was saying to Captain Gordon. "At least, the last man we can get to."

"I understand, Commander Keir," Gordon said quietly. "I regret we do not have the time to try and free the men trapped in her engineering spaces."

"If we could have only had another hour, we might have saved her," Keir said, his voice breaking. It was obvious the man had been through hell, his uniform blackened by soot and other stains that Eric didn't care to look into too closely.

It's never a good day when you become commander of a vessel simply because no one else was left. From what he understood, Keir had started the day as chief of *Hood*'s Navigation Division. That had been before the vessel took at least three 15-inch shells to the bridge area, as well as two more that had wiped out her gunnery directory and the secondary bridge.

Captain Gordon was right—she was a very powerful warship. Unfortunately that tends to make you a target.

"Commander, you are *certain* that…" Gordon started, then collected himself. "You are *certain* His Majesty is dead."

"Yes sir," Keir said. "His Majesty was in the conning tower with Admiral Pound when it was hit. The Royal Surgeon positively identified His Majesty's body in the aid station before that was hit in turn. We cannot get to the aid station due to the spreading fire."

"Understood. His Majesty would not have wanted any of you to risk his life for his body," Gordon said.

"I just…" Keir started, then stopped, overcome with emotion.

"It is not your fault lad," Gordon said. "Her Majesty will understand."

Gordon turned and looked at the *Exeter*'s clock.

"Very well, we are out of time. Stand by to fire torpedoes."

"Torpedoes report they are ready."

"Sir, you may want to tell your torpedo officer to have his weapons set to run deep," Keir said. "She's drawing…"

There was a large explosion aboard *Hood* as the flames reached a secondary turret's ready ammunition. Eric saw a fiery object arc slowly across, descending towards the *Exeter* as hundreds of helpless eyes watched it. The flaming debris' lazy parabola terminated barely fifty yards off of *Exeter*'s side with a large, audible splash.

"I think we do not have time for that discussion," Gordon said grimly. "Fire torpedoes!"

The three weapons from *Exeter*'s starboard tubes sprang from their launchers into the water. Set as a narrow spread, the three tracks seemed to take forever to impact from Eric's perspective. *Exeter*'s torpedo officer, observing *Hood*'s state, had taken into account the battlecruiser's lower draught without having to be told. Indeed, he had almost set the weapons for too deep a run, but was saved by the flooding that had occurred in the previous few minutes. In addition to breaking the battlecruiser's keel, the triple blow opened the entire aft third of her port side to the ocean. With the audible sound of twisting metal, *Hood* started to roll onto her beam ends. She never completed the evolution before slipping beneath the waves.

Made in the USA
San Bernardino, CA
16 April 2017